This is a work of fiction. Any resemblance to real characters, locations, or events is strictly coincidental.

Edited by Andrew Bunker

English-to-French Translation by A. Sokolowski

Published by The Bournbrook Press

ISBN: 978-1-7395829-5-1

This labour of love is dedicated to the following, without whom a childhood dream would be just so.

To Andy Bunker, for his timely and diligent editing. To the staff and proprietors of Anke's Tea Lounge, and Utopia Coffee Lounge, for keeping me fed and caffeinated while I wrote. To my friends and colleagues at Bournbrook Magazine. To BB, BL, and DB. To my father, and my sister. To my Grandmother, who first encouraged me to write, all those years ago.

And lastly, to my mother.

I hope I have made you all proud.

Preface

To quote William Somerset Maugham, whose deft and effortless touch can be felt throughout this work; *this* is an embarrassingly long book, almost unforgiveable for a debut. And yet, after two years of work, no more can be done. No word can be cut, no sentence can be slimmed down and made *punchier.* No conversation can be altered, no description made more apt, for in the novel that follows, I have simply emptied my heart. Every drop. In the process of writing, and re-writing, and waiting, and writing some more, I have sharpened by pen into an instrument of incison, sliced open the aortic valve, and positioned my gorging chest above the paper - letting time, and gravity, and experience do the rest. I shall not delay your reading any longer, for I - and Maugham - have already said, this is an embarrassingly long book. Read on, and perhaps you shall know me better than you had before.

THE PASSENGER

By S.D. Wickett

Published by The Bournbrook Press

PART ONE: *FABULAM DE NEMO*

1

I was born on a Tuesday in the August of 1933. On the Wednesday, my mother died. My father died too on a Wednesday, twelve years later. In lieu of them, I became aimless and senseless, and lived out my years with a twin chasm of absence and vague loss. I carried that loss to all places and into all relations. Perhaps this is the key to understanding a man such as myself; self-raised and educated by error. And now, in my expiring embers - as I dwindle and flicker, and the cancer spreads - I seem to know myself truly at last. Now, at death's door, with all in the rear-view - wisdom is so very easy to come across. And amidst a host of other revelations, one is written in bold italics. For when, at last, a life is confined entirely to memories, and no more can be made, then he who has lived shall become one with his recollections, for memory is the only evidence of life.

A life is but the creation of memory.

Mine began in the Autumn of 1951; my first Michaelmas term at Camford. I had a life in those prior, formative years; but it had not been *lived*. Rather, it was spent awaiting the day I moved to Camford, for it seemed a birthright of sorts, a tether to my father and to his father before him. We were, in his words, *displaced aristocrats*. There had been a Marquis somewhere in the tree I was told, though all that seemed to remain was a townhouse in Bayswater.

And so I went up to Camford, aflush with neuroses and trepidations; as if I were a diver on the water's edge, stripping to the waist and readying the jump, though not knowing if the water was hot or cold, or full of sharks. There were intrigues too as I boarded the train at Paddington, the imagined outcomes of every possible scenario. So bound was I to my neuroticisms that they no longer seemed to be quirks or faults in my psyche, rather a built-in characteristic. So bound was I to tragedy and heartache, having become so familiar, that no other way of living seemed right. And yet, on the train - somewhere between London and High Wycombe - a miracle of sorts occurred. I was lifted, and free, and suddenly I felt a gravitational desire for more. I suddenly craved music, and drink, and dancing, and women. And so, armed with my few belongings and a *tabula rasa*, I rode on to the rest of my life. And after what felt like the flick of the switch, I was there. Camford entered the senses and stayed, seducing me in moments and whisking me into a taxi as that city of eternal, transient youth, and learned stones floated on by. It asked no questions, and demanded no more than two essays per week, and an acquiescence into blissful, geranium odours and plentiful wine. When I arrived at my digs, having fallen in love for the first time, I felt as groomsmen do on their happiest day.

Richard Belling was halfway asleep when I first met him. He was sprawled across a leather armchair, two feet from a gramophone that roared Beethoven's Ninth, that was nearing the end. He smiled contentedly, with a cigarette perched on the left bank of his grin as the sun shone through a vase on the window sill, and his face was a glorious blue. After a minute or so, the music stopped. His eyes opened and narrowed upon seeing me.

"You," he said. "Are you our new lodger?"

"Lodger?", I asked, caught off-guard by his wording. "Y-yes. I'm R-Robin, how do you do?"

"Richard," he said, standing and taking my hand. "Surname?"

"Fitz—w-warwick."

"Fitz-Warwick?", he asked with a slight chuckle.

"How interesting. I know a few *Fitz's*, and a few *Warwick's*. I didn't realise they'd smashed them together. You're not a relation of Alfie Warwick, are you? I should hope not, he's been *such* a terrible ass to me of late."

"It's just F-Fitzwarwick. One word. You'll have to excuse the speech, it was never my biggest s-strength."

"Mm," he grunted. "*Fitzwarwick.* Goodness me, your hair is very black."

"Oh, yes. I believe it's on account of my mother being Cornish."

"Half Cornish?", he enquired. His hair was a golden blonde.

"Yes."

"Well, would you look at that. I'm full-blooded Cornish as it happens, or at least that's what father likes to say. Oh well, we can't have it all, can we? Do you smoke, old boy?"

"No."

"You do now," he said, taking a cigarette and placing it into my breast pocket. "D'you drink?"

"Yes."

"Good. Here," he said, gesturing at my bags. "Those look heavy, let me lend a hand."

I replied with a simple *cheers* as he ushered me out of the way and picked up the bags, before turning to face the hall. "Fucksby! Fucksby get in here!"

Within seconds, the hard-wood floor pitter-pattered with hurried steps, as a slim and slightly wet-looking young man, of about our age, flung himself into view.

"Yes, sir?"

"Take these," he said, passing over my bags clumsily.

"Yes, sir. Very well, sir," said *Fucksby* before turning and sprinting back out of the room. I looked at the now-vacant doorway, and then back at Richard, who smiled, knowing how bizarre the scene was.

"Fucksby?", I asked.

"Yes, Fucksby."

"How are you spelling that?"

"*F-U-C-K-S-B-Y*"

"I see. W-why?"

Richard sighed, as if this explanation was a regular chore. "His name is Francis Uxby. F. Uxby. *Fucksby*. It's hardly a complicated evolution."

"And is *Fucksby* a friend of yours?"

"Oh, the best of friends. He's the Watson to my Holmes. Fucksby! Get in here!"

Fucksby darted back.

"I fancy a round of drinks."

"Of course, sir."

"Rather. I'll have a gin and tea; dash of milk, no sugar—you know how I like it, my dear. And—the newbie will have the same."

"Very well sir," the errand boy blurted before turning to run.

"Actually. Red for me if you have it."

The butler looked at Richard for approval and turned back to me after getting a nod. "Very well."

He ran faster once unburdened by my bags.

"He's the wind beneath my wings," said Richard, with a great sentiment.

"I must say, I am quite impressed. He ran faster than I ever could; indoors, w-while carrying everything I own."

"Oh, yes. My dear Fucksby is a mighty fine mule. The best you can get really."

"A mule?"

"A mule, yes. It's a term at Eton. I believe you'd call him a *bitch* elsewhere. But I find that *mule* has a much softer touch. Mules are reliable, friendly. A perfect companion."

"I see."

"Fiercely loyal, the old boy. He volunteered to stay behind for a year while I travelled to South America after the sixth. I mean, it *was* my idea, but he did it so he must have wished to."

"How very charitable."

Richard smiled, in that moment taking me as a friend. "Indeed," he beamed after a few moments. *Fucksby* came back in, not running but walking at a brisk pace, a tray balanced effortlessly on his outstretched palm. "Gin and tea, sir."

"Thank you, Fucksby. And for yourself old boy?"

"For me? Oh—nothing, sir."

"What rot, Fucksby! Fix yourself a drink at this moment. And take the evening off while you're at it."

"Yes, sir," said *Fucksby* as he turned for the doorway.

"Wait."

Fucksby turned, with a simple expression of listening. "You're forgetting something."

He froze for a second, in thought. The penny dropped, and he handed me a glass of wine.

"Thank you, Francis."

He tried to hide a burst of joy, but failed. Richard looked amused.

"Yes, I suppose his name *is* Francis," Richard remarked when it was just us in the room. "I've called him *Fucksby* for so long I forget the old boy has a civilian name."

"How long have you called him that?"

"Eight years."

"And how long have you known him?"

"Eight years."

"Did you ever call him Francis?"

"I did. But as soon as I learned his surname I simply couldn't resist."

Francis came trotting back into the room, with a smartly prepared Gin and Tonic in hand. He'd even garnished it admirably, with coiled cucumber. It was then that I saw something unseeable in Francis, a quiet brilliance. I didn't then and still do not know why he put up with all he did. He seemed genuinely fond of Richard, and Richard seemed genuinely fond of him. It was six when I left them. The record had been replaced and the gramophone hummed once more. I hadn't seen my room yet and wished to know my quarters. It was nearest to the back of the flat and I passed the other rooms on my way. Richard's was large but a mess, Francis' small but well kept. Mine was intermediate between them. It was a perfect cube decorated with various shades of timber. A deep brown wooden floor and desk with a light brown wardrobe and bookcase. I'd unpacked by seven and was hungry.

"I'm heading out," I called, poking my head into the living room.

"Not so fast!", Richard countered, springing to his feet. He leapfrogged the armchair he'd been laying on when I first met him, stumbling into me upon landing.

"Where are you going?"

"Just out."

He raised a brow, instilling in me a hungering desire to say more. "For something to eat. Maybe a cup of tea as well."

"But we have tea here," he protested. "And gin."

"I think I'd rather go out. I haven't seen the city yet."

"Fucksby!", Richard called, as Francis stirred from the window he'd been looking out of. "Ready the flask, Fucksby. We're going out."

"Where to, sir?"

"Don't call me that, Fucksby. You're off duty. Robin wants to see the town."

We ate in a small and forgettable bistro. All the while, Richard moved and jittered, filling my ears with his fantasies of the drunken night ahead. He paid and whisked me out of the restaurant the moment I'd finished eating, and was restless as we walked into the heart of the hum. There was a dancing Autumn breeze on my fingertips, and soon I had begun to share his sense of thrill. *This,* I kept thinking to myself, *this is how the eve of battle must feel.*

"I'll have a gin and tea, please," said Richard in the first pub we entered.

"We haven't got any hot water," replied a bemused barmaid.

"We're leaving," Richard declared after a moment's thought.

"Well, we tried," he continued as we stepped out into the street. "I suppose there's always the college haunts. Though I'm not giddy about it. I can't stand to be around other undergraduates, you see. We all know each other, much more so than I'd find desirable."

"I see," I said, not really listening.

"They're all the same, really - the *Old Boys* - you know the next fellow from all the things you do outside of school, the Summers and Winters. A few from the same county. I'm an Eton man myself. Have you ever heard of Eton?"

"I'm aware of Eton, yes. And I happen to have gone to Charterhouse."

"Really?", he asked, stopping in his tracks.

"Yes," I said, half-amused.

"But—I've never heard of you."

"I—kept a low profile."

"What did you say your surname was again?"

"Fitzwarwick."

"Hm. *Fitzwarwick*. I'll check with my sources. It's not that I don't believe you or anything, but I'd assumed you were of the middle class. There's no shame in it, old boy. It's a new age, you know, as we keep on hearing."

"So you *don't* believe me?"

Richard paused for a moment. "No, I suppose not."

During our brief sojourn into that first pub, some new life had been breathed into the city. Students now rode about gaily on bicycles, calling out to one another about *this* party or *that* party, all happening at some indeterminate point in the late hours. A few parties had already begun, and every fifth house seemed to have undergraduates spilling out of the doors and windows.

"Nope. That one's full of pricks," Richard declared with contempt at the first party he saw, before pointing at another. "And that one's full of even bigger pricks!"

He sipped intermittently from a silver flask, which bore the monochrome of a fox with *Belling* typed underneath. "The family crest," he said, after catching me staring. "*To the cunning go the spoils.*"

Francis had taken to walking a step behind, as the pavement became narrow at points, and no more than two could fit side-by-side. He examined Camford much in the way that I did; quietly, contently, and seduced. "Here, Fitzy—yes, Fitzy, that's what I'll call you from now on. Have some of this. It's good for you, good for healthy bones."

Richard extended the flask, and I took a small sip. A great shudder shot from the base of my skull to my knees as that utterly horrid liquid, which I can still taste today, molested my tongue with bitters and sickly sweets.

"Christ!", I blurted. "What's in that?"

"Ah, you know. A bit of this, a bit of that. We call it the *real Eton mess*."

"It's ghastly."

"And not for the faint of heart."

"How on earth have you not grimaced once? That—*concoction* is utterly horrid."

"It is second nature to me now, dear boy," Richard smiled boastfully.

Though his confidence would not last long; and within moments he was keeled in a cramped alley, expunging what he had consumed. He writhed in agony as the day's contents fell out of him and accumulated on the cobbled floor.

"Oh God, I feel like a sewer."

"Anything I can do to help, sir?", Francis enquired, sheepishly.

"Yeah—fuck off." Richard said, in between dry and heaving breaths.

"Indeed, sir."

When Francis had rounded the corner, Richard turned to me, with some unseemly fluid dangling from his lip. "You too, Fi-fitzwarwick. I can see you judging me with those *baby browns*. Out— of—— my sight."

I did not need convincing and turned away. Strolling out of the alley, I found Francis admiring a church. The sort that one felt had always been there, and this great city of knowledge was simply built around it.

"14th century," Francis said as I joined him. "Gorgeous thing, don't you think?"

"How'd you two become friends?", I asked.

The question had weighed on me all through the evening. Before he could answer, Richard emerged; wiping his lips with a spotted handkerchief and staggering as if he had died and been reborn.

"Sorry for the spectacle, chaps. Had to get this rotten waste out of my precious body."

Richard gestured at the flask, before unscrewing the top and drinking what was left. He wretched. "Never again. Now, chaps. I've got a nasty hangover and a creeping anaemia. I need some iron."

"I think the pharmacy is closed, sir."

"Not pills. Fucksby. Too small a dose. No. I need some stout." Richard looked around in a focused daze, searching for a point of delivery. "Ah, this is familiar territory. Now, if I'm not mistaken—I believe some good old chums of mine are to be spending this evening——"

Richard paused, lost in attempted recollection. He snapped his finger like a gun, his target the *Bull's Head* pub. "There. Onwards!"

Before either of us could react, Richard was through the door. When I caught up with him, he was scanning the room greedily. He spotted a seat and directed Francis and I towards it. "I'll get these one's in."

It was just Francis and I, as Richard waited impatiently at the bar, I wanted to ask him that same question, but decided instead to enquire in general. "So, Fu—Francis. Where are you from?"

"Oh. Nowhere really. But also, many places."

"Oh?", I asked, imploring him to continue.

"Well, um. Forgive me, Robin, if I speak plainly?"

"By all means."

"Well, I am an orphan. I lost my parents in the war. So, I just got passed around really."

"Like a bottle of Christmas gin," I said, giving him a look. Our fates were the same, and nothing he could say would shock me.

"Yes, I suppose it is like that. Is there anything else you'd like to know?"

"W-where have you lived?"

"Oh, well. I was an evacuee when it happened, I think a stray bomb got them. I was in Herefordshire at the time, so I stayed there a while. Then with family in Pembrokeshire, then London for a while after the war. Then they sent me to board and sort of forgot about me. That's where I met Richard and became such friends with the Belling family. They've been ever so good to me."

I did not reply, instead choosing to let my smile remain in place. In an instant, he and I were bonded - tethered by loss - and our misery made us brothers. Francis pivoted the conversation to a worn out and chipped fresco on the ceiling, and I listened as he imparted upon me what he knew. Before long, Richard returned with three pints of dark stout. Just as he took a greedy first sip, an uncannily identical young man approached the table. Richard's posture indicated that the young man was an old friend.

"Alright, Bellers? Fancy seeing you here, I figured you'd be stuck in some Bolivarian foxhole. Jarves said he left you in Caracas."

"I came back for the Belling place at Camford. Say, speaking of Jarves, is he here?"

"Yeah, he's just around the corner."

"Oh, good. I must speak with that great ginger beast."

The two exchanged a few more pleasantries, before the doppelgänger left. "That's Maz," Richard said, once he had vanished into the crowd. "Complete prick. Biggest of the bunch really."

Richard turned and began craning his neck for a better view around the bar. "Jarves!", he called across the room.

"Yeah," called a disembodied voice around the corner

"Relocate your ginger self to whence I call your name."

"Shag yourself, Bellers," the voice replied. "I'm not done with my pint."

"If I have to drag you here I will!"

Presently, *Jarves* showed himself. He had a thick head of bright orange hair and a beard of brown patches, the sort that the university would declare unseemly and have forcibly shaved before the term began. He was scruffy and familiar, and I recognised him immediately as being in the year above me in school.

"What is it?", he groaned, pulling a chair out and sitting abruptly. "Hello, Francis."

"Hello, Matthew," Francis replied with a smile.

"See him?", Richard declared, pointing right at me.

"I see him."

"Claims he's a Carthusian."

"Oh yeah? House?"

"Grownboys."

His eyes narrowed. I held firm, as it became clear that he had remembered me. "Who was your beak for English?", he asked with a smirk.

"Harding."

Jarves scoffed. "Well, he's telling the truth, I'll tell you that much. Fitzwarwick, right? Yeah, I remember you," he said, turning to face Richard again. "He fancied himself a writer," Jarves continued. "A real *sensitivo iuvenis* People used to say that he wrote because he couldn't speak, and all the energy went there. Always scribbling away in a battered old journal. Harding was a right bastard to him, so I heard. Right?"

I tightened.

"Why? What did he do?", Richard asked, keenly.

"Oh, it was brutal. The kid had a stammer like a broken-down car, and Harding knew it, the sadist," Jarves explained, before realising the impropriety of his tone and nodding a sort of apology. I accepted without fuss, as pretending not to be phased by Harding's antics was just how I coped with school. "Apparently, Ol' Bastard Harding would make him stand up and recite Byron, over and over and over. And this other time, he—"

Jarves was suddenly interrupted as a glass thundered against the floor and shattered. We looked over and saw that Francis was the culprit. "Fucksby you plum!", Richard exclaimed as he roared into laughter. Jarves chuckled silently. I looked at him in disbelief.

"Sorry, sir. Must've just—slipped."

"You are a damned fool my dear boy, but you do provide the most abundant mirth," Richard chortled, roughing up his hair as he smiled vacantly.

Richard bored of the ribbing and engaged Jarves in a conversation only discernible to their ilk. Francis caught my eye and winked. And with that, I had made my first friend in Camford.

The next day I awoke to an awful drowse. I grimaced and rubbed my eyes as the room grew focused and I saw that it was ten past eleven. As the various sounds of the day wafted in, I heard collective voices in the lounge. Richard's voice rose above, and I recalled that he had invited the faces from the night before to luncheon. They were all dressed exquisitely. Silks and tweeds, that emanated all relations of the system from which they had emerged. The same, yet possessing a well-tasted and minute touch of their own. Jarves, and Maz, and Portnoy, to whom I was a stranger.

"Fitzy do get dressed," groaned Richard. "We're going to be late. You *do* remember that you agreed to have lunch with us?"

"Of course, just give me a moment."

I slipped back into my room and picked out a slim blue two-piece, my favourite tie, and a simple white handkerchief. There was a boutonniere, which I had reserved for a special occasion, but not this. Richard was impatient when I returned. "Do hurry, old boy. The cab's waiting." I gestured to the door, and we left the flat. Jarves fell into step with me on the stairs. “I remember you a tad bit better now. You were Monty’s friend, right?”

“Yes.”

We emerged out of the front door. Immediately, I spotted Francis standing by a car, and deduced that he was our driver. We piled in and headed for town. Francis drove like a ballerina dances.

2

The gramophone roared as we pranced about the living room, three sheets to the wind. It was just the three of us, as it would so often be in those years. I believe now that those hatchling steps into adulthood, right on the cusp of that first Michaelmas term, were among the happiest days of my life. I would never feel as young as I did in those halcyon days of my eighteenth year. Some part of me knew it, and on occasion in the weeks to follow, I'd stop, look around, and say silent thanks for all that lay about me.

Drinks had been flowing since we returned from the luncheon. Jarves, Maz, and Portnoy, who were all in their second year, had returned to their digs, on the understanding that they would rejoin us with company. We had almost cleared the flat of its stock, and felt the absence in our plenty. I stuck to wine, for it was all that my tongue could handle. It was a good wine, from the south of France. I was drunk. Quite possibly for the first time in my life, I was truly drunk. I'd taken to wine early, around fourteen, when port was routinely smuggled into the dorms at Charterhouse. My friend Monty had a knack for sourcing it, yet I never had enough to get tight. The warmth of two glasses always sufficed. I have ascribed many reasons as to my avoidance until that day; perhaps it was a fear that I would lose control, and do something foolish, or inflict some humiliation among myself. Hu

-miliation, it seems, was my defining fear. Though, like most things, the cause was most likely something familial.

My first sight of the drink came from my father, who took a single glass with dinner, and was only ever tight at the new year. When he died, and I was sent to live with various aunts and uncles, I came to know the puritan mind. I was naturally curious about that liquid seduction, kept hidden in cases of glass; however, their reprimands, and warnings of that brutish beast, Bacchus, had been stored deep within, and emerged each time I refused a third cup. Yet today, I did not flinch in the face of the *eros*. Instead, I disrobed and flung myself into its waters.

I drank, and danced, and drank some more. Richard was erratic, and switched between various interpretations of swing, and a delicate waltz, with Francis an unwitting partner. He, though an impotent toff with little grace and the twin habits for boasting and lying, seemed just a boy to me. And there sat his charm. He was selfish, obnoxious, and chaotic, yet also endearing and quite funny. Richard, too, was beautiful, his golden hair and hazel eyes spoke to a distant sense of the divine within me, that only emerged around that which was beautiful. He was not bound to the frantic insecurities and moral prejudices that defined the twitching cadaver of his social class; the upper aping the middle. Francis remained a mystery. I knew virtually nothing of his background, save that he was also an Etonian; from which I had deduced that he too came from money; though if it was old or new, I would never know. Though, the manner in which Richard discussed new wealth told me that Francis' was as old as time itself.

And so, this day cemented itself in my habits, as the blueprint for those Camfordian years; when I slept under the stars and woke to the rising sun. When I acted on impulse and made my formative mistakes. Shortly after six, the others arrived.

"Evening gents," chipped Jarves, as he took a seat. "Mind if I smoke?"

"Please do," Richard replied. "Say, where is the company you promised?"

"Getting ready, apparently."
"How long will that be?"
"Well," Jarves pondered. "If my sister is anything to go by, it could be hours."
"Eleanor's been talking about you all day, Bellers," Portnoy added. "Methinks she has unfinished business."
"Enough about her. I'll see to it when they arrive."
"Women are coming here?", I asked.

Maz took great amusement in the question. "Yes, you silly old bugger," he quipped. "The *real world* is nothing like school, you know. They do exist, and they go places. In this instance, *they* are some wonderful ladies, of good means, who we know from the London season, and *their* destination is *here*."
"In the meantime," Richard interrupted. "I suggest we play a game or two."
"Such as?", asked Jarves in a nervous tone."
"Comprehension," Richard uttered, with a gravity.
"Oh God, Bellers!", Maz exclaimed in disgust. "It's too early for that."
"Comprehension."
"I feel like I'm back at Eton," Portnoy scoffed. "Drinking that ghastly *Special Tea*."
"It helped us to study."
"No, it didn't. We always forgot everything by the morning."
"We're playing comprehension."
"What's Comprehension?", I asked.
"It's a game from Eton, very simple. One recites a passage to the group, and the others compete to see who can name the text first. You must empty your glass before you answer, first to finish gets the floor. If you get it wrong, you must empty another glass."

The others seemed resigned to play. "Jolly good," said Richard. "I'll begin."

He poured five glasses of gin, before reclining back with a sly smile. "Gentlemen, on your marks."

Reluctantly we all picked up what he had poured. I gave the glass a smell and shuddered.

"Are we ready?", he asked. "Very well, here we go."

He steadied himself, and contemplated for a moment. "*I, who prays to no God bar Bacchus. I, who walks no sands but Thracian, who wakes upon the shore, shakes off the night before and glistens once again.*"

The group looked confused, whereas I just stared at the floor, a temperature rising within.

"I don't know," said Jarves. "But it's jolly pretty. Who is Bacchus?"

"*Dionysus*," Francis replied. "The god of wine."

"Rather!"

Richard scanned the room and its faces, his lips perched on a word. "Anyone?", he asked, and was met with silence. "Why, it's our very own Robin!", he exclaimed. "I found it in his room earlier. "Isn't he clever?"

"Is that so, Robin?", Maz asked. "D'you fancy yourself a writer?"

"Oh," I said meekly. "I don't know."

"Well," Maz continued. "I think it's very pretty. Fix your posture and you'll be *very* popular with women. They do like a poet."

"Right," Richard interrupted. "Everyone drink. You too, Robin, you didn't give an answer."

"But —", I began to protest, before Richard silenced me with a hand, and poured another glass for the room. "I'll give another. *Virginity breeds mites, much like cheese, consumes itself to the very paring, and so dies with feeding his own stomach.*"

Everyone bar Francis and myself conceded defeat and launched gin into their throats, each with a gasp of varying depth and tone. I consumed mine with three clumsy gulps, and Francis with two elegant swigs. Maz, and Jarves, and Portnoy each gave wrong answers, gleefully accepting their punishments of more drink. Richard turned to me with a raised brow; half of inquisition and half of drunkenness.

"All's Well that End's Well," I said.

"Bravissimo!", he cried. "Alright, Fitzwarwick. You're up."

I was contemplative for a moment, before recalling a book I had read over the Summer. "*My theme is memory, that winged host that soared about me one grey morning of wartime. These memories, which are my life; for we possess nothing certainly except the past, were always with me.*"

"The Idiot?", Jarves winced.

"Drink."

"All's Well That Ends Well?", Portnoy asked, knowing he was wrong, and what his recompense would be.

"Drink."

I turned to Richard. "Samuel Whiskers?", he asked.

"Drink."

I then turned to the last bastion of silence in the room. "Francis?"

"Brideshead."

"Well done."

Richard grew elated. "Jolly good, old boy! Very wicked, isn't he? How wickedly smart!"

Another set of glasses were poured. Though before Francis could speak, the doorbell rang. "They're early," Maz observed.

Richard rose and strode to the door. "Gentlemen, I believe our company has arrived."

On that evening, when I was just eighteen-years old; the fairer sex was an enigma. I was lumped into a school for boys, and boys were all that I knew. At no point in my formative years had I felt love, or lust. In fact, I had rarely even seen a woman my age. I was wholly naïve, afraid, and pristinely virginal. And now, in this flat were four women. I knew not what to say, nor where to look; what I was to do with my hands, or feet was a bleak mystery. I was introduced but said little. Music played as Francis and I took the back seat, and observed the others in their competition. Like deer rutting, they postured for battle of words, seeing who could emasculate the others fastest, and with the most brutality; the spoils of war were to be a night of company.

Eleanor was introduced to me as Eleanor Andress. Though I knew her by name long before I'd seen her porcelain face. *Andress* was but a publishing company with a family conjoined to the hip. It was the largest publisher of fiction in the country. She carried herself like an heiress, and her presence drew the most fierce of competition, and yet Richard emerged early like the champion jockey, the *bookies' favourite*. The air seemed to part around her, dispersing all in her way. Every atom and molecule scrambled to move. She was a law unto herself.

"It would appear that we're out of gin, old boy," Richard called to Francis as he took a seat on the couch and lit a smoke. "Gin and tea for everyone!"

"*Gin and tea?*", Eleanor asked between giggles.

"What else would such esteemed guests of mine drink? It is the absolute finest of English beverages."

"Wine, Robin?", Francis asked in a hushed tone.

"Yes please, Francis," I smiled.

Five minutes later, he returned. In his absence, I hadn't said as much as a word. To fill the time, I pretended to examine the books that had been left by the previous tenants. Francis returned and served tea and gin to the others, before discretely laying a bountiful glass of red beside me. The discretion of the affair was gone as soon as I raised the glass to my lips.

"No tea for you, Fitzy?", Richard enquired.

"Afraid not. It doesn't go down too well."

"Perfectly foolish," he snapped, before turning to Eleanor. "Robin's a writer, you know."

"Oh, is he?", asked Eleanor, as if I were in another room. "He any good?"

"I wouldn't dare say yes or no. I'm hardly one to judge, I find novels far too boring and mature. Now, if he were an adventurer, or a matador, I'd take more of an interest. His poetry is quite pretty."

"Indeed. Mother and father are obsessed with finding the *next great writer*. I've had to shut out all thoughts of writers for the sake of variety."

"I hope no offence is taken, Fitzy."

"Oh, none. D-Don't worry about it."

An hour or so passed and our guests grew more comfortable. Francis and I had paired off and were discussing some matter that I can no longer recall. Richard held Eleanor close; like he was going to war and asking her to wait for him. She investigated him, without attachment of the heart, rather with a more guttural yearning. It seemed that their departure into another room was imminent.

My face had gone numb from the drink, and I still hadn't said much. The four pairs had taken to light whispers into ears and giggled responses. One such whisper was the final straw for Richard, he led Eleanor by the hand, out into the hall. My gaze followed them as they took a sharp right into Francis' room.

"Francis, I think they've gone into your room."

He seemed neutral on the matter. "Yes, I suppose they have."

Before I could respond, Maz stood to address me.

"Mind if I use your phone, squire?"

"Of course."

"Cheers."

He darted out of the room for the kitchen, as an uneasy silence descended. A few of the girls looked Francis and I up and down. Satisfied, they turned back to their dates. Footsteps entered as Maz returned to the room, bouncing.

"Just spoke to Crowe and his lot, they're heading to a club in town and asked if we'd fancy it."

There were murmurings of excitement as a consensus of '*yes*' quickly formed. Maz turned to us. "Well," he paused, awkwardly. "I shall hope to see you chaps around, do let Bellers know that we appreciate his hospitality."

I nodded.

Francis set about tidying up after they'd left in giggles and cries. I recall stories from school, some of the lads in my year, including my oldest friend Monty, would sneak out and supposedly liaise with the girls from a nearby grammar school. I never went, nor was I invited. *How* I envied

Monty, and his smooth, suave ways. Quickly, and without warning, I desired solitude, as I so often suddenly did. I slipped outside, trotted down the stairs, out the door, and rested my back on the building's wall, gazing up at a dark and clouded sky. The fresh Autumn air was like a drug, and within moments the odours of the evening had passed.

I drifted from quiet street to noisy street, and to quiet street again; eventually stumbling upon a picturesque fountain of an enchanted look. There were cherubs etched into the stone, and the rhythmic splatters of water was a hypnosis. Once more I was away, in some meadow or by some stream. I sat on its rim and cared not that my neck and back were damp. The clouds seemed to dissipate, and before long the cosmos came into view, as if just for me. I caressed my breast pocket and found the cigarette that Richard had put there the day before. A young couple strolled past, from whom I borrowed a lighter, and smoked my first cigarette. That was the first in a long and winding gallery of cigarettes, that would one day conspire in unison to kill me.

I stayed by that fountain and drifted around my head for a while, I'm not sure how long. I was happy there; alone, and yet among fantastical company. Eventually, I was snapped out, like the latter half of a baptism, by the noise of a party. The distant hum of festivities had been ceaseless since I arrived. So much so that they made up a general ambience and were indistinguishable from one another. Yet this one called to me, as if it were a siren, cooing me further out to sea.

It came from a darkened alley by the adjacent street. I wandered towards it like a shark to blood; knowing instinctively that for some reason, my fate lay in this direction. I was not wrong. Of all the parties, in all the flats, in all the streets of Camford. I felt drawn to this specific hum. It was as if I were chasing destiny itself. As it happens, I was to have numerous destinies. A dozen cars with a dozen drivers; all waiting to drive me some place I could never reach by foot. It would transpire that two of these cars were just around the corner.

I walked into the alley, keeping to the shadows as my

eyes and ears worked in unison to locate the sound. I spotted it though a first-floor window. There, I saw a man of his mid or late thirties, forty at the eldest. He was speaking to an older gentleman, who I recognised from magazines as Eleanor's father, Donald. Through the shadows I made it so that I could no longer see them but could hear them perfectly.

"I think you're perfectly mistaken, Mr. Balloch. The best is yet to come. These young writers; they're hungry, ravenous even."

"I'll believe it when I see it, Mr. Andress. I'm afraid I don't share your faith in the new lot. They seem far more intrigued by music and women than by words."

"Perhaps they are. And yet, I'd gladly read a book about such things."

The younger man chuckled. "Well, Donald, you're the magnate. I suppose what you say goes. Or rather *who* goes."

A woman's voice entered the fray. Her voice was like a velvet blanket for the ears, and I was entranced.

"Come along now, Donald darling. I believe the young professor has heard quite enough."

"Nonsense, Mrs. Andress. I find your husband just as charming as you. It's a simple matter of disagreement."

"Indeed, it is. Mr. Balloch believes that there are no good writers left, they've all died, gone to shit, were shit to begin with, or have died and been replaced by shit. Was that what you said, Bill?"

"I said words to that effect."

"Whereas I believe he is somewhere in this city."

"Perhaps Winter days will bring something new," said she. "And all will be well."

I felt a shiver in my spine, as that ghost named *epiphany* shot down it and barked at my legs to run. Just as my desire to escape the flat descended in a hurry, the desire to return came just as fast. Still hugging the shadows, I retreated towards the orange glow of street lights. And as I left the shadow, some unknown force coerced me into turning back.

When I did, that voice had a face. Her lips that spoke had eyes that met with mine. She was mesmerising and I could not look away; nor would she, and we were locked in place for several pulsing moments. She smiled, with a subtle twitch, as I remained still. I stumbled on some obstacle and glanced down. And when my gaze returned, she was gone.

Hurriedly, I jetted through Camford. The parties were winding to an end and crowds emerged from houses and flats, as each street became harder to traverse than the one that came before. I burst through the street-level door as the clock struck twelve. Feet descended the steps as I ascended, and within moments I crossed paths with Eleanor. Through excitement and fear, I could not speak and instead gave her a firm and chivalric nod. She giggled at my attempt to be suave and bade me a good night.

"I'm sure I shall see you again, Robin."

I entered the flat to find Richard, wearing only a finely made robe, laying across the armchair, listening to the radio, with Francis at his feet, finally allowing himself the night off. "Ah, Fitzy. I'd assumed you'd gone the club with the others."

"Oh, no. I was just taking a stroll."

Richard chuckled. "*Writers*. What a ridiculous sort."

I got to my desk and readied the typewriter. I had desired, long before I consciously knew so, that I wished to be a novelist, and that anything I did would be in service to this end. All I needed was a word, and in that perfectly-squared room in Camford, with the early-Autumn wind howling through the trees - signalling that Winter was nearby, and would not keep us waiting for long - I had six words, spoken by a woman I had never met. And yet, lingering in the walls and on the pavements of this postcard town, was the sense that Winter would come, that is a given, and with it would come—*something*. And so, under candlelight, I took a fledgeling step.

It was then, in that moment, with the day's alcohol wearing off and my head beginning to throb, that I took the first steps of what was to be my career as a writer. That woman's voice had lingered in my head, harbinger of Winter days.

And from there it emerged; those six words that would dominate me for the rest of my life, and drive me to near madness.

All is Well in Winter Days.

3

That first week came and went with ease. And by its end, I had settled on the fact that Richard and Francis were my designate friends, with Jarves, and Maz, and Portnoy on the periphery; Eleanor in the shadows. After I had officially matriculated, a week of gentle habit followed. On Monday, I stared at the page. On Tuesday we lunched and drank; and did the same on Wednesday. On Thursday, I walked the college grounds alone, and on Friday, Richard took me to get a lighter and cigarette case.

"About forty should get you a good set," he said, once we were in the city proper. "Fifty if you want them engraved."

"Fifty shillings?"

"Pounds."

"Fifty pounds?!"

Eleanor soon emerged from her shadow, and Richard declared his love when they had met for a third time. He came to me while I wrote, and requested I draft a poem for her.

"For her?"

"Yes. I hear you're rather clever with words."

"Why me? I'm not the one who's in love with her."

"I know that, Fitzy. I'll obviously pass it off as my own."

"I'll dumb it down then."

"Thank you."

All Richard truly knew of Eleanor was that she liked daisies. So, I went with that. It was rough, raw, and written in twenty minutes. Yet it had a nice sound to it, as if every word had been suffered over and extracted at great personal cost. It worked, and the next day, she flung herself into the flat, and pulled a half-dressed Richard into Francis' room.

"My toast!", he cried, as she dragged him. "My toast!"

Later, as I read by the lounge window, he slapped me on the arm with gusto. "Nice bloody work, Fitzy. You are a genius!"

"I'm glad she enjoyed it," I said, disinterested and concerned with my book.

"Oh, more than! You really are a gem my old boy. Say, have you considered becoming a writer?"

"Yes, Richard. I have."

"Well, carry on old boy!"

"Christ, Richard!", I said after turning to face him and seeing him in an entirely *natural* state. "Put some bloody clothes on."

By my book's end, another week passed, and so began the Michaelmas term. Awkward clusters of young men had started to form by lunch on the first day. They typically came from the same digs, but not the same schools. Each member seemed just as desperate as the other to shed old skin and reinvent. Hastily, and with their affected accents of the lower classes, they made plans for lunch or drinks, that would pour cement onto their fates. Like jaded men, the wrong side of eighteen, they cast away the fruits of excitement, and settled for what was nearest and most routine. These men would go on to play squash together, do business, and live side by side; though they would do so without a sense of fraternal love.

As I walked into the theatre, among some forty others, I felt a strange sensation. As if I was in some great danger, and I responded thus, looking for a threat, a reason to turn around and scurry away. Instead, I saw a familiar face, to whom I was a stranger. I had seen him a few weeks earlier, at the window by the fountain.

"Good morning," he said, once the room had filled. "My name is William Balloch. I shall be instructing you all on the *ways of modern and contemporary literature*—much to my chagrin. Some of you may perhaps know me as William Balloch the playwright, but that man is gone. *I* have taken his place. I will not read your work, irrespective of how good you think it is. Whatever, or whomever, you may know me as, do know that I consider myself, quite strictly, to be a Camford don. I shall require an essay, worthy of discussion, per fortnight. Starting with the art of writing about nothing. The *Fabulam de Nihilo*."

Once the pleasantries were up, he gave the lecture; and when he began to speak of literature, I fell into a sort of awe. I felt as if he had reached into my mind; its most shallow points, and its deepest recesses, and extracted every word that I wanted to hear. When I had first heard him speak, it was in lambaste of literature, yet today he defended it; as a principle, a fact of life, as the fifth limb. It was ruggedly angelic. He was funny, cynical, crass, and cool, so damn cool. He spoke perfectly, methodically, with a swagger and a bounce. And when he had finished, the room emptied in a flash, as the unappreciative hurried to lunch. I felt, in that moment, anger. I was outraged that such a sermon had gone unheard, and before I could pack my things, it was just he and I in the room. I approached him, and he glanced up toward my pattering steps. Yet, as it had so many times before, my throat closed, teeth chattered against one another, and I found myself unable to speak. For several seconds I just stared at him, praying for some verbiage to come.

"Well," he said once I had given up. "By the look on your face, you're either going to praise or punch me. Please, young man, I implore you to consider the former. I've had a very long night, and a very short morning. My head hurts already."

"Y-you spoke about the *Fabulam de Nihilo*."

"I did."

"I've n-never heard that phrase before. B-but I believe now that favourite book is one. *Of Human Bondage*. M—M—Maugham used surrogates. He based Philip C-Carey's club—foot on his own stammer, he walked just fine."

"I suppose you'd know a thing or two about stammers."

I flushed, and he softened, and smiled with a guilty pity. "I'm sorry about that. Truly. Please do forgive me. As I said; long night, short morning, and I'm feeling a bit—prickly."

I just smiled and nodded.

"You know," he continued. "There's always one."

"One what?", I asked.

"One who didn't listen."

"Oh I listened. Every word."

"Not about that. *You,* young man, are a budding writer."

"Yes."

"*Penny a pound, one born every minute*. Novelist or playwright?"

"N-Novelist. I think. Though I've never written anything truly."

"You know I had an aunt who stammered. She used to take a large breath right before she spoke, and would begin to annunciate on the exhale. Perhaps you should try that."

"Perhaps I shall."

"My answer is no, by the way."

"No?"

"No, I won't read your novel."

"Oh."

"What's your name?"

"Robin."

"Robin?"

"Robin Fitzwarwick."

"Are you one of those puritan upstarts?"

"What could you mean?"

"You know, those middle-class kids, who shall inherit the earth."

"Why does everyone have that impression of me?"

"You have a very middle-class air about you."

"Is that an insult?"

"It is what you make of it, boy."

"I just like to watch people."

"Why?"

"Because I find them interesting. From afar, that is. Up close they're all the same to me."

He smiled. "Well, you've got the instinct. But have you the bug? Do you drink?"

"I do in the evening."

"It's 7pm in New York. Come, let us drink and be merry."

We migrated to a nearby pub, known for professors and their favourite pupils. He ordered what he referred to as a *hat-trick* - a pint of beer, a gin and tonic, and a shot of whiskey -, one for me and one for himself. "Something from when I was once here," he explained. "So, what *is* with the stammer?"

"Oh," I said, with a slight gasp. "I've just——always had it."

"Does it ever go away?"

"It didn't used to, but these days it's only when I'm nervous."

"And you are nervous currently?"

"A little."

"Don't be. Drink up."

Balloch sank his whiskey and gulped from the pint. "So," he said, wiping his chin with a sleeve. "You want to be a novelist."

"Yes."

"Like I said, you have the instinct. I can see that a mile off. We never change, do we?"

"*We*?", I asked. "I thought you were but a Camford don?"

"I just say that to scare off the hopefuls. Though I can assure you that I am of very little interest."

"I don't think so."

"No? You find me a *muse*?"

I chuckled, as did he. "No," I dismissed. "B-But there is a story there."

"Perhaps there is," he ceded. "At least to the tragedian among us. The playwright who had it all and lost it all, and then some. Thirty-eight and teaching; following a short, but decisively unsuccessful battle against a cancer of the career. The *Camford man*, who instead of making a generous donation to his college, suckles on its teat. Oh *how* the mighty fall."

I thought for a moment. "At first. Until you become the r-rustic, cynical, possibly alcoholic m-mentor figure."

He smiled. "Perhaps."

He lit a smoke and offered me one as the bartender meandered over with a new round of drinks. Once he had left, Balloch leaned in and looked me in the eye. "So, about this fixation on Maugham. It's perfectly okay, you know. It is very normal for a young writer to fixate on a particular work and try to be it. Perhaps one day a wide-eyed fresher will do the same with one of yours, if you can navigate the maze that is. *The Game*."

"The game?"

"With a capital 'G'. There is plenty for you to learn, young Robin."

"Is there something wrong with having a favourite novel?"

"Not if you grapple with it correctly."

"Right."

"Tell me," he said, moving along. "What's your Lotte?"

"My lot?"

"Lotte. L-O-T-T-E."

"My—"

"You're a smart lad, Robin, well-read I presume. And if I were to really go out on a whim, not educated for free. You've read Goethe, you know exactly what I mean. You need that little spark of pain, it makes us all a bit more interesting. So, what is it? The stammer?"

"It's been a great source of m-mockery. But no."

"Family?"

"Or lack thereof."

Balloch grimaced, "I'm sorry."

"It's okay."

"Recent?"

"Yes and no."

He raised an eyebrow, silently imploring me to continue. "My father. He d-died in the war. He went to France in '39, I only ever saw him once after that. He died in '45, very close to the end."

"How close?"

"The last few days of the war."

"Was it a slug?"

"A slug?"

"A bullet. Did he get shot?"

"No. He died of an allergic reaction."

I looked down at my drink and sat in the silence. I shot back up when I heard his muffled laughs. He looked embarrassed, like a scolded schoolboy. "I'm sorry. It's not funny, just—"

"Ironic?"

"Ironic, yes."

"Did you fight?", I asked.

"I was in the navy. Pacific theatre, didn't see much though. I spent most of it moored off of the coast of Fiji, watching the Americans doing their bit."

Another silence came upon us, in which I could see the next question stewing in his eyes; held at bay only by a sense of shame at the intimate. "She died in childbirth," I said, pre-emptively.

Balloch grimaced again. "That's a pretty good *Lotte*."

"Oh, there's more. I was the black sheep, the family spectre."

"Go on," he implored.

"I never saw her side of the family. But my father's side, they loved her. They'd known her for as long as he had. They used to say that I murdered her. My father tried to protect me all he could, but he went to war when I was six. When he died, I—"

"Didn't stand a chance."

"Indeed. I inherited a lot, and they tried to take every last penny. If they'd had it their way, I'd have been dropped off at a convent and never heard from again. But my father saw it coming, and spoke to the lawyers. So one day they drove me to Godalming, and that was it. I haven't seen them since."

"So you went to Charterhouse?"

"I did."

"Ah! A blue blood. I went to Repton myself. Quite the commute for a Devon boy. Where did you go out of term?"

"With my friend, Monty, on occasion."

He posed in thought for a few seconds, as if trying to craft the wording of what he was to say. He chose to abandon all plans and ask another direct question.

"What is it that you want?"

"Excuse me?"

"When you are on your deathbed, what is it that you want? What ripple would you like to send into the water?"

"I—I want to be the mortal enemy of schoolboys throughout the country."

"*Schoolboys*?"

"Yes. I w-want them to hate me, to despise me, even."

"Why?"

"Because they have to study my books in school."

He laughed mightily. "Oh, that is excellent."

The day moved along like a breeze, and we spoke little of real things after that. We drank some more and moved on to coffee. We ate in a cheap restaurant as the sun fell. After, Balloch stopped me with a sincere look in his eye.

"You really want this?"

"Yes," I said. "More than anything."

"The business is brutal, you will have no true friends within it. You will be a cash-cow if you're lucky, and then a steak fillet. That's if you make any money at all. It's more likely that you won't. You'll lose friendships, be a terrible romantic partner, and you'll never truly feel good enough. It may even drive you to madness. Do you still want it?"

"Yes."

"You want to be the enemy of schoolboys everywhere?"

"Yes.

"Then you shall have to be great. Do you want to be a great writer?"

"I do."

"Do you want to be *one of the great writers*?"

"I do."

"And do you promise to complete and submit your essays to a satisfactory level?"

"Yes."

"Then report to me once a week. Fridays at six. We will make a writer of you."

He walked in the opposite direction before I could agree to his terms, and turned the corner into the night. And so it was that the Friday Club was born. It was in these meetings that I would construct, and mould, my earliest works. Where my blood, and tears, would indeed turn to ink.

I returned home giddy, and spent another debauched evening in the flat. That night, as I readied myself for sleep, I made a promise to myself, that I would since label the *Camford Declaration*; that I would not ever lead a normal life; at least not for long.

4

"Richard, why are we doing this?"
"Tell me old boy," he said, without answering. "What do you recall about last week?"
"We drank in the Wellington," I began. "You passed out and we carried you to the canal."
"What else?"
"Something about Portnoy, and a fifteenth-century window."
"So what you mean to say is that what you recall from last week is us being drunk and foolish?"
"I suppose so."
"Not your studies?"
"No, not my studies."
"And therein lies the truth, old boy. You see, *a life is but the creation of memories*. That, Robin, is why we are drinking instead of attending our lectures. Now, be a good boy and drink your tequila, it'll get cold."
I took an obedient swig. "Say, where is Francis anyway?"
"He is at his lectures."
"I see."
"Yes, education is very important, Robin. It evolves the mind into a *sharp instrument*. Now stop asking

questions and drink your dry vermouth and coffee."
"I just have one more."
"Fine."
"What is it exactly that you are studying?"
"I don't understand the question."
"How could you not? It's a very simple question."
"No it isn't. It's like asking a man what colour the back of his neck is, he simply cannot know such a thing."
"You're being an ass, Richard. Do tell me, I've been dying to know for months."
"Um—the natural sciences, I think."
"You think?"
"Yes! It is so complicated for me, you ask *such* rhetorical questions."
"You study the natural sciences?"
"Yes," he said in a pondering fashion. "I'm fairly sure that I do."
"*You* study the natural sciences?"
"Yes!"
"In two and a half years, you will collect a degree in the natural sciences?"
"Yes."
"And then what? You'll—become a scientist?"
"If my heart wills it."
"If you complete the work that is."
"Oh, I needn't worry about that. Fucksby handles all of that nonsense."
"He does your work for you?"
"Except for when he is unwell. Then I pay Portnoy to do it."
"So Francis is doing two degrees?"
"You said only one question."
"This requires investigation."
"No he doesn't do two degrees. In the eyes of the university, he *is* Richard Belling. Now stop being such a bore and drink your whiskey sour and daiquiri."
"So," I said, emptying both glasses. "Francis does

all of your work, attends all of your lectures, and has assumed your identity?"

"That is correct, yes."

"And at the end of it all, he won't even have a degree?"

"As far as I am aware, no, he will not."

"And he's okay with this?"

"Of course."

"Why?"

"Because the old boy knows that for as long as there is air in my lungs, he will want for nothing."

That drunken day, so hazy and yet so clear in my mind, was in the first week of November; when the wind howled and the trees were stripped nude - their discarded remains had vanished from the pavement, and I grew to miss the rustle as I walked hither and tither. The Friday Club had been well established, and I met with Balloch twice a week. I lived for the novel, still then an embryo; there were a few chapters, and I intended to write as I went. As far as I knew, a young man, with an awkward nature and a nondescript face, had arrived at an opulent country home, that housed the souls of long-gone relatives. It wasn't a dazzling, heroic story, and nor was it meant to be. But it was the story of life. It seemed so perfectly natural for a man of eighteen to reach far beyond the tips of his fingers, into uncharted territory. Yet, I had not lived, nor loved, nor passed a lot of time and there sat the issue, the clog in my machine; I had no muse but death.

Eleanor's shadow retreated more by the day, and Richard was smitten. She had that moreish quality. She lived as if each night, while she slept, her skin was shed, and a new woman was born by morning light.

"I think I'll write some poems of my own," Richard proudly proclaimed one day after she had left. "How hard can it be?"

A week later, while I was at my desk, Richard's hand slammed upon the oak. In it was a scrawled note. "What do you think, Fitzy? Up to your *high and mighty* standards?"

'Your hips, just as your lips
Do brim with subtle grace,
Darling, would it be rude,
To request both meet my face.'

"It's lovely, Richard."

"Yes. I thought as much."

Eleanor found it to be amusing and wholly unserious.

"It's you, isn't it?", Balloch asked, when we met on a Wednesday.

"More or less."

"Well, you wouldn't be the first. Writers always seem to write themselves. Particularly with the debut."

"Maugham's debut was about a woman."

"Oh, here we go again," he said, before catching himself. "Wait, how did I get roped into this? Wednesday meetings are to discuss your studies, and it is Wednesday, not Friday. Also, I must tell you off, Robin. I heard that you skipped your lecture on continental literature."

"I know, Bill. I was writing."

"That *wasn't* our arrangement."

"Perhaps I'm not supposed to be a scholar."

"You need a contingency plan, young Robin. If it all goes to pot. Success has eluded better writers and met the less talented. Make time for your studies. This is good, your poem was good. Balance is all I am proposing. I wrote my first play as an undergraduate, but I listened, attended my lectures, and wrote my papers. Do you know why?"

"Why?"

"You know why. I want to hear you say it."

"Because it can all go away."

"It can all go away. I don't say this to be cruel. I'd be crueller to not say it. All you can do is write something great, the rest is up to the whims of other men."

"But this could be great."

"And you have the rest of your life to write it."

We paused and stared each other down for several tense moments. He blinked first, silently declaring me to be the victor. "So," he said with a sigh. "Your novel?"

"My novel."

"Tell me about it."

"Well. I haven't quite figured it out yet, but I'm close. It's sort of about everything, but also nothing. Life, love, the passing of time. My protagonist—"

"Is he named Philip perhaps?"

"Not this again."

"Be careful, Icarus."

"Why do you keep saying that?"

"Don't wish away your youth. My first play was a jumbled mess. It was too complex, and no one cared a dot about it. It took me years to climb out of that hole. Don't make my mistake. Don't be me. Don't fly too close to the sun."

He stood from the chair and walked past me to a green metal cabinet in the corner, next to the bar. Three shelves down, he withdrew a vanilla envelope with some clippings inside. He read aloud from the first sheet.

"*William Balloch, while clearly a talented playwright, has made a crucial error of judgement with his debut work, The Harbinger. No one can understand a word of it, nor glean any of its meaning. Verbose, cryptic, and thoroughly unenjoyable. One out of five.*"

"Brutal," I said with a shudder."

"That was in the Herald. Never trust the Herald. Thanks to them, I was seconded to the *great tower of niche*. Banished if you will. Anyway, what's it called, your novel?"

"All's Well in Winter Days."

"What does that mean?"

"Just something I heard once. I'm still figuring that out."

He examined the first page, as I sat unnerved.

"Well, your prose is fine. It's clean, blunt, masculine. And I would, in no manner, ever tell you to discard this. What I'm saying is '*not yet*'. Sit on it, meditate, age a bit. Let your life inspire you, and let yourself take joy from it. You know what the greatest experience of life is? It is drinking with friends and laughing. You will soon learn two things; nothing is greater, and it will not last forever. One day you'll be married, with children, and all the better for it, for it is a man's duty. However, you *will* look back on those halcyon days with such a despicable nostalgia and regret, that'll bore into you, if you do not acquiesce to that simple pleasure while you are young. In the meantime, write something simple. A farce, or some poetry."

"Why does everyone want me to write poetry?", I sighed.

"Poetry is the most natural of all literature. We use it to understand ourselves, our environment. History, for generations and generations, was passed along through poetry, through songs. This flatmate of yours, Bellend?"

"Belling."

"Right, Belling. You wrote something for him, right? For his lady?"

"I did."

"And it worked?"

"It did."

"Well, there you go. You know it can reach people, whatever the intention."

"So, I become a poet?"

"No, you become a writer."

"*A writer,*" I pondered, aloud.

"A writer."

In the silence that followed, we met eyes and shared a smirk. By Friday, I had written a few more poems, all drafted while taking my evening walks, and refined by candlelight. I showed them to Balloch in the afternoon.

"Robin, these are excellent."

"They are?"
"Yes! A tad rough around the edges, formulaic at times, but you'll improve."
"Formulaic?"
"Indeed, strict couplets can be rather hit or miss. But this is inexperience, not a lack of talent, or a lack of respect for the form. You see, there's a tight rope walk one must do to write good poetry. To have a formula, but not be formulaic. To play around with, and bend the rules, while acknowledging that there are rules, and that they serve a legitimate purpose." He angled the notebook towards me. "See, here. The words are good, and you have painted quite a pretty picture, but it's rigid. The use of couplets boxes you in. Rhyme is important, as is rhythm, theme, a total expression of the senses, but you *are* allowed to have fun." He picked one out of the pile. "This one here, it's flawless. Perfect even. I must show people, you must let me."
"Of course."
He leapt with joy, almost right out of the chair.
"Come with me tonight, Robin. I must go to one of those painful college events, but I know just who to show this to."
"Who?"
"Donald Andress."

5

The banquet room was a living spectacle. The ceilings were high, and the windows were ornate and coloured in tessellations of red and green, that blasted the room with colour. We had arrived twenty minutes prior and made slow, deliberate strides around the room. Balloch was serious and severe.

"Now," he said upon our second rotation. "Despite the leisurely appearance, this is very much a work event. If you are to succeed in this world, you must learn the dance."

Balloch excused himself and wandered off to speak with a couple of the elder dons of the college. I could tell that at some point in their brief exchange, my presence had been the topic of conversation.

"Pardon me," called a voice behind me. I turned to see a frightfully old man, who seemed that he would drop at any moment. "Could you fetch me a gin and tonic?"

"I don't work here."

"Oh," he said, before scurrying off.

Before long, Balloch returned to me, amused from the misunderstanding. "I'm afraid you may have to get used to that. These lot aren't used to youngsters."

"And where do the youngsters typically reside?", I asked.

"You tell me. The Albert Village perhaps?"

We made another lap of the room, sharing brief nods with various professors and benefactors of the college. There were esteemed guests dotted around the room, and I was introduced to more faces and names than I can recall. We found our way to the bar, and I ordered a glass of red. Balloch ordered whiskey and encouraged the barman to keep pouring until it came to three fingers.

"Is everything okay?" I asked.

"Fine. Just a bit of Dutch courage." His eyes widened as he made out a target across the room. "Okay, there he is."

Donald Andress walked like a tiger stalking deer. He was precise, poised, almost predatory. His aura was the most powerful in the room; he knew it, and the room knew it too. He was the *big fish.*

"We'll let him navigate the room for a bit," Balloch whispered to me. "Then make our entrance."

"Why the tactical approach? Are the two of you not friends?"

"Donald Andress doesn't have *friends*. You have much to learn, Robin. This evening shall be an education. You see, it's all a game. Think of it like the playing field at school."

He gestured across the room to two men - one young, and the other of middle age. They laughed and joked as old friends do. "You see those two?"

"Yeah?"

"They seem chummy, right? Thick as thieves?"

"Sure."

"Don't be fooled, dear boy. The older chap is John Rawlinson. Associate Professor of Classics. And the young man is—"

"James Matheson," I interupted. "Of the Camford Review."

"You know him?"

"Same school."

"Ah! And do you see *her*?"

He took me by the shoulders and tilted my gaze until it rested on a woman in her early forties, in a red dress.

She watched the two men intently, as if a scuffle between them was brewing. To anyone else, the scene was perfectly sound and free of conflict.

"I see her."

"That is Mrs. Rawlinson. Jane. You see, the three of them share a secret. Some time ago, perhaps a year or so; our friend John comes home early, and I believe your imagination can do the rest."

"So?"

"Matheson sleeps with Mrs. Rawlinson, and Mr. Rawlinson knows - or *thinks* that he knows. And yet, no one knows. You know why?"

"Why?"

"Because they understand The Game; they play The Game, they do the dance."

"Why?"

"Symbiosis. They need each other. Therefore, in the eyes of Camford society, they are just the whipper-snapper, and his wise old friend."

"How do you know?"

"I visit Mrs. Rawlinson from time to time. Jane has many secrets. Now do excuse me, dear boy, I must play the game myself." He walked into the stand-off and raised his arms. "Johnny! How the hell are you?"

Balloch sauntered off and took Mr. Rawlinson's hand in his. And just like Matheson, he acted as if nothing were out of the ordinary. Matheson approached me after a few moments. "Is that one yours?", he asked, gesturing towards Balloch.

"Mine?"

"Yeah. You know, your elder, the one who brought you into this world."

"Yes. He's mine —I suppose."

"A good one to have, just be weary of the drink. It's gotten him into trouble before. You do look familiar. Have we met before?"

"We were at school together."

"Oh?"

"Robin Fitzwarwick."

"Oh, yes. You had that mighty stammer."

"Yes."

"And you wrote that short story, right? The one about the fox?"

His words caught me off guard. I had expected that any Carthusian of my age would have known me for the impediment alone. Yet none, bar Monty, knew me for my words.

"I did."

"It was good. D'you still write?"

"Yes."

"Well then. Keep on."

And with that, he left. I looked down and saw an empty glass, so I walked to the bar for more. It must be said that I took some joy as a man, twice my age, refilled my glass. I surveyed the room from the safety of my corner. Then, I saw her; the woman from the window. She moved about the room, not walking, but gliding. She charmed and disarmed every set of wandering eyes. The strength, and desire, to look away only found me when her gaze met mine, and suddenly I felt hot, and dizzy, and craved the Autumn air.

The cold breeze was indeed a drug, and I fell into a stupor as cars buzzed by, and the nightly charms of Camford filtered into my senses. The bliss was broken as a familiar voice rang out through the clouds.

"You fool! You damned fool! I am an esteemed student at this college, and you *will* let me into this event."

It was a voice, and a nature of speech that I could only credit to Richard. I glanced over and saw him; with Jarves, Maz, and Francis in tow. As I stared over, he caught my eye and lit up at the sight of me. "Robin! Hey, Robin, over here!"

I walked over, knowing the reason for my summons.

"Good evening chaps," I said. "Say, where's Portnoy?"

"He got sent down."

"Already?"

"Yes, it has been a most hazardous week. Could you help us, Fitzy?"

"With what exactly?"

He gestured at the doorman. "This brute, this—*neanderthal*, this *troglodyte* won't let us in. Give us a hand will you, old boy."

I turned to the doorman. "Uh —they're with me."

The doorman looked me up and down. "And are you a member of this club, sir, or are you a guest?"

"A guest."

"Well, I'm afraid to say that they cannot come in. Only card-carrying members of this club can vouch for non-members."

Before any of us could react, a secondary voice rang out from behind us. "It's okay, they are with me." We swivelled to see Eleanor, strutting towards us.

"Oh, absolutely, Miss Andress," cried the doorman. "My sincerest apologies."

"That's perfectly okay, Gill, I applaud the grace and duty with which you keep us safe from riffraff. Are my mother and father here?"

"Indeed, they are, Miss Andress."

"Splendid. Onwards!", she called to her retinue of drunkards.

We moved inside, back to that magnificent hall. Richard spotted the bar immediately. "Oh, excellent. Booze!"

He moved decisively straight for it, the others, including myself, following closely. "I'll have a gin and tea, my fine sir," he proclaimed proudly.

"We don't have any hot water," the barman rebuffed.

Richard turned back to us, looking lost and confused. "What on *earth* is wrong with this place?"

I slipped away from the group, with only Francis noticing. In the far corner, by a large window that led to a balcony, Balloch was speaking with Donald. They both noticed that I was awkwardly lingering some ten feet away.

"Ah! Speak of the devil. Robin, I'd like to introduce you to Donald Andress."

Donald took my hand in his, gripping it warmly and with a smile. "So," he said to Balloch, "This is your prodigy?"

"Indeed, it is."

"Balloch's just been telling me all about you. Though I must say, it's given me a bit of a chuckle, just last week he was telling me that there are no more writers, and now he's brought one to my soiree, a young one too. So, you fancy yourself a poet?"

Balloch interrupted before I could speak. "A writer. Poetry is just one of his many forms."

"And does your prodigy speak?"

The two chuckled and the onus now fell on me to speak. "I speak too. B—But I'm better at writing."

"I can see that," he replied, as if testing my resolve.

What struck me most about Donald was that, despite his wealth, name, and rank, he had maintained a cockney accent. As I would later learn, it had been a great obstacle in his come-up; and as such he clung to it like a badge of honour, a scar from the war. His focus was pulled to the right, past my vision, by the approach of someone else.

"Ah, darling!", Donald bellowed. "The apple of my eye! Come over here and meet my newest project."

I turned to inevitably see the woman from the window, making her way over to our little group. "Cynthia, I'd like to introduce you to—what's your name, kid?"

"Robin, Robin F-Fitzwarwick."

"Yes. This is Robin Fitzwarwick, vouched for by the illustrious William Balloch."

She took my hand gently, looked me dead in the eye and spoke. "Charmed."

"Likewise," was all I could say.

The conversation flowed, mostly between Balloch and Donald. I could hardly focus with such grace in my presence. On occasion, I drifted back into the room, just as I was addressed directly.

"Okay," Donald beamed, gripping my shoulder with a monstrous hand. "I'd say if you can have a collection together by Christmas, we can talk then, and I can see about getting your name out there."

"That would be excellent, sir."

"Please, call me Donald. We'll start with poems, see how you do, but the real work is in novels. People like romances. Exotic locations, passionate speeches, all that lovely old trite."

"I don't suppose any of you has a spare cigarette," said Cynthia. It seemed as if she stared right into me, into my soul, as she asked the question. "I'm all out."

"I do," I said, hand trembling as I reached into my breast pocket and withdrew my case.

She took one and placed it in her lips, before angling her body towards me, as if implying that I was to light it for her. I did, and while the flame torched the front end of the cigarette, her fingers danced upon the hairs on my wrist. I made some excuse and removed myself from the corner, finding stability in a chair on the far side of the room. Before long, Balloch joined me.

"*Careful, Icarus*," he said.

"Oh, God," I groaned.

"Trust me, Robin. I know. She is angelic. Cleopatra would blush. But she will break you if you let her."

"How do you know that?"

"I visit Mrs. Andress from time to time. Cynthia has secrets of her own."

I shot a glance at him, to which he chuckled and patted me on the back. "I'm just kidding. Even I know better than to mate with a black widow. Did you think that you were the first upstart fresher to catch her wandering eye?"

"I caught her eye?"

"And then some. And you're not the first."

"Am I the first to meet with you every Friday?"

"Yes. Are you the first student in whom I saw potential? No. Are you the first who tried to recruit me? No. But you have something; like a sort of disconnect. You very well may have spent your life thinking that this makes you cursed, but I see it as the writer's gene. You can only observe the world. You have that

neuroticism too, the self-awareness. It will make you great - though, you are impatient, and insecure, a simple matter of age. But I think you are going to be an excellent writer. A great writer. One of the great writers. Now, if you want to pursue her; or more realistically, allow her to pursue you, I won't stop you. I won't help you, but I won't stop you. But she will break you if you let her. But, she'll whisper in Donald's ear. So, what I'm saying is—"
"Careful, Icarus?"
"You're beginning to understand."

6

By Sunday, that night was but a hazy memory. And yet, Cynthia stayed with me like an omnipresent scent, like a childhood memory. Throughout the weekend, Richard had boasted of his drunken escapades; of climbing the college bell tower, and falling some twenty feet, only to bounce back up. It was later, and in private, that Francis had quietly corrected the account. The truth of the matter was that Richard had been ejected for drunkenness, fallen from the bell tower while trying to scale it, thrown up in front of the chapel, and required three men to carry him home.

Eleanor had not been seen on the Saturday, nor the Sunday morning; and Richard spoke as if she had never existed. "Emancipated women," he'd say from time to time. "If only there were ten of me."

After the party was over, Balloch had invited me to a luncheon at his on Sunday, which I accepted. I had known of his famous luncheons since we first met, and they were much talked about in the college for their propensity to spill into drunkenness and debate. *Witans of the college*, he'd call them. I awoke that day, and readied myself in a suit and hat. I was eating the last crumbs of my breakfast when Francis came into the kitchen.

"Ah, good morning, Robin," he chirped.

"Morning, Francis."

"You are looking swell today."

"Thank you, Francis."

"Hungry?", he asked.

"Just ate."

He set about preparing breakfast, setting up two plates and filling the kettle with water. Richard stumbled out of his room as the kettle hit a fever. "Oh, Christ. I feel like I've been punched."

"Perhaps you have, old boy," I called with a smirk.

"I hear the college green has a *mighty* right hand."

"Easy there, lad," he growled.

I laughed to myself, and Francis did too.

"Anyway," he added. "Where are you off to looking so fancy?"

"I'm going to a luncheon."

"Will there be drink?"

"Yes, I should think so."

"Can I come?"

"No."

I walked along the pleasant streets of Camford, as a rare hint of Autumn sun illuminated the streets, cut up by large trees, themselves preparing to undress. I had a sheet of paper with Balloch's address scrawled onto it. Number fifty-six. It was a townhouse with a red door. Balloch stood in the doorway as I approached.

"Robin, my dear boy! Come on in, there are some people I'd like you to meet."

I stepped into the flat and heard voices that blended into a low grumble, all men from what I could tell. I followed Balloch into the room to find four faces.

"Robin, you've met James Matheson, right?"

"Yes, I have. It's nice to see you again."

He nodded and took my hand. "I hear you've moved on from the Fox and into greener pastures. Bill's just told us that you've caught Donald's eye."

"Apparently," I said.

"Well then, long may our careers intertwine."

"And over here, we have Matthew Jenkins, critic for The Herald."

I shook his hand, yet his eyes did not meet mine They remained fixed on a half-drunk mug of coffee on the table.

"Rawlinson, from the Classics Department."

He nodded, as did I.

"And this is Wallace Mitz, final year PhD candidate in literature, and the man who will one day knife my back and replace me."

A roar went up around the room and Balloch grappled with the young man's shoulder. He stood to address me. "Pleased to meet you," he said in a thick, east-coast-American accent. "I must say, I found your poem to be quite brilliant. So, you are Balloch's poet?"

"He's a writer, actually," Balloch countered. "Poetry is just one of his forms."

"My most sincere apologies, allow me to rephrase. You are Balloch's *writer*."

We sat, and the conversation returned to the state of adversarial discomfort that was established before I entered. Balloch and Mitz were locked in debate.

"Look here, Bill," Mitz said, sternly. "You're not mistaken, the book may die out before we do, but literature? No. Literature will live on. As to my mind, literature is but the stories we tell. The radio and the television will not kill these things, movies are no threat, and even if they were there's little we can do about it. Talkies are going to stick around, and get better - so much better in fact, that reading, and listening——well, they'll become things that only snooty dons in armchairs do. They are not guns, these movies, they're vehicles. They will carry literature into the modern day. It, and we, shall evolve."

"Some things are better left the way they are," was Balloch's retort.

"Granted. And some things will be, the things that deserve to be."

"Does literature not deserve to remain as it is?"

"I didn't say that."

"You implied it. Tell me this; what is the greatest story ever told?"

"Objectively?"

"What to *you* is the greatest story ever told?"

"Well, it's Huckleberry Finn of course."

Balloch swivelled to Matheson. "And for you?"

"The Odyssey."

Balloch then turned to Jenkins. "And you?"

"Don Quixote."

Finally, he turned to me. "And you, my dear boy?"

"Oh, I couldn't say."

With a mocking grin, he turned back to the American, as did the rest of us. "Do you see a pattern here, Mitz?"

"Right now? In this moment, sure. But these stories will be told again, and not on paper. While you seem so content on clinging to the past like—if you'll excuse the expression, a number two that just won't flush. I'm talking about the future. The Adventures of Huckleberry Finn, The Odyssey, Don Quixote, whatever Robin decides with the graces of time. All will be told to future generations in voices, and pictures."

"God help us all."

"You see Robin over there?"

I felt uneasy, as all eyes turned to face me.

"I do," said Balloch, cautiously.

"He's your prodigy, right? Or Donald's? It's not exactly relevant to whom he reports."

"He is."

"He'll be making movies in ten years."

The two seemed to agree on an uneasy truce, and the conversation moved on. A degree of tension lingered between them for the rest of the afternoon. It seemed to me that said tension had been in place since long before that day, and would linger for days to come. And with good cause, in later days Mitz would indeed fulfil Balloch's premonition.

An hour passed and drinks began to flow. First coffee, and then wine and gin and whiskey. By the time food had been served, we were merry and in light spirits. I sat next to Mitz, and we spoke casually of London life. Though I knew little outside of various houses in my particular neck of the woods, he seemed to know the place like the back of his hand.

"And this other time," he began, after several boisterous anecdotes of the city. "I awoke to find myself quite nude, on the floor of a cheap hotel room, with a warrant out for my arrest."

"Whatever for?", I asked.

"Corruption of the youth."

"Like Socrates," I quipped.

"Yes!", he cried, grabbing a cup, and hoisting it in the air. "There'd better be Hemlock in here!"

"Okay, Mitz," Balloch intervened. "Now the real reason."

"I urinated in an alley."

"Ah," I said.

Mitz was born in Chicago, ten years before myself, and was raised in St. Louis. He had studied at Princeton, prior to Camford. He spoke confidently, even on matters in which he knew little. Though he was some way older, it felt that we were the same age.

We ate. I observed as Balloch and Mitz sparred a little. After, we rotated back into the living room. It was 3pm when there was a knock at the door. Balloch retreated out of the room and returned shortly, followed by pronounced and domineering footsteps.

Donald Andress entered the room and we all stood to greet him. Working his way around, he found himself taller than all the men apart from me. I had an inch or two on him.

"Good to see you again, Mr. Fitzwarwick. How goes the collection?"

"On its way, sir."

"Please, it's Donald to you."

It seemed a mystery to me just why Donald had shown up here. He was quite possibly the most important man in publishing, and his Sundays would normally be reserved for the cultivation of business, in church yards, members clubs and golf courses. He meandered to the corner of the room and prepared himself a stiff drink.

"Smokes, anyone?"

We all agreed, and he produced a shining gold case from his pocket. Inside were smokes, quite unlike any I had seen before. They glimmered, and the butt was coated in gold.

"This'll be the best smoke you ever had," he bragged, as he lit mine. It was.

"Where do you find them?", I asked.

"I know a chap, don't worry about it. You want some more, I can get you some. You see, kid, I have a very careful image to maintain. The old lot, you know the sort, only take me seriously when I have more money than they do, which is every day it seems. I need to remind them of this, and it makes me giddy to rub it in their faces. That's one thing you should know about me, Mr. Fitzwarwick; I am *not* a gentleman. I don't dress like one, I don't speak like one, and I don't behave like one. Chivalry is lost on me."

A few minutes later the telephone rang, and Balloch retreated from the room to answer. Donald followed him with his eyes, before snapping them back to me. "What do you make of this crowd?", he asked in a hush.

"They seem nice," I whispered.

"Being nice won't get you anywhere, Robin. You've got to isolate what you want, and pursue it, to the point of near-violence. Crush anyone in your way. I've been seeing Rawlinson's old lady, you know."

"Oh?"

"Strictly business."

"Any other old ladies?"

"Of those two?", he nodded in the direction of Mitz and Jenkins. "No. Not a woman between them. You know, they're a tad bit *closer* than you'd think."

"How do you know these things?"

"It's my job to know. It's good for business. I'm not a gentleman, Robin. I am under no obligation to be gentle."

"And for Bill?"

"I can't be the one to say, kid. He's your elder."

Balloch reappeared in the doorway and snapped his fingers to gain my attention. "Robin, it's for you."

I stood, and felt every eye in the room. Once I was through the door and out of sight, Balloch followed me for a few paces and gripped my wrist lightly. I swivelled to see a concerned look on his face. "Careful, Icarus."

By the time I had reached the phone there was some clarity in my mind as to who would be on the other end. I was not disappointed when I heard her voice. "Are you alone?", was the first thing she said.

"No. I'm at Balloch's."

"I meant is anyone near you?"

I made sure that Balloch had retreated. "No."

"Is *he* there?"

"Who?"

"You know who. Is he there?"

"He is."

"I thought as much. You know, Robin, a man is very little without his wife. No matter the man, the voice of his woman is always in the back of his mind. Guiding him, planting little seeds, little words of who he *should* and *should not* associate with."

"What are you implying?"

"You'd be wise to not disappoint me, Robin. You'd be very wise."

"Are you threatening me?"

"Threatening you? I'd do nothing of the sort. I'm

simply explaining something that any young man with aspirations such as yours should know. You have my husband's attention, your talent has gotten you to his influence, and he can open many doors for you. But talent can only get one so far. Tact, Robin. It is tact that will carry you much farther than talent. My husband makes writers. He decides who people read and who they don't. And a man is very little without his wife. I wish to meet with you, Robin. I wish to meet with you this afternoon. Make your excuses and go to the Galveston Arms, on St. Nicholas' Road. Order a pint of stout with no ice."

"No ice?"

The line clicked, and I stayed in place for several seconds. "I'm afraid I must be off," I said upon returning to the room. Balloch stiffened and stared me down.

"Oh, so soon?"

"I'm afraid so. There's been an emergency at my flat. It's my friend Richard—he is far too drunk."

"Invite him here!", cried a jolly Mitz. "I should like to meet him."

The others ignored him, and rose to see me off, I shook hands but avoided eye contact. "I'm sure I shall see you soon, Robin," said Donald when it was his turn to bid me a farewell, he handed me another of his golden cigarettes. "One for the road. Do let me know how the collection comes along. I shall be keeping a close eye on you."

"Yes, y-yes I will."

"And remember, we look after each other in these circles." He slipped a card into my hand. "No more middle-men. Anything you need, call me."

I left the townhouse and moved towards the centre of the city. I stopped in a shop to ask directions to the Galveston Arms and was informed that it was nearby.

"A pint of stout please, no ice."

The barman looked me up and down. He prepared the drink and served without charge. While I took my first sip, he placed an antique looking key on the counter.

"Room five. Second floor."
"Do I take the drink with me?" I asked.
"Nah. Enjoy your drink here."

And so, I did. Looking around the room, I knew that I had been summoned to a less seemly part of the town, far from the University. The stout went down easy, and soon I'd had my fill.

"The stairs are in the far corner, just past the loo," said the barman as I rose.

I paused at the door and readied myself before knocking. "Come in," she called.

She was laying effortlessly on the bed; her hair unfurled and one leg over the other. There was a cigarette in one hand, and a hard-covered book in the other. "What are you reading?", I asked. She didn't look up and answered slowly.

"Lady Chatterley's Lover."

"That's fitting," I said, nonchalantly.

"You think so highly of yourself?", she retorted, still not breaking her gaze from the page. "Pity. I prefer my men to be inexperienced and unassuming."

"Is that so?"

She finally looked at me, and pivoted into a sitting position at the end of the bed and tapped the linens next to her, inviting me to sit. When I look back upon my life, now in its flickering and expiring embers; I consider this to be the first of many milestones. It was the day that I became a man. And on that day, my wings of feather and wax were fixed. And I flew, straight for the sun.

7

I had come to know the Andress family rather well by the end of 1951; Donald, as he had taken the embryo of my career into his hands; Eleanor through Richard, and Cynthia through my own atavistic explorations.

They lived in London, and kept a small flat in Camford; though it was under the constant guard of watchful eyes and blabbering lips. So, we met at the pub, and on occasion at a tavern in the country.

One day in late November, I returned from my lectures to find that my typewriter had mysteriously fallen from the desk and broken into fragments. I interrogated Richard, and after trying to scapegoat Francis, he admitted to the accident. I told Cynthia of this during one of our lunches and was bought a replacement that same day. She would summon me with brief notes that a hired hand would slide under the flat door. Each was on an off-white slip of official paper with a simple 'R' stamped onto the front.

'Robin,
Your presence is required at the Galveston Arms, Camford.
Make haste.
C.'

One such notice came while Eleanor was in the flat, and

had been for several days. Her and Richard had seemingly reconciled whatever rift had formed between them. I cared not to ask. "Robin!" I heard, while at my desk. "Mail."

I scurried into the lounge, where she met me, wearing nothing except Richard's opulent robe. "Who's this from?", she enquired with a bounce.

"Oh no one, I—"

She interrupted me with a hat-trick of condescending tuts. "We don't like secrets, do we, Robin?" She leaned away from me with the note in her far hand, our faces came close.

"Give me that." I said, snatching the note from out of the hand and moving towards the hallway. I heard feet running behind me and suddenly she was on my back, attempting to snatch the letter.

"Now, now, now," called a voice from further down the hall. "Let us not be uncivilised about this."

Richard emerged, grinning as it became clear that I had been boxed in on all sides, and that the ambush had been a success. "I've been meaning to ask you for some time about these—summons. Give it here and we can put this all behind us."

"Oh, fuck off, Belling." I snarled, bumping past him and into my room. A few minutes later, I emerged from the room, fully dressed, and the two had seemingly forgotten about the confrontation. "I'm going out," I called.

"Out?", Richard called back from the couch. "Wherever to?"

"Just out."

And so, these excursions, as well as those to Balloch's office and my various academic requirements came to form the essence of my eighteenth year. Soon enough Christmas came and went. I had written home, to enquire about my staying for the holidays and received no reply. I wrote to Monty but was informed that he was in Cap Ferret and could not host me.

This was not my first Christmas alone, far from it. Most were spent at Charterhouse. I phoned Balloch and received an invitation to his Christmas luncheon. I was with

Cynthia in the morning, and arrived late, to find Balloch and Mitz in another spat. Seeing the fracas, and wishing to play no part, I retreated to the terrace, where Matheson stood already. "It's a lovely little picture is it not," he said, gesturing to the city. Smoke plumed from chimneys and added a haze to the various churches and steeples.

"Truly."

"I can imagine you'll get a pretty poem or two out of this. I heard about the collection, congratulations."

"Thank you, James."

"I suppose you'll be seeing a lot more of me. You must be initiated into The Game by now."

"Somewhat."

He noticed my expression and laughed to himself.

"Yes, I know it's all bullshit too. It's just how things pan out here."

"How is it that you're already in work? You are only two years older than I."

"I got sent down. It just happened to be so that my elder had strings to pull. You, however. Your fortunes point in the other direction."

"You mean Balloch?"

"I do. You'll probably end up writing the best works, but he doesn't open doors. With him, you're in a bit of a mare, success or bust."

"Meaning?"

"Meaning that you will either become a great writer, or nothing at all. Most likely both."

Before I could speak, the door opened behind me. Balloch strolled out and lit a smoke. "Mitz had to leave," he announced after a puff or two.

"How terrible," Matheson added, before we all broke into laughter.

"Of all the men to come along and knock me off," Balloch pondered. "It'd be like a knight riding for battle, knowing that some village fool would be the one to end him."

"Surely it isn't set in stone?", I asked.

"The die is cast," Matheson remarked with a melancholy.

"The die is cast," Balloch repeated.

Richard and Francis returned for New Years, and we attended a party, hosted by Jarves and Maz. By now, several of my pieces had been featured in the Camford Review, and I had become known as a writer. For the first time in my life, the prospect of womanising became quite real, and yet I was repulsed. Women, my own age and far prettier than I, could not keep me at that party. Just as I had done on that second night, I stepped outside for a smoke and never returned. Chorus counts from ten rang out in the city as I strolled on home. News had spread of my finished collection, but I had been secretive, and it was not until after the new year that I showed Balloch the finished work.

"Spectacular!", Balloch exclaimed when he read the collection on the second day of 1952. "Quite simply spectacular my dear boy. You really listened, by God you listened!"

"*Formula without being formulaic.*"

"Andress is going to shit when he reads these."

"I was hoping so."

I phoned Donald that same evening and he suggested we meet for lunch the next day. "I must say, kid. I wasn't sure if you had it in you. Fifty pieces, fifty publishable pieces, in six weeks. How very impressed I am."

"Thank you, sir."

"*Donald.*"

"Donald, right."

"I'd say we're looking at an Easter release. We can have it approved by Matheson in a few weeks, and the nationals by March. Those guys owe me a favour or two anyway."

"Dare I say, Donald, that we don't need favours?"

"Such is the nature of The Game, young Robin. I wish it was not so, but favours are the currency of this world. You could be Wordsworth, on mescaline and by a pretty lake, wouldn't be a lick of paint if you haven't earned yourself a few favours."

"I see."

"Are you a single man, Robin?"

"Yes, sir."

"*Donald*," he said, with a stern look.

"Donald."

"No lady in your life?"

I paused, stunned and slightly unnerved. "No."

"A pity. Love would be good for business. It's all well and good writing about rain and trees and woodland critters, but it can only go so far. People go mad for a young man in love."

"I suppose they do."

"Heartbreak too. If there's one better muse than love, it's a broken heart. The women love it. It triggers some sort of maternal instinct. So if I were you, I'd fly, recklessly into a doomed relationship, get the old chest torn open. Who was that sad German chap?"

"I'm sorry?"

"You know, from that novel, the one who topped himself at the end?"

"Young Werther?"

"Yes! That's the one, something like that would be great, without the——of course. Yes, a forbidden love. That would do mighty well."

I was eager to take the subject away from the amorous. "I cannot fault your logic there, Donald."

"I presume you'll move onto novels eventually."

"Yes, that's really where I want to be."

"I'll get you there, kid. Say, have you met my daughter?"

"I have."

"Right, yes. I should have recalled. She's dating that Cornish fellow of yours."

"How do you—never mind."

He smiled. "You're learning."

I returned home at three, safe and content in the knowledge that my first collection would see the harsh light of day. I entered the flat to find Francis alone.

"Good afternoon, Robin."

"Afternoon, Francis. Where's Belling?"

"Out with Eleanor. I believe his sister is in town."

"His sister?"

"Yes. Adeline. I believe she's interested in coming up next year."

That name slipped out of my mind as quickly as it entered, though I would soon come to know Adeline quite well. I strolled into my room, where I noticed that same off-white paper on my desk. I bolted back into the living room.

"Francis!", I barked. "When did this arrive?"

"Half an hour ago, I think. Why? Is something wro—"

Before he could finish speaking, I was out of the door. I took off down the stairs and almost fell once or twice. Out of the door, my pace only quickened as I surged into town, and through the quagmire of winding streets. I threw myself into the pub and collided with the bar. "Stout—no ice," I blurted between heavy breaths.

"You're late," said a disinterested barman.

"Is she still here?"

The barman said nothing, and quietly retrieved the key. I took off running again, up those crimson steps and along the hall. I paused outside the door to catch my breath before entering. "You're late," she said, reading and smoking, just as the first time I was stood there.

"I know, I was out with—"

"With my husband," she interrupted. "Yes, I know. *Easter release, Matheson's favour*. Did he say the thing about Young Werther?"

"Yes, and of forbidden love."

"Forbidden love? He must have improvised that. Did he say anything else?"

"That I should date your daughter."

The cigarette fell out of her mouth. Her head swivelled, so that those emerald eyes shone into mine, but they were relaxed. We held firm in that moment for a few seconds before laughter rose within us both.

By sundown I was in her arms, and we lay there in silence. A thousand thoughts swirled in my mind, but I dared not utter them. Another half hour passed before I spoke.

"How old are you?", I asked.

"Oh, let us not go there. The less you know about me, the better."

"You're much younger than your husband."

"Indeed I am. You know I'm not his first wife."

"You're not?"

"No. But I am the first to give him a child. He was married once before. A frightfully boring woman she was. His age. She hadn't the stomach for it. She was incapable of brutality."

"And you are?"

She didn't answer, and so we fell into another silence. Eventually, she took her gaze away from the ceiling and it rested on me. "I'm forty-four. Any other questions."

"What do you make of the Game?"

"Oh, that's Donald's business. None of mine."

"You must have some opinion."

"Only on the things that concern me."

"So, on me?"

"You're cute, Robin. Don't spoil it by loving me."

"I'll try not to."

"Perhaps you *would* be good for Eleanor. Once she dumps the bumpkin of course."

I returned home at night. As I entered my room, suddenly my youthful obsessions subsided, and I found the affair to be a matter of great disturbance. Eleanor was in the flat and I found her to be disturbing too. She had Cynthia's face, and Donald's laugh. I retired for the evening.

Weeks passed. I attended a few more parties and met with Cynthia a few more times. By Spring, the affair had become a simple obligation, where it had once captured me in every sense. There was little in the way of passion when I met with Cynthia on the final day of the Hilary term.

"*I should visit Monty*," I said to myself, as I drifted to sleep, next to her.

8

My first collection, *Songs of Merry England*, was released over the Easter vac, and had done well in the local hum. While I was far from known in London, it was received well in University circles, and I came to possess a stature in the stoney halls of my college. Second and third years would nod at me on the quad, having bought themselves a copy, and then given it to girlfriends back home; or typed up one of the more amorous pieces and proclaimed it to have come from their own beating chest. The collection was a source of concern among dons in the Literature department; some felt, earnestly, that such pursuits were an unwelcome distraction, others projected the anger felt at their own careers, which were invariably short, lamentable, and finished off externally. The reviews were generous, and I had made a modest sum. However, I felt an imposter at times; asking myself on occasion if it really was good writing or, by the luck of fools, I had charmed Cynthia into charming Donald into charming the critics on my behalf. There was a row of toppled dominoes, with her scent lingering upon the first.

"A volume of poetry in your first year is plenty for now, Robin," Balloch said in one of our meetings.

He had joined up with the concerned dons, and collectively they applied pressure on me to focus on my essays and exams, which came and went without hassle and soon my first year at Camford was at an end.

"It's good," Balloch reassured me over a drink once we had left the college. "Really. I'd dare not spend so much time on you if you didn't have some knack for it."

I had sat my last exam in May and was summoned by Cynthia that night. "I have bought you a gift," she said as I arrived. "It's in the wardrobe."

Inside was a perfectly-cut suit of brown tweed, which she had furnished with a dark green tie, and a white handkerchief with navy-blue spots. It fit like a glove, as if she had measured me in my sleep. "You have a suit for the city, and now one for the country. A young man of your position needs both. Especially one who intends on getting ahead."

"I thought you had no opinion of such things," I said, modelling the suit for her.

"I don't, but if you wish to be more than a one-time poet, you shall need to play it. And when anybody asks, it was made on Savile Row."

I was a creature of habit in that final Term. I attended my lectures, met with Balloch, and with Cynthia, and occasionally indulged Richard in the great game of drink. My novel had roared back into life, and then stagnated again. It was like some inadequate bicycle going up a tall hill; yet manned by a determined jockey. Life grew to be pleasantly monotonous. Though my concerns around the affair had not ceased, and yapped at my heels daily. We never left the room above the tavern; where all appetite for food and fresh air seemingly vanished. In there, she was a schoolmaster for unsure young men, and there I learned to *dance*.

At times she was feeble, and kitten-like, at others she prowled and stalked. The latter was her dominant disposition, when she'd play with me, delicately hinting at what we both knew; that in her palm sat my fate; so too in the lips that whispered into Donald's ear. And her presence was a stiff drink; and soon I grew discombobulated and unfocused, left with no other choice but to submit to her whims and fancies, to play her little games and dress myself in her gifts. Her affection felt as if it were grooming, stalking, as did Donald's. In tandem, they carried my career in its gestation and birthed it into the world. He had commanded that all makers of taste and shapers of consensus loved my work. He had bent the Camford Review to his will; and as such the public knew me to be the new poetic voice in England. And there was born an infant of doubt; had I earned this? Soon, in the eyes of that world, I stood at the centre of a fashionable clique, though I had never met my supposed compatriots, and was not sure that they were even real.

I left Camford in June, in a state of anxiety, and travelled by train to London. The city had barely changed, save for a few new builds upon the horizon; where the noise, scale, smoke and chatter found new points of entry. All through the journey, I pictured the conversations ahead. Monty was my oldest friend, whom I had met on the second or third day of school, one year after the war. He was beautiful, in a sharpish sort of way, as if he were a finely-tuned instrument. Not a follicle of hair was out of place, ever, it seemed, and he held within him, and carried daily, the ease and grace of conversation that lives down-wind of beauty. Monty had walked through life, leisurely and in total command. He corralled the pimpled and awkward young men of our year into his discipline, and I was only mocked by them in his peculiar absence. He seconded the girlfriends of our classmates, and it was known - so clearly that it often resembled memory - that he would marry well and achieve much. He had shunned Camford, and was reading chemistry at Imperial.

"Oh, none at all," I replied, when he asked me, by way of introduction, if I'd gotten any hunting done. "There's no time to get out of the city. Plus, the dons—"

"It's a changing time, Robin," he said, gravely. "Soon enough we'll have very little to say for ourselves except how grand our fathers' houses used to be."

We found a restaurant near to Paddington Station, and I offered to pay with my newly-found petty wealth. Monty was not the type to envy success and accepted my offer with grace.

"So," he said once we had ordered and the waiter was out of sight. "*Robin Fitzwarwick the poet*. Well, I knew you'd do well for yourself once Harding was out of the picture. Are there many of the old boys at Camford?"

"Yes," I said. "Do you remember Jarvis?"

"Oh christ," he groaned.

"He goes by *Jarves* now."

"Of course he does. They always try to reinvent. I was telling Vera that just the other day."

"Vera?"

"My angel, the love of my life, and if I had your temperament then she'd be my *muse*."

"I'm happy for you, Monty."

"And for you?"

"For me?"

"Have you found a lady yet?"

I fidgeted, trying to avoid the inevitable. Monty sat up straight and stared me down. "Well that's a yes," he said with a grin.

"I actually wanted to talk to you about this. I—could do with some advice."

"My, my, my. Robin Fitzwarwick the *Lothario* poet."

I opened my mouth, but could not find the words. He interrupted my silence. "Is she a classmate?"

"No."

"Year above?"

"No."

"Is she a graduate?"

"I suppose she is."

"When did she graduate?"

"1929, I think."

His eyes widened. "My God."

"She's somewhat older."

"Well, yes I'd gathered that, Robin. Not unless she is England's youngest genius, I'd say so. And how did you meet this—*exalted elder* of the college?"

"Monty!"

"Answer the question."

"A party at the college—for the dons."

"Is she a patron of the arts?"

"Of sorts."

"Oh God, she's not an *Andress* is she?"

I looked down and flushed. I saw Monty stir in the corner of my eye before he gesticulated violently, almost knocking a glass across the room as heads swivelled and snapped towards us. "No!", he said, raising his voice.

"Keep your voice down."

"Robin Fitzwarwick, you feral dog!"

"Alright, Monty. Keep your hair on."

"I was wondering how you managed to get picked up by Andress. I said as much to my Vera, I said *how on earth has a young whippersnapper like my good friend Robin managed to swing this*. And now I know. Charming the old man while bedding the wife! Oh, how far you have come."

"Okay, enough of that—"

"*And when you look at me the same, I feel not a thing, but guilt and shame*'"

"At least you've actually read it."

"Of course, *Into Cold October's Night*. Vera and I wept to it after we made *furious* love."

"So you see my predicament."

"Indeed, I do."

"So, what do I do?"

"Well, start by telling me everything. Leave no detail untold."

And so I told him, without self-censor, everything. I told him of that night in the alley, the call to Balloch's house, the Galveston Arms, the typewriter, the suit.

"Well it's a lovely suit, I must say. She's got lovely taste, the old geriatric minx. It's bit of a *country* look though, isn't it? Are you sure you're supposed to wear it in the city?"

"It was cut on Savile Row, apparently. But a nice suit doesn't change the hole I appear to have dug for myself."

"No, no it does not. Do you want to be with her?"

"I don't believe I have a say in the matter. It feels like being in a zoo, really."

"Does he—"

"Know? No. Of course not. My head would be on a pike outside the Bodleian if he knew."

"So you've been ensnared by the wife of your publisher."

"Yes."

"And you believe that she has convinced him to publish and promote you."

"Indeed."

"And you feel that if you displease her in any way, she will speak to her husband and have you sent packing. You'd be unpublishable, buried by the literary press, exiled and washed up before your nineteenth birthday."

"In effect, yes."

"Well," he said, descending into thought as a pregnant silence brewed. "How about a holiday? The year is up, you have a bit of money in your pocket. And that novel you're working on—"

"All's Well in Winter Days."

"Yes, that one. Then I'd say that it's rather obvious, Robin. Get away, get off this island and find somewhere new. Write your novel, and see if she follows you."

"Would she follow me?"

"She must have taken some liking to you. Camford is full of hopefuls I can imagine. She'd have her pick of the lot. Or at least the lot not stupid enough to go to bed with her. So you must have just been the prettiest. And if she's the sort to only seduce freshers, then you've got a few months until the new batch come in. So—get out of the way."

"It's that simple?"

"Our most pressing concerns usually are."

And so, I resolved to go away. Monty and I took

in the British Museum before I caught the evening train home. We wished each other a fond farewell and Monty promised to visit me wherever I ended up. I got into Camford at eight, and back to the flat for half past. I crossed Eleanor on the stairs, but she said nothing, and stormed past me and out of the door. The flat was still and Richard sat motionless in his armchair. "You okay, Belling?" I asked. He said nothing. "Richard?", I repeated. "Everything okay, chap?"

"Get out of my sight, Fitzwarwick."

I was stunned, and lingered for a moment, almost paralysed.

"Leave me, Robin. Before I put you through that wall."

"Which wall?"

"The one with the window. I will defenestrate you if you say another word."

I made my way into the hall, spotting Francis sat on his bed, reading.

"Francis," I said, leaning into the room. "Is Belling alright?"

"I'm afraid Eleanor has decided to end their courtship."

"Oh," I said, glancing back into the living room and seeing his back shudder with heavy and laboured sobs. In that moment, Richard's annoyances faded into the fog, and he became something new entirely. I grew desperate to rid him his pain. "Richard," I whispered upon re-entering the room. He turned around with tears in his eyes and I laid a hand on his shoulder. He crumbled at my touch and wept openly. "I wrote her such a wonderful poem," he whimpered, between sobs.

"I know you did, Richard."

"Why are they like this?"

"I don't know."

After a few minutes, his eyes dried and he returned, somewhat, to his former self. "What was it you wanted to say?", he asked, staring at me with boyish innocence.

"How about a little trip?"

9

"I am a pulchritudinous god!"

"Richard, get down from there!"

"Camford! She stands before me, trembling at my splendour! My beauty! Oh, how she shakes and murmurs!"

"Richard! For God's sake, Francis, do something."

"Um, Richard?", said Francis, feebly.

"I'm a pulchritudinous god, Fucksby!"

"Yes you are, Richard. But I really think you should get down from there."

"God's do not care for the whims of mortals, old boy. I am a god. I *am* God. I am the night sky, I am the morning sun! I am dew drops on the grass, rain in a heatwave! I——I——am very unsure as to how I got here."

"If he falls," I said, looking at Francis, who was just as unnerved as I. "He'll bounce his head on the floor, and drown—or freeze to death. And I won't jump in after him."

"I fear I shall," he said, more to himself than to anyone else. Jarves and Maz snickered behind us.

"I say, you're like a circus performer up there," Jarves cracked.

"Yes!", Maz added. "Do a tightrope walk!"

"Don't encourage him," I snapped.

"He won't fall," Maz retorted. "Look at him, he's a natural."

"Did you hear that, Bellers?", Jarves cooed. "You're a natural."

"Thank you, mortal. And yes, you are right. I am also a pulchritudinous god!"

"Has he just learned the word?", I asked Francis, who moved, cautiously towards the ledge.

Our drunken escapade had led us to a bridge, that arched from one end of the river to the other, separating the students from the locals. Goaded on by none other than himself, Richard had scaled one of its stoney limbs, and swung precariously on it. One hand had a tenuous grip on a lamppost, and the other swigged from a bottle of Bordeaux wine.

"When'll they put gin and tea in one of these bottles, I wonder?", he asked, rhetorically, before giggling to himself. "Something for you earthlings to figure out. After all, I am not one of you, dear chaps, I am a pul——"

His words trailed off into a hearty cry as he slipped and plummeted into the dark below. "Fucking hell," I groaned, as the others raced to the edge. Francis, without a thought began to strip and scale the wall.

"I—" we heard from below. "—am a pulchritudinous god! Though I am a bit wet and very cold."

"Swim, Richard!", Maz shouted, between fits of laughter. "Swim to the bank and we will come and get you."

"It's okay!", said Richard. "I can stand, it isn't very deep. Oh, I say, the wine is here, it must've just floated towards me."

There was a splash as Francis dove in to join him. Jarves and Maz moved around, off of the bridge and toward the bank, as I stayed put, straining my eyes to make out the figures of Richard and Francis. "Is he okay?", I called. "Yes," Francis called back. "He's drinking wine."

"I cannot feel my feet," Richard said, as his delusions began to fade. "I say, how did I get here?"

"You fell, you utter pillock."

"I sense, Fitzy, that you are mocking me. It is very unwise to mock the gods, Robin, we too have patience and it too expires."

Jarves and Maz reached out into the water, and each grabbed a wrist, as Richard and Francis were hauled onto dry land. Francis panted a little while Richard just laughed, lighting a cigarette he'd taken from Jarves' pocket, and laying on his back. It was the late Spring and fortune had it that the air was warm and not one to punish such feats with shivering death. We had been out since three and it neared ten. The sun, emerging from the prudish Winter and the stuttering Spring, now extended itself much further into the night, and there was still a glimmer of its rays residing in blueish clouds, and the pulsing air. Moonlight gave the water a shine, and much could be seen. Richard, however, did not dry quickly. And while he was still dripping wet, he bored of the act and sought more drink.

"I say, where did that *ludicrous* bottle of wine get to? I haven't scared it off, have I?"

"It must've floated away," said Jarves.

"How unseemly," Richard tutted. "What a rude thing to do. That pompous little bottle. I was just starting to like it. Oh well, that's the French for you."

I made my way down from the bridge, just as Richard sprang to his feet and cast off his jacket, throwing it into the water with a loud screech.

"Argh!", he cried, as it left his grip. "Begone, rotten tailoring! Let the eels wear you, not I! Fucksby, I am very cold, may I have your jacket? It would seem that I've lost mine. There must be a thief in our midst."

"Of course," he said. Francis had removed his jacket before jumping in, and thus it was bone dry.

"Francis, don't. You'll freeze. Here, Richard, take mine."

"No!", he snapped, like a stubborn schoolboy. "I want Fucksby's. He's *my* mule, Fitzy, not yours. Get your own, old boy, they're a penny a pound if you know where to look."

I waited until Richard donned Francis' jacket before giving Francis my own. "Are you sure, Robin?", he asked.

"Keep your voice down, Francis," I said with a wink. "I dare say he won't notice."

Richard was still damp and dancing when we entered a pub on the edge of town. "Maz, old boy, do go up and get me a gin and tea. I fear I've misplaced my wallet."

"It was in your jacket," Maz snarled.

"My dear boy, you shall be recompensed. *That* is a certainty."

"Fine. I'm too tired to argue with you."

Jarves returned to the table. He'd fled to back corner to fetch an ashtray. "I'll get yours, Robin."

"You will?", I asked.

"Yeah, why not."

"Are you trying to achieve some leverage over me?"

"Maybe I am, maybe I'm not. Perhaps I'm just being nice. What'll it be?"

"House red."

"You're too kind. I'll get us a bottle. Uxby?"

"I'll take a gin please, Matthew."

"Stiff?"

"With tonic."

Jarves headed to the bar just as Maz turned back from it. "Bellers! They say they're not doing gin and tea."

"Rot!", Richard cried. "Rot! Rot! Rot!"

"I already told them that," Maz protested.

"Might I enquire, Mr. Barman. Do you serve tea?"

"We do," the barman replied.

"And, given that this is a public house, one that sells, I presume, alcohol, you might have some gin?"

"Yes."

"*Wünderbar*," said Richard in a cartoon German accent. "I vill have ze gin and tea, bitte."

The barman grunted a noise of defeat and set about making the drink. "How d'you take it?"

"Dash of milk, Mr. Barman. No sugar."

The barman grunted again. "You see," Richard boasted to

Francis and I. "Ask and you shall receive."

"It's a good thing he stopped when he did," Francis said to me once Richard was distracted. "Last time he did the German voice I had to wrestle his arm down."

"And ve vill march into Paris in ze morning!"

"Oh, no," said Francis.

"You're going to Paris?", asked Jarves, returning to the table.

"Ja!"

"Alright Bellers, you can cut the German act now," he groaned. "Uxby had to wrestle your arm down last time."

Francis turned to me. "You see?"

We stayed put for the evening, as Richard settled back into an English accent. We drank more wine, and jaunted home. And with the ill-effects of drink forming behind our eyes, we departed for Dover the next day.

France wept in thick blankets as we arrived at the port of Calais; from whence we boarded a train to Paris. We had arranged rooms by the Seine, and it offered a handsome view of the left bank. This was where a lost generation found its words. Where Brits, Americans and continentals, all fleeing something or *someone*, were united by the same creative impulse that now had me in its grasp. I found Paris to just as seductive to the sense as Camford. It was inexpensive in those days, which made it all the more attractive place to write. The cafe's and brasserie's were rousing, and seemed to wobble with the jolly, drunken patrons, and the air seemed to breathe something else entirely.

I had pitched All's Well to Donald a week earlier and he had arranged a generous advance. I was due to have a first draft by Christmas. "I still think you're flying too high, Icarus," Balloch warned me, on the morning of our departure. "Though I wish you the best. I wrote my second play in Paris, I think you'll find it agreeable."

In spite of my resolve, it was impossible to write in those early Parisian days, as our attention was so often drifting towards the bottle. Richard saw no use in me spending those days at my desk.

"There's a city out there, Fitzy!", he'd cry whenever he found me at the typewriter. "A city of dogs, of animal lusts and wonderful flesh!"

"That's rather poetic, Richard," I'd say, meaning it more than I wished.

And so, we'd head out into the night, in search of cheap drink and blameless debauchery. As Richard saw it, it was our right; as young men spared the horrors of war, and from too high a strata to fight in the next one, we were the inheritors of fun. "Je vais prendre un gin et un…uh…tea, s'il vous plaît." Richard said, sheepishly, at the first bar we entered.

"Oui, monsieur," chipped the barman.

"Oh God, I love this city."

We had found ourselves in a watering hole a short walk from the apartment. We were in the Latin Quarter; where they say that Paris '*learned to think*'. The bar was once a hub of intellectuals, and it still maintained such an image, yet the clientele seemed to resent what they, and it, had become. I looked around the room and saw silent, glum faces, all staring into their drinks. An American played away on a piano in the corner, moving and swaying with the music he conjured. He was the sole spark, and dragged the room to his level.

"Say," said Richard, gesturing at the sound. "That chap over there plays a mighty fine piano."

"Joplin," said Francis. "A slight deviation, but that is most certainly Joplin, *Bethena*, the concert waltz."

"Indeed, it is, my dear boy," Richard replied, patting Francis on the head as if he were a child. "My Fucksby is a cultural genius, and a scientific one."

The American finished playing and stood to a quiet room. Richard stood up and called across the room as heads shot up from their drinks and fixed on us.

"Excuse me, sir!"

The American turned.

"I don't suppose you could be so kind as to join us for a drink?"

The American grunted. "If you're buyin'."

Richard kicked his chair a few inches back and walked across the room to the bar. A minute later, he returned with a tray of drinks, the American following behind. He had grey hair and a bushy grey beard, a haggard look. His jacket was worn to the fibres and his shirt had most of its buttons undone, which revealed a boney, hairy chest.

"Gin and tea?", he scoffed, pointing with his head at Richard's drink.

"Oh, yes."

"So, like an Irish coffee, except——"

"Gin instead of whiskey."

"And tea instead of coffee?"

"Precisely."

He smirked. "You know, I've been to many places and seen many things. Very little surprises me, but this is something new. Life is funny like that I guess."

"Indeed," dismissed Richard - who, inspite of his ways, did not enjoy being laughed at. "Let me introduce you to my retinue. This is Robin, the writer. And this is my closest associate, Fucksby."

"Fucksby?"

"Francis Uxby, F—"

"Fucksby, I get it. That's funny."

He shook our hands with a mighty grip and introduced himself as Andrew Finnegan. He was of Irish stock, born in 1896 and had fought in the Great War. In the 20s, he'd taken to Socialism, and edited several small but fervently Marxist journals. An avowed Trotskyist, he had fought in Spain, with Tito's Partisans. He had not seen America since leaving in 1935.

"I'm probably on a list somewhere," he said, two drinks in. "I can't imagine I'll see the States again." He didn't seem upset by the idea. After a while, he began laughing to himself. "I'm definitely losing some of my credentials here. Sat in this bar, breaking bread with blue-bloods."

"Pigs and farmers," I said.

He chuckled and nodded. "Exactly. Well, in my own

defence, you guys don't seem so bad. You know, I met Eric once."

"Oh yeah?"

"Yeah. He and I narrowly avoided a firing line in Spain once. Stalinists. Animals."

"Walking on two feet," I added.

He chucked. Richard entered the fray clumsily. "If the two of you are referring to Animal Farm, I'm afraid you may be mistaken. Animal Farm was written by George Orwell. Not some tit named *Eric*."

Andrew and I caught each other's gaze and laughed while Richard fiercely stared the two of us down. Andrew finished his drink and stood from the table. "Well, gentlemen. I appreciate the drinks, and the company, but my night has come to an end. I have a train to catch in the morning and must rest."

"A train?" Richard enquired. "Wherever to?"

"I don't know yet. Until next time, gentlemen. Adieu."

And just like that he was gone. I wondered then if I'd meet that haggard American again. The rest of the evening came and went without incident, and by midnight we were back in the apartment.

The window of my bedroom overlooked several streets that coalesced around a single point. On the corner of that point lay a little cafe, '*Le Coin*'. One could sit by that window and watch people come and go all day, as I did whenever the chance appeared. Richard would drink himself into a stupor each night, and sleep until noon. Francis wouldn't disturb me. And so there I stayed, until Richard stirred and our day would begin. I'd spend my mornings sipping on coffee and watching people come and go. My eyes fell upon one figure each and every day. A waitress in the cafe, who'd ferry drinks, hot and cold, to those dining outside. She didn't walk, rather she bounced. I could not hear her, but she seemed to sing each time she spoke.

I found in those days that there was something in people who didn't know that they were being watched; a natural, candid exposure - a true humanity. This, in essence, was that first week in Paris. I would wake to the traffic and bustle, and stay motionless in bed for some time, as I had nowhere to be. By ten, I had prepared a small coffee and some toast, and would sit by the window, watching the cafe and its patrons, and her. My peace would be disturbed by Richard calling out some rallying cry to attack the bottle, and we'd be off.

After a week, Monty joined us, and my mornings would change irrevocably. He, Francis and I would take morning walks along the river and practise our French with the merchants and fruit sellers. The French don't like to speak English.

Monty and Francis got along well as they were both students of the sciences, and I got along with them as I still had a youthful curiosity in those days. Science did not appeal to me, but the fired eyes of passion did, and I adored to speak to people on the subjects they cared about.

One day, when it was just me awake after a heavy night of drink, I took the morning walk alone. Returning to the apartment around noon, I walked past Le Coin, felt a thirst, and figured I'd go in for a drink.

10

And so it was that I now took my morning coffee at Le Coin, and my observations of Paris life migrated to the street level. A fortnight passed in that gentle isolation. Monty had returned to England a week after Richard and Francis, as they were due in England for the debut of Richard's sister, Adeline. While of their blood, I was not of their world, and as such I remained in Paris alone, and took new rooms in the same neighbourhood. I spent my mornings in the cafe, my afternoons at my desk, in a writing fervour, and my evenings in stroll around that magical city as my novel slowly grew into fruition.

"Do return to England at some point, old boy," Richard said as we parted. "I don't know if I can handle a new lodger."

"I'll return, Richard. As soon as I am done here."

Cynthia had slipped away from my mind, just as easily as she had slipped into it. She was a creature of proximity, and while I was in France, our affair seemed but a strange dream. All that mattered to me now was Paris, and that embryo of a novel. However, with each word, and sentence, and paragraph, it made less sense to me. I had managed to write myself into a labyrinth by the first day of August. I felt, with some shame, that Balloch had been proven right about my ambitions, and that I'd undertaken too large a task for a kid of eighteen. I continued on, desperate in my attempts to justify Donald's faith in me. I grappled with the story but came up empty handed as a sense of foreboding grew. "You fool!", I'd scold myself, over and over again. "You damned fool."

Twice over, I scrapped all prior progress, and started again. Though I maintained that first sentence, which to me seemed crucial and assumed.

"*Little did I know, that when I walked through the gates of Old Burgh House, I'd leave as a man, quite unrecognisable from the boy who entered.*"

I phoned Balloch for advice. "What did I tell you about writing something complicated?"

"Yes, I know."

"I told you that you're too young."

"Yes, Balloch, I know. Just tell me what to do."

"You mean aside from bench it and write something simple?"

"Yes, aside from that."

"Read."

"Read?"

"Yes, read. Take the pressure off of yourself and read something great. Read Dostoyevsky, or Tolstoy, someone——*Russian*. Fall in love with reading again, and you'll fall in love with writing again."

"Russian?"

"Yes. They have a profound sense of tragedy. Perhaps it's the cold, or the boot-heel."

It was sound advice, and I wandered throughout the Latin Quarter in search of a book. I found a few bookshops, but was met with glares when I asked for books in English. Eventually, well into town, I found a shop, owned by a Canadian, and purchased Dostoyevsky's *White Nights*.

I took the book back to the cafe and read over a strong cup of coffee. Balloch was right, and I fell back in love with words. I read half of it and resolved to read the rest the next day. That night I took my usual stroll and ended up back in the same watering hole I met Andrew in. I heard the piano playing on my approach and hoped to find Andrew inside, playing and swaying as he did. Alas, it was not him, rather an African. I stayed and listened intently to his musings on the moonlit sonata. He refused my advances at a conversation, claiming to speak no English, and I left after a glass of wine. I was restless and could not sleep. I went back to the typewriter but could only stare at that inaugural sentence. It was not until well into the early hours of the morning that I managed to fall asleep.

I slept until one. That day was sluggish and I didn't go to the cafe until it was time for my supper. I ordered a sandwich and a beer and sat in my usual spot outside. And then, as I read, and drank my beer, a funny thing came my way.

"Qu'est-ce que vous lisez?"

I was shaken out of my reading by the words, spoken so soft and fragile, almost like a lullaby.

"Pardon?" I replied, blinded by the low, setting sun and speaking only to a silhouette.

"Le livre là."

"Je ne parle pas français."

"Anglais?"

"Oui."

All of a sudden, the owner of that voice stepped forward, out of the shadows and I saw her. I had seen her before. She was around my age, with shoulder-length auburn hair and a dimple on her left cheek. She spoke to me in English, revealing an English accent. "The book. I'm talking about the book. What are you reading?"

I angled the book towards her; stunned by the conversation that had found me and out of practise due to several days of solitude. She examined the cover keenly.

"*White Nights*—I can't say I've ever read it."

"It's good. Very sad."

"Funny and sad are the only ways of being that truly exist. It doesn't surprise me that you move in the direction of *sad*."

"Excuse me?"

"I've been watching you for a while. Normally you write, but today you are reading. It's funny. See? I'm *funny*, and you're *sad*," she chirped, before giving a slight bow and turning around to retreat.

I could not rid my thoughts of her, and returned the next day where I was met with a similar interaction. I had sat in my regular seat at my regular table outside, watching the street when a shadow appeared behind me.

I ordered, while removing a notebook from my bag, eager to make some sense of All's Well.

"En français, s'il vous plaît."

I glanced up and met her, she was barely holding the laugher back and gave way as soon as our eyes met. "I'm only kidding," she giggled. "So, you are writing again today?"

"I'm trying to."

"Then I shall leave you to it," she said, without a hint of offence taken. "Oh, hey," she added, as if suddenly remembering a message of vital importance. "Wait here."

I waited as she trotted into the cafe, soon returning with worn-down paperback. "It's poetry," she said as the book slapped the table. "I don't know if you like poetry, but I adore it."

I briefly considered mentioning my recent exploits; the volume, and the name I had garnered at home. Though I figured that braggadocio would work against me, and decided against it. "I do."

"Oh, great! Well, I hope you enjoy it."

She lingered for a moment, before turning to leave. "Hold on," I called as she was halfway through the door. I went into my bag and pulled out White Nights. "Here."

"Wow, this is for me?"

"It is, I've finished with it."

"Thank you."

"Thank *you*," I replied, gesturing towards the book of poems.

She turned to leave, but swivelled on her heel. "I'm Francine, by the way."

"Robin," I replied with a smile.

I read the collection that night, and again the next day. By mid afternoon, it was complete. I chose not to go to Le

Coin that day, instead I ventured further into Paris. On the way back, I stopped by the river and observed commuters making their way home. I spotted Francine, on a bench just outside the cafe. I could tell from the size and colour of the book in her hand that she was reading White Nights. I smiled to myself and resolved to see her the next day.

"You are aware that term begins in two weeks, right?", Balloch asked when I called him that night. "And you shouldn't call so often, it can't be cheap."

"I know. I'm just not done here yet."

"Well, hurry up and be done. These college Summer parties are painful and I need your success to distract from my own failures."

"Soon, Bill. I promise."

The next day came and I felt anxious to go to the cafe. Idly, I waited until noon before making my way through the meandering and narrow streets to Le Coin. Once more, I found my regular seat unspoken for and made myself comfortable. By now I had come to know the shape of Francine's shadow and it appeared before long.

"Un café noir, s'il vous plaît," I said with confidence, having practised my French.

"Oh, I'm not actually working today," she said as I glanced up. "I was wondering if I could come and sit with you."

"In French, please," I replied with a smirk.

She giggled. "Puis-je m'asseoir avec vous?"

I gestured towards the empty chair across from me, and she sat, with a huff.

"I love my days off," she began. "I get to do whatever I like."

"And yet you came here?"

"Yes," she chuckled. "I wanted to see you."

"Me?"

"Yes! I think you are very interesting."

"Really?"

"Yes, I don't know many artists, or any really. I thought I'd meet a bunch in Paris, but I think the party ended before I arrived."

"How do you mean?"
"Well, my parents met in Paris. My father is English, which may explain a few things."
"It does."
"Ha. Yes. Well he is English and my mother is French, which may explain some other things. They used to tell me all of these wonderful stories about Paris and London before the war. There used to be artists everywhere, then I suppose they all just turned on each other. Some became Fascists, some became Communists, and some of them were normal. That's a little joke I like to say."
"When did your parents meet?"
"1923."
"Mine too."
"How funny! Well they met in 1923, and it was all so exciting back then, the first war had worn off and the new one was nowhere near. They used to come to this café, it's owned by her family. I think about that time, even though I hadn't been born yet, and wish so much that I could have been there. But as I said, I missed out on the party."
"I feel that way too."
"What are you writing? I've wanted to ask."
"A novel, but it isn't going very well."
"Oh?"
"Yes, my friend thinks it is too complicated, and that while I am young I should write something simple."
"What do you think?", she asked,
"That he is probably right."
"What's it about?"
"That's a hard question to answer, Francine. It's very long, and not really about anything. But there is one thing, a house. I've never been there before, but it's some opulent country house in Bassetshire, where my parents met. Everything else keeps on changing though."
"Maybe you'll finish it when you're old and grey."
I laughed. "Perhaps it'll be the last thing I ever do."

We shared a moment of silence, in which our eyes spoke in a tongue that neither of us could decipher. There was, undoubtedly, a connection. So quiet and pure, that the thought of spoiling it with action was forbidden in my mind. We spoke some more, and I learned more of her life. Her surname was Jones, and her father was a self-made man. She was born and raised in Kent. She holidayed in France and spoke French fluently.

"Will you return to England?", I asked.

"Perhaps. Though I am in no hurry. I intend to leave as soon as Paris offers me nothing."

"That may be a while."

She agreed with her eyes. "And you?"

We spoke some more, of my life at Camford, and hers in Paris. Some time past and I got up to leave. She bade me farewell and I bade her the same. Some way down the street, I suffered a change of heart and turned back to see if she was still there. She was not. I ran back to that point where three streets meet and looked down each one to no avail.

"Are you looking for someone?"

I turned to see Francine, there with a mocking smile. I spoke before I could think.

"Dine with me tomorrow."

"Ask me in French," she said with a smirk.

I looked at her as if asking for mercy. She laughed at me and acquiesced. "Do you have a pen?"

I removed a pen from my shirt pocket, and broke off some notebook paper and handed them to her. "Turn around," she said. I obeyed and, using my back for support, she wrote a number on the sheet and handed it back. "Until tomorrow, Robin."

"Until then."

I walked back to the apartment, high from the rush of conversation. I got to the building and was stopped by the doorman on my way in. "Monsieur, this arrived while you were away." He handed me a folded note and I took it before walking up the stairs to the apartment. I dropped my bag onto the dining table before unfolding the note.

'Robin,

Your presence is requested.
Papal Hotel, Avignon.
Make haste,
C.'

11

I paced about the room, trying to figure out a plan. It had been almost a day since I had received Cynthia's note, and I was no closer to knowing what I was to do. Frustration only grew with each rotation of the apartment. The view of the Seine became ghastly and unremarkable as a more important thing had arisen. I tried to call Balloch, twice, but there was no answer.

I emptied my pockets, hoping to find some sort of sign. My pockets were bare, except for the note containing Francine's phone number, and a single coin. And it was then that I did something. Something I had not done before and have not done since. I ignored my senses, my gut; disregarded the call of my soul to dine with Francine, and the call of my head to go to Cynthia. I let blind, stupid luck guide my decision.

"*Heads for Cynthia, tails for Francine*."

It was heads.

I glared at the coin, gradually coming to terms with the decision that fate had made. "Allo?", called a male voice on the other end of the phone. I froze briefly, expecting Francine.

"Oui, allo. Parlez vous anglais?"

"Oui," he said with a frustrated resignation.

"I'm looking for Francine."

He stepped away from the phone and called out.

"Francine! Your English boy is on the phone."

A few moments later, I heard her delicate voice.

"Robin?"

"Francine, hello. Listen, I'm really sorry but I cannot dine with you tonight. Something has come up."

"Oh."

"It's just—well, I must leave Paris and—"

"Robin," she interrupted. "It's okay. Really, it is. Go."

"I'm so terribly sorry. I—"

"Don't be. Fate is mean like that. But it can also be kind. I'm sure I shall see you again, Robin. And if I do ever see you again, then it shall be a good day."

"If, Francine, the stars see fit to align; then I shall find a nice patch of grass, lay on my back, and enjoy the constellations.'

"Oh, Robin. You are such a *beau parleur*."

"A what?"

"A beautiful talker. Adieu, Robin."

"Adieu, Francine."

And then she was gone. I lingered for a moment, and just listened to the tone. I knew I had made an error in judgement, but also that it had now been cast into cement, hardened, and rendered permanent. I read Cynthia's note again. Alas, her pull was so great that not even random chance could resist.

"*To Avignon*," I said to myself.

I boarded the train at noon. Before leaving, I said farewell to the sweet old landlady and wired the Papal Hotel to inform Cynthia of my evening arrival. The train was scarcely packed and I had moved, without notice, from standard into first class. I arrived at 7pm and called and cab to the hotel. "Fifth floor, room sixty-seven," said the concierge when handing me the key.

"Thank you."

"I hope that you shall enjoy your stay Monsieur Andress."

"*Monsieur Andress*?", I asked myself.

I entered the lift, alongside an assistant, and felt my chest squeeze tight as the door enveloped me. The five floors up felt an eternity and I had filled my head with all sorts of nightmares as to what would be waiting for me when I arrived.

"I can take it from here," I said to the aid, tipping him several crumpled notes, as I took my bags from his grasp and made way along the hall. I knocked in a way so unnatural that it could only have been me. "Come in," she called.

I entered the room and saw Cynthia sitting on the balcony. The laced curtains swung and fluttered in the evening breeze and she was poised, like a black widow.

"Cynthia?", I called.

"Come and join me, Robin. I have wine."

I laid my bags down and ventured forth. "How was Paris?", she enquired.

"Three sheets to the wind, for the most part. Then productive for a short while."

"Hm," she chuckled, as if she possessed her own drunken memories of Paris. "Paris has that effect on the young. You are so young, aren't you, Robin?"

"Yes."

"How old? I forget."

"Almost nineteen."

"Eighteen then. How charming. And how goes the novel? Donald has high hopes for you, you know."

"It goes well, it's—"

"I don't need to know, Robin. The business, the *Game*; that's his world."

"And what is yours?"

"Wine, music, flesh."

"Perhaps you and Richard would get on."

"I doubt that. I hear Eleanor's dumped him."

"Did you not hear it from her?"

"We rarely speak."

"A pity."

"Do you speak to your mother so intimately?", she asked.

"My mother is dead."

"A pity."

We paused for a moment and both sipped our wine, before she spoke again. "How about your father?"

"Dead too."

"Hm. You make more sense to me now."

"Excuse me?"

"The war made orphans out of many. And if it wasn't the war, it was the depression. Your associations with those of a—let's say greater experience, makes sense. Balloch, Donald. You really are attached to them, and now it makes sense. Boys need fathers. It helps with the transition."

"The transition into what?"

"Manhood."

"And how is my transition going?"

She avoided the question, instead throwing one my way.

"Are you hungry?"

"I am."

"I'll order us something up."

"Do you not want to take a walk?"

"Not tonight. We must conserve our energy."

"To what end?"

She laughed to herself and finished her glass. "Don't be so naive, Robin."

She stood and walked past me into the room and sprawled herself on the bed. "You know," she said, at the evening's end. "We must return to England at different times. And no one can know that you were in Avignon."

I knew why, but asked anyway.

"*Discretion*, Robin. The less savoury elements of the Game are reliant on discretion, and discretion will spare us a lot of trouble."

"I thought you didn't care for the Game."

She fell asleep before answering, and I watched her for a few moments of disquiet before falling asleep myself, but I could only dream of *tails*.

12

I fell quickly back into Cynthia. Five days in that city of story and stone, and England felt a distant alternative to the life I was living. On the sixth day, we took our lunch out of the hotel and had found a charming cafe by the river's edge.

"You look happy," I said to her, once the waiter had taken our plates away and gone to fetch coffee.

"Do you take credit for that? I feel free."

"Free from what exactly?"

"Eyes," she replied, removing her sunglasses and showing hers off. "*Prying eyes.*"

"Oh?"

"England is my home; it is yours too. But one needs to break away every so often. Don't you agree?"

I nodded.

"England talks," she continued. "It watches, and it speaks, so carelessly, about what it sees. Such little care. 'S*he goes here, she does this with him*'. It is all so tiresome."

Thus far I had held back from mentioning Donald. Despite the water between England and France, and Cynthia's assurance that he was on the other side of it, I still feared him seeing us. He'd kill me with his bare hands, or worse. Yet, today I had felt a confidence, bolstered by Cynthia's willingness to lunch in public.

"Do you find your marriage tiresome?"

"Oh, constantly."

"Then why do you stay?"

"You are straying into deep waters, Robin, and I fear that you don't know how to swim. Divorce is not the done thing. It's bad for business. *I inspire him and he inspires me*, that's the official line."

"Does he inspire you?"

"Not particularly."

"Do you love him?"

"On some level, yes. Yes, I still do."

Something about the conversation has spurned, within her, a fire tantamount to the Summer heat. Her relaxed demeanour vanished into the southern sun and she sprung forward, elbows on the table and spoke directly, albeit softly, into me.

"You know, Robin. You and I are not totally unalike. I too was orphaned. Granted, I was a little older than you were. But I lost them both, in one swing. 1928. You may look at me and see the golden girl, the money, the prestige, the wife of the man who made himself indestructible. But it was not always this way. Donald wasn't the only one who came from nothing. My mother and my father worked the skin off of their bones to put me through university, but they never got to see me graduate. They were of the middle class in the age in which middle class kids did not rise above their station. I moved to London after I graduated and could only afford to share a house with seven other girls from my college. Two to a room, it was like being in a dormitory again. I worked as a typist. I had a university degree, and all that I could do was work as a typist. I may as well have gone to finishing school. I made nothing. I ate two meals a day, walked everywhere. And then I met Donald. He was the only person I knew back then who drove a nice car, who wore nice clothes. When he asked me on a date, I knew that he was my only hope of escaping. I had no contacts, no connections, no dowry, nothing. No one had any reason to marry me, save for the beauty that I knew would some-day wane and falter. And then, I had him. He told me that he wanted to marry a common girl, so they could capture this world together. His first wife was of the top and he hated it, he felt like an imposter. But he was powerful, so powerful. And people were nice to me. He opened doors that once were bolted shut. So, you ask me if I love him, and I do. Does he take me dancing? No. Does he buy me flowers? Or write letters? No. Does he make love to me? Or look at me from across the room? No. Does he see other women? Most certainly. But I will always be grateful for what he made of me, because I will never go back to what I was before him. *Never*."

I was stunned. Her answers to me were typically collected and distant, as if they had been written prior, at great labour, and rehearsed to perfection. She finished speaking and held my gaze; her green eyes on fire. After a moment or two she sat back again and returned to her composed normal. "Any more questions?"

I thought for a few seconds. "How did you know I was in France?"

"Your friend, Balloch, is very helpful."

"Hm."

"Are you not pleased that he was?"

I smirked, trying to elicit something playful. "Indubitably. But I was making good progress."

"On your book? And how is that going?"

"Do you care?"

"No. Well, only if I am in it."

"You are not."

"Then write me one. I'm sure Donald would love it."

"You cannot be serious."

"Oh, I am."

"You want me to write a book about this? Us?"

"Yes."

"You want me to go to your husband with a book about an affair with the wife of a publishing magnate?"

"Yes."

"You are mad."

"Relax, Robin. I'm only playing a game. There would be an element of thrill though, wouldn't you agree?"

"I don't do this for the thrill, you know."

Her eyes widened, and I continued towards the cliff's edge. "I do this," I continued. "Because—well, because I very well think that I—"

She interrupted sharply. "I'm very tired, Robin. The sun has beat a mighty lethargy into me. I think I may retire back to the hotel for a bit. You should walk over to the cathedral. It is quite the muse."

"Oh—okay," I said, deflated by the interruption.

Cynthia left and settled the bill. I finished my coffee before leaving too. I strolled to the cathedral and found it to be just as Cynthia has described. And yet, despite the beauty around me, all I could think of the women I had come to know. Cynthia and Francine jostled for position in my mind. And then, as the swirling faces hit a fever pitch, I decided to purge Francine, at least from my mind, and consummate the decision I had made.

I returned to the room and found Cynthia on the balcony, the way she was when I first entered. She joined me on the bed where we began to drink. There was a brown oak door directly across from us which had been a mystery since I arrived.

"It's twin room," she said when I enquired. "There's another bed in there."

"Oh?"

"Discretion, Robin. It'll —"

"*Save us a lot of trouble*, yes. I see now. And that is why the concierge greeted me as *Monsieur Andress*."

We drank some more and soon I had hit the spot one finds himself in after two drinks; a slightly bolder version of what came before. Good features pronounced, and bad ones disarmed. I decided to confess to her again, this time in a manner which could not be avoided.

"And what if I *did* tell you that I loved you."

"I'd say that you were drunk, and leave it at that."

"I've had two glasses."

"Then I'd say that you cannot handle two glasses."

"I'm sober."

"Then I'd say that you are young, and don't quite understand the words that you are saying, or their implications."

"We could stay."

She scoffed. "Stay?"

"Yes."

"Did you not hear what I said to you earlier? You want me to give up everything?"

"For a new *everything*."

She laughed, falling back onto the bed. "You see," I snapped. "You're not utterly repulsed by the idea."

"You have lost your mind."

"Maybe I have. I'd write so much here. You were right, about the cathedral. It is wonderful. Truly wonderful! I could find a new publisher, maybe write for an English-language paper. And you could—"

"Give up *everything*."

"We could stay."

"You will not let this go, will you?"

"Not until I have an answer."

"It is late, Robin. I must bathe, and sleep. And think, too. You shall have your answer by morning."

She got up and moved towards the bathroom with elegant and deliberate steps. By the threshold of the bathroom, she turned and looked over with a slight grin. "Are you going to join me?"

I could not sleep, and lay motionless in the dark; weighed down by my coming fate. I rose and stepped out onto the balcony and watched the city slumber as several cigarettes came and went. My last memory of that night was watching the stars, as I drifted to sleep in the chair, with my feet perched on the balcony's edge. Alas, I woke in the late morning, with the sun beating my brow, to find that Cynthia was gone.

13

I sat on the bed and stared at the wall, though I looked at nothing, felt nothing, could hear nothing. As if a switch had been turned off. I don't know how long I was there; if it were minutes or hours. All I knew was that she was gone. Though my heart was not quite broken, what I felt was a regret that squeezed it tightly. Eventually I had gathered myself and made my way to the concierge. He greeted me from a distance with a smile and open arms.

"Ah! Monsieur Andress. Your aunt checked out this morning, and all outstanding fees have been paid. She said you will be staying for another night?"

"Oh, no. I'll be checking out today. I just need to fetch my things."

"Oui, monsieur. I shall send someone up."

"Thank you."

"Is there anything else I can do for you, Monsieur Andress?"

I thought for a moment. Suddenly, it became clear.

"When is the next train to Paris?"

I watched the French countryside as it passed. Much as I had on the way to Avignon. Though what differed was my destination, and what awaited me there; mystery in the stead of certainty. The train was light and scarce, owing to it being a weekday afternoon. I got to Paris in the evening and jumped into a cab that took me to the Latin Quarter. I found a hotel that asked for little, and booked a small room with an underwhelming view. I figured that the cafe would be closed but walked there anyway. It was and I made my way home after dining in a small restaurant. The next day I was frayed, and fidgeted without end. The hotel offered breakfast and I ate a bland meal. At noon I again strolled to Le Coin. In a way I was tricking myself into a state of calm, by meandering slowly, and in a carefree manner, despite the fear and anger that had gripped me since the day before.

"Hello, is Francine here?"

"No, monsieur."

"I see. Will she be working in the evening?"

"No, monsieur. She is not here any more. She left Paris yesterday."

"Oh. Where did she go?"

"Back to England."

"Do you know where exactly?"

"No, monsieur. Sorry."

"Do you know when she'll be back?"

"No."

I walked out into Parisian day. The switch, that had been turned back on after periodical rest, was closed off again. Paris fell quiet and numb, and the gaps between particles felt a million miles. I looked, suddenly with a scorn I had not known before, around the streets, at the men in hats, rushing about the day. "*So, this place offers her nothing now*," I said to myself. Paris did seem to lose its shine in that moment. "And now it offers me nothing as well."

Rain began to fell, but it felt like the rain in London rather than Paris; drawl, oppressive, and a stain on the day. I returned to the hotel and made a call to the only person I still felt I knew. "Bill, I'm coming home. I'll be on the ferry tomorrow."

"Have the winds changed direction?"

"Let's just say that my initial enthusiasm has expired."

"Cynthia?"

"Gone."

"Novel?"

"In the Seine."

"Too—"

"Complicated. Yes."

"I'm sorry to hear that, kid. But it is better late than never. Come and see me when you are back, and we will get something new started."

"Something simple. I'm ready for something simple."

"You'll have something by Christmas, I promise."

"Thanks, Bill."

I arrived back in England after an odyssey of trains and buses and boats. It rained when I reached London; for a moment it was like I hadn't travelled at all. The English Summer had truly ended, and I arrived in Camford much in the same way as I had a year earlier. It was early evening when I got back to the flat.

"Fitzy!", Richard called, clutching me in a bear-hug before I could drop my bags. "I never thought I'd see you again. I figured Paris had gobbled you up like a little sandwich."

"Christ, Richard. I was only gone for a few weeks."

He nodded and smiled, before turning to the hall. "Fucksby! Cancel the newspaper ad, the prodigal son has returned!"

Francis trotted in. "Oh. Hello, Robin."

"Hello, Francis." I shook his hand and was happy to see him again.

"I think a round of gin and tea is in order," said Richard, placing a hand on either of our shoulders.

"You know what," I said. "I'll have a gin and tea."

Richard gasped with delight as Francis filled the kettle. A drink and a short conversation later, I excused myself and went to bed. In the morning I walked to Balloch's flat. We sat in silence for a moment, waiting for our coffee to cool to a drinkable temperature.

"So," he said when the time came.

"So."

"I know it's not exactly my place to ask. But if you do want to t—"

"I don't want to talk about it."

We sat in silence again. Balloch had a way about him, that extracted secrets and soon the quiet became too much to handle. I sighed, breaking the silence. "I flew too close to the sun."

"Well, you lived to tell the tale. Is there anything else to report?"

He caught my eye and carved me open with a grin.

"I met a girl."

Like a porous wound, I spilled and spilled. I told him of Le Coin, of Francine and of my error. He listened intently and I saw the gears of his mind working. "That actually happened?", he asked when I was done.

"Yes."

"In the exact manner by which you describe it?"

"To the best of my recollection."

"Then I think you have your '*something simple*'."

"Yeah?"

"Oh, Robin. You naive young tit. Yes! How dare you come here all forlorn, with that sitting underneath you. It's perfect. Perfectly simple. Boy meets girl, exotic location, horrible ending. I wouldn't change a thing. Though, Donald will of course. He'll have a happy ending, '*for the spinsters*', he'll say."

"I don't want to write for spinsters."

"We all have to write for the spinsters at some point. It's best that you get it out of the way sooner."

"I can't write about the affair, Donald will know something is up."

"Or he'll think that you made it up."

"That's even worse, fantasising about his wife."

"Then change the ending."

"To what?"

"A happy one."

"Just like that?"

"It's *simple*."

"Yes. Yes it is."

"I think this will be good for you. There's a function tomorrow, the usual lot. Donald should be there. Do come along, he's been asking about you."

"Okay."

Some time passed and I got up to leave. In the doorway, I stopped myself and turned back. Balloch had anticipated it and not taken his eyes off of me. "Will——will *she* be there?"

"I think so."

I had come full circle. I had been without love, and then I had known it, only to be where I was before. The next evening came in a flash and we stood in the middle of the room as familiar faces spun around in rings. Balloch had gotten merry rather quickly and before long, we spotted Donald across the hall.

"Okay, there he is," Balloch said with a blurred focus.

"So, let him work the room, right?"

"No. He's just spotted us."

"I say, is that the young Fitzwarwick?", Donald called, as eyes turned to us. He walked over and gripped us both firmly. We jumped straight into talking shop and I told him of the new novel.

"Wonderful! Absolutely wonderful. The last one sounded awfully complex anyway. What was it called again, Summer Is Hot?"

"All's Well in Winter Days."

"Save it, son. Save it for the end. You'll write it in a flash when you're old enough. But this new one, *English love in Paris*. How wonderful! The spinsters will shit!"

Donald continued to talk, but his voice trailed off into white noise as I looked past his shoulder and saw Cynthia. She watched us intently with a glimmer of fire in her eyes. As if this was all of her doing, and some nefarious plan had come together perfectly.

Donald's voice grew back into my mind as he gripped my shoulder like a vice. "Balloch, do excuse me. I wish to borrow our young writer here for a moment or two."

Donald, in effect, carried me away and we found

ourselves secluded in a sort of drawing room. One that belonged more in a country house than a college hall. There were two red arm chairs. He sat in one and gestured to the other.

"You know, my wife was also in France. Avignon, I believe. Lovely old town, have you been?"

"No, I have not. This was actually my first time abroad."

"Oh really? Pity, it broadens the mind, my dear boy. It opens the senses. Oh well, you are still young. Eighteen, right?"

"Nineteen."

"Really? As of when?"

"A few days ago."

"Many happy returns my dear boy."

"Thank you, Donald."

"You're so young, Robin. I could almost envy you. These things, experiences, will all happen in good time. The only thing the young lack is money, but I take it that's not an issue for you. A young man of your station, your name, mixed with your——unfortunate family circumstances. I understand that you are well taken care of."

"Actually, Donald, no."

"Oh. Well then, I shall make a wealthy man of you. Anyway, as for the book, I cannot imagine anything will change. I shall still require the manuscript by December, and we want to have it on shelves by March. Would that be agreeable to you?"

"It would."

"Good. I've earned a new round of favours that I shall be calling in. And for now, I must return to the festivities. But it's been a treat to see you again, young Robin."

"Likewise, Donald."

"Do come and see me when the novel is finished."

"I shall."

He stopped by the door. "Robin."

"Yes, Donald?"

"Do you still have my card?"

"I do."

"Good. Don't hesitate."

And then he was gone. To this day, I'm not sure why I chose to linger, but I did. I sat in that red arm chair for several minutes and finished my drink. I was still firmly in the dark as to what Donald knew, if anything at all. The angel on my shoulder told me that he knew nothing; for if he did know, I'd have been in a gutter by night's end. And yet, the corner of my mind that produces words and proclamations and poems, as well as crippling neuroses, told me that I was a fly caught in a spider's web. Trapped, and paralysed, and waiting to be consumed. I finished the wine and readied myself to leave. My heart throbbed when I opened the door and saw Cynthia standing there. Before I could say a word, she handed me a note and scurried away.

"I have to go," I whispered to Balloch, once I had found him.

"Go? Where?"

"Home."

I was gone before he could respond. Just as in that Avignon hotel; I heard nothing and felt nothing as I walked through Camford and to my digs. Richard and Francis were up to something when I entered, but cared not, and went to my room without a word, shutting the door behind me. I opened the envelope and withdrew the letter. I lit a cigarette, threw open the window, and read the contents.

'Robin,

I must apologise for all prior conduct. It was not my intent to leave in the way that I did. However, it must be stated clearly, and without ambiguity, that I consider this affair to be over.

It was fun, but you fell in love with me. For reasons I have given directly to you, I can not leave my marriage. Although, this affair, and its end, may prove serendipitous for us both. I implore you to use the pain and confusion that you may feel, and direct it into writing.

You have it within you to be an excellent writer, you just need pain. Please do not contact me. Donald does not know..

C.'

I crumpled the note and threw it against the wall.

"I need pain?", I growled to myself. "I'm a fucking orphan."

That was how my first experience of love came to an end; alone in a room. Later, I would come to know the true nature of my role in Cynthia's life. I would learn that there had been young men before, and after me, all of whom saw the same fate. They all spent time at the Galveston Arms, all tried to flee and were reeled back in. All confessed their love, and tried to pry her from Donald, and all awoke one day to find her gone. The depression that ensued was made no easier by the completion of my first novel, in the November of 1952. For days after, I languished in a despair felt only by those who had lost something. I was warned of this by Balloch near its completion, that no greater pain is drawn from the scribbler's stone, than by finishing the first true work.

Cynthia was true to her word, and never told Donald of our affair. Though she did tell Eleanor; who I met in the Summer of 1994, long after Cynthia had died. Eleanor told me the truth of our affair. It had not ended because I loved her, but rather that she had loved me. Though, I never saw, or spoke to Cynthia Andress ever again.

14

Six months had passed since that night. Donald had remained a fixture of Camford society, but Cynthia stayed in London. Her absence had been explained by Donald, when after a respite of some months, we met for dinner in the centre of town.

> "She's gone off classical architecture, it's the most peculiar thing," he said. "I can't seem to get her to come up any more. She is transfixed on modernism these days."

My first novel had been completed by November, and was written in ten intense sessions; interwoven by fierce exchanges of critique and defence with Balloch. He had moulded me as if I were in his school for wayward writers; putty in his hands. Through him I had found that loose brick in the wall, and unravelled the entire facade. The life of a writer, Balloch said, was lived in sole pursuit of the singular masterpiece, which all over works only seek to serve. They, he would add, simply built the stage. Despite the anger I often felt towards him, his methods had worked, and the novel was received well. It was published in March and had gained me some notoriety. Publications to whom Donald was not entangled had written positive reviews. One such publication was the Herald, and Balloch read it to me one day in his office.

> "*Combining delicate and sensitive prose, with witty dialogues, and that hazy glow of youth; Camford upstart Robin Fitzwarwick has made his name irrevocably linked to the university's new liter-*

ary scene. One year after the release of his debut volume of poetry, and under the tutelage of the once promising playwright William Balloch, this novel is a must read for the romantic heart, and the intellectual mind. 'The Way We Went' tells the story of two strangers, in a strange location, finding a familiar comfort, love."

Balloch folded the paper and threw it onto the table that stood between us. "I must say, it's quite the review. Though it is in the Herald, do keep your distance from the Herald."

"At least you got a mention."

"Oh, yes. '*Once promising*', '*once*'. No thanks to them."

"It's the same critic, too."

"Bastard. I figured he'd have scurried back to the shadows by now."

I chuckled. As I did the door behind me opened and a disembodied American accent called in. "Hey, Bill. I'm going out. Do you need anything?"

"I'm okay, thank you."

Balloch nodded and the door closed. I perched forward. "Mitz?"

"He's a research fellow now. Good for him."

"Oh yeah?"

"Yeah."

"How do you feel about that?"

"What could you possibly mean?"

"For a start, you hate him."

"Granted, the slimy little prick is after my job, with his dagger sharpened. But, young Robin, you underestimate the job security I enjoy. I'm nothing short of a total nervous breakdown away from dismissal."

I glanced at the empty gin bottle on the windowsill behind him. "Are you still drinking?"

"Don't you worry about that. I have it perfectly under control."

I feared, and had feared for some time, that Balloch was *not* in control. He had always shaken off the failures of his career in writing, and even joked about them carelessly. However, I saw in him a man numbing a pain that does not subside easily; that of a man on a leash, a man whose wings were clipped before he could truly fly; a tiger in the zoo, who once stalked the Bengal plain. I feared for my friend. And without knowing, I had begun to mourn him prematurely. Balloch did not drink as a man does, when accentuating a mood, celebrating a hard-fought victory, or burdensome achievement; nor even to simply pass the time, or to birth a brotherhood among men. He drank as if he was thirsty, as if the bottle were an oasis in the desert, and he - a weary and sun-beaten traveller of some forty days and forty nights - had no other choice available to him but to drink, and slurp, and gulp. As the months went on, I seldom saw him without a drink. Sometimes it was disguised in a tea-cup or water bottle, other times it was flagrant and out in the open for all to see. He drank shamefully, and he drank without shame, depending on the mood and setting. Our Friday meetings would invariably, and if given enough time, migrate to the pub. And there he was at home.

"Ah, Fitzy. There you are," Richard said as I arrived home. "Your friend is here."

"My friend?"

"Indeed. He is in your room. I let him go and wait in there because we ran out of things to talk about."

Cautiously I walked into my room to find Monty, sat on my bed with what remained of All's Well in his hands. "Monty?"

"Robin!", he stood and gripped me firmly. "I had a long weekend and figured I'd visit. You did not answer the phone."

"I must have been out. It's good to see you, old friend."

"Robin," he said, gesturing towards the unfinished manuscript. "This is very pretty. How'd a whipper-snapper like you get so wordy and deep."

I removed my jacket and hung it up, before taking a seat at the desk and lighting a smoke. "Thanks. Pity it'll never see the light of day."

"Oh?"

"I'd rather not talk about it, Monty. Besides, there are more pressing concerns, now that I am a *best-seller.*"

"So you are, and with your newfound riches, you can buy me dinner."

I smiled at my friend, and he smiled back. "Fine," I said, stubbing out the cigarette and putting my jacket back on. Monty took point and entered the living room, where Francis had now joined Richard.

"Richard, Fuc—Francis. We are going out. Do join us."

Richard sprung to his feet. "At last, a man of action!" I've been starved for entertainment I tell you. Starved! Monty, is it? I like you, Monty. I like you a great deal!"

We strolled into town and found a small restaurant to dine at. Monty seemed satisfied and Richard did not. Once more, Francis was difficult to read.

"I say," Monty whispered to me when the meal was done. "This town is awfully pretty. I can see why you fled London in such haste."

"It's not terrible, is it?"

"I wouldn't say. Forget Paris, dear boy, you should write about this place."

For reasons that still, over forty years later, baffle me; I did not ever write about Camford. It was, as it seemed, just for me. I would go on to write of all corners of the earth; but Camford, that painting of a town, that gave me so much, never made the cut. We finished our food and moved on to a watering hole. It was the very same one I had indulged in on my first night in Camford. We had returned numerous times since arriving, and Richard had, reluctantly, accepted that he would not be able to drink gin and tea here. He ordered a gin and tonic and called it '*the closest thing*.'

We chatted gaily over cheap beer, and soon the late afternoon had turned into the evening. Eventually, Jarves - whom I had seen sparingly, and then very often in fluctuating patterns - appeared from nowhere.

"I say, chaps. Fancy seeing you all here."

"Jarves," we all said in a stagger.

"It's a good thing I've found you lads, there's a party on tonight, an off-college thing. I'm just about to head there myself. Wait a second, is that—oh shit, is that Montgomery Villiers?"

"Hello, Jarvis," Monty replied.

"Christ, what are the odds. What on earth are you doing up here?"

"Visiting a friend," he said, nodding his head towards me.

"Oh, yes. I forget that Robin's an old boy too, he has *such* a middle-class soul. Well, it's good to see you, chum. How's London treating you?"

"Just fine, Jarvis. It's been a while."

"Far too long, lad. Is your sister still asking about me?"

"Only if you've gotten the message yet."

The two let out a laugh and embraced each other as old friends do. We told Jarves that we would meet him at the party, and returned to our drinks. We arrived at the house off-college, and were met by Jarves, Maz, and a few others I had come to know in Camford, whose names have since slipped my mind. A tour of the house brought me back into the kitchen, where I found Richard in a dispute with the tenant.

"What do you mean I can't have a gin and tea? I can see the kettle, it's right there!"

"Listen, Belling. If you fire up the kettle, everyone is going to want a cup of tea. I can't have that."

"What rot! I demand a gin and tea, right now."

"The best I can do for you is straight gin."

"Sold."

Sufficiently amused, I moved on. Monty and I found ourselves on a balcony, looking over the city. We stared out into the stone and cobble for some time in silence. After an amount of time I cannot recall, Monty drew my focus back into the party.

"Your friend is quite a wise fellow."

"You can't mean Richard."

"No, of course not. I mean the butler."

I followed Monty's gaze and found Francis in the midst of a heated debate. He was surrounded by others, equally invested. He gesticulated and made his case with passion and the group stopped and fell into a rhetorical retreat; having been soundly defeated by whatever Francis had said.

"Why does he put up with it all?" Monty asked.

"I've been asking myself that question ever since I met him. I've asked him a few times. He just changes the subject."

"Any theories?"

"Richard's family took him in, he's——like me."

"I see."

Some time passed, and I entertained the fancies of various freshers who'd liked my book. Monty beamed on like a proud father, and the evening passed with a gentleness. I had hit the right level of drunkenness, and my anxieties faded into the February night.

"You have a good little life here, Robin," said Monty, as we shared a smoke. "I worried so much for you."

"Really?"

"Well, I don't want to sound like I'm patronising you, but I did often fear how you'd get on without me. You've done just fine, mate."

There was a moment of intimacy between us, the sort that arises between lads who've been through it all together. A moment of fraternal bliss hung delicately in the air, until we were brought back into the party, by a chorus of muffled laughs inside. We looked in to see Richard, soundly asleep in an arm chair. Jarves sat next to him, drawing on his face with a pen, which drew much amusement from those nearby. Francis noticed what was happening and moved swiftly over to wake Richard from his slumber.

"Come on, sir. Let's get you home."

I turned to Monty, knowing he shared the endearment that Francis had implanted in me.

"You know," I said. "Despite all Richard puts him through, I'd say it is a fair trade. Francis gets a family, and Richard gets a friend; the only true friend he has. Apparently, he has known Jarves since they were kids. Yet Jarves draws on his face and Francis takes him home."

Monty smiled. "Come on, let's give him a hand."

We carried Richard home and cleaned him up upon arrival. All the way he muttered about Eleanor. "I loved her. Why doesn't she love me back?", he repeated; over and over. "I loved her. I loved her. I loved her."

Francis retired once Richard was put to bed. I took Monty by the shoulder, and led him back to the front door.

"Come with me," I said. "I want to show you something."

We walked back into the city. Despite a distant glow of sound here and there. It was that hour in which Camford slept, and all was still. We meandered through winding streets and alleys until we came to the fountain, from which I had smoked my first cigarette. I had returned here many times, though Monty was the first guest I had brought.

"You know," I said, lighting a cigarette. "I'm baffled by this fountain. Anywhere else in the world, anywhere else in Europe, you'd build some opulent public square around this fountain, it'd be a tourist trap. Yet, whenever I come here, day or night, it is only ever me."

"Perhaps it was built only for you. You and esteemed guests of yours."

I chuckled. "Fate would never be so kind."

"You're too pessimistic. This fate has brought you great things. You have the ability to command words, and how wonderful they are. You were blessed with that instinct, the one that separates Waugh from Watson, Yates from Yardley."

"Who are *Watson* and *Yardley*?", I asked.

Monty just smiled. "Nobodies."

"You know," I said, gesturing. "I saw Cynthia for the first time down there."

"Are you still beaten up about it?"

"I suppose. I don't know, I keep trying to find meaning in it. She said that I needed to have my heart broken, and sometimes I think it all goes through Donald, like he'd put her up to it or something. And then, it becomes obvious, and I feel a fool for trying to find meaning in it. Some people just come into your life, stay a while, and then leave. That's it really. There's no use in trying to make it make sense, you'd wait forever."

"And what of the expat?"

"The expat?", I asked.

"The girl from the book. I take it she was real."

"She was. I'm glad that you read the novel, Monty. I didn't want to ask if you had."

"Of course, I did. *Suzanne*."

"Francine," I said, gravely.

"And where is *Francine*?"

"Haven't a clue, Monty."

"You don't know?"

"She left Paris, while I was——"

"While you were in Avignon."

"Yes."

"It happens."

"What does?"

"The wrong decision."

"Some part of me thought that it would all work out."

"Yes. The part of you that is between your legs. Ask yourself, Robin, what was the best-case scenario? A life of secrecy?"

"Okay, I get it. I'm a fool."

"You're not a fool. You just did a foolish thing. There's a difference. Much in the same vein, you could do an awful thing, but you'd still be a good man."

"Am I a good man?"

"Who's to say, Robin. We're hardly twenty. I don't even know if we're *men* yet, let alone good men. But I can say this, I enjoy your company. I always have. You're not an ass, but you can be. Just, enjoy feeling something, even if it's pain. And what now? Nothing. We're young, too young to realise just how young we are. And one day we'll be old, and even older the next day. I never saw much point in doing anything other than just enjoying the nice things in life. College won't last forever, and soon we'll spend every day doing things we really don't care about. I think about that all the time, how bored we'll be in a decade. Our entire lives are ahead of us. Study, write, do what you were doing before you became entangled in this mess. Just live. Maybe go away again."

We wandered home without saying a word, the whole time I thought of Francine. Early the next day, Monty left for London, and I walked him to the station. My head swirled with a thousand thoughts as I made my way home, and I found myself unable to speak once I arrived. Richard came to me and broke my self-imposed silence.

"Say, Fitzy. Fucksby and I are headed down to Cornwall once term ends. Summer in the *Belling patch*. Do join us!"

15

As my second year came to an end, I fell into a mundane sort of sickness. I had lost the bounce with which I walked from the lecture hall to my digs, and from my digs to the pub. I wrote my essays, attended my lessons, and waited for Friday in a haze. I lived as I had in my first year, but the sense of fun grew distant, and hummed in agony from the rear, like a widow. Perhaps owing to Cynthia, and the manner in which she had left my life, or perhaps just due to the gentle passing of time, I had become a man in my nineteenth year. I focused solely on the fruits of my labour. I drank until morning, dined expensively, and would only address my scholastics in brief fits of output, and yet there was something eerily mature in it. As such, I had cracked the code of Camford academics, and allowed my name to carry me the rest of the way. I became a respectable member of my college, and was hosted, on occasion, as a guest of honour.

The last Friday of the term came around, and I sat across from Balloch, just as I had countless times before.

"So," he said, sipping a cup of tea. "Another year done."

"And one more to go."

"How would you say it has gone?"

"Must we discuss my education?"

"I think so."

"I just—keep asking myself what I'm still doing

here. All the work, the essays, exams. All the hours spent in lectures and seminars, for what? I have my career."

"And what is keeping you here?"

"You, I suppose."

"And your friends?"

"Yes, them too."

Balloch stiffened and leaned into me. He froze, as if curating the right words in his head. "I wrote my first play when I was an undergraduate. I sat where you're sitting and thought what you are thinking. And you know what?"

"What?"

"I am glad that I stayed. For one, my father would have killed me, but that's a matter for a psychiatrist to unpack. I'm glad because things didn't go as I had expected them to go. But I had a contingency, a good one. And all it cost me was three years of my youth. Besides, it's a hell of a place to be young. "

"To hell with you, Balloch. I can never contest."

He grinned. "It is a simple matter of age, young Robin. One day you too will impart wisdom upon the youth."

"And I shall ask you to shoot me when that day comes."

"What are your plans for the Summer?", he asked after a while.

"I've been invited down to Cornwall for the season."

"Oh, yes! You should go. Have you ever been?"

"I haven't."

"You'll like it. Cornwall is a magical place. *Paradise beyond the moors*."

"Have you spent much time there?"

"Not since I was young. But it doesn't ever leave you."

"Oh, do join me. I don't know if I can go three months without a Friday."

"I wish that I could. Alas, Camford is a spider's web, and I am but caught flea."

We chatted for a while longer and soon I got up to leave.

"When do you go?", he asked.

"Three days."

His demeanour changed as I went to move for the door. He took my hand in his and gripped my shoulder, as if he desired to never let go. "I'm really proud of you, Robin."

"Relax, Bill. It's only the Summer. I'll be back by August."

He just smiled.

I found Richard in the living room when I got back. A book perched in his hands which came as a surprise, as I had never seen Richard read a book in the near two years I had known him.

"Good day to you, Fitzy."

"Good day, Richard. Are you—reading?"

He looked up with a defensive glare. "Yes. I'm frightfully smart you know."

I placed my jacket on the table and sat in the armchair across from him. "Granted. Otherwise, you wouldn't be here."

"Precisely."

"Well, what are you reading?"

"Jemima Puddle-Duck," he said, turning the page deliberately, as if he was pretending to read.

"Oh, right."

"What?"

"Nothing. It's a good book."

"It's a brilliant book. Jemima Puddle-Duck is my favourite of all Blyton's works."

I made an indeterminate noise, choosing not to correct him. "Fancy a drink?"

"No," he said, turning back to the book. "We're out of gin."

I nodded and got up to leave. "Wait," Richard called once I'd made towards the hall. I turned to see an envelope in his hand. "This came for you. It's from Eleanor's dad."

"How'd you know?"

He swivelled the envelope to reveal the trademark Andress wax seal. "Oh, thanks," I said, picking it out from his grip.

"Have—", Richard began, but trailed off, I looked up to see him struggling to get the words out. "Have you seen her, Fitzy?"

"Have I seen—"

"Eleanor. Have you seen her?"

"I'm afraid not, Richard."

"Oh, okay."

I smiled at Richard in a way that failed to conceal the pity I felt for him. And then he surprised me. "It was the mother, wasn't it?"

"Excuse me?"

"The summons. Those pretty little envelopes. I opened one of them once. It was Eleanor's mother, wasn't it?"

"Yes. It was."

"*C.*"

"Yes, *C.*"

He smiled. "We are kindred spirits, Fitzy. Both broken-hearted at the hands of an Andress."

I opened the note and read its contents. "And another wants to dine with me."

"When?"

"Tonight. I wish he'd give me a fair warning when he decides to come up."

"I lied. We do have gin. Would you care for a gin and tea?"

"Just a tea, please."

He glanced uneasily at the kettle. "Well, you see, Robin. Dear Fucksby typically does that part for me. Could you—"

"Sure. How much gin do I put in?"

"A lot."

We drank gin and tea and chatted some more. At seven, I left for my dinner with Donald. He had picked a restaurant far beyond my budget. I had learned by now that Donald took great pleasure in paying. The conversation went in whichever direction he chose it to. We ordered and our bottle of wine arrived. He poured two mighty glasses and laid one in front of me. Once the pleasantries were through, he asked if I shared Balloch's view that there *were no more greats*. By way of answer, I told him of my own ambitions.

"I'd hope so. It's just a pity that such books aren't in a great demand. The people don't want a character study, or an epic anymore. They're perfectly content with love stories. Granted, your prose is good, it's clean, and I go where the money is. That's where we seem to have slotted you in, Robin. You write like a great, for an audience who've forgotten what it means to read something great, who'll pay for the reading pleasure."

"I suppose that's something."

"Very few men do *something*, Robin. That is what I can offer you, and have offered you, and given to you. Though of course, I'm merely talking shop. I did invite you to dine with me for a reason, and you may be wondering what that is." His tone was impossible to decipher. His coldness sang praises and his warmth heralded warnings. In this, he was neutral, and then he burst into a fit of mirth, and pounded the table, so that we became the focal point of the room. "But I've forgotten the damn thing! Oh, age. Age, age, age. Do yourself a favour, Robin, and top yourself when you're north of thirty, it's only downhill from there."

"I'm sure it's not so bad, Donald."

"Oh, spare yourself. I don't like it when you tell me what I want to hear, Robin. My daughter's getting married, what d'you make of that?"

"Oh, right. That's good news, no?"

"Allegedly. I will concede that this new suitor is not an oaf like that pillock friend of yours. But I always imagined that she would end up with a writer. I always wished for it, and the two of them would run every press in the country. It's conquest I'm after, young Robin. It's conquest that gets me up in the morning, conquest that keeps me moving. My wife was a conquest, the most beautiful girl in London; Andress House is a conquest, and you could fill a hall with the skulls of the men I've crushed to be here, because my goals are simple, like yours. I want to *be* publishing. I want to *be* the English language. But, it's a generation game. I'll die long before I run the world, but my grandson will have a good shot. He works in politics; which is just theatre for goblins and the like. There are obvious benefits to having relations in the Commons, but it's the business I care about. I always hoped that she'd end up with you."

"With me?"

"Yes, I think you'd make a handsome pair."

"Hm," I chuckled.

He chuckled back.

"Why are you telling me all of this?", I asked.

"Well, it's no secret I always saw the two of you as being compatible. And if I am being completely honest, I am sorely lacking in confidantes. Vulnerability is bad for business."

"I appreciate your candour, Donald."

He smiled and then became serious. The food arrived and he readied himself for consumption before speaking again. "There is one more thing, but it seems to have slipped my mind."

He thought for a moment, looking around the room as the tension grew.

"Oh yes," he snapped after a while. "My wife."

My heart thumped as he took a bite of his steak. We held each other's eye as he chewed. I broke the silence once he swallowed. "What of her?", I asked.

He took another bite and chewed for a minute that felt like an eternity. "She was very fond of your novel and wanted me to ask you when you will have another one ready."

"Oh," I said, with relief. "That is very kind of her." Donald had a habit for sudden shifts in tone, and one never felt quite at peace in his presence, which I have since come to believe to be a cultivated, and entirely conscious part of his character. His goals were simple, just as he said, he wanted to be the King, and a King has no friends. After we ate, had a coffee, and found ourselves on the curb, smoking his golden cigarettes, he asked me about my plans for the Summer, and shifted his tone again when I said I'd be in Cornwall with Richard.

"Be mindful of the company you keep, young Robin. Do not let your associations bring you down. A man's circle is his destiny. A man is his peers."

"I have Balloch."

"Oh, yes. *Dipso Bill. Balloch Brandy-for-Breakfast.*"

"He's been very good for me."

"I should hope so, he is your elder after all. Just be careful. That man is on the edge of a cliff. Hold on too tight and you'll be pulled over too."

"He has been through a lot. The critics were not kind to him."

"No, they were not. It was certainly one of my tougher decisions."

My eyes widened and he gave a tense smile. "I'm just kidding," he said with a slap on my arm. Night came and I bid Donald farewell. He left me with instructions to visit him in London once I had completed a novel. I arrived home to much commotion, that I could hear from the stairs. Richard roared with laughter as I heard objects drop and be knocked over in the flat. I opened the door to find Richard wheeling Francis around the flat.

"What on earth is happening in here?"

"I'm using Fucksby as a mop," Richard said, as if there was nothing peculiar about it.

"Okay."

I went into my room and began packing for Cornwall. Richard came in and sat on the bed.

"So? Do you bring me news of Eleanor?"

I didn't have the heart to tell him. "I'm sorry, Richard. It must have slipped my mind."

Long into that sultry night, I rolled about the bed,

and paced about the room, as a pulsing discomfort came rolling over the cobbled hills and penetrated the walls. I thought about Balloch until it pained me to do so. What had disquieted me so about our last meeting was how barren his office was, as if it had been packed. His last words to me before I left too had imparted a sour taste.

And so, I waited until the sun rose, and left the flat, having not slept a wink. There was a distance between my thoughts and warmth in my bones, a pale hue in my skin, as I walked through the city, past Merton, and Oriel, Mansfield, and Trinity, until at last I came to Balloch's leafy street, and climbed the steps. Alas there was no answer to my call.

16

At noon, on a Saturday in the middle of June 1953, we boarded the train to Cornwall. It was a journey of three parts; to London, to Wessex, and then to Cornwall. '*The New Asturias*', as Richard called it. "This is the beginning of our revolution," he said, as we rode to the station. "Our revolution against all that is boring, and all who are early to bed and unused to drink."

We were to stay at *Belling House* for the Summer. Even before I had known Richard, I had heard stories of it from school friends. It was, as they said, the greatest of all the houses in Cornwall. It sat on a hill, by the village of Molt Bay on the north-western coast. I stared out the window with content as England floated on by. Richard snapped me back into the train with a raising of his finger.

"Right, I've got a nap-sack of gin for us to get good and merry with. Wine for you, Robin. And then it is just five short hours down to Cornwall. Charles and Mary will pick us up from the station, it's a bit of a drive from the village."

"Charles and Mary?" I asked.

"His parents," Francis interjected.

"Right."

"Oh, it is going to be a *feast* of a Summer. A feast, I tell you! The parents go away first thing in the morning and then it belongs to us. It all belongs to us. Oh,

I'm so excited that I could weep. Fucksby, pass me the thermos would you, old boy."

Francis went into his bag and retrieved a thermos full of tea, he then handed me a bottle of wine, hidden in a paper bag, as Richard set about preparing his tincture.

"Oh, and if anyone asks," he said. "Just say that you're drinking a blackcurrant cordial."

Those five hours came and went with haste. We were drunk by Bristol. And when we reached Devonshire, Richard summoned a waiter. "I say, we'd like some coffee please, squire, and make them strong. And some bread." He turned to us. "We need to sober up. Charles and Mary are of the opinion that the public intoxication is unbecoming."

"How intolerant of them," I chipped, as my mood lifted.

"Indeed. That's exactly what I say of them. So horribly intolerant. So stuck in their *ghastly* ways. If I wish to get merry on the noon train from Camford, then I *shall* get merry on the noon train from Camford. It is no business but my own."

Some more time passed, and we arrived at our destination. Richard's father, Charles, stood alone on the platform, eyeing each carriage for sight of us. I had managed to suppress the dizziness I felt, as had Francis. In the usual course of events, Richard was the liability.

"Okay chaps, walk straight," he said as the door's hissed and opened, before tripping and falling out of the train, landing face-first on the platform. He rolled and writhed in pain, while clutching his wrist. Charles walked over and stood over his son.

"Oh, hello Richard. I see that you are on the floor. *Why* are you there?"

Richard staggered to his feet and shook his father's outstretched hand. "Hello, father."

Charles looked stern and spoke to his son as if no one else were around. "You'd do well to not burn my name and reputation, Richard. Now fetch your bags, your mother is waiting."

Richard nodded and went off to retrieve our luggage. Charles turned to Francis and myself. "Hello, Francis. It is good to see you again."

"Hello, Mr. Belling."

"Are you keeping well?"

"Oh, yes sir. As well as can be."

"Good to hear," he said, turning to me. "And you must be the writer?"

"Yes, sir. Robin Fitzwarwick."

"A pleasure."

Richard returned with our bags on a trolley. Francis took over as we made our way to the car. It was a thirty-minute drive to the house and we winded through country roads, lined with trees and hedges, and the occasional farm. Richard sat in the passenger seat with his head out the window while Charles drove.

"Do you smell that?", he asked from the front seat, in reference to the general scent of country and farmland. "Nothing quite like it."

Eventually he bored of the routine, as some peculiarity struck him, and he turned to his father. "Why do you drive, father? Where is the chauffeur? Richmond, or whatever his name is."

"I had to let Raymond go," Charles said, with his eyes fixed firmly on the road "Some of the other staff as well."

"Why?"

"Times have changed, Richard. Money is not what it used to be."

"So, who has been relieved?"

"A few of the maids, the physician, and the tennis coach."

"The tennis coach? Why on God's green would you let him go?"

"Do inform me, Richard. When was the last time you played tennis?"

"I figured Adeline still played."

Charles continued on, as if nothing had been said. "And we are selling the townhouse."

"Fuck off!"

The car slammed to a halt and Charles snapped his neck towards Richard, who immediately recognised his error and apologised. What followed was a pregnant silence, in which it was clear that Richard had much on his mind. "And what of Bilkins?", he asked, in a sheepish tone.

His father settled for a moment, before he allowed the car to move once more. "*Bilkins* is going nowhere. As for the house, it is already settled; I shall stay at my club when in London, and you shall stay in hotels."

"So, we are homeless now?"

"Yes, we are vagabonds, *tramps*. I'm driving us to an empty field, that is where we'll stay." He laughed to himself before continuing. "No, of course we are not homeless. The house on Corfu is still ours. Two homes is plenty, and a trimming of fat is much needed in these—uncertain times. My great-great-great grandfather bought Belling House, and I bought the townhouse It hardly defines us."

He trailed off, as the house came into view over a winding hill, with the village just beyond. It all seemed to curl above, like smoke from a cigarette, and I knew then that I was to find something hidden in myself this Summer.

I could write forever, and yet never quite find the words befitting Belling House. Everything I had heard was true. No painter or poet could do it justice. It felt of another world entirely, of another time. The sole word that came to my lips on that first visit, same as my last, was *palatial*.

The man known as *Bilkins* met us at the door, he was around the same age as Richard's father, and had dressed exquisitely. Not in a servants garb, but rather a finely cut suit of tweed and amber. "Ah, Bilkins," Mr. Belling beamed. "Please, do take our guest's luggage."

"Pleased to," he replied in a simple elegance. "Welcome to Belling House, Mr. Fitzwarwick."

Something about him seemed odd, it had not yet struck me why I found the man, and the circumstances of our meeting, so bizarre. He took my bags as I followed the others into the house. "I must give you the tour, old boy," Richard said, taking an apple from a display in the drawing room and taking a bite.

We left, without Francis, and over a dazzling half hour I saw all of Belling House. Each room was decorated with an air of thorough-bred English gaiety, within the confines of pure ostentation. Charles Belling seemed a fool to me on that day. He had sold a London townhouse, and thrown several good men to the scrap-heap, when all he had to do in order to balance books was sell a tenth of the decor. Each room was stacked with art and ornate furniture, from all corners of the world, and the view from every window was its own work of art. We crossed paths with Bilkins again on the stairs.

"Your room is ready, Mr. Fitzwarwick. You'll be staying in the *Beech Room*. And I'd say it'll do. I find it to be the most beautiful of all the guest rooms."

"Thank you, Bilkins."

He nodded, and strode away.

"What's his first name?", I asked Richard.

"Couldn't say," he shrugged.

"*Beech Room,*" I said, aloud.

"They're all named after trees, the bedrooms. Mother and father have the *Oak;* Francis has the *Pine*, and I have the *Willow*. Adeline renamed hers."

"Whatever to?"

"*Dionaea muscipula*."

When we returned to the greeting room, Richard's mother had appeared, and seemed to lay in wait for us. She jolted to her feet when we began down the stairs. "Hello, dear," she said, as I reached her. "*You* must be Robin."

"Yes, Ma'am."

"Please," she said with a flip of her hand. "Call me Mary."

"It is a pleasure to meet you, Mary. I must say, you have a wonderful home."

"The pleasure belongs to me and me alone. I loved your book; it was frightfully good."

"Based on a true story too," said Richard.

"Is that so?"
"Yes."
"Well, where is she? I'd love to meet the ingenue."
"I'm afraid that I don't know."
"Oh, what a shame. I'm sure you'll win her back."
I smiled, but inside I still loathed myself for leaving Paris in the manner that I did.
"Darling," Mary said to Richard. "Where is Francis."
"If I were to guess, father is showing him the botany room."
She chuckled. "That is *so* Francis. Are you boys hungry? Supper won't be long. Mrs. Ambrose got to work as soon as your father left for the station."
"Starved, mother. Say, would anyone care for a cup of tea? My treat."
"Yes, that would be lovely, thank you dear."
"Robin?"
"Sure, thank you."
Richard left the room and I sat with Mary. Not long after, he returned with a tray of tea. "Here you are, mother. Robin."

I took a sip of tea and almost spat it out as a strong hit of gin struck the back of my throat. I looked up to find Richard, staring at me with a devilish grin. "How is your tea, Robin?"

I fought to speak with a composure, so as to not afford Richard his victory. "It's delicious. Thank you, Richard."

I put the tea down, and Richard decided to make my ordeal worse than it had to be. "Drink up, Robin. I would hate for it to go cold."

Evening came, and dinner was served. We spoke little during the meal. Charles had watched us pensively, calculating his after-dinner words, and at last he addressed us once the puddings had been taken away.

"So, boys. Your final year is approaching."
"Yes, father," said Richard.
"I shall make arrangements for you in London. I think stocks will suit you very kindly."

"Yes, father."

Charles raised a single brow, expecting more in response. "Thank you, father," came the desired words

"And Francis, I expect you shall take care of my son while he is there."

"Of course, sir."

"Good lad. And for you, Robin? I suppose you are set up rather nicely. I hear you publish with Donald Andress?"

"Yes, sir."

"That man opens doors. At least that is what I have heard."

"I suppose he does."

"You are a very fortunate young man. I believe that all men are born with the desire to create. This is why we become fathers, build nations and empires, establish fortunes. But the arts, that, Robin, is the truest form of magic. One that cannot be squandered."

"I agree, sir."

"Charles, please. The age of deference is long gone, and informality reigns supreme, so why fight it?"

I smiled and nodded. His words seemed genuine. As if he had once dreamed of the arts. Richard interrupted. "Say, father. Where is Adeline? I figured she'd be here by now."

"She is due to arrive tomorrow, I doubt we shall see her before leaving. I'm sure she would have liked to tell you herself, so do be a good chap and act surprised when she tells you."

"Tells me what?"

"That she is engaged."

"Oh, heavens. Not to that Bruce fellow?"

"*The upstart*," Mary resigned. "It's too horrible. You know, he came for dinner right after the engagement. I knew she'd shine at her debut, and shine she did, but I couldn't imagine she'd agree to marry in such a hurry. And to *him* of all people."

"Regretfully so," Charles added. "She seems dreadfully keen on the matter. So, I suppose there is little we can do about it."

Richard grew hot and spoke in a manner I hadn't heard before. "He does not belong in our family."

"And she does not belong in his. If one had told me before the war that one day my little girl would be wed to some—*upstart*, I'd have dropped dead on the spot. Alas, times have changed. It is not *our* world anymore."

He looked sad about the matter. As if Adeline's engagement symbolised directly to him that the world he knew was no more. He leaned forward and picked up a bell that lay in the middle of the table. He rung it twice and Bilkins entered, wheeling in a globe bar and opening it before departing. We all rose and helped ourselves to whatever tickled our fancy. Charles stood once we all sat and began a toast.

"Well, there is no use in getting forlorn about the state of the world. We have been dethroned and usurped, and our old crown is waved in our faces. Our skin has been flayed and worn as a trophy. But we have something these hoarding vulgars do not possess; we have class. It is the one thing that money cannot buy. They can throw their gold at a bigger house, a faster car, a sturdier boat. But they cannot buy the blood in my veins, our veins. We had a good run, but our time has come, and we are strangers in the sequel. Aristocracy is dead, long live aristocracy! To our twitching cadaver."

"To our twitching cadaver!", we all repeated before drinking.

"Francis," Charles said, once he had settled. "I was hoping you could do myself and Mary a favour tomorrow morning."

"Of course."

"We need you to drive us to the ferry and return the car without a scratch. Are you up to it?"

"Yes, sir."

"Thank you, Francis."

He nodded, before returning to his contemplative state. "Oh, Francis. There was just one more thing."

We then found ourselves in the drawing room, sat in awe as Francis played a perfect rendition of Chopin's Nocturne. His fingers danced on the keys; light, and yet so dominant. He swayed side to side and up and down with each rise and fall, and it was truly spectacular. In that moment of bliss, my eyes moved and danced around the room; resting, momentarily, on various ornaments and trinkets that were dotted about. Eventually I fell onto a family photograph. And that was the first time I saw Adeline. Her golden hair, pixie eyes; her delicate, feminine frame.

"She's beautiful," I said to myself as I grew weary and ready for bed.

17

I awoke the next day; late morning, to hear the scattered fragments of some conversation downstairs. In my haze, I could pick out the voices of Francis, and of Richard's parents. For half an hour, I drifted in and out of the day, eventually rising to the sound of a car turning over gravel stones. I looked out the window, as my eyes and ears became one. I dressed myself, half conscious of the fact that Adeline would be arriving today and made my way downstairs. Richard sat and read a newspaper with breakfast as I entered the dining room.

"Good morning, Fitzy. You hungry?"

"Famished."

"Very well." He picked up the bell, rang it twice, and Bilkins entered. "Robin is famished, Bilkins. What do we have?."

"Same as what you had, Your Lordship. The continental."

"Very well, he shall have that."

"Of course," said Bilkins, before leaving with a bow.

"*Your Lordship*?", I asked.

"A mere honorific," he replied. "Doesn't count for much these days."

I ate and drank coffee. And after went to light a smoke. Richard shot up before my lighter's flame could.

"Not in here! Either go outside or to the botany room."

"Fine. Where is it?"

"Hallway. Last door on the left."

"Cheers."

"Help yourself, old boy. I am going back to bed. Fucksby! Run me a bath!"

"He's gone."

"Yes, I suppose he is. Oh well, a cold one for me then."

Richard got up and strutted out of the room, swiping a stray bottle of gin on his way. I stepped into the hallway and saw the door he was referring to. The botany room was, in essence, a small greenhouse. Various exotic plants grew ferociously on walls and and the wall cried beads of sweat from the humid heat. A small fountain sat in the centre of the room. It splashed gaily and without a care.

I lit the smoke but quickly became uncomfortable. The room was sweltering, and with each inhale, it felt as if my lungs were melting, and my insides cooking. I began to sweat and palpitate, as a level of panic rose within. I had to get out, and so I did. I burst through the door and into the hall as tepid air hit me and was not enough. I looked out of the window that was immediately to my left and saw an oasis. There, in the large, opulent garden, sat a pond. As if it were made just for me, just for the situation I had found myself in. I ran outside and stripped off as I bolted for the pond. I stopped on its rim to remove my trousers, socks, and shoes before hurling myself into its cool embrace. It was better than any smoke I'd ever had or would have.

I swam around for a few minutes, with calm and deliberate back strokes as the sun beat upon me. Eventually, I crawled out and lay on the grass as the few clouds in the sky floated and dissipated. I lit another smoke and lay there in bliss. I thought of Balloch's words on Cornwall when I last saw him; '*paradise beyond the moors*', I said to myself.

I was pulled back into the world by the slamming of doors and the shuffling of feet in the distance. I looked toward the house to see a taxi driving away. Sensing that I was not alone, I dressed myself and sat up with my feet in the water.

Once more, the world evaporated, and I fell into bliss again.

"Hello."

The words were like a thunder-clap and my entire body jolted; I turned, almost falling back into the water, and there she was. Those blue eyes and golden hair, just as I had seen in the photograph.

"Are you one of my brothers' friends?", she asked.

"If not, then I think you are trespassing."

"I believe so."

"What? That you are a friend of my brother's? Or that you're a trespasser?

"The former."

She looked puzzled. "You believe so?"

"It's hard to tell with Richard, but we seem to get along."

"Indeed," she chuckled, extending her hand. "Adeline."

"Robin."

Before I could take her hand, a devilish grin shot across her face and she pushed me with all of her might, back into the water. I splashed and spluttered, robbed of all elegance, and only noticing, once I had stabilised, the pack of smokes in my pocket. Adeline had taken off running as soon as I hit the water.

"Hey!", I called. "You owe me a pack of cigarettes."

She didn't say a word, preferring to turn to me and smile. Once I had dried in the Cornish sun, I walked back to the house and found Richard exactly where I had seen him in the morning. This time he ate lunch.

"I hear you met my sister."

"Not quite. She pushed me into the pond."

Richard burst into laughter and slapped the table several times. "Addy you funny little thing, did you push Robin into the water? That is a classic."

"Yeah, yeah," I said, making for the door. "I'm going for a shower."

The staff only worked breakfast and supper on Sunday, and took their leave after ten. I nodded a farewell to Bilkins on his way out, and got a nod in return. I showered and wrapped myself in a robe before leaving the bathroom. As it happened, Adeline's room and my own were only separated by a handful of doors and she lingered by hers as I came into view. She laughed gaily and walked into her room.

The day floated from that point, Richard had gone back to sleep, and I spent the afternoon alone until evening came. I read in the drawing room, and swam in the pond once more. I ate a quiet meal with Richard at seven.

"It's not the same is it?", he asked in a melancholy. "Without the old boy."

"No it isn't. Won't Adeline be joining us?"

"She is dining out this evening. I heard the car outside and ran out thinking it was Fucksby. Alas it was a school-friend of Adeline's and her chauffeur. I miss our chauffeur. Ryan."

"I think his name was *Raymond*."

"Yes, Raymond. Oh how I miss him, and Fucksby."

Richard took his bath after dinner. I sat alone in the drawing room, until I heard the car returning. I walked out to find Francis in a high spirit. "Hello, Robin," he chirped.

"Hello, Francis. How was the drive?"

"It was heavenly. There was a performance of *The Marriage of Figaro* on the radio. It made the journey soar by."

"You like your classical music, don't you?"

"I do. Thank you for noticing."

"How could I not? You play so wonderfully."

"Only as wonderfully as you write, Robin. Say, is there any supper left over?"

"I believe so."

"Would you join me while I eat?"

"Of course."

We sat, and he ate a meal that was now cold, though he didn't seem to mind. So superlative were his manners that the meal could have been ghastly, and one wouldn't have known. As it happens, the food at Belling House was very much to my liking.

"Do you read my work, Francis?", I asked, as he

swallowed the last mouthful.

"I do. I haven't gotten around to the novel just yet. But I keep a keen eye on the poetry," he said, as we rose, and made way for the library. "It's very necessary in our time. I fear that beautiful things are simply out of fashion. The new stuff is all well and good, but it is fleeting, ephemeral. It won't be here tomorrow, figuratively. Whereas beautiful things are immortal. I like what you do, it bends the line between the old and the new. Poetry can be too rigid, but as recent trends tell us, it can also be too—— elastic. Contemporary writing is but a diagnosis of the post-war condition. Whereas Romance is a diagnosis, prognosis and treatment. One says '*there is depravity, let there be more*', the other seems to say '*there is depravity, it will poison man's soul, let there be wonderment instead'*."

"Well, Francis. You are much cleverer than me."

"Ah, Fucksby," said Richard, entering the room, "There you are. I have a mighty thirst and could do with some gin. Would you be so kind?"

"Of course."

"You are my wings, Fucksby."

Francis then turned to me. "Wine, Robin?"

"Yes please."

"There are cold meats in the kitchen if you're hungry," Richard said to me once we were alone.

"Maybe later."

Francis returned with a tray of drinks; gin, a pot of tea, some tonic and garnishing, and a bottle of wine. "Say," said Richard. "Adeline should be back soon."

As if on cue, and entering from stage left, Adeline appeared through the door. "Here I am."

She sat across from me and gave me a look up and down. Francis addressed her first. "Would you care for a drink, Adeline?"

"Whose wine is this?", she asked.

"Mine," I said.

"Well, it is *ours* now."

She leaned over and picked up the bottle and examined the back of it, before pouring herself a glass. I stood Francis down with a gesture and went into the kitchen myself to fetch another glass. Once all of our drinks had been prepared, Richard stood up. "And to what shall we drink?"

"To new friends," said Adeline.

"And old ones too." Richard added.

Our glasses met and we each took a sip before silence descended again. "So," Richard enquired after a moment or two. "What shall we do with this evening?"

Adeline perked up. "I have an idea. There is this game that Bruce and his friends play. A terribly fun game."

"A game?", Richard asked. "What sort of game?"

She giggled, as if her parents were in the next room and we were discussing some sordid secret. "Why, a drinking game of course!"

"Oh, Addy," Richard tutted. "You forget where I've been in this world. I've played every game under the sun. What is it called? I can guarantee you that I've heard of it."

"It's called tee-dee-dee."

"I've never heard of it, how fun!"

"*Tee-dee-dee*?", I asked.

"T.D.D., it stands for 'truth, dare, drink'. We each take it in turns to either answer a very embarrassing question or do some awful dare. And the only way out of it is to drink an entire glass of alcohol."

"Oh heavens, yes!", Richard exclaimed. "Perhaps I like this Bruce fellow after all."

"I'm not sure," I said. "I—"

"Absolute rot, Fitzy. This game sounds like marvellous fun."

And so, we played. Eventually we had all warmed to the game and grew to greatly enjoy it. Either through ignorance, or simply a desire to get drunk, Richard would drink his concoction with each question or dare, despite answering every question and doing every dare.

An hour passed and each of us found ourselves craving more drink, more dares, and more exposure. The line of questioning fell back onto me. Richard, slurring and drooling, tried as best he could to speak.

"Okay Fitzy; here's one for you. Wha—what's it like to bed a woman as old as your mother?"

Adeline gasped and laughed. "Oh, Richard that is terrible."

"If he doesn't want to answer the question, he knows what to do."

I don't know if it was the wine, or a wish to rob Richard of his laughter, but I answered the question bluntly. "It'd be much stranger if I'd have known my mother."

"Oh," said Adeline. "Why is that?"

I put the glass to my lips and consumed all it could carry. Richard continued.

"Okay, who has one for Addy?"

I spoke immediately, without censorship and without even truly knowing what I was about to say. "Do you love your fiancé?"

She stared right at me. "Why would you ask such a thing?"

"Well," I began. "Some people marry for love. Some people marry for money."

Adeline gave a mocking smile before drinking her glass too. She grimaced, innocently, on its completion.

"Okay," Richard interjected. "Now it is Fuc— Oh."

We followed Richard's gaze to see that Francis was sound asleep on the couch. Richard's eyes lit up with delight. "This is too perfect! I must fetch a pen."

He got up and darted out of the room, leaving Adeline and myself alone. She did not say a word, just picked up the bottle and poured two more glasses. This was the second bottle and had been fetched from the cellar a half hour earlier.

Several minutes passed and Richard still had not returned. "It does not take this long to find a pen," Adeline scoffed.

"I'll go and check on him."

I walked into the foyer to find Richard also asleep.

He was planted, face-first, on a decorative couch, and I rolled him into his side before moving back to the drawing room. "He's asleep," I said upon arriving.

"Amateurs."

We both laughed and she continued. "Let's take a walk. Bring the wine with you."

I followed her out of the room and along the hall, through the kitchen and out of the back door into the fields that surrounded the house. We passed the wine back and forth, each taking a sip or two. After a few minutes, we came back to the pond at which we met; something that was not lost on either of us.

"Here we are again," she said, looking into the darkness below.

"Yes," I replied, before laying a hand on her back and pushing her in. She burst out of the water and cursed me between spluttered breaths.

"Robin! I am going to gut you like a pig!"

"Consider us even."

"Well, you could at least have the decency to join me."

"Right you are," I said, slipping off my shoes and stripping to the waist before jumping in to join her. We swam circles around each other, as the moon illuminated our faces.

"You could have killed me you know; it is freezing in here."

"Here," I said, retrieving the bottle. "Have some wine, it'll warm you up."

"Thank you."

"You are most welcome."

We passed the bottle back and forth until it was empty. We swam there in silence, under the moons light. I waited intently for her to say something. Soon enough, I could tell that some confession was on her mind.

"No," she said, pensively.

"No?"

"No, I don't think I love him."

"Then why are you marrying him?"

"I suppose I married for——"

The words froze in her mouth as I swam towards her and took her into my arms. We kissed with soft touches as she wrapped her legs around my waist, and her arms around my shoulders. She held a look of fear in her eyes when we parted. "I'm sorry," I whispered

"No, don't be."

We held eyes and smiled at each other. "Hey," she said with a renewed light. "Close your eyes, and count to ten."

I did as she said, and when ten seconds had passed and my eyes were open, she was nowhere to be seen. "Up here," she called. I glanced up to see her on the bank of the pond, with my clothes in her hands.

"Hey! You put those down."

"I'll see you around, Robin," she said, before winking and turning. She ran into the darkness and was out of sight within seconds.

'*Here we go again*,' I said to myself.

18

A week had passed since that night, that kiss. Adeline and I had kept our distance, yet a certain gravity had formed; meaning that despite not speaking, we were never more than a few dozen feet apart. And when we were, her eyes would dance, and her hips would sway ever so slightly from side-to-side. Though she was wholly innocent. I called Balloch for some advice but was met with no answer, I called again the next day and there was no answer again. Rather, my advice would come from an unlikely source.

As had become common, I sat alone one evening in the library, while all of the others were occupied elsewhere. Adeline was in Truro with friends, Richard took his bath, and Francis prepared his wardrobe for an expected downturn in the weather.

"Any more drinks, Mr. Fitzwarwick?", Bilkins asked, poking his head into the library.

"Another glass of wine, thank you Bilkins."

"You seem to be rather fond of the library, Mr. Fitzwarwick."

"I—it's my favourite room in the house."

"Of course," he said, retreating. He returned after a few minutes with a replenished glass, and lingered at the door while I sipped. "Is something the matter, Bilkins?", I asked.

"I was hoping to show you something."

"Oh?"

"Yes. Would you be so kind as to follow me?"

I got up, and clutched my drink as I followed him out of the door. He led me out the front, and up the small hill toward the servant quarters. "Belling House is unique in that there is no proverbial *downstairs*," he explained with a vague pride. "The servants live up the hill. We've come to know it as *Help Village*. It is a most bizarre house."

We walked past the cottages and huts, and around a threaded corner in the hedgerows. There, some ten feet away, stood a grand mausoleum of black marble and golden lettering.

BELLING, it read.

"I didn't know that this was here," I said, mesmerised by the revelation.

"So few do. Yet it is much closer than you think. It is only a few dozen feet from that pond you seem so fond of."

"Really?"

"It's just on the other side of the hedge. However, it is something else that I would like to show you."

He approached the door and unlocked it, with a fanciful key of solid gold. Inside, were a myriad of paintings, curated in order of chronology. The men in each had Richard's golden hair. "What is this?", I asked.

"These," he said with a wide gesture. "These are the Belling men throughout the years. The *Earls of Warren*. Does anything about these portraits stand out to you, Mr. Fitzwarwick?"

I scanned the paintings for a moment, before it became clear. "They're not alone."

"No, they are not. You see, behind every Belling, is his helper, his right-hand man. They walk, and we run. They eat, and we digest. They are born, and *we* are chosen."

"Chosen how?"

"We are the orphans of England's great public

schools.."
"Is that you?", I asked, pointing at a picture, dated from 1923.
"It is. I was a far younger man then, but it is me. I was twenty-three when this was made. You see here, this is Anthony Belling, the first Earl, and next to him is Holdsbridge. Here is the Viscount Walter Belling, founder of the line, behind him is Hartley. The third Earl, and Arnold. The fourth, and Brewster, and so on. Soon, there will be another portrait, of Richard Belling, and his loyal helper, Uxby."
"Do you think he'll be known as Uxby?"
"I fear not. Nevertheless, he has taken his place in the minutiae of petty history."
"Is he aware of this?"
"He and I have had many conversations on this matter. After all, I have known him since he was a boy. It is the Belling's form of charity you see, they take us, the lonesome and homeless, and they cure both ills. They give us work, security, and companionship. The world is a much less brutish place when you have well-to-do friends. We serve the Belling family, and we serve it with pride."
"Why are you showing me this?"
"Because, Robin, it could have been *you*. I have seen the way that you look at Francis, and I know that it boggles your mind why he, a perfectly reasonable and kind young man, possessing all of his faculties, would put up with it all. And now you know, because it is his place in history, his destiny. It chose him, and he accepted it. Your destiny is elsewhere, Robin. And I suggest that you pursue it."

I would heed Bilkins' words, in some form or another, for the rest of my days, and it was these words that cemented me to the concrete walls of my decisions. They became my antidote for doubt.

Alas, the downturn in weather did not come. The Belling residence was built with Winter refuge in mind, and thus was rather useless on sultry days. When those days came, I often found my room - and all others - too stuffy to bear and I took to writing outdoors. Gradually, I etched a further radius with each journey. I wrote on the banks of the pond, I wrote at the cliffs which overlooked the Atlantic, and I wrote on the water's edge, my furthest excursion yet. It was at the latter that Adeline found me, engrossed in my latest chapter.

"A new novel?", she called from some distance.

"What are you doing this far from home?", I called back.

With each call and response, the distance between us closed until she sat directly across from me. "I'm afraid you are blocking my view of the ocean," I said.

"Then I shall sit next to you."

"So be it."

"What are you writing?", she asked, perching herself next to me, and peering over at the typewriter.

"What the people crave. Romantic dross for the aspiring classes to drool over on their commutes."

"You don't like romances?"

"It's not serious work."

"You take yourself very seriously."

"Yes, I do."

"If you want to write more serious things, then why don't you?"

"Because that isn't how the Game works."

"Then the *Game* is stupid."

"Perhaps it is, but that doesn't mean I don't have to play it."

"What would you write then?"

"I don't know. My publisher tells me that I write like one of the greats, but that their subject matter is no longer in fashion, so this is my compromise."

"That isn't what I asked you."

"Okay. You want to know what I really wish I could do?"

"Yes," she said.

"I want to disappear one day."

"Disappear?"

"Yes. I want to disappear, and for everyone to wonder

where I got to. Some will say I've died, and some will say I've found a little corner of the world that no man has ever seen before. And wherever I end up, I'll write, without money to weigh me down, or critics to please, or Donald Andress to appease. And just when people have started to accept that I'm gone, and move on with their lives, I'll return, with the finest novel that anyone has ever read."

"What'll it be about?"

"Nothing."

"Nothing?", she asked, unconvinced.

"Nothing," I repeated.

"You know, I've never met a writer before. But if they're all as cryptic as you then I'm glad of it. And shall hope that I don't meet many more." She gestured at my notes. "What sort of romantic dross is it?"

"It's about the area really."

"Is there a love story?"

"It wouldn't be a very good romance without one."

"Am I in it?"

"Behave yourself, Adeline."

"That's not a definitive *no*. So I presume that I am in it."

"For that, Adeline, you shall have to wait until it is finished."

"And then what?"

"And then you shall purchase a copy."

"And then what?"

"Read it."

She huffed and stood up. "You know," she said with a turn that flung her hair across her face. "Being written about is such a lovely thing. It may just help a girl to fall in love."

And with that, she left. I watched until she was out of sight. I had not planned to write about her, or anyone for that matter. Though, her words had planted an intractable seed in my mind, and so without true intention, my heroine would begin to resemble her. I had restrained myself from describng the girl in the book explicitly, but as she walked away, occasionally looking back, I found the words I was looking for.

'Golden hair, with a halo around it, for she always stood in view of the sun. It was her only competition.'

It would turn out to be easy fodder, and I wrote about her, for days on end. One day, we drove to St. Agnes, and found ourselves on the sand, with the remnants of the afternoon's picnic scattered at our feet, drawing in the gull's from afar. I was writing in my notebook, glancing at Adeline for reference while behind the shield of my sunglasses.

'*It was a day to remember in the height of Cornish Summer,*" I wrote. "*I had woken late and missed the train down from Exeter. Hurriedly I made way to the station, knowing I had only one shot. With haste, I made it to the next train and fidgeted my way to Molt Bay; glancing every few minutes at the slip of paper that told me where to be. She waited for me by the water, so caught up in the sparkles that rippled that she had barely noticed the time going by.*'

I paused for a moment and looked around, taking in the scenery and the ambience. I was struck by inspirations arrow and flipped the book to the front, where a blank title stared at me. I wrote in its stead; '*Loving Saint Anne*'.

I continued: "*She spotted me from some twenty yards away and uncrossed her legs in a rehearsed and graceful move, stretching the toes of her right food to take in the last of the sun's rays. She was new to adulthood, and exhibited the excitement, the impatience of a debutant. She wore a slender light blue dress with sunflower patterns, and a broad straw hat. She was beautiful, knew the fact, but wasn't swayed by it. It did not affect how she spoke to the ugly and unfortunate. I was doomed within seconds.*"

"Say, what are you writing there?", I heard.

Adeline had taken notice and leaned over, trying to see the page.

I closed the book and guarded it with a hug into my chest. "That is a secret."

"Now, now," Richard tutted. "Our artist is not to be

disturbed. I disturbed him once and he almost threw me out of a window."

"You broke my typewriter."

"And you got another," he protested

"Come on," Adeline blurted desperately, tossing a leather-bound book that she was reading into the sand. "I want to read it. I'm so bored of Austen and want some new material."

"You should listen to your brother, Adeline."

She huffed and turned to face the sea. "Boo to you. And boo to the lot of you. I want to go home and drink some."

"I concur. Fucksby?"

"Yes, sir."

"Righteous. Robin?"

I looked over at Adeline and gave her a mocking look. "Not just yet. I feel I am on the precipice of a breakthrough here. Really riveting stuff."

"Oh, piss off you bore," Adeline scoffed.

"If you fancy some refreshment, I believe I saw a pub on the way in. It looked positively charming."

Richard shuffled awkwardly. "Ah, yes. You see there was a spot of bother. And, well—"

"He is barred for life," Adeline giggled.

I found the escapade amusing and laughed too. "Alright," I said, shutting the book and putting it away. "Let's go home."

On the drive back to Belling House, I asked Richard why exactly he'd been barred for life. "Shenanigans," was all that he said. We arrived home and made ourselves scarce, each retreating into our rooms until dinner was served, which we ate in a relative silence and scurried away again. Adeline to her room, Richard and Francis to the botany room and myself to the library. It was a room that one could expect from the private library of a Lord. It was wooden, elegant and designed with a maximalist intent. Naturally, I circulated around the room, until at last, I came upon a gramophone, with a recording fully packaged and sat upon its rim. It was a Korsakov recording, *Song of the Indian Guest.*

In that moment of my life - nineteen years old and with little to say for it bar a book and a singular love affair - I had two things to say of crying. The first is that my earliest memory is of crying. I recall weeping uncontrollably while my father and a retinue of relatives tried in vain to make me stop. The second is that, since that day, I had been unable to shed a single tear. I did not cry when my father died. I did not cry after every rejection, abandonment, or public embarrassment. I did not cry after any public fit of stammering, nor any horrid lesson with Harding, nor after any berating from my family, or accusation of matricide. No event, pain, or sensation had drawn tears to my eyes, and caused them to flow as water does from a tap. That was until I listened to that Korsakov recording.

As I have since done with all music spoken to me in a foreign tongue, I dared not attempt to decipher the words. Instead, I let that alien whisper woo me, and woo me it did. I knew nothing of what he sung about. I knew not if he was driven to song by pain or by pleasure, pure love or abject heartbreak. It was, quite simply, the most beautiful sound that I had ever heard, and I wept like a child. In that moment, my entire life and every single moment of it - every minute and memory - found itself sandwiched in the grand timeline of my life, between two bouts of crying.

The record crackled to a halt and the room came back into view. I placed my hands on either side of the gramophone and leaned forward, as tears streamed down my face like droplets of rain on a window. So transfixed was I in that moment, that I did not hear the door open, nor too Adeline's approach.

"What are you doing?", she asked.

"Oh. Nothing. I—"

"Are you crying?"

"No. Well, yes. I—I don't know why."

She moved towards the record, and I moved with instinct. Before either of us knew it, we came face to face and were locked there for some time. She broke our frozen state by ushering me out of the way and examining the record. "Hm," she said, with no clear emotion at all. She swivelled and skipped over to the couch, sprawling herself across it in a way that was still, inexplicably, flattering.

"I am deliciously bored," she said. "Richard has gone to bed, Francis is no fun, all he wants to talk about is oratorios and flowers. You must entertain me."

"Must I?"

"Yes, you must."

"When did that become my job?"

"About three minutes ago. When I realised how boring oratorios and flowers are."

"How exactly would I entertain you, Adeline?"

"Oh, Robin, please do away with the politeness for a minute, you are so much better than that. And while you're at it, you can read me something."

"Read you something?"

"Yes! Read me some poetry."

"Okay."

I walked over to the first bookshelf and scanned the bottom two rows, which housed *Lord Belling's* collection of poetry. Adeline scoffed audibly. "No, no, no! Read me something of your own."

"Absolutely not."

"Then read me your favourite poem. From memory."

I thought for a moment and recalled one that stood alone in my memory. "*Into my heart, an air that kills*."

She perched forward and engaged me with her eyes, and so I continued. "*From yon far country blows. What are those blue remembered hills? What spires, what farms are those?*"

I paused and she gestured for me to continue. "*That is the land of lost content, I see it shining plain. Those happy highways where I went and cannot come again*."

She pondered the words for a moment. "It's a bit sad."

"I think that's the point."

"Why on earth would one focus on the sad things?"

"There's a beauty in sad things. The sad things in

life are unavoidable."

"So are the happy things, you just have to wish for them."

"And if I wished to sit next to you?"

"I'd say your feet look *awfully* weary."

We smiled at one another, and I took a seat next to her. Our heads gravitated towards one another before a knock at the door forced us apart. I moved into the adjacent armchair as Adeline called out. "Come in."

The door opened and Francis appeared. "Oh, hello Robin. Adeline, you have a visitor."

"A visitor? At this ungodly hour, so close to midnight. Who on God's green would be calling at such an hour?"

"Well," Francis said with some discomfort. "It's Bruce."

"I beg your pardon?"

"Bruce. He's in the drawing room."

Adeline looked at me before looking back at the door. "Send him in."

Francis disappeared, and I got up to leave. "At least stay and say hello," Adeline called.

"I think I'd rather just see him at breakfast."

I walked into the hall and hid in a shadowed corner as Bruce and his thumping footsteps approached. He slipped into the library as I listened in. "Hello, darling!"

"Bruce? What on earth are you doing here?"

"I figured I'd surprise you, I'm so glad you're not in bed."

"Indeed, I am not."

"Well, let's get you there. What do you say?"

I had heard enough and made my escape to the stairs. Francis emerged from the drawing room, and we met by the first step. He placed a hand on my shoulder and gave me a smile. "I'm sorry, Robin."

"What could you mean?"

"I saw the two of you in the pond."

"It's okay, Francis. I know better than to entangle myself in the romances of others."

19

July became August as the late Summer air tingled and danced upon us all like some rare blessing. Cornwall was suited, quite perfectly, for these months. However with August being the month of my birth, and thus a near constant reminder of my misfortunes, it never meant that much to me. And yet I swelled with a silent pleasure as I walked, bare foot and barely clothed, around the grounds of Belling House in a perfect solitude.

I saw very little of Adeline in the week after Bruce had arrived. The two had secluded themselves, in what I assumed had been a decision taken by Bruce, in the guest house that lay a half-mile-or-so from the big house. My suspicions were answered on one hot day, when I found myself in that usual spot on the edge of the pond. Bruce approached without a sound, and sat next to me.

"Robin," he bellowed in his brutal tone. "May I ask your opinion on a rather delicate matter?"

"Of course."

"What do you make of that fuck-head chap?"

"You mean *Fucksby*?"

"Do I?"

"You do."

"What an unfortunate name," he said to himself.

"It isn't his real name?"

"It isn't?"

"His name is Francis."

"Oh. Well, what do you make of him?"

"Of Francis?"

"Must we walk in circles, Robin. Yes, of *Francis*. What do you make of *Francis*?"

"A paragon of morality."

"And does his eye wander?"

"Excuse me?"

Bruce refused to elaborate and walked back towards the guest house. I realised then, to my twin mirth and bafflement, that Bruce had taken Francis to be some sort of romantic threat. When I did see Adeline, it was from afar and she walked with a slight limp, which led me to suspect the worst.

"Just an injury that she picked up playing bowls," Bruce dismissed when I asked him one day."

What I remember most about the company of Bruce and Adeline was a sort of hostile stillness. Everything lay still when they were around. Bruce had a penchant for removing all joviality from a room. He took every joke literally, and walked with a chip firmly fixed to his shoulder. He was not of the world in which we lived; the world of public school, black tie, and country sports. He knew it, and despised us for it. We woke in the late morning and seldom ate breakfast as a group. By lunchtime, Richard had drunk himself into a merry stupor and set about entertaining himself. Francis either played the piano or taught me to play chess, and we'd play most afternoons.

"You see," he began during one such game. "The wonderful thing about chess is that one cannot lose a game by accident. If one loses, one made a mistake. I feel it good preparation for life in general."

His gentle company was all that had seemed right in the world. I tried on several occasions to contact Balloch to no avail, and I began to worry for my friend. Said worry evolved into a grave mourning as time grew. In the evenings, when it was just me, I wrote in a fervour and had resolved to return to civilisation once my novel was complete. As I wrote, I simultaneously plotted my escape from what I perceived as the harsh confines of writing romances. Although I was still young, not yet twenty, and what I wrote back then was all I could amount to, it still felt as if it were beneath me. Yet I wrote on, and with each passing sentence I fell more in love with the facsimile of Adeline I had created. "*This cannot end well*," I'd say to myself.

One night, a storm came from the blue and battered all that was not fixed to the earth. Items of clothing that I had put to dry were carried into the night and never seen again. I sought comfort in that Korsakov recording, I drank wine and smoked while the storm played out beyond the window. By midnight, I was merry, and the storm had brought with it a great distraction. The next day, shortly after breakfast, I took a walk to the nearby cliffs, and when I had returned, a panic had set within the house. All four of the others were congregated in the drawing room, and each looked as flustered as the other.

"What is happening?", I asked.

"The power has gone," Richard sighed. "That bloody storm took it out. We may as well relocate to the caves."

"Don't be so dramatic," Adeline hissed. "It isn't so bad. Who needs the television or the radio? We can entertain ourselves."

And so, we did. Initially, it was by way of playing bowls on the sodden grass. We graduated to cards, and then to alcohol. By night's fall and the stars debut, we found ourselves in the drawing room and in high spirits.

"Bruce is an oil man," said Adeline, attempting to force some conversation between us. "He comes from a very humble family, but they got rich from oil. Isn't that lovely?"

"Is that so?", I asked.

"It is. It's a good time for business, lots of money to be made."

"Right," I said, uninterested by the world of business. "I didn't know we had any oil."

"Oh, it's not here. You have to go abroad for it. We're based in London, but operate mostly in North

Africa; Egypt and the like. There's a few deals in Iran too that I've got my eye on."

"Right," I repeated.

"It's funny, you lot probably think a house like this is a palace of some sort. Don't make me laugh. My family came from nothing, and we could buy this place and turn it into a knocking shop. You should see the place we have in Sinai, it's twice as big. No, three times."

"Mhm."

"Are you from Cornwall too?", he asked.

"London."

"Oh, yes. Which part?"

"Bayswater."

"Oh, really? We've a house in Kensington, and one in Hampstead Heath."

"I'm very happy for you, Bruce."

"What is it that you do, Robin? What's your line of business?"

"Books."

"Oh yeah?"

"Yeah."

"D'you publish them? Or produce the paper?"

"I read them. I'm an undergraduate."

"Where do you study?"

"Camford."

"Oh, yes. I should have presumed. I suppose that's where you game-bred lads go to become men. I never saw much point in it all, books and capes, old buildings and the like. Who wants to waste three years reading and studying? The family business is oil, so I figured why wait?"

"That's riveting," I said, focusing on Francis, who'd begun to play the piano.

"Robin is being modest," said Adeline. "He's a writer, a published novelist—and poet."

"Oh, right," he scoffed, casting into stone my dislike toward him. "Do you make much doing that?"

"I get by."

“Well then, I had no idea I was in such *esteemed* presence. I never got the point in such things, but perhaps I can be persuaded. Would you read me something?”

“Oh, yes!” Richard chimed in. “I must say I’ve never read your works, that’ll be such great fun.”

I grimaced, knowing that I had been routed. The pressure from the room mounted until it was insufferable and eventually, I caved and went away to retrieve a notebook. On the way, I threw two glasses of port down my throat as to gain some last-minute courage. When I returned, the others had seated in a crescent and eagerly awaited. Throughout the day, I had lost the tactful touch that sobriety brings. And the last-minute port had inserted a seed of carelessness into my heart, and I decided to recite something I’d written about Adeline.

Once I had finished, the room clapped to me as I sheepishly took a seat, still and forever uncomfortable around appraisal. Francis smiled at me and laid a hand on my shoulder. “That’s really something,” said Bruce after a few moments of contemplation.

“Thank you, Bruce.”

“Though I must ask, what exactly are the practical applications of such words?”

“I’m sorry?”

“You know, what does it do? What does it provide?”

“I don’t follow.”

“You see, uh—how can I best explain this? You see, in my world we have pretty words of our own; *profit, yield, growth.*”

“I do not inhabit your world, Bruce.”

“No. Perhaps you do not. What I mean to ask is, in our new world, is there even any room for what you do?”

“If I may interject,” Francis called, perching himself forward to address Bruce and myself. “Poetry, as with all of the fine arts, exists entirely independently of money and of economics. Words like ‘*profit*’, and ‘*yield*’, and ‘*growth*’ are not in the vernacular because those words describe the material world, and poetry is fundamentally immaterial. It does not exist for any particular purpose, it just exists. It is not a means to an end, rather it is an end of its own. Right, Robin?"

I smiled at him, knowing that once again he had found the words that I could not. "Right."

"Well, I think that sounds like awful tosh."

"Bruce!", Adeline yelped. He ignored her and maintained a forward pressure.

"Perhaps you do," I said with a blank expression, meanwhile an intense hatred was forming. Far greater than the one I had already felt.

"I mean, what do you expect to do with it?", he asked.

I began to grow frustrated. "Once more, Bruce. I'm afraid that you and I live in different worlds. I seek only moderate comfort and creative fulfilment."

"You don't want money?", he scoffed, as if the idea was ludicrous in the extreme.

"Having grown up with money, I can tell you with absolute certainty that I do not."

"And if it comes to you?"

"Then I shall be gracious."

"And if it does not?"

"Then I shall be humble, live within my means, and be safe in the knowledge that I'll always have my words."

"You sound a fool."

"Your money, Bruce, however much of it you choose to throw around, will never buy you class, or pedigree. Just vanity, and fleeting material."

"Oh, you think you're better than me?"

"Your words, Bruce, not mine. My vocabulary, I'm afraid to say, expands slightly further."

"You're a snob," he said, with a slight tremor.

"And *you* are an ape."

Suddenly and without warning, Bruce lurched forward and stopped himself only a few inches from my face.

"Listen here, mate. I am no fancy poet, but I do care very much for fighting. I was a boxer in my day, a good one at that. And I reckon I could take you out back and beat you into a—"

"Get him, Robin!", Richard called out, only to go quiet when Bruce shot a glance in his direction.

"Bruce!" Adeline whispered fiercely. "Don't be such an antagonist. They mean no harm."

He relaxed and sat back. "Okay, darling. I'm sorry, my love. I cannot help my temper sometimes, outnumbered by these old-world artsy types."

"I do not mean to cause a row," I said with my eyes fixed firm, holding a view deep into that angry little soul of his. "My way of life, and my means of work are all that I know. They are all that I desire. Do you desire a line of work outside of business?"

"No, I do not."

"And would you tolerate any effort to induce you into the arts?"

"No."

"And what is it that draws you into business?"

"The thrill, I suppose."

"I too am thrilled."

"I see. Well, why don't you give me another chance to understand what it is that you do. Won't you read us something else?"

"Indeed, Robin," Adeline added. "Be a dear a read us something from your new novel."

I considered the proposition for a second and had decided after a moment that Bruce had irked me. So much so that I figured I would play around with him a little. "With pleasure," I said with a smile. I retreated to my room and picked up a sheet of paper off of the desk. A cocktail of fear and excitement had me in its grip and my feet grew heavy as I returned to the drawing room. Along the way I detoured to the dining room and drank two more stiff glasses, before preparing a third.

And so, I read once again to the room. If my poem was cryptic, then my passage was an overt confession. I had written of that night in the pond, and as I read the room became divided into two parties; one consisting of Francis and Adeline, who knew exactly what I spoke of, and the other which included the oblivious Richard and Bruce.

"*And as the moon stood naked above us, and the stars became voyeurs, we separated and swam rings around one another. From that day on, and on each day since, I found myself hopelessly, chronically, in love.*"

I placed the page on the table and looked around the room. Each face met with its level of understanding. For every blank face given to me by Richard and Bruce, was a knowing one from Francis and Adeline. Francis smiled to himself, and Adeline smiled at me wickedly.

"Who is that?" Bruce asked, causing me to fear, briefly, that he had cottoned on.

"Who is who?"

"The girl. Who is she? Is she someone you know?"

"No," I said, looking past Bruce and onto Adeline. "I made her up. It's part of the magic, you see."

Later that night, Bruce came to me while I smoked by candle-light in the botany room. "I'm sorry things got so tense back there, chap. I fear we have gotten off on the wrong foot."

"It would seem that way."

"Adeline is mighty mad at me for it. She said that she wants to sleep in her own bed tonight, and I don't blame her for that. I was an ass, and for that I'm sorry."

"It's okay, Bruce."

"God damn, I can never figure you *noble* types out."

"There is little to understand, all is forgiven. And for what it is worth, I am sorry too."

We shook hands and he disappeared. A few minutes later I saw him trudging under moonlight, back toward the guest house. Satisfied that he was gone, and would not return before morning, I took myself to bed. I found myself unable to sleep and sat immobile by the window. Where I smoked and watched the clouds envelope the moon, only for it to reappear some time later. After midnight, when I was motionless in bed, there were footsteps in the hall; which grew closer and headed towards my door. I felt an odd vibration as the knob turned and the door opened. Through the pitch-black hall, I could not see a thing.

"Robin?", she whispered.

"Adeline."

She did not say another word. I was reliant on my other senses and charted her progress by the creaking of floorboards under her feet. She found the bed and crawled in. Her body was warm and pressed up against me, so much so that I could feel her beating heart. We lay there for an hour, saying nothing and not moving. I woke the next day to find that the power had returned, and that Adeline had fled the scene.

20

I lay there in bed for an hour. Hungover, and not quite sure if the previous day's events had happened. Music roared and reverberated around the house as electricity returned, with triumph, to Belling House. I had taken my time getting ready, before seeing what the others were up to. I left my room and walked towards the stairs, only to be met by Adeline, who walked towards me with purpose. It was not until we were a handful of feet apart, when I saw the clawhammer in her hand.

"Say, what are you doing with——"

She struck me on the wrist as I yelped in pain. "What on earth did you do that for?", I snapped.

"Tell them you fell."

So taken aback was I by the incident, that I simply did what she said. Using only my right hand, I picked myself up and made down the stairs, clutching my wrist.

Richard, Francis and Bruce were drinking coffee in the drawing room when I entered, still agonised and confused. "Oh good, you're up," Richard said when I came in, clutching my arm. "Say, what's wrong with your hand?"

"I fell. I think it is broken."

"Broken you say? Well, it's a pity father dismissed the physician."

He and Bruce laughed in a way that indicated they had become firm friends since last night. Francis walked over and took my wrist in his hands, probing with caution. "It's a sprain. Still a painful business but keep it on ice and you'll be fine in a few days."

"A few days?" Richard said with concern. "Well, I suppose that's you out of tomorrow's hunt."

"Hunt?", I asked.

"Yes, the Summer hunt. The whole village takes part."

Adeline entered as Richard spoke. "Oh dear, Robin. What happened to your hand?"

She played the role of the hatchling perfectly, and I began to wonder if I really did just fall. "I—fell."

"Clumsy. Is it bad?

"Not fatal," said Francis. "But he shouldn't make much use of it for a few days."

"Does that disqualify him from tomorrow's hunt?", she asked.

"Afraid so," said Richard.

"Oh well, you can keep me company then. I'll inevitably get bored. We shall have a tea party and cake ourselves in make-up!"

She gave me a wink, that was masked by her golden hair, which at times fell over her sapphire eyes; blocking them from unwanted view. Bruce spoke to me something of a continued apology from the night before, but I could not listen. I was disinterested and in pain.

"What on earth were you thinking? A bloody clawhammer?", I hissed to Adeline when we were left alone for a moment. "You could have broken my arm!"

"It just made sense to me at the time."

"Well give me a fair warning next time you decide to take things into your own hands. I could just as easily have lied to them."

"Yes, I suppose they could have. Oh well, it's done now."

"You're telling me."

And so, the day passed without further incident. It blended into the background of those other days at Belling House. We lounged, or swam, or entertained ourselves with parlour games and music. Francis and I played chess. Nightfall was our call to drink, and by eleven we were all in bed. The next day came, and the entire village descended on the house, and it pullulated with activity; with horses and dogs, and no one seemed to be in control. Eventually, the boundless energy that had amassed was brought into control by one Mr. Ellis, a village elder, who barked commands and allied men with horses.

I sat with Richard and Francis, as they readied the final touches on their hunting gear. Adeline read a magazine in the corner, so quietly that periodically I would forget that she was there. Presently, Bruce came in, unlike the others he did not wear the traditional red. It seemed as if he had purposely foregone comfort and flexibility, in favour of ostentation, and of one-upping the aristocrats with his splendour.

"I went to Mr. Pratchett's on Savile Row," he began. "Asked him for the most expensive hunting garb, and cleared out the lot. How's that for *pure-blood nobility*?"

We didn't say much in retort. He looked plainly ridiculous, like he had no business in the country, which was indeed the case. He turned to Adeline, who hadn't glanced up once. "This is your last chance, Addy," he called. "You sure you don't want to come along?"

"Positively sure, darling," she replied, without looking up.

"But you love horses."

"Only from afar. And while I do love horses, I also enjoy the other animals; in particular, the ones I'd be required to slaughter."

"This one," he said to the three of us directly, and as if Adeline were elsewhere. "Always a crusade with this one."

Adeline let out a single syllable in response, and Bruce let the matter go. "I suppose we'd better be off."

"Indeed," Richard said, checking his watch. "Fucksby, be a dear and hand me my thermos."

They left to join the others and I watched them from the window. With an eclectic range of grace, struggle, and outright foolery, they each mounted a horse, and set off for the fields when Mr. Ellis gave the order. There must have been at least thirty, and the sea of red coats brought my mind to the Light Brigade, and its fabled charge. Bruce stood out in his golden coat, and it shimmered in the morning sun. Soon it was just Adeline and myself, and I grew weary of her intent. It was clear that she had injured me purposefully, as the lynchpin in some plan of hers.

I stood, uneasily, in the corner and watched her read, awaiting some sort of signal which did not come for a while. Growing bored, I wandered into the dining room, where Mrs. Ambrose readied a tray of coffee, before moving to my preferred spot on the water's edge. It was there that, at last, she made some sort of advance.

"I've just sent Mrs. Ambrose off to fix some lunch. Would you join me?"

"Yes."

She nodded her head and retreated to the house. A half hour later, I sat across from her and we ate in relative silence; only breaking it for pleasantries of a vacuous nature. I became curious and spoke while she chewed. "Are you really opposed to the hunt on a moral level?"

"Oh, heavens no. I adore the hunt, I just didn't fancy going today."

"Why is that?"

"I have better things to do."

"Such as?"

"Well, drink port of course. Would you join in me in having a bottle."

"A bottle?"

"Yes, they'll be gone all day and I cannot withstand boredom and sobriety, not together at least. Oh, no I cannot. I must have no more than one at the same time."

"Richard told me you were planning on coming up next year."

"Did he?"

"Mm."

"Well, I don't think that'll happen now. I should think I'll be in London by the time matriculation comes around. How silly of him. Doesn't he know that it is far easier to marry rich."

"I suppose it isn't on the curriculum."

She chuckled and rung the bell for Bilkins. Before long, I had a full glass and half-empty bottle of port in front of me. We chatted some more, and the conversation increasingly resembled an unsanctioned biography of Richard. As a boy, he had almost drowned in the very pond that I had taken much pleasure from. He had been, to my surprise, a quiet and precocious boy, sensitive by nature and introverted beyond compare when he was sent to Eton. As Adeline recalled he cried whenever he had to return; but that, with age, he grew into what he was now. She loved him, quite dearly, but was unsure as to whether or not she liked him as a person.

"Loud," she kept saying. "Loud, loud, horribly loud. Isn't he loud?"

"Horribly so."

"You know, Robin. It is poor form to simply agree with everything a woman says. We don't like that sort of thing."

"Is that so?"

"Indubitably."

"Well then, I think you are completely wrong—and a wretched cow."

She laughed and lightly threw a teaspoon at me, it bounced off of my chest. "That's more like it. Though do you make a habit of such language in the presence of a *lady*?"

"It's bold of you to assume that I'm often in the company of ladies."

She giggled and wiped some port away from her lip.

"You seem to come alive when it is just you and I."

"I am not a pleaser of crowds."

"Meaning?"

"Meaning I feel that I am at my very best when it is just me and one other. In crowds I do not function as well."

"Define a crowd."

"In our case, five."

"You find our current setting uncomfortable."

"Incredibly so."

"Is that why you are always by yourself?"

"I figured we all were."

"You figured wrong," she said. "I'm with Bruce and Francis is with my brother. I suppose that's the bastardly part of an odd number."

"Someone is always alone," I said, examining the bottle

"Someone is always alone, yes. Anyway, what shall we toast to?"

"To even numbers."

"The happiest numbers."

Adeline had walked over to my side of the table in order to touch my glass with hers. In a smooth and fluid motion, she took the seat next to mine. She asked me a question that I had asked myself several times since arriving here.

"Do you ever get concerned about Bilkins?"

"In what sense?"

"In the sense that we go about our business, and speak rather openly, while he is so often in the same room. Granted, he's essentially part of the furniture. But he still has eyes and ears, and people to talk to."

"It is quite disconcerting."

"Do you feel the same at your home?"

"We don't have a butler at my home."

"Not even a cook?"

"No, it's just Richard, Francis and myself."

"No, not your college digs. I mean your family home."

"I don't have one."

"Oh, right. Yes. Well, where do you go when you're in London?"

"I haven't stayed the night in London since I went up."

"You don't have aunts and uncles?"

"I do."

"And yet you do not stay with them?"

"I do not."

"Why?"

"I have never met half, and the other half want nothing to do with me."

"I think I met a Fitzwarwick once. At my coming out party. Jasper Fitzwarwick."

"Yes. He's my cousin."

"Now I think of it, he did mention a black sheep in the family, who they'd sent off to school and forgotten about. He said it as if it were some family joke."

"That would be me."

"What made you fall out of favour?"

"They think that I killed my mother."

"Did you?"

"No. She died in labour."

"Oh, Robin. How on earth could they blame you for that?"

"They just do."

"When did you see them last?"

"1946. The year I went to Charterhouse. The year after my father died."

"Was he the same?"

"You mean to ask if he also accused me of killing my mother?"

"Yes."

"No. He was different, a good man. He died in the war."

She placed a hand on my shoulder, and I placed my non-injured hand on top of hers. Her head fell and landed on the soft pile of interlocked fingers. Almost as if an alarm had gone off inside her head, she rose and removed her hand from mine. Only to pick up the bell and ring it twice. Bilkins came in.

"Yes, Lady Adeline?

"We shall not need any help until the others return. Do take the afternoon off."

"Of course. Very well, my Lady."

We waited until we heard the final set of steps leave and trudge up the hill to the servant quarters. "*Lady Adeline*?", I asked, with a smirk.

"An honorific. Bilkins is very precise about these things. He's *very old school.*"

Adeline took point, grabbing the half-empty port bottle and leading the way into the library. She examined the Korsakov recording, still where I had left it. "You know," she said after a quick scan. "Father had this recording commissioned."

"Did he?"

"He heard it on the radio and loved it so much that he contacted the BBC and found the composer. He loved it so much that he gathered the very same composer, and the very same musicians, and had it recorded. Only that one piece. Do you know what it means?"

"I don't want to know."

"Father said the same thing."

She walked past me and sat, cross-legged, on the sofa and lit one of my cigarettes.

"So," she continued, before exhaling. "Where did you spend Christmas?"

"Occasionally with my friend, Monty. But his family travelled often, so I spent most of them at the school."

"And birthdays?"

"It has become something of a personal ritual to spend that day alone."

"I think that is the saddest thing I've ever heard. Spending Christmas alone in that school."

"I wasn't the only one. There were a few of us."

She grimaced and poured herself another drink. "Oh, Robin. I fear you've lived such a horrid life."

"Not exclusively."

"No?"

"There have been many wonderful moments. Moments of bliss, or inspiration, awe in the face of beauty. It's a simple matter of scale. The bad moments tend to be rather traumatic, grandiose. Whereas the good ones are the little things in life."

"Like a lovely bit of lemon drizzle."

"Yes, I suppose so. Or, in my case, the oblivion one feels after a bottle of port."

"You are funny."

"Am I?"

"Yes. I don't know what I'd have done today without you."

"Gone hunting?"

"Oh, heavens no. I am *morally opposed.*"

"Did I ever mention how wonderful I find your home to be?"

"Oh, you should have seen it."

"Yes?"

"Yes. Back when father was a young man, long before Richard and I were born. This place used to be teeming with servants, and it hosted the most incredible parties. The king came here once, you know?"

"Which king?"

"I'm not sure, George the fifth, I should think. Yes, it was such a wonderful house then, there are pictures somewhere."

"I often think about that time. My parents would have met around then as well."

"Does it not feel as if we missed the greatest party that there ever was?"

"How do you mean?"

"Well, I had my debut last year, you see. And it was a wonderful affair, so very glamorous, but I could not help feeling that I simply arrived at the party just as all the guests were leaving. The King and the Prince of Wales were at my mother's debut. Victoria was at my grandmother's."

"I know how you mean. It feels so close, yet of a different age entirely, as if we were discussing another species who just happened to look very human."

She let out a laugh. I did too, and we were locked once more in a comforting stalemate. "And then," I pondered aloud. "Like an ambush in an alley, came the age of Bruce."

"You have a way with words, Robin."

"It's my job."

We caught eyes and laughed, just as we did the door flung open and Bruce stormed in angrily, his left side covered in mud, and with a large tear on the thigh.

"Oh, darling, what's happened?", Adeline asked, exerting some effort not to laugh.

"I fell off the damn horse. Your imbecile brother told me she went very well. Yeah, about as well as well as a lit match in an oil field. Look at my new coat, it's ruined! I spent hundreds on this get-up."

Adeline gave up the fight and began to laugh. Sensing that Bruce valued his pride above humour, I did not join her. Instead, I rose to my feet and bid the two a good evening.

Francis and Richard sat and ate bread and butter in the dining room. "Fitzy!" Richard called. "I must say, you missed a day of almighty mirth. Bruce fell off his horse."

"So I heard," I said, allowing myself to laugh at last.

"Oh, Fitzy, you should have been there, I was on fire. Jokes here, jokes there. Perhaps I shall set about becoming a comedian."

I was endeared and sat with them to join in the laughter.

"I said to him," Richard continued. "I said '*Bruce, you ought to be careful, mummy is deathly afraid of ghosts and the house doesn't need haunting*'. My God, I'm such fun!"

"It sounds a riot."

"Oh, it was. Fucksby here nabbed a few of the little orange pricks."

"Is that so?"

"Indeed."

I had always held the red fox in a strangely high regard. And thought it darkly ironic that a Belling man chose to spend his day hunting down the symbol of his house. I recall one Winter day at school, when it was just myself and the other rejects sitting around, a fox had gotten into one of the cloisters.

There was such commotion, as the fox darted throughout, scaring the schoolboys. I kept my head while all lost theirs and observed that conniving little creature, mesmerised by its vaguely-tamed wilderness. And so the thought of killing one did not interest me.

Richard spoke on while I remained tethered to my thoughts. Bruce came in after some time, which snapped me back into the room.

"Adeline and I shall be going to bed. I won't see you boys for a few weeks now, so do take care."

"A few weeks?", Richard enquired. I had thought the same, and like Richard, had heard of no such plans.

"Yes, business calls. We cannot all lounge around in the country all Summer. I'm due on the first train to London."

"Fare thee well, Bruce. I shall miss you so. Thank you for the mirth."

"I'm sure I shall see you soon, Robin."

I shook his hand without a word, and he was gone.

I would only see Bruce once more after that day in his ridiculous golden coat, and on that day, he'd strike me in the face. But that is a story for another time.

21

As August stretched its limbs, and my return to Camford grew closer, I had begun to shut Adeline out. As I came to the novel's final chapters, I could bare no distraction. I would be remiss if I did not also point out my apprehensions around her status as an engaged woman. This, however, would not last long, as evidenced by one day in the middle of the month. Bruce had been gone for a week and had not written as much as a postcard. One night, shortly after he had left, Adeline confided in me that she believed Bruce to be an adulterer. He was seven years her senior and had been engaged once before.

I had kept largely to myself. I was beckoned from all corners of the house, and yet I never answered. Richard called upon me to drink, Francis to discuss my work, and Adeline for a multitude of reasons. Despite all that lay before me, my resolve held, and I successfully barricaded myself in, where I spent six consecutive days and nights in a trance. I had informed Bilkins of my desire, and he had understood. It was thus that he was the only face I saw in those days, when he brought my daily food and drink. I wrote faster than I could think and would, at the end of each day, find myself surprised at the things I had written. It was like being drunk in every waking moment, and yet maintaining one's core creative faculties. I was high and sober, messy and ordered, dangerous and floral.

Adeline, or '*Anne*' in this case, was no mirage, no type, trope or fantasy, she was real. To this day, I don't think I ever wrote a more real character. She danced and spoke with a grace and youth, yet she was conceited, scheming, deceptive. She was beautiful and she was insecure. She loved, and withheld. Laughed and cried. Joked and jabbed. In her I found the true duality in us all. As my thoughts caught up, and fell into synergy with my hands, I looked down one day and found that I was finished.

"Fitzy!", Richard exclaimed, when I walked into the dining room. "I figured you'd gone back to civilisation."

"I've been taking meals in my room. I asked Bilkins that I not be disturbed."

"Oh really? Why would that be?"

"I've been writing."

'Writing? Oh, yes. The novel. And how is that going?"

"Well, it's finished."

"Oh, marvellous. Fucksby! Did you hear that? Robin's finished his novel."

Francis trotted in with a look of excitement. "Is that so?"

"Indeed, it is."

"Oh, well done, Robin. Very well done."

"Thank you, Francis."

"It's not that one you were groaning over in Paris, is it?", Richard asked, while preparing a celebratory toast. "Leaves Fall Down in the Autumn?"

"All's Well in Winter Days. And no."

"What a pity," he said. "The title is so memorable." He poured a glass of wine for each of us. "So," Richard started again, with an arm raised. "To my very clever friend, Robin Fitzwarwick."

Adeline walked in just as our glasses touched.

"You're still here? What are you toasting to?"

"Robin has finished his novel."

"Oh, has he? How lovely. When can I read it?"

"Christmas. When it comes out."

"Don't be such a bore, Robin. I want to read it now."

"Ask me again tomorrow."

She grunted and left the room. Richard turned to us with a flame in his eye.

"Right. Right. We need to celebrate, properly this time. Gin, tea? No. It's been done before. Whiskey! That's it, I shall go and get us some whiskey. And Fucksby——prepare some coffee."

"Yes, sir."

"Oh yes!", Richard sang, as he ran out of the room. "We are cooking!"

"I shall meet you gentlemen in the drawing room," I said. "I have a call to make."

I dialled for Donald and he came to the phone soon after learning the caller. "Robin!"

"Hello, Donald. I have some good news."

"Oh?"

"My novel is finished. I shall stay another week in Cornwall and then come up a week tomorrow."

"Well done, young Robin. Yes, a week would be lovely. Cynthia is out of town, she fancied Avignon so much that she's gone back for a few weeks, so it'll be just me."

"Of course, Donald. I shall see you soon."

"It is so good to hear your voice, my dear boy. I figured you'd be all cut up about the news."

"The news?"

"Oh. Yes, no need to worry about that just yet. Enjoy your holiday and I shall see you in London. I assume you already have the address."

"I do. But, Donald, what news? I know nothing of any news."

"Farewell, young Robin. I shall look forward to seeing you."

The line clicked into a hum before I could say another word. I was overcome by vague concern, I decided to drink myself into a firm merriment, and that I would reserve my worry for when I returned to civilisation. I was unused to whiskey, and quickly became drunk, and passed from the right sort to the wrong sort. Francis had met a similar fate and jammed, clumsily, on the piano as Richard roared with laughter.

"Yes! Yes!", he roared with glee. "Try playing Chopin now that you cannot tell your arse from a hole in the ground!"

Adeline was not seen in that hazy afternoon. Not at least until around seven, when I excused myself and resolved to take an early night. I entered my room, where she had made herself comfortable. Reclined on my bed, and sipping a cup of tea, she read my manuscript.

"What on earth are you doing?"

"I don't like to wait for things, Robin."

"You give that back to me, this instant."

"What use would that be? I've already read half, what harm could the other half do?"

"You know what harm it could do. You know that very well."

"Well, allow me to read on and we shall see."

"No. You've read plenty."

I lunged for the manuscript, and Adeline rolled herself back, so that I fell and landed on top of her. "Oh, my," she said. "What a predicament."

"I'll take that."

I snatched the manuscript and retreated to my feet, as she bounced up in a similar manner. "You bloody bore," she hissed. "I was just getting to the good part."

"Which part?"

"The *Hail Mary*. The part where our hero simply cannot stand the sight of Ann in the arms of that beastly Scottish industrialist. But he must accept that his time is over, and the swindler runs the show now, the swindler gets the girl. And he falls into a deep depression, and grows jaded with love. Perhaps one day, he is in a quiet town nearby, where he sells books, or does something completely unrelated to the passions, and finds her once more. Or, he finds someone else."

I scanned the manuscript and found where she had read to. "You are nowhere near that part."

"But I predicted it. You writers are far less enigmatic than you make out. Behind your wall of indifference is a beating heart, just like mine. You dream of grandiose adventures in love; form and custom be damned, and all you were left with was the crushing realisation that you were too late to the party, just like me. It matters not that I am engaged to be wed."

"And what if I do?," I burst, chucking the novel on the floor and pointing at it. "Who cares? Beside the spinsters."

"The world isn't just a dichotomy of spinsters and illiterates, Robin. You never know what is in front of you until you reach out and touch it."

"Don't."

"Don't what?"

"You know what."

She stared me down as a smile gradually curved up from her lips. Naturally, within a few moments I had softened. Suddenly, it became of little consequence to me whether or not Adeline read my manuscript. As I saw it, she would read it eventually; either in this moment and free of charge, or bought new from a shop. In fact, it struck me as more convenient for her to read it now. By the Winter, she would be wed to that beast, and I would be alone once more, exactly where I was before I came down to Cornwall. As I saw it, in that moment, I had nothing to lose.

"Here," I said, passing her the manuscript. "Just try not to annotate it. It's my only copy."

"I shall. Thank you, Robin."

"Goodnight, Adeline."

"Walk with me tomorrow. Early, before the others wake."

"I shall."

"Wonderful. Goodnight, Robin."

"Goodnight."

The next day, we did just that. We went further than she or I had at any other point in the Summer. We departed before breakfast, and by eleven, had cleared the village and found ourselves on the moors. Without let or hindrance, without aching feet or weary minds, we walked in each other's company, straying no more than a few feet from each other at any given time. Cornwall, in those days, was England's last true frontier. Pockets of society sat adrift, with the great, unfurling moors in between. On the horizon, we saw one such pocket, and ran to greet it. When we arrived, it was worn to its bare foundations and the walls were charred.

"I know this place," she said. "This is the old Boden House."

"The old Boden House?"

"Yes. The Boden's, they used to be the other old family in these parts. All of the sons died in the Great War, the Marchioness died in the Spanish Flu. The house burned down during the Depression, and the Marquis took up residence in Bath. It's been abandoned ever since."

"Bath? Why Bath?"

"He couldn't stand the thought of staying in Cornwall. Without the house, he had nothing left here."

"How sad," I said, mourning for people I had never known.

"One day I should like to live here, Robin. With a big, beautiful family, and not a care in the world."

"It'd need some deal of repairing."

"No. Just as it is. You'd get such a wonderful airflow in the house."

She looked at me and giggled. That was one thing I truly admired in the Belling children, something I saw so rarely in others except those with that family name; a desire, above all others, to amuse one's self. We walked around the battered gate, and into the grounds. From behind, the house sat on the precipice of a lake, that stretched out and glimmered, fetching the sun and returning it, like nature's deep cover.

"I've bought us a lunch," she said, revealing a sack that I had noticed throughout the walk, and not thought to ask about. She removed some sandwiches, fruits and wine. We lay a blanket down, using our shoes to keep it in place, and bathed under the sun.

"So, what'll you do now that the novel is finished?", she asked as we stared at the clouds.

"Take it to London, I suppose."

"What's it even about?"

"You tell me, you've read it."

"I want to hear it from you."

"Young love I suppose."

"How drawl," she teased, rolling onto her front and lighting one of my cigarettes. "I want to read about *old love*. People who are young, and beautiful are easy to love, and love easily. No. I want old love. Don't you? Love that passes the test? Love that can withstand wrinkles, and bad knees, and foggy minds. Isn't that just the most wonderful idea? To sit on rocking chairs, knowing that your love has beaten the world, swatted away all of its distractions and temptations? Oh yes, sign me up for that."

I was speechless, for she had taken my words. And hidden them away in some corner of the golden halo, that hung all about her, a hair's length from her skin and swinging with the ocean breeze. She noticed me in that haze, and laughed to herself, changing the subject with ease.

"You know," she said. "I've almost forgotten what London is like."

"Almost not worth visiting."

"Well, it'll be my home before long. Bruce is set on the idea."

"I wish to hear no more of Bruce."

"Do you get jealous?"

"Supposing I do?"

"I've said it before, Robin. I am right here."

I took her words, however vague to be in invitation of sorts. To my joy it was just that; and when I kissed her, she kissed me back. And when I took her in my arms, she wrapped hers around my shoulders. She trembled, ever so slightly, at my touch. I knew then that she hadn't been touched in that way before. Bruce, with his battering rams of cash, and bulldozers of classless intent - his oil rigs and foreign apartments -, had been kept at bay. We made love on the lake's edge. She whispered to me throughout, and I whispered back. It was a language of our own, and today I cannot recall a single word. We moved in that state for a while, until, satisfied, we rolled onto our backs and watched the clouds go by, dissipate, and allow the sun onto our faces, both fundamentally altered by what had just occurred.

"You are my first," she said, after a silent interlude.

"You beat him to the punch."

I said nothing. I just rolled onto my side and watched her. She did not look at me, her eyes were closed.

> "I am not attracted to him," she continued. "I think that he repulses me. He cannot dance, and he speaks so carelessly—not in a good way. All he cares about is money, and he has *such* a chip on his shoulder. He chews with his mouth open, and laughs with it still full. He drinks wine as if it were beer, and beer as if it were water. But you, Robin. You are beautiful in your own way."
>
> "In my own way?"
>
> "Yes. Your beauty is unassuming, it means no harm. It does not force its way into the world. Rather it knocks, politely, at the door. It is innocent. I think it's because you're sad all the time."
>
> "Am I?"

She said nothing, and so no more words were said. We returned to Belling House in the early evening, having waked in a contented silence, and staggered our arrivals as to not arouse suspicion. We went to our separate rooms and retired for the night. And, for the remainder of that week, an undeniable bond was there. Passing by in the wind, like gulls above a languid hill, looking down on the fools below, who've never known love as we had found it by that lake. It is that very lake that I overlook now while writing this. And of all the memories I have come to possess, in that haze of my youth, that day with Adeline ranks among the happiest, and most often recollected. It was in the final days of my boyhood, while twenty loomed, like an cloaked assailant, sharpening a knife or loading a pistol.

It was the final time I would taste young love; before the bitterness, found only in the heartache of mid-twenties and beyond, came to me like an ambush in an alleyway.

22

I held within me a slight bounce in those final Cornish days. Adeline and I had our little secret, that none were to know; not even those closest to us. When I walked around the house, I felt as if I floated. When I swam in the lake, I glided. When I wrote, I sung. Though, in spite of the joy I felt around Adeline, and the way I knew we both felt, we would have a conversation of a particular peculiarity in the midst of August, as it happens, it would be one of our last.

"Was I really your first?", I asked her one day.

"Of course. Who else could it be?"

"Your fiancé?"

"Like I said, he repulses me. How'd you think I got that limp?"

"An accident while playing bowls."

"Excuse me?"

"That's what I was told."

"By whom?"

"Who d'you think?"

"*Guilty men lie*. He wanted to have his way with me and I said no, 'not until we are wed'. And he got angry."

"He strikes me as the angry type. Are you alright?"

"I shall be. But are you, Robin? That is the true question."

"Excuse me?", I asked.

"Are you going to publish your novel, with the ending as it is? Even though you know what'll happen?"

"As long as men write, they shall write wishfully, correcting the errors of fate."

"The errors?", she asked.

"The errors," I repeated.

I knew I couldn't save her. Even in the highest flights of fancy, I knew that I couldn't save her. She was to marry into a world of dirty money, a world of chips on shoulders and malignant rumours. The world that Bruce inhabited, and thrived in, was ugly where she was beautiful. And when I speak of the women I have loved in my life, I would be remiss if I did not impart the same wisdom that they had imparted onto me. Adeline was young at heart, but wise beyond her years. And there was a hidden well of strength in her, that took every beating - both real and in effect - that Bruce would inflict upon her, it would strengthen her until the bloody end. Her words, *I shall be*, have since become something of a mantra. With each new low, those words of indifferent confidence, that all would figure itself out, were etched into my mind.

Bruce had returned two days before my departure, and in those two days I saw nothing of Adeline. It was on a Monday morning that I left Belling House, and made way to London. Adeline and I had shared one final kiss in secret the night before.

"Do return to us safely, old chap. I have grown quite used to you," Richard said as I placed my bags in the car.

"I shall see you in Camford, Richard."

Adeline waved from the window as the car left Belling House. Francis drove me to the station and we spoke little. Upon arrival at the station, and with half an hour until my train, Francis parked the car and turned to me.

"Best of luck with the novel, Robin."

"Thank you, Francis."

"I know—that you're not writing what you want to write, but you will be soon. This is just a step towards it."

"I hope so, Francis. Anyway, I must get my train."

"Indeed, I shall see you in Camford next week."

"I look forward to it, Francis."

"Farewell, my friend."

He stayed behind to wave me off as the train left the station. It was a long and anxious journey to London; marked by extended views of rural anonymity, and the occasional large town. When I reached the Home Counties, and London grew closer, I planned out what I'd do. Two things went without saying; I would see Donald, and I would see Monty. I arrived at Paddington in the early evening, and checked into a nearby hotel that asked for little. I felt a general sickness when in the western part of London. I had grown up in Westminster, and its memories were barely pleasant, so I avoided any sort of evening out. Instead, I drank in the hotel bar, and ordered a sandwich to my room. I called Donald and was given an address for a home in Marylebone, where I would go the next day.

"Robin!", Donald cried when his maid had shown me into his study. "Do come in."

"Hello, Donald."

"Good to see you, dear boy. I trust that your Summer was fruitful?"

"Indeed, it was."

He made a gesture that said, without saying, that I was to hand over my manuscript. It was widely said of Donald that he knew, within the opening paragraph, the potential of a novel. "My, oh my. Very pretty. This'll fetch well."

"I'm glad that you enjoy it."

Donald called for a maid, and when one arrived, he dictated a message to be sent to various literary critics.

"Tell them that Robin Fitzwarwick has a new novel, and that it is perfectly delicious."

"I think this one shall make for a fine Christmas release," he continued. "Now, where are we in terms of your studies?"

"My final year begins in the Autumn."

"Crikey. It *has* gone so fast. That is Camford for you; fleeting, transient, seductive."

"Are you a Camford man, Donald?"

"You know the answer to that, young Robin. Now, that's enough business for the time being. I have something I need to discuss with you, of a—personal nature."

"Oh?"

"Yes. My wife."

"Your wife?"

My chest tightened. I had not spared a thought for Cynthia in some time. "Do you believe her to be an adulteress?", he asked.

"An *adulteress*?"

"Yes. I was reviewing her spending habits. Two Summers in a row, she has absconded to Avignon. Nothing out of the ordinary there. However, she used double rooms each time. How bizarre."

"Very bizarre."

"And it gets more so. I telephoned the Papal Hotel; it seems to be a particular favourite of hers. And they told me she had visited with her nephew."

"Is that so?"

"It is. And here is where it gets stranger, my only brother died at war, long before he fathered any children. And Cynthia was herself an only child. We have no nephews, no nieces who could be mistaken for nephews, and Eleanor has spent the Summer with me, preparing for the wedding. It's all so strange."

"It's very strange."

"Are you sure that you were in Cornwall, Robin?"

I held his gaze for a couple of seconds, before he roared into laughter. "I'm playing, Robin. Though I shall be having words. God, send your mightiest angel to defend the man dumb enough to screw *my* lady, lest I disembowel him. If you see anything that raises a brow, do let me know."

"You have my word, Donald. Though, I must say

that I so rarely see your wife, and haven't at all in over a year."

"Yes, I suppose that is true. She does seem so unwilling to venture up with me to Camford these days. Here's another oddity; she and I were great supporters of Sandhurst when it first opened. We'd go once a month, and she lost her appetite for that in exactly the same manner."

"It's a true mystery."

"I'd say."

I left Donald's not long after that, and returned to the hotel and telephoned Monty. We arranged to lunch together the next day. When I arrived at the restaurant, he was already there. We carved our way through the standard pleasantries of old friends, and discussed our Summers. Monty had been through Italy with his elder brother. "Cornwall," he said upon hearing of my Summer. "I do wonder what Belling's house is like."

"Spectacular."

"I bet. I hear that his sister is something of a delight."

"Where'd you hear that?"

"In Tatler, just after her debut, and this morning in the Times."

"She's in today's Times?"

"Yes. Her wedding to some oil brat was announced this morning, the date and all. In a few weeks, at the big house."

I went as white as paper. Though in those Summer months, Adeline never called off the engagement; and as far as the world was concerned, the wedding would go ahead unimpeded, I held hope that something, or *someone*, would derail these plans. Monty, being someone who had known me for many years, immediately noticed my change in demeanour.

"No," he gasped. "Not her."

I looked up at him and spoke with my eyes. "Robin," he continued. "I must ask if this is some sort of brewing fetish. Is this your thing? Married women? And, by *mar-*

ried, I specifically mean to other men."

"It just happened."

"That's a lousy excuse. What's the chap like anyway?"

"He's an ass."

"Oh yeah?", he chuckled.

"You've no idea. Christ, Monty, you'd have tried your luck with her if you'd met him. For no other reason than to spare her the trouble. I don't believe I've ever met a pair less suited."

Monty and I took a short walk after we ate; down to, and then along, the river. And when we parted, I rushed to the nearest newsagents and purchased a copy of The Times. Sure enough, the marriage of Bruce and Adeline was confirmed.

'*In the rural splendours of Cornwall's north coast, a blending of world's is set to take place. Adeline Belling, 18, the recent debutante and gem of the south-west, formally announced her coming wedding to the son of London Oil International founder, Alexander Campbell. Bruce, 26, while born outside of the gentry, possesses all of its charms and dignities. Their wedding is set to take place in the second week of September. After which, the couple plan on relocating to London society.*', read the article.

The notice was like a swift punch. I felt as if I were a castaway on some disparate island, and that all I could do in this predicament, was throw a letter out to sea. I gathered my equipment, and a sheet of hotel paper, and wrote.

Adeline,

It is with great sorrow that, today, I read of your announcement. With regret, resentment, and a longing to call you my own, I shall ask you once and once alone, to leave this rotten place with me.

That day by the lake, on the moors, with the Cornish sun beating down, was a day that I shall never forget. And one that I dare say you will not either.

I shall be at the hotel marked above, a short walk from Paddington Station, in room 42. Knock three times and then once, so that I know it is you.

I trust your intuition enough to know that this goes without saying, but if I do see you again, in the manner that I imagine, then I shall pledge my life to you.

With love,
Robin.

For four days I waited. At last, on the fifth day, while I sat in the room staring out of my window at the city I detested, there was a knock. Three, and then one. That morning I had woken with a sense of foreboding. As such, I had dressed in a black mourning suit. I opened the door to find Bruce; with my letter in his hand and a fire in his eyes, and what happened next needn't be said.

23

I walked around London, without direction or guidance, I simply walked where my feet took me. Two days had passed since my encounter with Bruce, and for my efforts, I had been rewarded with a large bruise beneath my right eye, that had since faded but was still noticeable.

Almost as if guided by something invisible, and incapable of reason, I ended up in Bayswater, and there something happened, which would happen again and again, during moments of significance in my life. I had ceased to drive the car, and now sat in the back seat. I was carried to the street I grew up on, and the house at the end, only to find it crawling with barriers and workmen.

"What's going on?", I asked a workman, who looked the least busy.

"The whole street's going. Block of flats going up."

It should be said that, at around this time, England was being rebuilt. Entire streets, just like the one I grew up on, were destroyed and a thousand towers of Babylon erected in their stead. I stood there, in disbelief, as the home I once had was blown into dust. Later that day, I arrived in Camford to find the city fast asleep. It was still August, and most of the undergraduates were at home or abroad. I entered the flat to find it empty. I knew that Richard and Francis were still a few days away from returning, yet their absence was still felt. The remainder of that evening was spent alone. I went for a walk and did not see a single face.

The next day, I tried at Balloch's home address, only for there to be no response. I waited half an hour, and still no one was there. I figured that he may have been in his office. Something odd struck me as I walked through those college halls, like I were being watched by a ghost, or from behind a two-way mirror. When I saw the door to Balloch's office, I made for it, not reading the sign on the front. It was only when I entered, that all made sense. It was not Balloch sat behind the desk, but rather another familiar face.

"Ah, Mr. Fitzwarwick. Back to school early I see."

"Mitz?"

"It'll be '*sir*' to you from now on, Mr. Fitzwarwick."

"W-where's Balloch?"

"I'm afraid to say that William Balloch is no longer a member of this faculty."

"What? Why?"

"Because he is a meritless drunkard, and I am not. You see, Robin, it's rather plain and simple. I won."

"You won?"

"*The great game.* I won it. Do you not see my gold medal? My crown?"

"Where is he?"

"I neither know, nor care. He's probably overdosing on brandy and barbiturates in a puddle somewhere," he said with a twisted little chuckle.

I turned and left, grief-stricken and numb, and took to walking around the city. All of a sudden, Camford had become a very ugly place. Its splendour became unsettling, and its silence grew deafening. I felt no desire to eat, or drink. No desire to read, write, or listen to music. The geranium flowers were grey, and carried the bitter scent of death.

Once more, I came home to that empty flat. I threw myself onto the couch and stayed there for hours. Said time passed, but only felt like minutes. My head was a whirlwind of Adeline, and Balloch, and Francine, Bruce, and Mitz. The latter stung the most, as his sardonic smirk lingered like a bad smell. He knew that I was Balloch's protege, and sensing that his victory would not be total until I too was ousted, he'd surely seek to torment me, and turn me out as well. Round, and round, and round it went, until suddenly a knock came at the door. It was Adeline.

"What are you doing here?"

"I told the others that I was going to a flower show in Bath, with some friends from school."

"Oh?"

She softened, and I gestured for her to come in. We made it no further than immediately inside the flat. She wished to go no further, and she was to go no further.

"Robin," she said. "I'm not here to elope. I will marry Bruce. I just had to say goodbye."

"Why?"

"He can give me the life that I was born to live."

"So can I."

"You can't yet."

"*Some marry for money.*"

"Quite," she said with a slight whimper. I sensed her regret; she had made a decision concerning the heart using the most coldly logical of her senses. In short, she was doomed. "Do promise me one thing, Robin."

"Of course."

"That *you* shall marry for love."

"I shall try."

"I have something for you," she said, reaching into a bag. "I just hope father doesn't mind."

She produced the Korsakov recording and handed it over. For a moment, I was speechless. So moved was I, that I began to mist and steam. "Th—thank you."

"No, Robin," she took a step closer. "You were my first, you always will be. Your gentleness will never leave my side. And now I have the courage to face him, knowing that whatever comes to me next, I have loved and been loved, which is all that I ever wanted. Thank *you*."

"So, what'll you do now?"

"Marry. Move to London, and one day become the *Queen of Crude Oil.*"

"Can you bear it? Leaving such a palace?"

"I suppose I'll have a new palace."

I smiled, as a recollection of youth came to my mind. "I recall the day I left my boyhood home. It was just over a year after my father had died. You see, my father was the——"

"Robin, I don't have long."

"You can afford me this, Adeline. For it is the last time we shall ever speak."

"Is it?"

"You know it is."

"Then go on."

"My father was the youngest son of three, he wasn't to inherit a thing. He had bought the house himself, and I was supposed to inherit it, but I suppose the others must have fiddled with the paperwork. The house didn't belong to the family, you see, it died with him so they sold it and gave me a little. It all happened so very quickly. They must have been eager to get rid of the place. Do you know what happens to a house when all of the furniture is gone? It echoes. It echoes just like a cave."

She said nothing, and so I continued. "And I remember the day I left. It was just me in the house, and so I walked around, to rooms where I had once been happy, now gutted and empty, and naked. At last, I came to the library, that overlooked the little garden we used to have. I must have stood there for a little while before something remarkable happened. Do you know what I saw, out in the garden?"

"What did you see?"

"A Robin. It lingered for a moment or two, just enough for me to see it clear. And then it flew away. That is when I knew that I was free of the place. Its memory could hurt me no more, and I never returned to that house, at least not until a few days ago, when I walked, inexplicably, to it. They're putting up flats, and I saw the place get blown to dust."

"Oh, Robin," she said, moving closer. "How sad your life has been."

Her words substituted a final farewell. One that we both knew was binding. She kissed me on the cheek and left before I could say a word. I stood still for a while, processing what had just happened.

In the years that followed, I learned of Adeline's life through Richard. And it was not a happy life. By all accounts, her marriage to Bruce was a miserable affair, defined by his repeated infidelities. She did not settle well into London society, and was forbidden - by Bruce - from returning home until it was too late. A decade after our final meeting, Adeline died while giving birth to Bruce's heir. He did not attend the funeral, and was married again three weeks later. She was buried on the grounds of Belling House, in the mausoleum, alongside her forebears, and not too far from that little pond, which gave us so much in that Cornish Summer; and now hangs in the rosey air of my memories, perfectly young forever.

24

That final year in Camford came and went without passion. A switch had been flicked, and suddenly a part of me that lived was gasping for air. The years before had been spent in a dance of innocence; a wonderment at art and music, but that all seemed to be irrevocably gone. I was innocent no more. Those experiences had ended in sorrow and disappointment, and I wallowed in the ill-effects of delusion and the crushing blows of reality. I came to see that *art* as I knew it was merely a game of social politics.

My second novel, *Loving Saint Anne*, had been released in the December of 1953, and I had spent the Christmas break on a promotional tour of the cities, colleges, and provinces. I detested them immediately, and felt an odd contempt for those who enjoyed my work. I saw little of Richard and Francis, and had become Donald's project all the more. Without Balloch to urge caution and guide, I fell further into Donald's debt. Despite the distance I had built, or perhaps because of it, my friends could tell that something was not right. When we hosted, I was barely seen, and when we went to parties, I took to leaving early. My studies became tedious, and then tormenting, and I considered leaving Camford without a degree. Part of me wished to get sent down, but it was Balloch's words of warning that stayed behind to keep me in place. For good or bad, I was still haunted by his ghost.

Mitz had vindicated my fears about him and his intentions. He could not, and did not, hide the contempt that he felt towards me. He bathed, daily, in the glory of his great victory over Balloch, and could not resist the urge to intimate more to come. In me, he saw Balloch and Balloch alone, or at least the final vestiges of him. It was not until he had taken his seat at the table, that I saw the full extent of the hatred that bubbled beneath his pince-nez.

I met with him on a Monday at the end of Michaelmas term. He had taken the liberty of redecorating Balloch's office, changing the order of furniture, and placing three copies of his own book, '*The Coming Death of Paper and Ink*', on the desk, in a manner so that the spine - and ergo the title and authorship - could be seen wherever one stood.

"I must say, Robin. I am very disappointed," he said, foregoing any pleasantries. "You were heading quite nicely towards a First overall, and now you're in a freefall."

"I wonder what's changed."

"Your attitude. That is what has changed. You publish a few books and think that you're too good for this place. Well, how about this; you're not. Many better men have passed through these halls. Men who had other things going on, great things. But, never did it get in the way of their academic requirements."

"With all due respect, Mitz—"

"Sir."

"With all due respect, *sir*, I do not compare myself to such men. In fact, I feel that Camford now offers me little."

"You would be a fool to leave."

"Perhaps."

"A damned fool."

"Perhaps," I repeated.

We walked in circles for a while longer until I left, dishevelled and apparently a graduate. Picking up wine on the way home, I intended to drink alone until the day was done.

There was no novel in the works, and instead I wrote prose and poetry for an upstart magazine out of Magdalen called *The Mollusc*, that had come to gain an image of ill-repute, much to the delight of its second-year founders. In the early days of January, when bitter frost gathered on every inch of cobble, I met with Matheson, who had become its editor.

"I see you've branched out, Robin," he said, warmly, as we sat down for lunch.

"As have you, Matheson."

"May I just say, I was very sorry to hear about Balloch. Are you coping well?"

"Not particularly."

"Yes, I could tell. These poems are—well, they are something else entirely. Although I never quite saw what the other critics say about your novels. They say you're gooey and sentimental, lofty, heartfelt, which is true, but I fear, Robin, that you are far cleverer than that. I think that you wear a mask."

"I just play the Game, Matheson."

"Of course. I hear you're nearly done here."

"I'm due to graduate in the Spring."

"Where shall you go?"

"Don't all writers end up in the Albert Village?"

"I'd stay away from the Village if I were you."

"You know me rather well, Matheson."

"Perhaps I do. I never had it in me to write, I always wish I did. But I do manage to play the Game rather well."

"Well, you're risking that with The Mollusc."

"The wind is changing direction, Robin. The tide is coming in. Something new is on the horizon, everyone can feel it. And it'll be filthy. I think the old way of doing things, the manners, are on borrowed time. I'm not pleased about this, but I am aware of it. That is my advantage"

My pieces for the Mollusc were generally dark and macabre. My humour grew twisted in those final terms, as I longed to leave. I found mirth in death, and war, and disease. I'd read through the papers, find the *grizzliest* story that I could, and write about it. Donald refused to touch them, and I understood why. They were not for the likes of him. One piece I wrote tickled the fancy of the college, and briefly spread rumours that I had fallen to darker instincts. It was titled *The Wishmaker,* in which a man resembling the *Countenance Divine*, grants wishes to the arrogant and ungrateful, only to interpret their desires literally. He grants an otherworldly beauty to one man, only to have him devoured by those who don't just wish to behold him, but to ingest and wear him. He grants immortality to another, only to destroy the world and humanity within it, leaving him alone in the rubble forever.

The Spring came, and with it, the end of my studies. I met with Mitz one last time, in that office he had usurped.

"Well, it would appear that you did not listen to a word I said, Mr. Fitzwarwick. I told you to improve and you only got worse. You could have rescued a perfectly respectable two-one with a finely written dissertation. But, this; '*The Permanence of Paper and Ink*'. I suppose that's an attempt at mocking me? Under sources, you've put *William Balloch.* This is quite simply not good enough. I have been left with no choice. You will graduate with a Third, and I consider *that* to be an act of charity."

I was unmoved by Mitz's words. He had won the victory he so desired, over Balloch and myself by proxy. It was a battle he'd carved out of a generations-long peace, his nemeses did not raise arms or banners, nor too did he really exist, and still he went to war. Balloch was gone, and by the decade's end the college and the faculty would belong to Mitz and Mitz alone; and from there he'd forge a little terracotta army of Mitz's - armed and well-versed in the latest fad theories - and send them forth, to bring fire and brimstone masked in consideration and concern. He would introduce a cinematic module in the years to come, and in a particular flight of vitriol saw fit to introduce my own works for ridicule. And yet on that day, knowing full well what was, and what was to come, I did not move an inch; for I was free of him.

"Thank you for everything, Mitz."

"It's *sir*."

"Goodbye, Mitz."

I laughed to myself as I left the office, and wondered down the hall, through the college, and back home. Once more, Camford was beautiful, and tickled the senses as I walked home; there were blissful geranium odours, and the gables and cupolas spun and sang with Spring in the air and I felt on that day as I had on my first - suspended in youth, and lifted a finger's breadth above the mowed and pollinated grass. Blissful geranium odours, and plentiful wine greeted me as I found my way home, and it was in this state of stupefied bliss that I encountered Richard, who was in a state of elation.

"I've only gone and got a bloody first!"

"And I a third!"

"Bravo," Richard cried. "Tonight we shall celebrate. After your little meeting of course."

"My little meeting?"

"Yes, Donald sent word for you to call him.

And so, I called Donald. "Robin! So prompt. I have news for you, my boy."

"Do go on."

"I've been reading your poems in The Mollusc. I must say, they are very grim. However, it is a new age, and one must move with the times. As it appears, there is an audience for this sort of thing."

"So there is."

"Well, I cannot publish this sort of thing through Andress House, wouldn't please the investors very much. But I *have* purchased The Mollusc, and it shall become a subsidiary, for what they call '*dangerous writing*'. I shall be richer than I could possibly imagine! Anyway, must be off. Do let me know when you have something new for me. It was *such* a shame about Balloch. And now I shall take care of you."

As the year ended, I felt some of my neuroses leave

me and drift off into the clouds. Once more I walked the city, and this time some of the colour had returned, some of the magic. Graduation came, and we were truant. "I'm sure they'll send ours in the post," Richard dismissed. Instead, we rambled around the city, drinking in bars we'd never before entered and talking to women far above our stations. The night ended with Richard finally climbing the clock tower, and touching the college bell. Upon his invitation, Francis and I also made our way up. And we sat there, in that frozen moment; a moment that all young men face when in the twilight days of youth. A moment that seemed to say '*life will never feel this good*'. '*Now, you are free. Fly on, young jackdaw, fly on while you still can.*'

And so I sat up there, with Camford in a panoramic view, and was the happiest I had been in many months. "I can't believe it's over," I said.

"The greatest years of our lives," Richard remarked.

"Were they?"

"I'd say so, wouldn't you say so, Fucksby?"

"Yes, I'd say so, sir."

I smiled at them both. "The greatest years of our lives."

"So," Richard said after the silence had worn thin. "What lays in store for us?"

"Let's not worry about that just yet," I said, placing a hand on his shoulder.

"Well," he said. "It's London for us, Fucksby and I; father has arranged for me to be a stockbroker. And you, Robin. You *must* come to London with us. We would not be complete with you. We are the three musketeers, not the two."

I thought about it, and suddenly it occurred to me that, perhaps my aversion to London was more of an aversion to loneliness. I had, until that day, connected London with orphanhood, bullying, and wicked relatives. But, as I sat there on the college tower, I realised that every soul I knew, and every soul I would not choose to live without, was to be there. '*Perhaps*,' I said to myself. '*Perhaps it is time I gave the big city one more chance*'.

I placed a hand on either of their shoulders and hurled myself down to the grass below. "Where are you going?”, Richard called, as I walked into the darkness.

“Home.”

PART TWO:
ICARUS FLEW

25

It had been fifteen months since that graduation night, and a year since I had moved to London. It was September 1955, and I was freshly twenty-two. I had published a second volume of poetry - all from my contributions to The Mollusc - and had since entered an intense period of writers' block, from which nothing had emerged. Though, in the unexpected tradition of luck, I had not stammered in some time.

I had taken rooms in Chelsea, five minutes from Richard and Francis. I rented from a bumbling octogenarian named Mr. Willowfall. He was pleasant and dim; and spent all day reading Wodehouse in a bottom-floor flat with the door wide open; so that he always saw who came and went, and greeted them sweetly. I was on the second floor, and had a view over the King's Road. Beneath me was a place to-let, and often saw guests from far-flung corners of the world. I had a balcony, a bedroom, a small living room and a kitchen. It was all I required and the rent came cheap. I cooked my own meals, washed my own clothes and generally kept to myself while I sought new words. Money trickled in from my prior works, and I did not want for any essential.

In the middle of the month, I met with Donald at his home. We had adopted a semi-arranged monthly meeting and he kept a good collection of wine. He looked awful when I saw him, and brushed it off as a rough night's sleep, though I sensed marital issues. We spoke of unimportant things for a while, and then of business. I had told him that I wanted to move away from romances.

"But the people love them."

"I don't, Donald. I fear that if I were to write another, it wouldn't be very good."

"I see. Well, what do you want to write?"

"I don't know. Something that actually captures the essence of being. A *Fabulam de Nihilo*?"

"Fabilam de Nihili?"

"*Nihilo*."

"Okay." He was unconvinced. "You'll have to sell me on that, young Robin."

"Would you at least let me write it?"

"I'll let you try."

I left after an hour, and wondered home. I greeted Mr. Willowfall at the door. "Ah, good afternoon Mr. Fitzwarwick, back again already?"

The question confused me, as I had left in the morning and it was deep into the afternoon. Such an ambiguity was clarified as soon as I entered the flat and found Richard, smoking a cigarette in my dinner jacket.

"Fitzy!", he cried.

"What are you doing here? And how did you get in?

"Your old landlord let me in. I told him that I was you."

"Right."

"Oh, Robin. You must entertain me, dear boy. Our Fucksby is off at the *Royal Hort*. We agreed that he can take his own pleasures on the weekend, and I feel quite lost without him"

"Fine. But you cannot make a habit of entering like this."

"Of course not. The old man will catch on eventually."

I thought, briefly, of Mr. Willowfall. "No. He probably won't now that I think of it. Dinner?"

"And drinks!", he added. "Do drink with me, Robin, I am so bored and you make for such good company."

"No I don't," I countered, putting my coat back on.

"Alright, drinks too."

We walked, side by side, down to the Kings Road and spoke pleasantly when we dined in a small bistro I had come to frequent, for the meals were cheap and well crafted, without pretension. After which, we moved to the Bull's Head Pub, at which I was also no stranger. Richard ordered a beer, which I did not notice as immediately odd.

"Anyway," Richard said. "I just spoke about myself at dinner. What have you been up to old boy?"

"Well. If I am to be honest, Richard, I fear that I'm in a most horrible rut. I can't seem to write anything. I started on a story, but no. No good."

"That's something?"

"It was a terrible story. I think you were in it."

"It can't have been that bad then. But I can see how that would be difficult for you."

"Indeed," I sighed. "It's no stock market I can tell you that."

"Can I tell you something, old boy?"

"Sure."

"I hate it. I hate everything about it, and I knew that I would. Oh, God, my ills have grown arms and legs—and a great big phallus to bugger me with."

"How did we end up like this?", I sighed. "I fear, Richard, that London has gobbled me up, and shit me out."

"I'd figured you were always unhappy."

"Not always."

"I suppose a slap-dash of the old misery helps with the craft."

"Usually it does."

"Well, at least you have that going for you. It's better than trading. The only words I know of these days are so boring; '*yield*' and so forth. Oh, Lord help me I've become Bruce."

"I thought you liked Bruce?"

"Have sense, Robin. No one likes Bruce. Bruce doesn't like Bruce."

I chuckled. "That's good."

"Speaking of Bruce, I hear he's in for a shock out in the oil fields."

"Oh yeah?"

"Yeah. Word on the market is '*don't invest in British oil*', we get all of it from abroad, and the taps are gonna close any day now."

"Is that so?", I asked, somewhat pleased at Bruce's coming misfortune, though cautious as they were Adeline's as well.

"Yeah. He's set up in Egypt, right? Well, I've heard that the Egyptians aren't best pleased about it. Nationalisation."

"I just hope it doesn't harm Adeline. Do you hear much of her?"

"Afraid not. That beast has squirrelled her away."

"Oh."

"Did I tell you Jarves got called up?"

"You did not."

"Yep. The army paid for his studies, and now he's theirs. Poor bugger is in boot camp as we speak. They're going to send him out to Malaya, to go and kill Communists in the jungle."

"How wicked of them."

"Indeed. He only missed Korea by a whisker, he said something about them deferring deployment while he completed his schooling. But he skipped around a bit in his last year and didn't get into the postgraduate school. That was his plan, you see. He was going to do the full route, PhD and all. But, he spent his final year getting tight with us. And now he's going to Malaya, to go and kill Communists in the jungle. Do you recall that Communist chap we met in Paris?"

"I do."

"What a funny fellow he was. But I can't dwell on such things, I'm concerned about Jarves. I really do think he'll die out there. I think we overestimate, quite severely, our ability to win a war. We followed the Americans into Korea, and I doubt we did very much while we were there. And if things do go stray in Egypt, they'll probably send him there instead, alongside the French and the Jews, to go and die for Bruce. The Yanks won't like it of course, and they'll say stop, and we'll say sorry."

"Something's changed in you, Richard. You're discussing politics, asking about my life, drinking beer. What's happened, old boy?"

"I suppose I'm just growing up."

In that moment, a lightning bolt cracked and whipped, and the path ahead was lit in a clear hue.

"Yes—I suppose we all are."

The words trailed out of me slowly, as I felt the epiphany coursing and careening. I, still to this day, find it difficult to describe the sensation I felt when inspiration struck. It *is* like a thunder-clap.

"I have to go," I said, before standing up and making my way out of the pub, with Richard's cries of protest ringing out behind me. I alternated between sprints, and paced walks, all the way up the Kings Road, and throughout various sub-streets and alleys until I found myself at home.

For ten days and ten nights, I barricaded myself into a single room, and forbade the world from entry. I had but a simple premise, graduates of an elite institution; each possessing their own flavours of genius and folly, attempting to reconcile their lofty idealism with the cold reality of the post-war city. It was fresh, interesting, and decidedly unromantic. I came alive in that week and a half; dancing spontaneously, and typing in a rhythm. I planned not so much as a word; all was improvised and made up on the spot. I lived on bread, butter, and coffee. When I was done, and the paper seemed to smoke and sizzle, I turned back to the front of the manuscript and wrote down its title. '*Growing Up.*'

'*Thanks, Richard,*' I said to myself with a smile.

That night, I took Richard and Francis out, and became the drunkest I'd been since Camford. I called Donald in the morning. "I have something."

"Already?", he said, with a disbelieving chuckle.

And so it was that my third novel came to be, born out of frustration and misery. The response to it was quite unlike anything I'd known before. It did not just sell well, it was not just received well, it was adored, and lauded. I came to know *stardom* in 1956. Even today, forty years later, it is perhaps the work that I am best known by. Though with it, and all of the fortunes and favours, came something strange. The more it became adored by the public, the more I grew to despise the public. The praises and the sycophancy blended into one continuous groan, and I sought immediate and permanent refuge from it. I fell into a form of sleep, and all became dreamlike and surreal. In that state of fugue, I toured the land, spoke on the radio and on television, spoke in theatres and at conferences. All the while, Donald stood at the back of the room, counting his money. When at last I awoke, it was the January of 1957; I was twenty-three, rich beyond all desire, and hopelessly depressed. I had remained in my old rooms, for I needed nothing more. Naturally, I sought out Monty.

"I don't know why you're so glum," he said when I had sat down and not spoken for a few minutes. "The whole thing was a positive success. The reviews—"

"I don't want to hear the reviews. They make me uneasy."

"Really?"

"Yes. It all feels like some sick joke at my expense."

"Ah, I've heard of this. *Imposter Syndrome.*"

"What's that?"

"It's when you don't feel deserving of your success. And that, with your success comes exposure. Exposure which will reveal you to the world as—well, as an imposter."

"Yeah. That pretty much covers it."

"Would it comfort you to know that you aren't famous on the continent, or in America?"

"Is that so?"

"Well, the French seem to have enjoyed it, but apart

from that, no."

"Then perhaps I shall go to Europe."

"And you've already been to France."

"But never America. You know, I always wanted to see Italy."

"Yes. I can see you enjoying yourself in Italy. It's a lovely place."

"And the Adriatic."

"One cannot forget the Mediterranean."

"Will you be joining me, Monty?", I asked, mockingly.

"Sure."

"Really? Won't Vera mind?"

"No. Not really, she's a good sport in that sense. You really ought to meet her. That aside, I'm free as a bird, let us go and see the world, like we used to always say at school."

"Then I shall pack my things."

I did just that, and it was only when we had spent several days planning meticulously our route of the south-eastern continent that I took seriously the prospect of travel. We set off on the Ides of March. "You will return to us, won't you Fitzy?" Richard asked on the eve of my departure, some four weeks later.

"I shall. Eventually."

We left England on a Saturday, and Vera drove us to the ferry. From there, we rode the train through France, and Switzerland, crossed into Italy, and rented a car that took us to Rome, and then to Venice, and then to Positano on the Amalfi Coast, which is where we stayed a while. As the clutches of notoriety slowly ceased, and anonymity pulled me in, I asked myself when, or indeed if, I'd ever see England again. As it happened, I would return, just under a year later.

26

We had lounged in Positano for some weeks. It was now May, and the Winter felt further away than ever. Eventually, we grew bored of the Italian idyll and sought some exotic danger. We passed through Greece, into Anatolia, and across the Sea of Marmara into Istanbul. Monty came to me on the boat, while I stood on the deck, as the thin crevice between Europe and Asia crept into view, over the glimmer and the waves.

"I think my journey ends here, Robin," he said, surveying the emergent city. "I'll see what the place is all about first, of course. But home calls."

"Vera calls, you mean." I laughed and slapped his arm.

"You say that as if it were shameful, Robin. Indeed I have found being away from her difficult, at first it was a welcome reprieve. But I see it all so clear now. Before this trip, I had grown complacent, far too casual about her love. And now, I see, just as plain as I see Istanbul over there, that I do not wish to see another day without her. I'm going to ask her to marry me when I return."

"Monty!"

"Ease up, Robin. She hasn't said yes yet."

"She will, old friend."

I shook his hand with a genuine warmth, and

an eagerness to see him happy. He stiffened up and spoke. "You know, Robin. It isn't really my place to dictate such things, but I feel you are missing out on the love I enjoy, and I want you to have it as well."

"I have known love, Monty."

"Not as one should. A married woman and an engaged woman are no true muses of the heart. They are like to slapping a snake, and asking it to love you. A married woman is like a crown court judge; you only see one when you've fucked up. What I mean is to say is that love, true love, with a woman who is truly yours, is what a man was put on this earth to experience. There's nothing like it, and I want this for you, Robin. I want you to know someone who makes you feel the way Vera makes me feel."

"There was someone."

"I know. But do remember what I said about her."

"Leave it to fate."

"Yes."

I looked ahead, at the city that grew nearer with each passing glance. I could feel Monty's eyes, I could feel them bore into the side of my head, and knew that he had more to say. "Love isn't sex. Robin. It isn't flirtation, or secrecy. It isn't some clandestine meeting, in a hidden corner. It is a total devotion. It is creating your own world with someone, writing a language that only the two of you understand. It is having someone who knows exactly how to make you laugh, and strives to do so every day. It is security, companionship, a future and a legacy. It is the little things too; her face when she sleeps, and her tired voice when she stirs. It is her excitement, her trust, her laughter. It's having someone in your corner."

"Perhaps I shall find these things in Turkey."

"I think not. But perhaps somewhere close, sometime soon."

Monty left me two weeks later. He had indeed seen what the place was all about. And we strolled the bazaars and night cafe's, carefree and young. It was to be the last trip we ever took together, and with his proposal to Vera imminent, we both knew it. We laughed and talked long into the night, just as we had at school. And when, I walked him to the docks, some part of me knew that I had lost my oldest friend in many ways. Our friendship would not, and could not be the same once the boat was out of sight. He called out to me when the ship took off. "Where will you go?"

"You'll know as soon as I do," I called back.

"Just don't miss the wedding," he yelled as he grew further away. "You shall be my best man."

"Indeed, I shall! Farewell, Monty!"

He removed his hat and waved it, gently. And just like that, I was alone once more. Monty and I had travelled for three months, and like he, I too had grown weary of Istanbul, and endeavoured to find another place. For a few days, I walked around that city of ancients, and its various stories came to mind, wafting through the air; so insufferably hot. I searched for a sign of where to tread next. I found it after a week, in a newspaper article that detailed life in Tito's Yugoslavia. I was staying in an English guest-house, and asked around. The consensus was that Serbia was no good, hostile to foreigners and crawling with secret police. I asked of Croatia, and it came recommended. It was all that I needed, and I boarded a boat for Athens, and from there, I travelled to the eastern coast of Italy. From there to Split, and there, I boarded a train to Zagreb. It may as well have been a different planet, populated by a different species. English would not suffice, so I picked up enough Croatian to get by, and found a boarding house close to Saint Mark's. My first few nights were made up of solitary walks, and little conversation. On the fourth day, I found a bar on a quiet street that had aimed itself, squarely, at the English and the American.

Inside there was a single Croat, who served the bar. Among the bustle, I heard Yanks, Australians, and a rogue Boer, though most were British. And as I moved toward the bar, one American voice trickled through. I recognised it immediately, and turned to see the source. It was Andrew Finnegan, who I had met in Paris, five years before. He had barely aged, and had retained his shabby look. His hair was still that same shade of grey, and his chest still adorned with hair. He looked more continental than he did when I saw him last. I watched him as he moved from one conversation to another, and then to the piano. He played a tune I hadn't heard before, and it injected a little life into the room. People swayed while they spoke, and the drunkards began to move with lucidity. He finished, and moved back towards the bar, where I made my approach.

"Hello," I said, with a false confidence. "Do I know you?", he grunted.

"Yes. We met in Paris, around five years ago."

He gave me a funny look, and then one of intense recollection. "Did you try to kill me?"

"No."

"Are you an aristocrat?"

"On a bad day."

He smiled. "Ah, yeah. I remember you now. The limey writer."

I returned his grin and nodded. "So," he said, getting a drink and downing it in one. "Did you ever make it?"

"As a matter of fact, I did."

"And how is that?"

"I ran away. And how are you?"

"Happy as the day I was born."

"I was born crying," I said. "Were you not?"

"No. *I* was born drinking a Croat wine."

He laughed and sat down at a table. He kicked out the stool next to him, inviting me to sit. "So," he said. "What makes you so unhappy, kid?"

"Well, it's everything I wanted. It's just——"

"Not what you expected."

"Yes."

"And they're making you write total shit. Buttering up your ego, telling you how fantastically you write, just to convince you to carry on."

"Yes."

"I see. So the money is good then?"
"And then some."
"Do you like your own books? Would you read them if you hadn't written them?"
"I don't think so."
"Then why do you do it?"
"Nothing else makes sense. It's not writing that I hate, I love writing. It's odd. When I am writing something, it feels so—-vital, so necessary, as if I were doing humanity a disservice by not writing it. And then, it is finished, and goes off into the world, and people seem to enjoy it. But I just despise it, it makes me feel sick. People approach me and tell me such lovely things about my work, and all I can think is 'Fool. What a damned fool you are for enjoying this.'"
"You know why you hate it?"
"Why?"
"Because it doesn't belong to you anymore."
"That's ironic."
"Is it?"
"Aren't you supposed to be a Communist?"
"These days, kid. I don't know anymore. You show me a working guy, who's gettin' shafted, and yeah, he's my guy. But all this grandiose shit, these *deep metaphysical truths* about '*ownership*', and '*solidarity*', and I lose interest. Maybe I'm just old."
"You know, when we last met, you said something that made me laugh. I still laugh about it. You told me you'd lost some of your Communist credentials by drinking with me and my friends."
"Ah, yeah. Your friends. How are they?"
"One's a stockbroker."
"Which one?"
"The one with no business being a stockbroker."
"Lord help us all. Say, I feel like getting a bottle of something, if you're buyin'."
"Me?"
"Yeah, you. You're the celebrity."

"In England. Why do you think I'm here?"

"Your money's good wherever you drink. Do you want the bottle or not?"

I did, and turned to the bar. He sat eagerly in waiting, and attacked the bottle as soon as it was laid down, pouring us a generous glass each. "How about this for *Communist credentials*," he said, after a thirsty gulp. "Those publishers, they're probably eating caviar in the Ritz, with money that you made for them. If that isn't theft," he tapped his glass onto the table. "Then I don't know what is. Who do you write for?"

"A man named Donald Andress."

"And he's some sort of big shot?"

"Oh, the biggest."

He scoffed. "The silver spoon."

"He's self-made actually, came from nothing as the story goes."

"That's worse! To be born with it is one thing, I can understand that to a degree. But, to come from the gutter, and send people down to it. No. That, to me, is treason."

"Mm," I murmured.

"You don't strike me as political," he said.

"I wouldn't say that I am."

"You gotta be something?"

"Is being anti-political a political position?."

"Just beauty, art, and books?", he asked.

"Something like that."

"You're an aesthete. Like that fellow from Brideshead, the cosmopolitan."

"Blanche?"

"Blanche! Yes, that's the fellow."

"*You've* read Brideshead?"

"Yeah, yeah, laugh it up. I like books, okay. Maybe I'll read one of yours. Have you taken an assumed name?"

"No. Just my real name. Fitzwarwick."

"Jesus. Maybe I have lost my credentials. But, look. Keep hold of that all you can, kid, that thing inside you that doesn't give a shit about money, or any other type of soma, just the art and the artistry. The world is cold, full of bad people, greedy people, and people who want nothing more than to take your talent and turn it into a well-oiled machine. Keep your head as far away from this shit as you can get it. And don't listen to anyone who says you can't. You got some books published, so you're at least half good, and there's no crusade for you to join. That makes you one of the lucky ones. You can make art; therefore, you can spend the rest of your life living in art."

"That's very good advice."

"I know. Here's some more. Get out of here, of Zagreb I mean. You'll never write anything here, it's too loud. Too many people shouting. You need to go somewhere quiet."

"Yeah?"

"Yeah, go find *Eden*."

"And where will I find it?"

He swirled the remnants of his glass and threw it down. "Kotor."

"Kotor?"

"Yeah, Kotor. Go to Kotor. It's in Montenegro. You can be there in a day or two. Go there and you will find it."

"Find what?"

He smiled, sardonically. "*It*."

"I am very glad I met you tonight, Andrew. You've done me a great service. I don't know how I can repay you." "Ah," he said, flapping an arm. "Name a kid after me."

It was thus that I found my true purpose in the year of 1957. It had a name and the name was *Eden*. Though the wind was not quite right, and my voyage south took two days, but eventually I did find my way to Kotor on the cusp of Summer. As soon as I arrived, I knew that I had come to the right place. I knew that I would not leave this place without finding *it*.

27

'Dear Robin,

I fear London has lost its wings without you, and has fallen, rather dramatically to the earth. Much like that Icarus fellow you used to go on about at college. Though I haven't the foggiest why he'd make wings out of feather and wax, did they not have compact aluminium in ancient Greece?

We miss you greatly, the old boy keeps asking when you'll be back, so I figured I'd write you and see to it myself. Though I have no idea where you are, so I left this letter with Monty. He didn't seem pleased to see me.

Fucksby is well, he goes to the Royal Horticultural at the weekends and helps me in the week. I am still a rascal, in spite of my mature line of work. Stocks are as stocks do, and I don't quite understand them just yet. I just make calls and hit buttons, praying that I don't start a fire. Do return to us soon, Robin, we're ever so lonely without you. No news of Adeline.

Inebriatedly yours,
Richard.'

I had received that letter several weeks into my stay in Kotor. The note gave me a quiet joy, and added to the general ease that I felt; for the Balkan coast was a river on which I floated, languid, gaily and without any trepidation. There was no distant pain, hidden deep within my soul as I had so often felt in England. Once more, I was happy and at peace, in some corner of paradise. Wherever I went, and whatever I did, I could not seem to find misfortune anywhere; not under any rock, nor behind any tree. Richard's letter had arrived with one of Monty's, giving me the date of the wedding. March 1958. I had written to him, with my address upon arrival.

I stayed with a middle-aged couple, who entertained foreign guests in a small shack on their land. I was the only to come from the Anglosphere, and as such was met with a linguistic wall. Milan and Danica Savic did not speak a lick of English; only Serbian, and a trace amount of French from an earlier guest. My excursions around the city bore no other fruits, and it soon became apparent that I could not speak to anyone in my native tongue, and would have to learn some Serbian. I did, just about enough to order a coffee, and enough to thank Milan and Danica for the food they made for me. In a way, I was thankful for the situation; not just because Kotor's charms rendered all of my troubles obsolete, but because isolation had worked so well for me before.

I had accepted the position of being an autobiographical writer. In my first novel, I wrote of my days with Francine in that Paris cafe. In my second, I wrote of my affair with Adeline, and my third chartered the oblivion I had found myself in after Camford. Perhaps it was why I was incapable of writing All's Well, as its events were not inspired by anything in particular. I tried for a few weeks, but gave up, and started to take longer walks into the old town. I had begun writing of an English traveller, in search of Eden; who sells all of his earthly belongings, save for a book and a pen, and endeavours to walk the earth until he is happy again. He travels far and beyond, to the furthest corners of this little speck of dust, searching for paradise.

He found nothing in China, India too, nothing in Africa, nothing at home. And when he had just given up, he discovered this little spot, hidden in the bay, with the Adriatic over the horizon. '*Adam of the Adriatic Eden*' I named it.

Just as I did in Cornwall, I formed concentric circles around the city, gradually moving further and further away. I walked through the old town, and marvelled at its churches. The language barrier never became an issue, until a day came, on which I found myself hopelessly lost and without the means to ask my way home.

"Zdravo," I called to an elderly man, who sat on the porch of his house with a pipe.

"Zdravo!", he called back, cheerily.

"Da li pričate Engleski?"

"Ne."

Such a conversation repeated itself over and over again, until I had walked so far in search of my own tongue, that, by pure accident of fortune, I found that I had stumbled home.

When I returned to the Savic property, I found a great bustle underway. Milan and Danica were setting up around the house, and the two seemed excited.

"Moja ćerka!", Danica would cry, again and again.

"Moja ćerka! Moja ćerka!"

It was two days later when I first met '*Moja ćerka*'. I sat, in the little part of the garden reserved for staying guests. It had the shack in which I slept, a small outdoor dining area, a hammock, and a fire-pit. I laid my typewriter on the table and tapped away on my opening chapter, with the water in view through the thin layers of tree.

When I wrote, I fell into a state of oblivion, a state of true flow. So engrossed was I in this state of affairs; in the fate of my hero, that I was impervious to all distractions around me. The passing of winds through branches did not disturb, nor did the occasional hum of passing conversation. Nor did approaching footsteps. Until a voice cut through it all, like a knife in hot butter.

"Hello."

I stirred, and stared directly ahead of me. Unsure if what I had heard was in my head, or was tangible. "Hello," the voice repeated.

I turned to see her. She smiled politely, and without assumptions or judgements. She wore a green he scarf, and a matching, modest blouse, tucked into a large skirt that flowed down to the floor, but stopping just above it.

"Hello," I replied. Stunned, as I had not heard English for some time. "Žao—mi—je," I continued, without confidence. "Ne govorim Srpski."

"That's okay," she said with a smile. "I speak English quite well."

"Indeed, you do," I replied. "It's nice to hear it."

"Yes. Not many people in Montenegro speak English. We have enough languages of our own to—how do you say, '*juggle*'?"

I laughed, with amusement and relief. "Yes, '*juggle*' is just right."

She beamed. "This is good!"

"Very. How did you learn to speak English?"

"I went to the university in Belgrade. It is the only place to learn English. Where did you learn your Serbian?"

"That question assumes that I can speak Serbian," I said, laughing to myself. She did not join me, and just smiled politely. I stiffened. "In the old town."

She laughed, and it filled the silence. Our eyes met and lingered for a few seconds before she looked away "Are you American?", she asked.

"British."

"This is nice. I like your British writers."

"Milena!", called a voice from inside the house.

"I must go, but it has been nice to meet you." She turned and walked a few paces before turning back. "I'm sorry. What is your name?"

"R-Robin."

"It was nice to meet you, Robin. I am sure we shall speak again soon."

"I'm sure we will."

Milena walked into the house and I turned back to the typewriter, though I soon found that, for now, my focus had gone. I packed the typewriter away and lay in the hammock. As I smoked, I looked up at the sky, and smiled, now that I had someone to speak to.

'*Milena*,' I said to myself, before going for a swim.

28

It had been two weeks since I had met Milena. We spoke little beyond the distant looks that we would occasionally share. It was late in July now, and the sun beat with a fervour I had not known before. I swam in the bay, wrote in the shade, and read by moonlight when the sun went down.

One day, as I wrote, my mind detached, she approached me in her unassuming way. "Are you hungry?"

Slowly, I turned, to see her holding a plate of food with a simple, yet sincere, smile upon her face.

"I am."

"Here, eat."

She laid the food before me while I examined it.

"What is it?"

"It is Kačamak, traditional Montenegrin food. Give it some time, it is hot."

"Thank you."

"Thank my mother. She made it, and asked me to bring it out to you. She says you look so sad and lonely all of the time."

"That's funny. I figured your mother and father didn't like me."

"They did not like you at first. They assumed you were an American. But I told them that you are British."

"Ah, the magic words."

"I'm sorry?"

"Never mind. It was a joke."

"I like jokes! Please tell me!"

"It wasn't funny."

"Oh, okay. Well, may I sit?"

I gestured at the empty chair and she sat while I took a bite of the food. "This is good," I said.

"It is comfort food, mother always makes it for me when I come home. She said that you probably miss your own mother's cooking, so she made some for you."

"My mother never had the chance."

A look of concern flashed across her face, and she went to speak, before stopping herself and retreating into the house. She returned promptly with a bottle, in it a light brown fluid. "What is that?"

"Rakija.."

"What is it?"

"Strong."

"And do you intend to get me drunk in the afternoon, Milena?"

"Yes," she giggled, before straightening. "We have a saying in Montenegro. It is better to drink and feel sick, than to not drink and feel sad."

"Well then, chin-chin."

"Chin-chin?"

"Cheers."

"No," she said, taking her glass and clinking it into mine. "Živjeli!"

I fumbled my attempt to repeat what she had said, and threw the shot into my mouth. Immediately it burned and lacerated my tongue. Like a fool, a swallowed, and my throat met a similar fate. "You don't like it?", Milena asked behind a laugh.

"It's—strong."

"I told you that, *Englishman*."

"Am I done yet?"

"No. Let us do another."

"You *are* trying to get me drunk."

"You're sad, of course I am."

"I never thought I'd say this, but alcohol is not the solution to every ill. You'd be better off having met me a few years back."

"You English are funny. Drink."

Begrudgingly, I did. Satisfied, Milena put the bottle away. "Okay, enough drink for now. I know what you western boys like to do after too many of these. And it is safe to say that you will not get it."

"I don't have time to think about sex, Milena. I'm writing."

"Yes, I have been meaning to ask you. What is it that you are writing?"

I stiffened and tried to shake off the alcohol before answering. "A novel."

"This is good! Is this what you do?"

"Yes, I suppose so. This will be my fourth."

"So, you actually are a writer then?"

"Excuse me?"

"You know, like, you are actually a writer, professionally. It is how you make a living. You're not just one of those people who says that they are."

"Do you speak from experience?"

"Oh, yes. I knew so many in Belgrade. They write about the most disgusting things and call it art."

"Oh, yes."

"What do you write about?"

"Life, mostly. My own to be precise."

"Your own?"

"Yes, I think the minute things in life are rather interesting. Don't you?"

"You are like a little old man."

"I've heard that before."

She giggled. "Do you like Kotor?"

"I love it. *Clarity in the cacophony.*"

"My English is not that good, Robin. You must speak to me like I am a very clever child."

"It's quiet here."

"Yes. But why did you come *here*?"

"I needed to flee England for a while."

"Did you kill someone?"

"Worse," I said, breaking into a gentle laugh. "I became famous."

"Have you travelled a lot?"

"I suppose I have."

"I have never left Yugoslavia."

"Do you wish to?"

She thought for a moment, and I saw the conflict behind her eyes. After a minute or so, she had reached a conclusion. "No. Home is enough for me. You see, I see home as being something more than just the people you know. It is like a chain. It stretches from today, all the way back to the very beginning of time. Some see no issue with breaking that chain, but I believe I would be letting them down. Do you understand?"

"I think I do. Though, I think that perspective depends on your family."

"You do not like your family?", she asked.

"I don't have one."

The look I gave her said all that needed to be said. She understood immediately, and retreated from the subject. We found ourselves in an identical situation one month later. I was sat by the shack, while she sat opposite. This time it was she who ate, while I drank coffee. We spoke again of home and of travel, and I could sense a question brewing in her.

"Do you believe that you will return home?"

"When I finish the novel," I said, typing away.

"Then I hope it takes a while."

Something occurred to me in that moment, and I stopped typing. "You know," I said, looking up. "Typically I don't let anyone come near me when I am writing. When I was writing my second novel, at the home of a friend, I barricaded myself into my room, and only let the servant see me, he was the only person I saw for two weeks. And when I emerged, my friends were surprised to see me, they thought I'd gone home. It was the same with my third book, I was a complete hermit while I wrote it. I didn't see a single other soul. But I don't mind you being here while I write."

"Servant?", she asked, with a raised brow.

"For my sins," I said, finishing off the chapter and removing a strip of paper. "But it wasn't *my* servant."

"May I read it?", she asked, gesturing with her eyes.

"Not yet," I said, readying a smoke.

"You must. It is a story about my home."

"How do you know that?"

"You told me that you write about your life, and you are here. But I think you are making a mistake."

"Am I?"

"Yes. You do not go into Kotor. You stay here, at the bay, but you do not see the real city. If you let me read it, I can help."

"Fine," I said, gathering the half-written manuscript. "It is not finished, not even close. But you can get an understanding of the story."

She picked up the papers. "Thank you, I will begin immediately."

With a smile and a slight bow, she turned and left.

Two weeks passed before she came to me on the water's edge. "I hate it."

"You hate it?"

"The writing is very pretty. But I hate it."

"Why?"

"It is too, how do you say, arrogant? It is all about you; *your* experience, *your* conversations, *your* opinions. You came to Kotor for inspiration, but this could be anywhere in the world. Where is Kotor?"

"What would you have me do?"

"Listen to what I say. This is what happens when you only write here. You barely leave the house!"

She was not angry, but wouldn't budge. I, as she repeated, wrote so well, and quality was not a factor of her complaint. She was right. I could not protest, or offer any explanation to my own defence. I found the city to be an endless charm, and yet it had barely featured. My story, so far, was about an expat finding an exotic paradise. And, as she said, that paradise could have been anywhere.

"I will take you into the old town tomorrow," she said with a simple certainty. "And you will throw away everything you have written and start again."

"Everything?"

"Yes, everything. Come on, we will go to the sea now and drowm it."

And so begun the second layer of writing, embedded in the morning walks I would take with Milena into the old town. She took me around the churches and walled fortifications, and omitted no detail of the local history. On one such journey, in the middle of August; when I felt I had enough to re-write the novel, entirely to her liking, I caught myself smiling during a tirade of hers, and asked myself if I was ready to love again.

29

It should be said about Kotor that it in those days it hosted very few tourists, and there were almost none when I walked its cobbles and causeways. This was where I found my bliss; in the duality of surrounding myself with familiar faces, and of discarding them all when I travelled. I sought only space and solitude when I left England, and thus felt throttled in the presence of the English. All of the tourists and expats who had found their way to Montenegro stayed at a hotel in the centre of town, and I had marked it out as a place to avoid at all cost. Luck being what luck is, I met an English couple one day in September, when Milena came to me as I swam in the bay.

> "You are wasting valuable time," she called to me from dry land one day. "You could be writing a masterpiece right now!"
>
> "Today, I shall rest, Milena! Rest is the most important thing for a writer. It keeps the mind able."
>
> "I can already tell you are English when you open your mouth. You do not need to prove it further with your actions. Anyway, it is not me to wants to speak with you, it's my mother."
>
> "Your mother?"
>
> "Yes! She has a surprise for you."
>
> "Well, why didn't you say?", I joked, wading out of

the water and drying off. We returned to the house, where I was ambushed by Milena's mother.

"Robin! Robin!", she cried. "Ima Engleza! Razgovarati s njima."

"Englezi?", I asked. I had collected some Serbian by now, and could converse a little more. "Ovde?"

"Da!"

The couple approached in a bashfully *English* way. They were in their fifties or sixties. The man was plump and held all the trappings of retired military, and the woman was spindly. They seemed a country vicar and his doting wife. "I say, old boy," the man bellowed. "Mighty strange finding a compatriot way out here. I figured you'd be at the Marigold with the rest of us."

"I prefer to live among the locals."

"Very bizarre. Well, you are in good company now. The household cavalry has arrived! I'm Captain John Harding, and this is my wife Carrie."

I shook both of their hands, as they examined me, like some beast; part wild and part domestic. "That's a firm shake," said the Captain. "A *public school* shake if I am not mistaken. Am I mistaken?"

"No, sir, you are not. Charterhouse."

"Oh, yes, yes. You are most certainly in good company. I'm an Eton man myself, the whole family are. However, my brother used to be a beak there. He got the sack a year or so back for the most *frivolous* of reasons, wound up at one of those new schools in the city."

I felt an involuntary clench in my jaw, as that name I had not heard for several years entered my mind once more. You may recall discussions from my first days in Camford, when the memory of a *Mr. Harding* came up. He was my greatest tormentor, more than any other wicked schoolboy, any relative, any lost parent. He was perhaps the only soul in this world that I truly hated. "Yes," I said, conveying an air of indifference. "I remember him."

"He's at the Marigold now, I'm sure he'd remember you."

"Oh, you must join us," cried his wife. "We're so starved of company, especially one so young. We're a bunch of old bores, really. Do come?"

"I'll consider it."

"Nonsense!", the Captain blurted. "We shall fetch a car and go there now."

Milena looked up as I swung my head into her room. She read, having made good her escape once I was cornered by the vicar and his wife. "Yes?", she said.

"I need a favour. It's rather urgent."

"What is it?"

"Dine with me, at the Marigold."

"The Marigold Hotel?"

"Yes."

"And I'd be doing *you* a favour?"

"A big one."

"I don't think a Slav has ever dined at the Marigold."

"Then you, Milena, shall be the first."

She dressed into her best clothes, and followed me outside, where the Captain had talked Milan into driving us. Milan shared a few words with Milena, before starting the car and carrying us off. I didn't say a word as we meandered through the town. My mind was fixed in place on the coming reunion with Harding. As the distance between us closed with each passing second, I became less convinced that I could face him.

"Have you been to the Marigold before?", the Captain asked, leaning back to face me. I was on the right window, Milena was in the middle, sandwiched between myself and Carrie.

"No. If anything, I've avoided it until now."

"Oh?", he asked.

"You see," I began, choosing my words carefully as to not offend. "I prefer to be with English people in England. When I am abroad, I like to mix with the locals."

"I see," he said, disapprovingly. "Well, we're here now."

He was right, and Milan pulled into a small parking bay, directly in front of some great wide doors of glass. A concierge flew into action, and opened both doors.

"Biti pažljiv," Milan said, as his daughter exited the car.

"It's the greatest luxury one can find in these parts," the Captain said, putting an arm around my shoulder as we entered. "Reserved for the Westerners of course."

We walked through the carpeted hallway, where paintings of London, and Bath, and Glasgow sat upon the walls. After a dozen or so steps, we came to a small dining room, with six tables spread out evenly. On each were six chairs. The Captain made for the table at the back of the room, that nuzzled the large window, overlooking the gates of the old city, into the harbour. I recognised Harding immediately, and he recognised me. In the seconds between our eyes and our hands, we jostled silently.

"Oh, brother, I've met a terrific young Englishman, over where the natives live. This is——"

"Robin Fitzwarwick," Harding interrupted. "I remember him."

"Oh, yes!", the Captain cried heartily. "The two of you must be acquainted."

"Indeed," said Harding, coldly, and yet with an air of humour. "How are you, Fitzwarwick? I hear you've made quite a success of yourself."

"Yes," was all that I could say. I felt Milena's eyes pierce the side of my head as we sat down. Perhaps the Captain and his wife did not see it, but Milena was wise and sober, and could feel my hatred linger in the air.

"Well isn't that just grand," Harding added. "I never got around to reading any of your books, but I'm sure they're just grand."

"An author?", the Captain asked. "Oh, how marvellous. You know, I got that sense from you, young lad. A writer, can you believe that, Carrie?"

"I can't!", Carrie exclaimed with a vapid joy. "How very exciting!"

"What do you write about?", the Captain asked.

"Romances mostly," I began. "At least on the surface. I suppose they are autobiographical in nature."

"I like adventures," said the Captain. "Give me a good military adventure, over any of that lovey-dovey stuff, but my wife adores romances."

"I do! I really do!"

"Do you have children?", I asked.

"Afraid not," said the Captain.

"Hm," I said to myself.

A waiter came over and took our orders. Milena tugged on his arm as he began to move away. "Rakija za mog prijatelja." The waiter nodded.

"Rakija?", I asked.

"Da vam pomogne."

"Is there something that the two of you would like to share?", Harding asked, with a sickly grin.

"Yes," I said. "We were going to order some Rakija, a traditional Slavic spirit."

"Oh, no," he replied. "If I wanted to be like a Slav, I'd put on a waistcoat and take everyone's orders."

"Need I remind you, *sir*, that you are in the presence of a Slav."

Harding stiffened. He seemed surprised that I had answered him back - something I had never done in school. Perhaps he expected me to be meek and afraid, as I was the last time we shared a room. Internally I was, and still found him to be intimidating. But, from where I knew not, a sly courage emerged, and I felt the need to challenge him on every syllable.

"I meant no offence," he said to Milena, who smiled back politely.

The conversation continued for another ten minutes, as drinks were served. The Rakija stung as it always did, and with it came courage. Harding did most of the talking, of his new school and the wretched children he taught there.

"I hear you got the sack, Harding," I said, caving in to the desire to continue my assault. "Did they give you a reason?"

"As you'll know, Fitzwarwick. Some might refer to my methods as being *direct*."

"*Direct*," I repeated. "Just a word really. One of many. Direct, unyielding, sadistic."

"To the weak, my methods may seem sadistic. But in a case such as yours, Robin, it seemed to have worked."

"Are you going to take credit for my success, Mr. Harding?"

"I'd do no such thing. However, it does seem that your *experiences* at school have shaped you, and you have succeeded because of them."

"Or in spite of them."

"I hear you're in bed with Andress."

"Yes."

"It must be nice."

"Yes, that's a man I can blame my success on."

"How's your Byron?", he asked.

"Immeasurably better," I snarled.

"Gentlemen," the Captain intervened. "Please. Let us find some peace. I'm sure that what has gone on between the two of you is not insurmountable."

"Yes, you're quite right, brother," Harding said. "Perhaps me and R-R-R-R-obin can f-f-f-find some c-c-c-common ground."

Before I knew what had happened, I rose to my feet and thumped the table with my fist, as heads swivelled and eyes shot towards us. "Would you like to step outside, sir?"

"So quick to anger," Harding sneered. "Like a common boy, no different to the low-cast boys I teach in the city. Perhaps you were never public school material, Robin, no gentry, no class. Perhaps if you'd had a father you wouldn't be so——"

His eyes widened mid-sentence as I lurched forward and struck him in the face, as hard as I could. The blow sent him tumbling as a shock of pain shot up my arm and into my shoulder, like a crack of thunder. I had never struck someone in the face until that day, and haven't since. It is perhaps for that reason that I never knew how much it hurt to strike bone with bone. Adrenaline alone kept me from succumbing to the pain, it was that same adrenaline that threw my legs into action as a giggling Milena grabbed my arm and led me out of the room, before our food could even arrive. The Captain called out behind us.

"Oi! You loutish boy!"

Laughing, and with the adrenaline wearing off, we emerged into the street, where Milan sat in a cafe across the street. Milena went to fetch him, as the pain came to me. My hand felt as if it had been set on fire, and I winced with each pulsing sensation. The Captain's wife came through the door. Alone, I braced myself for a dressing-down. Alas, that never came.

"You know," she said. "He's a rotten man, my brother-in-law. I've always prayed that someone would strike him in the face like that. It'll do him such a lot of good." She smiled, and placed a gentle hand on my shoulder. "I shall keep an eye out for your books, Robin. And don't you worry about this little incident. In this room it shall stay."

Milan emerged from the cafe, having been briefed on what had happened. He laughed and gripped my shoulder. "Kao ratnik," he said, as we entered the car and readied ourselves to drive off. The sun was falling when we arrived at the house, and by the time we had eaten, the sky was dark save for the moon and the stars. I excused myself and did what I had come to do in those deathly-still nights. I scaled the shack I lived in, and sat upon the roof, admiring the cosmos. Before long, I heard footsteps on the weeds, and Milena came into view.

"Do you wish to be left alone?", she asked.

"No," I said. "Join me."

She did, and I could tell that she was concerned about something. "Are you going to tell me about what happened earlier? He was a horrible man, but horrible men don't get struck for just being horrible. He was a teacher of yours?"

"Yes. My father died a year or so before I went to that school. Up until then, I had lived in London, and was sent out to a boarding school after. Charterhouse, it was called. I don't know if it was the grief, the fear, or just rotten luck, but I developed a severe stutter. It was so bad that at one point I couldn't say my own name. The thing is with those schools is that if you can be picked on for something, you will be picked on for it. The only things that can protect you are friends and family. I had one friend and no family. So I didn't stand a chance. The other kids were horrid, but Harding was cruel. I can understand what the other kids did, I can forgive it, and I have forgiven it. For them it was a simple matter of survival; if someone else is getting picked on, then you aren't. But Harding, a teacher, had no such excuse. He did it because he has something rotten in his heart, some broken mechanism that leads him to do something like that to a defenceless boy, thirteen years old. He mentioned Byron, because he used to make me stand up in front of the class, and recite Byron over and over again, knowing that I couldn't. I've wanted to do that to him for longer than you can imagine."

"And now you have."

"Yes," I laughed. She joined me, and soon we were laying on our backs. Silence fell, and we watched the moon fall behind a cloud. In the darkness, she spoke. "I noticed that you haven't written for a while."

"Yes."

"Will you finish the book?"

"Yes. I've been here before, and will no doubt return at some point in the future."

"For a twenty-three-year-old, you have quite the old man's temperament."

"I'm twenty-four."

She sat up. "You are?"

"Yes. It was my birthday last month."

"Why didn't you say?"

"I didn't want to make a fuss."

"A *fuss*?", she asked.

"It's another way of saying attention, I don't care much for attention."

"Then you picked the wrong job."

I chuckled, as the roof gave a disconcerting little noise. "This roof won't give way, will it?"

"I don't know. But it would be funny if it did."

"For you perhaps. Where I'm sat, I'm pretty sure I'd land straight on the drawers."

"A slightly less comfortable seat than the roof," she laughed.

"At least you'd get your wish and no longer find me swimming during prime writing hours. A broken spine would leave me no choice but to write all day."

"At least you'd have me to talk to."

"And to bring me food."

"And Rakija," she added.

"Oh, no. I can only handle so much. Wine, perhaps."

"Of course."

She jumped down from the roof and vanished into the darkness for a few minutes. She returned with a bottle of wine. We passed it back and forth, much in the same way that I had with Adeline, four years prior.

"This wine," she said, before taking a sip. "Comes from the market. It is made locally by a farmer called Dravoc. His son, Luka, has asked me to marry him. Twice."

"And you said no twice?"

"Yes."

"Poor bastard."

"What do you mean?"

"To be turned down is one thing, by one such as yourself is another."

"Oh?", she asked with a total innocence.

"You do realise that you are completely angelic, right?"

"I am just me."

"You've really never been in love?", I asked.

"No. Just as you have never known God."

"I wish I did."
"You do?"
"Of course. Death is so utterly terrifying. Faith seems to be the only cure."
"Why do you fear it?"
"It is so final, so constant. If it is too hot, I fear dying of sun-stroke. If the water in which I swim is too deep, I fear drowning. I fear cancer, polio, influenza."
"Do you always think of death?"
"No. But when I do, and cannot find it within myself to believe in anything other than infinite black, nothingness, the whole thing becomes a great terrifying beast."
"You know, having faith is similar. I do not believe in nothingness, but I do believe in two things; endless reward for a good life, and endless punishment for a bad one. I do not think about death in the way you do, but I think that when I die, everything I have done could be used against me."
"What do you do with such a fear?"
"I behave. I treat my father and mother with respect. I go to church with them, and I worship. I live a good life, I keep my appetites under control."
"Perhaps life is just terrifying, regardless of what you think happens after it is over. Death is too great a thing, too large a spectre, to ever just ignore and enjoy life."
"Not always. My life is not difficult. If you waste all of your time thinking of these things, you will never experience life. You may as well be dead."
"How does one feel alive?"
"That is an unanswerable question, Robin. And it is late."
She jumped down from the roof again and turned back to face me. "I shall see you tomorrow, Robin."
"No," I said with a smile. "I have a novel to finish."

And so, once again, I found myself in a fervour of writing. I had collected half a notebook's worth of Milena's critiques of the story, and another half of her thoughts on life and death. And that is what I wrote; Eden through her eyes. I became secluded, hermetic. The burgeoning winds led me to stay in the cabin, where a small furnace calmed and comforted. Each morning, there was breakfast and coffee at my door, and in the evenings, there was dinner and wine. I was left alone with my words, and as a result of my cabin fever, organised themselves in a hurry, as to escape the clutches of my weary mind. One week became two, and then three. By the fourth week, I was onto my final chapter. Until now, I had fought the urge to include Milena in the story, and no such character bore her likeness. I wanted to give my protagonist, Adam, a reason to stay in Eden, so I gave him an Eve. In the blink of an eye, three months had passed.

"Hello, Robin," Milena said when at last I emerged.

"I figured you had vanished and returned home," she said with a mocking chuckle.

I just looked at her, overcome with joy and relief.

She tilted her head in a way that asked me what was going on. "Milena," I said after a few moments. "It's finished."

"Robin! Congratulations!"

"Thank you. It was something you said when we spoke last. It put the last piece into place."

"You can thank me with a dedication."

I chuckled. "Perhaps I shall."

"Would you like to join us for dinner?"

"In the house?"

"Yes."

"What's the occasion?"

"Are you joking?"

"No?"

"Robin. It's Christmas Day."

"Oh, is it?"

"Yes, how did you not realise? I am surprised you are still here. I thought you would have gone home for Christmas and just not said goodbye. The only sign you were still here was the empty plates."

"I typically spend it alone."

"Well, not this year. Come, join us."

"I figured your people celebrated it in January."

"We are catholics."

I obliged and spent Christmas afternoon with Milena and her family. We ate richly, consumed wine and sung songs. Though I knew not the words, I hummed in time; which greatly amused them. I pointed at a tree that lay in the corner of the room. "I say, what's that tree doing there?"

"It is *Badnji Dan*," Milena said with a smile. "A local tradition. The men, in this case my father, go into the woods the prove their worth by cutting down a tree."

"Prekasno je za tebe," her father said. The others laughed and I gave Milena a puzzled look.

"He said it is too late for you, to prove yourself."

I joined in with the laughter and Milan gave me a playful slap on the shoulder. After dinner, we had wine and danced. Milan took his daughters hand, and I danced with Danica. I moved until I could no more, and excused myself for a cigarette and some cool Winter air. Before long, Milena joined me. "Are you having fun?", she asked.

"I am. I just needed a moment."

"That is okay. Christmas spent with another family can be a bit—much."

"I figured that Christmas in this part of the world would be a large family affair."

"It is for most. However, this is all we have. Unfortunately, war is no stranger to Yugoslavia. And many died in the last one."

"Yes. My father died in that war."

"As did my brother."

Death was something I had always known. Perhaps it was my first true realisation, that my mother was dead and would not return. When my father died, I accepted death is something that can strike anyone at any time; prince, pauper, it matters not. At the end of it all; coin, courage, brains, brawn, nothing can keep it at bay. With this, came a commonality among others who had seen it take their loved ones. As soon as I heard of someone afflicted by death, a deeper connection was born.

"I'm sorry."

"What for? You didn't kill him." She changed the subject with an ease, which told me she had deflected interrogations on her brother and his demise many times before. "I have a gift for you."

"A gift?"

"Yes. It is getting late, and my parents will go to bed soon. I shall give it to you then."

That time came a few hours later. I had retreated to the roof of my shack as the wind had settled. Wrapped in a blanket, and with a cigarette perched within my lips, I watched the clouds dissipate and the stars come into view. The moon was full and lit up my corner of Eden with a metallic sort of glow. Milena's voice called out through the reverie, and caught my attention.

"The way you perch up there is very poetic. Some passer-by might mistake you for a writer of some sort."

"Hurry up and give me my gift," I quipped.

"Patience, Robin. Life moves slow here. You are not in London."

She took her time climbing up onto the shack. When she made it, she sat next to me. We had been here before, but never had we sat so close. "Wrapping paper is hard to come by. So, I wrapped it in a newspaper."

I opened the parcel, inside was a leather-bound book. It was filled to the brim with hand-written notes, lists and illustrations. Clearly, it was the fruit of a significant labour. "It is a book of Montenegrin recipes."

"Did you do the illustrations?", I asked.

"Yes. I suppose we never spoke much of our studies, but my discipline is design."

"It shows," I remarked.

"Now, wherever you are in the world, you can make my food, and know that with each mouthful, Kotor is in you."

"Milena, this is incredible. Thank you."

She smiled. "You are welcome, Robin."

"I—I didn't get you anything."

"Yes, you did. I dreaded coming home. Since my brother died, my parents have not been the same. He was my father's pride and joy, the apple in my mother's eye. Sometimes, when they talk to me, I know that they are picturing him and hearing his voice. And whenever I did come home, the guests we had were always so boring; boring and old. But, you, you are interesting. Sometimes you are too English for me, but you have been a gift this Summer. And for that, we are even."

"Milena."

"Yes."

"May I kiss you?"

"Do not ever ask a woman that question, Robin. If you want to kiss a girl, just kiss her. She will know what you are about to do, and move out of the way if she does not wish to."

And so I kissed her. Initially, she moved away, but laughed at her own joke, and kissed me back. For a few moments our lips were locked, and for a few moments more, our foreheads touched. When we parted, I carried a face of sadness, the cause of which became immediately apparent to Milena. "You have to return to England."

"Yes."

"May I read it before you go?"

"Of course."

Just as I spoke, the heavens opened and rain came pouring down. Hurriedly, we jumped down and fled into the cabin. Our haste was so that we were still dry. I handed the manuscript to her and lay on the bed. She sat at its foot, and began to read.

"Sleep if you must," she whispered. "I shall be here a while."

I tried to dismiss the notion, but was asleep in moments. In the morning, she was still there, asleep next to me. I stirred, and so did she. "Robin," she said, in a sleepy tone. "It is wonderful."

"I'm glad you like it."

"I really do."

We sat up and I looked into her eyes. This time, she kissed me. After a few seconds, her face betrayed the exact same sadness that I had exhibited the night before. "How long will you be in London?"

"I have to get the novel published, and then do some press. And then, my friend is getting married, and I shall be his best man. The short answer is, I don't know. It could be a year."

"Will you return?"

"If you would be so kind as to wait for me."

"Of course."

"Then I shall return."

"Here," she said, removing her necklace and placing it in my hand. "This is something to remember me by."

I tried to protest, but she just waved a hand. "I shall expect it back. You can give it back to me when you return to Kotor."

I left the following week. I bid Milan and Danica a farewell, before taking Milena into my arms one last time. "I do not know when I shall see you again, but rest assured that I shall."

"Goodbye, Robin."

"Goodbye, Milena."

30

I arrived in London on a Friday. It was the midst of January and England had met me with a cold and shivering hug. My journey from Kotor was not as arduous as the one that brought me her way. I travelled by boat to Italy, and then flew from Rome.

"Where'll it be?", said a jolly taxi driver when I arrived at Paddington from the airport.

I thought about it for a moment, and decided that I did not wish to stay in a hotel, and that it was worth checking if my old rooms were still available. "Chelsea."

I arrived at the building, that overlooked the Kings Road and where I had spent many hollow months. In the year of absence, little had changed, except that a few, uglier, buildings had been erected around the neighbourhood. The people still wore the same clothes, and hurried about their days in the same exact manner. The clash between the culture I was in, and the one that I had just left, was obvious.

"Hello, Mr. Willowfall," I called when I entered the building.

"Oh, hello. I haven't seen *you* for some time."

"Yes, I've been away, on the continent."

"How lovely. I believe your friend is in."

"Excuse me?"

"Your friend, I presume you're here to visit him."

"Which friend might this be?"

"Good God, you're a forgetful fellow, aren't you. Why, Robin Fitzwarwick of course, the famous writer."

"Robin Fitzwarwick is upstairs?"

"Have you hit your head, dear boy? Yes, Robin Fitzwarwick is upstairs."

"But—but *I'm* Robin Fitzwarwick."

Mr. Willowfall gave me an odd look and burst into laughter. "What mirth! Yes, I remember now, you must be Richard, *the Cornishman*. Robin told me you were a mighty fine trickster, and would try to pull the wool over my eyes. How naughty you are, playing pranks on the elderly like this."

Immediately, it became apparent to me what was happening. "Excuse me," I said, before making haste up the stairs and bursting through the door. Richard lay prone on the settee, and smoked a thick mist into the room. He sat up when he saw me.

"Fitzy! Do my eyes deceive me? Have the Winter winds that took you from me, brought you back unharmed? Oh, what a day! What a lovely day!"

"Just what the hell are you doing here?", I snapped, weary from the journey.

"That Mr. Willowfall is a gullible old fellow isn't he. I told him that I was you, and he gave me the key. I haven't paid rent in six months!"

"We'll forget about the identity theft, and the fraud, for a little while. But just what exactly are *you* doing here? Don't you have rooms of your own?"

"Yes, but not a place of my own. Old Fucksby lives there, and I live here. He comes by in the day and leaves in the evening. It is a *wonderful* arrangement."

"*Was* a wonderful arrangement. Leave, and clear up this whole mess with Mr. Willowfall on your way out. The old man thinks I'm you."

"It *is* quite funny though, is it not?"

"Okay, fine, it is quite funny. But I need my room

back."

In that moment, Francis came through the door, carrying a bag of groceries. "It's over, Fucksby," Richard cried with a melancholy. "The jig is up. Robin has returned and I am to come back with you."

Francis was happy to see me, and shook my hand eagerly. "It's good to see you again, Robin."

"And you, Francis. I trust you've looked after this one?"

"Of course."

"Do dine with us tonight, Robin," Richard interrupted. "You *must* dine with us."

"Of course. Though it shall have to be tomorrow. I need to square some business with Andress first."

"Will you ask him about—"

"No."

"Is it at least good to see me?"

"Yes, Richard. It's good to see you."

I met with Donald the next day. He had moved to a flat in the Albert Village; known for its debauched artists and impoverished folk singers. Later I would discover that he was in the early stages of a divorce from Cynthia. However, now, I went into our meeting with little else on my mind.

"Robin," he said, unenthusiastically. "Good to see you, old chum. I trust your travels were fruitful."

"Indeed, sir."

He didn't exert himself to correct the formality.

"Yes, well, I suppose we'd better get this book published. Andress House will sort out the usual deal. Do tell me about it."

"Well, it is about an English expat, who finds himself in the Balkans and—"

"Yep, that's fine."

"Is that it?"

"Yes, yes, fine, jolly good. We shall have to converse in more detail at a later point. I have a meeting with Elias Woodbridge at four."

"The American?"

"Yes, we're all so very excited about him. I'm scouting him for Firebrand. It's all very exciting."

"*Firebrand*?", I asked.

"Yes, Firebrand Books! I must have launched it while you were away, with a few of the investors. It's for what we call *dangerous writing*. It's all the rage now - the sort you'd see in The Mollusc; which I have closed down, by the way."

"Right."

"It is very exciting."

"Would it be better for me to write for the new publisher?"

"Oh, no. You are much more suited to Andress House. It's where we house the—*old guard*. We save Firebrand for the younger crop."

"I had no idea that I was the '*old guard*'."

"Oh, yes. And Woodbridge is the new crop."

"I believe Elias Woodbridge is older than me, by quite some margin."

"It's not a matter of age. It is the movement. It's fresh, new, virile. It concerns blood and guts and sex and rock and roll. It's sexy! People like your writing because it is romantic, nostalgic, all that warm stuff. It's safe, reliable, profitable. We can punt out one a year and watch the money trickle in."

Safe, reliant, profitable. The knife in my abdomen, the poison in my gut, the bullet in my head. They say that fame comes fast, and that which lays beyond comes faster still. And so I was forlorn when I left Donald's. My book had been accepted for publishing, but on a *legacy* publisher. I was a Jackdaw with its wings clipped, on the bow of a sinking ship. Commercially, the book would sell poorly, but was received well by critics. In a sense, I preferred the outcome of this novel. My fame had died down, and was replaced with a quiet acceptance; a simple recognition that I, Robin Fitzwarwick, was a writer of solid reputation.

I returned home, and half-suspected Richard to have wriggled his way back in. Alas, he was not there and I showered and dressed in peace. I found Richard and Francis in a booth at the back corner of the pub. "Here he is,"

Richard announced when I was ten feet away.

"Hello, chaps."

"So, did you ask about her?"

"It didn't come up, but they've accepted my book."

"Good going, old boy."

We ordered food and chatted for a while, and fell silent once the food had arrived. I had not quite re-adjusted to English food and quickly became full. Wine followed, as did beer. Soon we were off, looking for a pub. We found one on a corner, and entered. It was misty and filled with smoke. Clawing my way to the bar, as if I were hacking my way through a translucent jungle, I ordered a bottle of wine to spare myself repeated trips.

"This is more like it," Richard declared, surveying the scene of provincial mundanity that lay all about him.

In spite of the fog and smoke, Richard was right. The place had a nice ambience and we drank ourselves merry. Soon enough, Richard spotted a group of women he wished to befriend, and darted into the thickets. He returned five minutes later, accompanied by them. One took an interest in me and sat between myself and Francis.

"Hello. What's your name?"

"Robin F—"

I froze, and could not speak. The remainder of my surname simply would not emerge. I felt as I did in those wicked school days, and flushed a bright red.

"Robin what?"

"Robin F—F—"

She looked at me, perplexed. "Go on, speak up."

"Robin F-F-F-FitzW-W-Warwick."

Another of the women noticed what had happened and raised it to the room. "Dear me, Lucille. You're such a knockout that this one is lost for words. You've frozen him."

All but Francis laughed, and with that my flashback to youth was complete. "Please excuse me," I said, standing, and making my way out of the building. My skin was hot to the touch, and I lit a cigarette with trembling hands.

A stuttered exhale came as I buried my face in my hands. I stood there for a while, until a hand rested on my shoulder. I looked up to see Francis. "Hey, don't worry about it."

"Humiliation, Francis, was never something I took very well."

"And nor should you. It's a horrible thing to happen."

He guided me to some steps and encouraged me to sit. "Robin, may I tell you a joke?"

"A joke?"

"Yes, I think that it could help you to put things in a new context."

"Okay."

"So, there is a caretaker, and he works at the village church. One day, a new vicar comes to the parish, and approaches the caretaker. The vicar asks him what his strengths and weaknesses are. The caretaker replies that he is excellent with people, the parishioners trust him, and respect him. The vicar says 'that's all well and good, what are your weaknesses?' To which, the caretaker says that he is illiterate, he cannot read. The vicar turns to him and says that he cannot have an illiterate caretaker, and fires him, gives him the sack on the spot. And so, the caretaker leaves with his head hanging low. And he says to himself 'you know, I have not touched a cigarette for ten years, but this is just about the worst day of my life and I need a smoke'. However, he finds that there is no longer a tobacconist in the village, nor is there one in the next village over. So, he takes his savings, and purchases a shop, opens a tobacconist, and it becomes a great success. He then opens a second tobacconist in the next town over, and two more after that. Then, one day, he owns a handful of shops, and is fabulously wealthy. One day, he goes to a bank in order to cash a cheque, and the bank teller says to him 'read this, and sign'. The caretaker replies than he cannot do that, because he cannot read. The bank teller is shocked, and says to him, 'you cannot read? You made all of this money, and you cannot read?' The caretaker confirms this, and the teller replies 'imagine where you'd be if you could read'. The caretaker replies 'I know where I'd be. I'd be caretaker of the village church."

I scoffed at the punchline. Francis continued. "You see, if we allow our weaknesses to define us, we will never succeed. Always lead with what makes you strong. So what, you stammered in front of a pretty lady, you know what you've also done? Written books, how many people can say that? You don't need to speak when you write in the way that you do."

"You know, Francis. I think you are the wisest person I know."

"Just give it time."

"Where'd you hear that joke?"

Francis smiled and put a hand on my shoulder. "It's an old story, by Maugham."

31

I met with Monty on the eve of his wedding. It was our third meeting since I had returned, and the first in which anything seemed to be the matter. "What bothers you, Monty?", I asked, once two bottles of wine had softened us.

"I don't know if I can go through with this."

"With the wedding?"

He nodded; breaking down and hiding himself as if it were the first time that he had admitted such doubts.

"Do you doubt how you feel?"

"Not at all."

"Then what is it?"

His words lingered, on the tip of his tongue, as he searched for the correct verbiage. "I've never known another woman," he said after a while. "When I marry her, that's it. She'll be all I ever know."

"That's not true? Surely not. What about all of the Italian women you'd meet on your family trips? Or when you and the others would sneak out of dorms, and head into town?"

"The advent of a teenage mind."

"Oh."

"You do realise that everyone at school was lying about their conquests, right?"

"I assumed most were."

"Everyone was, Robin. You were the only honest man there, the only one who didn't have high tales about chasing women——and catching them. We were fourteen, fifteen, sixteen. Of course it was all a myth."

"Now that you say it, of course it was."

He grumbled and we fell silent while I considered what to say next. "So, what? What does it matter that you never slept with a harem of women, has it not occurred to you that this is a good thing?"

"What if I have regrets?"

"Let me tell you about regrets. Did I ever tell you about how I chose Cynthia over Francine?"

"Go on."

"I tossed a coin. That is how I decided."

"Did you really?"

"Yes."

He laughed. Subtly at first, and then haughtily. "You are a fool. You really are an imbecile. But I appreciate it, all I have to do when I feel a fool is listen to you tell me about your decision-making."

"Yes, I know. Don't join the club. You know, I'll never forget what you said to me on that boat, Monty. About the magic of love; the language that the two of you create, the security, the comfort, the little routines and idiosyncrasies, the laughter. I want that, the proper way. You have it, and tomorrow it becomes an adventure, for life. You feel nervous and that's okay. You ask yourself if you are making the right decision and that's okay too. But let me tell you this, you are making the right decision. You may spend the rest of your days occasionally doubting that, but you are. When we stood there on the bow of that boat, and you'd told me of love, and love without deception, and I distinctly recall thinking '*I want what Monty has*'."

I stiffened and was lost in thought for a moment. He snapped out of it and faced me. "Thank you, Robin.

You've talked some sense into me."

"Anytime, Monty."

An hour later we parted, and I wandered home in the dark, seduced by a few glasses of wine. The next day, I awoke and put on my finest suit. It was the day of the wedding and I called a cab that took me to Hampstead Heath, where the two were to wed at a large Anglican church. I stood at the altar, with Monty by my side and few of his college friends there too. The church began to fill with friends and family, as I scanned the room for familiar faces. I saw some Old Carthusians, and eventually Richard. He amused himself by loudly gaining my attention, and that of everyone else in the church, before giving me the finger, much to the chagrin of Monty's grandmother, who sat next to him.

An organ began to play as the bride's entourage filtered in. First, her mother, and close family. Then, her bridesmaids. I watched them intently, until one stood out. She, like Francine, had ear-length and light brown hair, eyes that flickered and danced, a slightly crooked smile and a mole above the right side of her lip. '*Perfectly imperfect*' was my first impression. She did not look my way.

Eventually, the bride entered as the room stood. I turned to Monty to see a smile on his lips, and in his eyes. He looked truly smitten, and I felt satisfied in my words of encouragement. The rest of the ceremony went off without issue. They held hands, pledged their vows, and kissed with resolute fervour. The room cheered, and just like that, it was over. I followed the newlyweds outside, and joined the myriad of suits, and hats, and dresses outside. I shook Monty's hand, for the last time as a bachelor, and then he was gone. I found Richard and made my way over to him. "Did you have to do that in the middle of a church?"

"In that moment, yes. It was like a possession; I was a mere passenger to my actions. You have to understand these things, Robin, I am at the mercy of my own whims."

"Of course you are. Where's Francis?"

"He's around here somewhere."

I looked past Richard, and saw her again, standing a few dozen feet away. She was in conversation with the bride's mother, but seemed uninvested, and looked around the church yard. I could not take my eyes away from her, but was forced to when she shot a glance in my direction, Swiftly, I looked away, and pretended to examine the church spire. When I looked back over, she was still staring and we locked eyes for a moment or two. She laughed, perhaps knowing that she had me there and then. Soon enough, we were all ushered down the road and into the banquet hall, where an opulent display of late-stage decency had been assembled. We were greeted with champagne, and informed of an open bar.

"This is absolutely marvellous!" Richard exclaimed, giddy at the prospect of free alcohol. "I've fallen from the horse, Fitzy. I'm back on the gin and tea. Do tell Monty I said my thanks."

"I don't know if they have hot water."

"Oh, don't you worry about that, old boy. I have a trick up my sleeve."

"Do I want to know?"

"Oh, you shall."

"Right. Anyway, I must go and prepare."

"Prepare?"

"For my speech."

I seconded myself to a lavatory and readied myself in the mirror. My formula was simple; in, humorous story about school, compliments to Vera, toast, and out. The speech seemed to have gone well. I shared a story of Monty being caught trying to steal the school flag, and of an unfortunate cricketing injury involving a friend of ours, who'd subsequently earn the name of *Lack-a-bollock Lawrence*. My jokes earned laughs, and my praises, blushes. Lastly, I told the story of Monty and I on the boat into Turkey, how in attempting to talk me into love, he talked himself into marriage.

"—I wanted to know the secret to a long and happy marriage, but I could not ask my parents. So, I asked an uncle, but he didn't know. And so, I trawled London, seeking out a happy, married couple. At last, I found one, preparing to board a boat to America."

Laughs rung out around the room, and I was happy that the joke had worked.

"And they told me that the secret to a long and happy marriage is three-fold; to always communicate, to always laugh, and to always be physically attracted to one another. So, if you will join me in raising your glasses. Here's to words, to laughter, and to staying beautiful. To the bride and groom!"

"To the bride and groom!", they called back.

All rose from their seats as the festivities began in earnest. Soon the floor was filled with dancing, and the bar bustled with life. I made my way over to get myself a drink, when a clearing emerged, and I saw a familiar face.

"Francis?", I said, approaching the bar.

"Hello, Robin. Are you enjoying the wedding?"

"Why are you behind the bar?"

"Richard got me a job at the wedding. It's good, right?"

"No. I'll have a word with him."

"Okay, Robin. Can I get you anything in the meantime?"

I paused for a moment, and looked at the busy bar next to me. "Red."

"Of course. Though I am only allowed to serve Richard, I shall get that for you."

"Thanks, Francis."

Richard called out from the dance floor. "Fucksby! I'll take a gin and tea."

"Yes, sir."

I paced toward Richard as he danced alone. "What are you doing? Let him enjoy the wedding, he's Monty's friend too."

Richard meditated on what I had said. "Well, who's going to make my gin and tea?"

"I don't care who, let him enjoy the party."

Richard could tell that I was serious, and gestured to Francis that he should come over. He trotted around the bar, and met us on the floor. "You're relieved for the evening, old boy. Go and have fun."

"Really?"

"Yes. But I shall expect a gin and tea once we return home."

"Of course!"

I nodded at Richard, satisfied by the agreement. "Oh," Francis said. "I don't have a jacket."

"Here," I said, removing mine. "Take it. I'm hot anyway."

"Thank you."

Francis put on the jacket, that was a few sizes too big, and followed Richard into the mist of moving bodies. I turned to see Monty moving decisively towards me; a bottle of whiskey in one hand, and two glasses in the other. "Follow me," he said.

We found ourselves in a billiards room, with dim lighting and red-leather arm chairs. I sat as Monty poured two glasses and handed me one. We tapped our drinks and took an exploratory sip.

"Did you have to tell the cricket story?"

"It's funny."

"I suppose it is. Lawrence is here you know, livid. I'd avoid him if I were you."

"Well, he shouldn't have told us."

"Mm," Monty said, examining his ring.

"Heavy?", I asked.

"You'll know some day."

"Perhaps."

"You spoke about when we were on that boat, heading into Istanbul."

"I did."

"Remember what I said? About love and whatnot?"

"I do."

"I wasn't talking to you when I said all that, I was talking to myself. The truth is, I love Vera. I always have and always will. But I was still terrified. I know that I want to spend the rest of my life with her, just as one wishes to swim in a cool lagoon on a hot

Summers' day. Yet, I felt I was standing on a cliff's edge. The lagoon is just beneath me, but I must throw myself off the cliff, knowing not how shallow the water is. When I spoke to you on that boat, I was preparing myself to jump, but I faltered. And when you came to me last night, you pushed me when I refused to jump. For that, I will always be grateful for you, Robin. Vera is too, she just doesn't know it."

"I want to swim in a cool lagoon too."

"You'll find one, Robin. Just wait for a hot day. Anyway, I just wanted to say thank you."

We finished our drinks and headed back into the ceremony. Richard danced, with a clear radius formed around him by those who wanted no part of it. Francis had let himself loose, and laughed with his dearest friend. I showed myself outside and lit a smoke. It was there that I saw her again. As I have mentioned before, Whiskey was never something I handled well. With it, came the discarding of all filters and proportions. Her and I caught eyes once more and I decided to approach.

"You know," I said. "I hear that it is something of a tradition for the best man and maid of honour to become acquainted."

When she spoke back, the first thing I noticed was that she was an American. Her voice was light, breezy and crisp. At points it gave way, and had a vulnerability to it.

"Are you trying to flirt with me?"

"I'm not sure."

"Well, just so you know. I'm not the maid of honour, just a cousin of the bride. The maid of honour is her sister——who is fifteen."

"Ah."

"So maybe you should become acquainted with her?"

"I'd rather not."

She giggled, extending a hand. "I'm Elaine."

"Robin," I said, taking it.

"I know who you are."

"Oh?"

"You addressed the entire room, about thirty minutes ago?"

"Yes, that was me."

"Also, Vera mentioned you."

"She did?"

"Yeah, that you're a writer. And something about you being in Yugoslavia, to write a book?"

"Yes."

"That's exciting."

"It hasn't come out yet, but yes."

"Is it your first?"

"Fourth."

"Oh, that's cool."

"Cool?"

"It's a word people say back home."

We spoke some more, and she told me that was an actress, or rather that she wished to be. She was from Los Angeles and her surname was Mills. Her father was some big producer, and could make her a star, but all she wanted was the theatre.

"Is that why you are in London?" I asked.

"Yes and no. It's either London or New York. I'm just here for the wedding, but I think I shall stay for a while longer and look at the West End."

"You know, I always wanted to write a play."

"Is that so?", she asked.

"Yes."

"Well, if you ever do. Write a part for me."

"In London or in New York?"

Only her eyes answered, in a tongue that I instinctively understood. And they said words to the effect of '*ask me*'. We went back inside and shared a drink, and then a dance.

Before long, we had spent some two hours in each other's company, mocking partygoers from afar, and emptying my pack of cigarettes.

"Who are those two?" Elaine asked, pointing at two familiar figures, still dancing with possession.

"I am the Duke, Fucksby!", Richard cried with animated laughter. "I am the Duke, and you are my buxom Duchess!"

"Richard, and Francis. Friends from college."

"What's wrong with them?"

"Eachother, I suppose."

"Are they fools?"

"One is."

"Well, which one is the fool, and which one is the genius?", she asked.

Just as she spoke, Richard's movements caused an ice cube to jump out of his drink and land on the floor, which he promptly slipped on and fell, crashing, into the laminate ground. "He's the fool."

The party was winding down as we smoked the last of my cigarettes. Men walked alongside their wives, draping their jackets over cold shoulders. The young played out their last chances of company for the night, while Monty stood at the door, bidding farewell to friends and family.

"It is getting late, Robin. The party seems to be over, and I must retire for the night, but I hope I shall see you again."

"As do I."

"Goodnight."

"Goodnight."

She returned to the building, and I lingered to watch the early leavers make their way home. I heard footsteps on gravel, and turned to see Vera walking towards me. I smiled and anticipated what she would say. "I cannot help but feel that today's success is something of your doing," she said.

"Is that so?"

"Yes. Monty has been so distant lately, but he met with you last night and today was his usual self. I don't know what was said, and I don't want to know. I just wanted to say thank you."

"You're welcome, Vera."

She gave me an odd sort of bow, before turning

away. She took a single step, but caught herself and swivelled to face me once again. "Oh, there was one more thing. Be careful."

"Be careful?"

"Around Elaine. She's a loveable little thing, but she will break you if you let her. Believe me when I say that there's a trail of bodies. Just don't get too close."

But I didn't listen. Before I could say anything, she was gone. I stood there, now completely alone. Everyone was either still in the building, or had left entirely. Once more the gravel made approaching noises, as a car drove past me and towards the exit. Elaine sat in the back seat and we caught eyes one last time, as she drove into the darkness, and out of sight.

32

When I was a boy, my father would tell me stories of Dorset, and the Summers he would spend there. As we'd sit, idly, in his study; he with whiskey and I with milk, he would speak so fondly of its Jurassic hills and cheap arcades. He would go down on the train from London, and watch England as it floated on by; much as I have done with the corners of this earth that I have come to leave some part of myself in. The journey, in his words, was as important as the destination. He, and his father would build castles in the sand, walk the proms and arcades, and hear the bands play long into the crisp Summer night.

He was also in Dorset when he wrote what would become his last letter to me; written while he prepared for passage to Normandy, in the final push of the war. He had been evacuated at Dunkirk, and spent some time in North Africa, before being reassigned to Europe. There, as you know, he breathed his last. When he wrote to me, in a letter that I still possess, he mentioned that Dorset had suddenly meant nothing to him; how the promenades that once filled him with such wonderment, gave way to a sort of melancholic disgust. He too had considered himself in possession of a piece of Eden.

Eden, it would seem, is ephemeral, and I had not thought of Kotor for some time. That land of Rakija and smiling Slavs, where I had been so happy and tranquil, had all of a sudden become backwards and jarring. The mere thought of a swim in the Adriatic, or a stroll in the old town, gave me a melancholic disgust of my own.

Perhaps London just has that effect on the senses. Perhaps London's seduction is one that drags its victim, kicking and screaming, into a moving tide. With hard-fought gasps of air the only available respite. So caught up was I in the bustle of the city, the constant noise, and the publishing of my novel, that August had come; and I had been away from Milena for seven months. I had not told my friends about her. Francis had read the manuscript, but not asked of its veracity. Monty had been too busy with wedding preparations, and Richard would not have thought to ask.

I telephoned Donald, and was met with the voice of an assistant. Donald's loss of interest in me as a writer was confirmed when, later that day, I received a telegram from him which informed me that he was no longer involved with the running of Andress House, and that I was to contact someone else. I did, and received a call, much to my surprise, from Matheson.

"Robin," he said, when we met for lunch in the centre of town. "How good it is to see you again, it's been a while."

"So, you work for Donald now?"

"Indeed, it *is* a changing landscape."

"I see. It would appear that we've both been relegated to the Andress House hinterland."

"Regrettably so, the ghosts of Charterhouse weep at our fate. Firebrand is where it's all at now."

"Do you still hear from Rawlinson?"

"You mean his lady?"

"I guess."

"No. That all went up in smoke, which is why I am in London."

"Right. Shall we discuss the book then?"

"Of course. I've been reading it this week, it's good. I just have one little nit-pick."

"Oh?"

"The conversations, with the local girl, do you see them to be wholly necessary?"

"What do you mean?"

"Well, it hasn't gone down too well with the editors. It's not *classic Fitzwarwick*, we want to hear streams of consciousness, the hero's point of view. If you'll pardon the phrasing, it's not *arrogant* enough."

"The novel is about the place."

"But should it be? The location is grand sure, and you make it sound so pretty, but you need to be at the centre of it, not some Balkan backwater."

"Do you suggest that I re-write the whole thing?"

"I'm afraid so, that is if you want to see it published of course. I tried to stand in your corner, Robin, but the editors insisted and I was outnumbered. We've established something of a democracy, in lieu of Donald's absolute monarchy. '*Robin Fitzwarwick*', I said, over and over, '*is an artist. And an artist needs space*'. But they wouldn't listen. Alter those conversations, place yourself back at the centre, and we'll have something ready for the general audience."

'*The general audience*', I thought to myself. Three more words. Knife, poison, bullet. "What does Donald think of this?"

"He doesn't."

Reluctantly, I accepted and bid Matheson a farewell. It felt as if, once I had arrived back in England, all had conspired to keep me from returning; including my own instincts and desires. And so, page by page and word by word, I removed Milena from the world that she had built, and as if her very essence lived within my words, as they were changed and altered, she occupied less of my mind with each passing day.

For two weeks, I worked on the re-write, cutting parts and inserting sections set before and after the voyage to Kotor. Matheson seemed happy and accepted my changes. As has already been said, the critics seemed to like it, but it sold poorly, and I was not instructed to tour the novel extensively. I gave a few guest lectures, and one or two interviews. Once more, my birthday came and went, and now I was twenty-five. I was intolerably lonely, and sought the comfort of friends. Monty was still on his honeymoon and would not return until the year's end.

One night in early September, I met with Richard and Francis, in that King's Road pub we had come to know so well. They were already there once I arrived. Richard seemed happy, as they had hot water in and he drank a gin and tea. Francis was his typical self and greeted me with warmth.

"I say," Richard enquired, ten minutes after my arrival. "Aren't you supposed to be abroad right now?"

"Not quite. I stayed behind as there were complications with the novel, but that's all been cleared up now."

"So you are free to return?"

"I suppose so."

"Well you are still here, so you must wish to stay."

"That, I still do not know."

"Perhaps it is a sign that you need," Francis interjected.

"A sign?"

"Yes. Something that tells you where to go, what to do. I mean something, not a person, a voice of reason. Something completely and explicitly irrational."

"What complete rot!" Richard thumped. "You do not need a sign, like some sort of occultist, summoning demons and awaiting a breath on his neck. Stay! Stay in London with dear Fucksby and I. We have such fun together."

Richard continued to speak, but I did not listen. As I am one to do, I scanned my surroundings; and as a result of sitting by the window, my scan covered the street outside, and fell upon a restaurant across the street. Also sat in the window, was Elaine. She stared vacantly up at the sky, and chewed morosely on her food. In this moment, a rotoscope in my mind roared into life, and showed me images committed to memory of our dancing at the wedding. I saw her dimples and moles, her unassuming, yet firm beauty. I dared not imagine days to come, and yet the memories of days gone by were enough to stir that thing in me that only arises when profoundly inspired to act.

"If you gentlemen will excuse me," I said, standing and putting some cash on the table. "There is a sign across the street, with whom I must speak."

"Oh, I see," Richard groaned, following my gaze.

Francis noticed as well, and turned to me with a smile. "Well, what are you waiting for, Robin? Go."

"Don't encourage him, Fucksby. He is to stay with us an—"

I was gone before Richard could finish. I crossed the street with a purpose, my eyes fixed upon her. As I approached the building, her eyes fell onto me and widened. She smiled and waved, which I reciprocated. She gestured for me to join her and I did. For a few moments, we just sat there in silence. We were both happy to be in each other's company. She spoke first. "I asked Vera about you, she said that you were to be returning to—wherever it was."

"Montenegro."

"You've no idea how happy I am to see you, Robin."

"I was held-up with the publishers, but I am free to return now."

"And will you?"

"No, I don't think so. Why are you still here? I figured you'd be back in America by now."

"I figured I'd try my hand at getting some work on the West End."

"And have you?"

"No. There are no roles for Americans, can you believe that? And besides, I can't get the English cadence down."

"How about New York?"

"Perhaps, but I think I shall stay here until I completely give up on the West End. London is something else. You all talk so funny."

"Aren't you used to how we speak by now?"

"Not you."
We spoke some more in the restaurant as an electric tension formed all around us. With each exchange, she seemed to grow closer. Soon enough, we left and embarked on a jaunt around the city. From Chelsea, we meandered through the great halls of power, and into Soho; then into Holborn, Bishopsgate, and The City. By 11pm, we had stretched from west to east, circled around, and found ourselves drinking gin in a tavern just off the Holborn viaduct. "You grew up here, right?", she asked, once we were onto our second glasses of gin.

"Not here."

"But London?"

"Yes. I lived in Bayswater until I was thirteen."

"Why did you leave?"

I told her.

"You're not missing out on a father."

"Oh?"

"Yeah, they're overrated."

"I fear that I am missing out. Mine happened to have been a good man, least as I recall."

"Mine is a piece of dirt. Ever since he took over the studio, everybody wants to tell me how wonderful he is, but they're just looking for a handout. Everyone in Los Angeles is looking for a handout. I know the truth. I know he betrayed my mother, left her for a younger woman."

"And what happened to your mother?"

"She died two years ago, they say it was an accident, but I know she took her own life. She was a dancer, the prettiest thing you ever saw, from somewhere out in the Mid-West, I can't quite recall. She met my dad, and he did what he always does to the teenage girls he meets; offers them everything. Says he can make them *America's Girl.* My mother just managed to hang on for the ride, but it got her in the end. Soon enough he got bored of her, but not before they had me, and moved along. Heck, he probably did when they were together, how many studio meetings end at 3am, I wonder."

"I'm sorry."

"It's okay. I don't like to talk about this stuff, but I hear about your folks and feel like I can, you know?"

"Pain can bring people together."

"Yes, it can."

We smiled at each other in silence, as the hum of the tavern faded away, and it was as if only she and I were sat here. "You have beautiful eyes," I declared, without warning.

"Well I think that you are a very flirtatious man."

"You do?"

"I do."

"Perhaps that's just your influence."

"I don't see how it could be. You approached me, remember?"

"Somehow I feel, Elaine, that you won't let me forget that."

She smiled behind the glass that was raised to her lips. "Perhaps I won't."

"If I am to be reduced to my flirtations, then what shall you be reduced to? Your beauty?"

"You're flirting again."

"Perhaps I am. And yet you are here, humouring my whims. So, what does that make you?"

"You tell me."

"Someone who appreciates good writing. Or at least good writers."

"Such as yourself?", she asked, wagging a finger at the bar to request more drinks.

"Perhaps," I said.

"You'll never know."

"I can only presume."

"And what do you presume?"

"Very little. I suppose I could begin by saying that you're not utterly repulsed."

"You are far too humble in your assumptions."

"Am I? Would you dare correct me?"

"That shall," she said, with a wink. "Remain a mystery."

"You sure do know how to bring a man to his knees."

"A lifetime of experience. Though which men, I couldn't say."

"Any man. Take your pick."

"It would seem that I have. Though, I humbly give you authority to choose for me."

"And I return to you your freedom of will."

She giggled, and threw down the drink that had just arrived, as her hair swished without effort, and without a single follicle landing out of place. "Then I shall say that it is late, and I am tired."

"Is our evening over?", I asked, doing the same.

She caught my eye and held it, squeezing out every second that passed. "Not just yet."

We stepped outside and hailed a cab. "To the Papal Hotel in Chelsea, please," Elaine said to the driver. '*The Papal Hotel*', I thought to myself, as I wondered how long it had been. It had been six years since I was there with Cynthia. I missed her on occasion, but took solace in knowing that our relationship had indeed given me something. It had prepared me for love, and all other things that fall just short, such as this night.

We arrived and lingered outside a while to smoke a cigarette. Elaine looked around with ease, making note of passers-by. "Hey," she said with a pointed look. "Aren't those your friends over there?"

I followed her gaze to see Francis, trudging along, with a barely conscious Richard hanging off of his shoulder.

"Yes."

"Shall we say hello?"

"No. They've got enough going on, I shall see them soon."

"Well, okay. Are you ready?"

"I am."

"Okay, I will go up first, wait a few minutes and join me. I'm on the seventh floor, room 59."

And so, I waited. And while I waited, I thought of Vera's warning. A few minutes passed, and while my head was still full of foreboding, my feet followed my heart and before long, I was outside of her door.

Suffice it to say that Elaine became the third soul that I conjoined to my own. Though when we made love, there wasn't passion. Her neck craned to the left, and her eyes did not meet mine. Yet, I felt an immeasurable gravity around her, and knew then that I was wrapped around her finger. And so began something of a masochistic affair, one that would carry me up to heaven, and toss me down to hell. The next morning, we had coffee and pastries delivered to the room, where we ate without dressing, smoked without care and made love again.

In the afternoon, I left the Papal Hotel, on the understanding that I would be seeing Elaine soon, and soon again after that. I was racked with guilt and shame, and resolved to write Milena a letter, which I did, but did not possess the courage to send. Quietly, and with a ruthless indifference, I moved on from Milena. That evening, in my flat, I set fire to the letter. Fire decimated the paper quickly, and before it reached my fingertips, I opened the window and let the wind take what was left.

> "*I'm sorry,*" I whispered to myself, as the ashes fluttered in the wind. "*I hope that you do not wait too long*."

I would never speak to Milena again, though I would see her again, from afar, some twenty years later. Though by then, she and I would be greatly different people.

33

"*——and so, it would seem that my stay in paradise had come to an end. England called, and I had answered. And as I boarded the boat, and gave my piece of Eden a solemn farewell with my eyes alone, I knew that I would never return, and should never return. Just as Adam could never crawl backwards, and see Eden again, for in his heart of hearts, he knew he had betrayed it, I would never again swim in the Adriatic.*"

I finished speaking as the scattered applause gradually widened into an ovation. There were thirty faces in the room; it was little compared to readings of my prior work, yet it was more dedicated. I scanned the room, and saw faces I knew at the back of it. Elaine was there, as was Richard, Francis, Monty, and Vera. Of all the clapping hands, and cheered cries; theirs were the loudest.

For a while, I signed copies of the book for those who attended. I never liked the cover that Andress House gave to the novel, it told me that they did not care all that much. Matheson was there too, he had indeed fought in my corner, and his design was far more suited; yet he was the arms and legs of Andress House, not its lips. Once I had signed the last book, and bid the last farewell, I sauntered over to the group, who had each taken seats but rose to greet me.

"Looks like no one else from the publisher came

along," I said, giving Matheson a polite nod from across the room that he returned.

"Ah," Richard dismissed, with a wave. "Forget about them. You were most excellent, marvellous. Superlative!"

"You read so beautifully," Elaine said, kissing my cheek.

"Well done, Robin," Francis said with a polite nod.

"Thank you, all."

"Right," said Richard, with a clap of his hands. "Enough of this dilly-dally. Let us go and get merry."

"Sounds good to me."

We moved along, and by ten, were sat in the third bar of the evening.

But I was not celebratory. Nor was I indignant toward Donald and the Press. I sat there at the table, with noise all about me, and all of the friends I had left, trying desperately and fruitlessly to fix my broken heart. Though I would forbid myself from admitting it then, I would awake the next day with a sinking realisation, that my literary career - or at least his phase of it - was gone, and I was no longer Donald's project.

Suddenly, the room became frozen still, as I glanced out of the window and saw a vagrant in the street. I, like many others, whether or not they will admit it, do not often notice such people. They are the great unseen, the great unloved. Though this one was different, and I could have sworn that it was Balloch. "Excuse me," I said to Elaine before darting out of the pub. The vagrant was crossing the street, his clothes shabby and hair unkempt. He was Balloch's height and build, walked like him, hunched over like him.

"Bill!" I called, to no response. "Bill!"

I ran to follow, but a small parade of cars and buses blocked my path, and when they were gone, so was he. I just stood there for a moment or two, so convinced that I had seen him, my old friend, without whom I felt so lost, that his not seeing me had brought a great pain. I returned to the group, sullen and sour. "Are you okay?" Elaine asked, with a gentle hand on my shoulder.

"Yes, fine. I just thought I saw someone."

"Our Robin is always seeing things," Richard chipped. "It must be something to do with the fact that he's a writer. I call them his *phantoms of creation*. You'll be sitting with him, all relaxed and comfortable, then all of a sudden, the old boy will dart up and run away. Chasing phantoms——It really is quite beautiful."

"How are the stocks, Richard?" Monty asked.

"It is entirely possible that I have bankrupted the country."

"Right," I said. "Drinks, anyone? I'll get a round in."

"I'll give you a hand," said Vera. We approached the bar and ordered for the room.

"Three glasses of merlot, a whiskey and water, gin and tonic, and——a gin and tea."

"Gin and tea?", asked a flustered bartender.

"Yes."

"It's not for that pillock mate of yours, is it? Do let him know that hot water don't come cheap."

"I shall."

I waited with Vera, while the water was heated by the bartender, who had graduated from fluster to anger. "So," she said, with a sharp stop. "You did not listen to my warning."

"I suppose not."

She sighed. "You are not the first, you know. And you won't be the last."

I looked back over to the table to see Elaine locked into a conversation with Richard. In that moment, I wish I could have seen what I see now, and can only see in hindsight. The way that she spoke to Richard; the way her eyes moved, the way she laughed, licked her lips, was no different to how she was with me; her supposed lover. In my folly, I was too captured by the whole affair to notice it. I was a man of mid-twenties, which is by no means infantile, I just did not, and could not, see it.

The night drew to an end, and a car came to collect the newlyweds. I got into a taxi with Elaine, and Richard, and Francis. We all got out at my building, and I bade my friends a good night. Elaine and I found ourselves in bed, talking on the pillow. "Robin?", she asked after some silence.

"Yes."

"Do you still want to write a play? I think it would be such fun, you can write it, and I can be the star!"

"Oh, I see."

"What?"

"It's about *you* being the star of a show."

"Oh, Robin, don't be an ass! Okay, yes, but, also you. Yes, I need the starring role, but you need the rebirth. You saw the crowd tonight, sure they cared, sure they think you're just the greatest, but you could fit all of them into a train car. It makes sense, no? I mean, we are something of an artistic power couple; the writer and the actress. Surely it is only a matter of time before we became collaborators, as well as lovers. And America, Robin! You think you know stardom, just wait until you make it in America!"

"Lovers?"

She giggled and gave my shoulder a little nibble.

"Perhaps."

"You love me?"

"Well, heck, Robin. At least write me a play first, before we start using such big words."

And so I did. For the next month, I wrote with that fury I had come to know so well. At first I struggled for subject matter, until a pub that I had come to frequent closed its doors. I was there on the last night, and spoke to its clientele. They felt such a misery at the prospect, as if it were the end of their own lives, and their sadness brought me words. I was, for all purposes, a part-time writer, in that I spent most of the year searching, without fruit, for inspiration. And when I found it, no force on earth could stand in my way.

"New York?!" Richard exclaimed when I told him,

some two months later. "Why would you *dare* go to such a place? It's—it's——not here."

"It was Elaine's father's idea. He agreed to fund production of my play, on the condition that we housed it in America. He owns a theatre in Manhattan."

"You wrote a play?"

"Yes, Richard. It is just about the only thing I've spoken about in the last few months."

"Oh."

"I recall," said Francis. "The one about the bar."

"Yes. Thank you, Francis."

"Fucksby, my dear boy," Richard called, despite the fact that Francis was only a few feet away. "Could you prepare me a drink?"

"Of course."

Richard waited until Francis had left the room, before turning to me with a soft expression, somewhere between a feeling of mourning and guilt. "Robin, may I ask you a question?"

"Sure."

"Do you think I'm too harsh on the old boy?"

"A bit."

"You know, Robin. I think I am coming to a rather horrid realisation."

"Oh?"

"That I'm not a very nice man, that I'm not good to my friends."

"You could be better."

He pondered for a moment. "Robin, I am ever so sorry. I've been ever so selfish all of these years; consumed by drink, my own amusement came above all else. I'm such a prick!"

"It's okay, Richard. Truth be told, you always amused me."

"Well, at least there's that. You *did* humour me. You and Fucksby both."

I just smiled, happy to see my friend come to an epiphany. "You know, Robin. I always respected you, I know I've been such an oaf, but it never really occurred to me before how difficult things were for you. I mean, my parents are no saints, but I don't know what I'd do without them. It's the same with the old boy, it has only just become apparent, that my two dearest friends in the world are orphans."

"Thank you, Richard. I appreciate that."

"Do you think I should let him go?"

"Francis?"

"Yes. Shall I let him go? Let him follow his own pursuits? He does seem to mention the Royal Horticultural Society quite a lot."

"Honestly, Richard; even if you did let him go, he wouldn't leave your side."

Francis returned with drinks, he laid them down and took a seat, as Richard looked at him with warmth. "Here you go, Richard."

"Thank you——Francis."

We arrived in New York in the dawning days of 1959, a year since I had left Montenegro, and two since my great foreign voyages had begun. Elaine's passage into the country was simple, and without interruption. I faced a brief interrogation at the border.

"Are you a Communist?", asked an officer in the airport, once I had handed him my passport.

"No."

"Okay. Welcome to America."

The play, despite my wanting desire to even produce it, and my forced hand, was a success. Elaine's father had made enough arrangements to ensure that the process was smooth. By the time we arrived at the *Mills Theatre* in the Upper East Side, the cast of five had been filled out by jobbing thespians. Though I had no role in the casting, and harboured some resentment for that, the casting had been done perfectly; as if each actor was not an actor, but the character. It was such that I viewed them, as I directed their utterances, and moulded them into the figures in my mind. They all looked exactly how I had imagined them. The leading role, of course, had been reserved for Elaine, and she was the sole point of weakness in the ensemble.

Two months passed, and the play premiered on a Saturday evening in March. After which, I received a standing ovation and a myriad of compliments and well-wishes. To them, I was so new, and so fresh, that my casting off by Donald mattered not. The name *Andress*, in this land, meant as much as '*Smith*' or '*Jones*'. It was an anonymity. News of my success did not reach England, but the American press was very kind. A week later, the last performance was given, at which Walter was present. He came to me after the performance.

"Say, kid. That was a fine play, a very fine play indeed."

"Thank you, sir."

"I wasn't sure what to make of you. In fact, I didn't know who you were until Elaine became so intertwined with you. But, I read some of your stuff, and think it's mighty swell."

"Yes, well. I'm afraid to say that England appears to have turned me away."

"Well, America would not exist if it wasn't for the exiles of England. That's actually what I wanted to see you about. The fact is, Elaine is going to be a star. I will make sure of that, but she is so dead-set on stage acting. What stars do you know from the stage?"

"Laurence Olivier."

"Okay, in England perhaps. But not here, no. If you want to be a star here, you'd better get yourself into a movie or on television. Listen, kid. Elaine is mighty fond of you. And if what you say about your flickering success in England, then I think I have a solution that benefits us both nicely."

"Is that so?"

"How would you like a job? People in your shoes would kill to work in Hollywood, and here I am, handing it to you on a silver platter. You'd love Los Angeles, it's always warm, the people are beautiful, and business is booming."

"You want to hire me?"

"I want you to write movies for me, for Elaine really. I'll let you ponder it. Here, take my card."

He left the room, while I sat in silence, and thought about it. Truth be told, I had agreed to the proposition as soon as it was offered, but I recalled Balloch's lessons in the Game. I waited; and dined with him the next day, where I accepted his offer.

Once more, I found myself in a position of passage. Life had a habit of snatching some things away from me, and of handing me other things. I wrote home to England, to inform all who cared that I intended to stay in America. I received letters back, wishing me well, and one from Richard, complaining of an incessant stomach ache. I felt content in my decision, and yet I was young. So little did I know then, that I had made a decision of irrefutable lunacy.

Even then I asked myself what exactly it was that I saw in Elaine. It could not have been loneliness, for there was a love - true, and honest, and pure - that waited for me in Kotor; nor was it companionship, for I'd still return home on some days to find that Richard had deceived Mr. Wilowfall and broken into my rooms. It was not *stimulation*, for I never quite had a libido of note or ill-repute; it was not conversation, because we never seemed to stray from either small talk or meandering flirtation, that truly meant nothing. I don't recall a single conversation we had that possessed more depth than a puddle. When I looked within myself, and the parts of me that concerned her, all I could find that drew me deeper was her simple, arresting beauty. Alas it was her beauty that caught me, and reeled me wriggling from the water. It was beauty that made me betray a promise, beauty that made me sightless and dim, and beauty that led me, blindfolded and expectant, along the hall and into the gallows.

PART THREE: A TEPID VIEW FROM THE PLATEAU

34

On occasion, I will ask myself what could have been if I stuck with various lovers from the past, with whom my affections were intense albeit brief. What if Cynthia had accepted my proposition to run away, or if Adeline had. It was through dreams - both of the day and night - that these outcomes were revealed to me. If Cynthia and I had stayed in Avignon, I would have sacrificed all opportunity. Donald would have sought to break me - not through the mechanisms of his heart, but rather through the shock to his pride - and broken I would have been. He'd have called in every favour he was owed, to sabotage what little I could grow. The papers and magazines would have buried me as an amateur. '*Vulgar*', '*sophomoric*', and '*crude*', and soon, Cynthia would have grown to resent me, as she would have also set fire to all that she knew. Our life together would have been loveless, passionless, and masochistic. And we'd have parted, worse off for the whole affair.

I would have been happier with Adeline. We both would have skirted around society, without much desire to partake in its games and rituals, except to mock them. We would have laughed, from afar, at the try-hards and social climbers; the grammar-school leg-ups and local councilmen; arms length at the masquerade ball. I'd have written her poems, and drawn paintings with my words. Though, her death was etched into the fibres of fate, and she too would have died in my arms after bearing me a son. And I'd have walked the earth, forever trying, without fruit, to love again. If I had stayed with Milena, I would never have seen England again. England could never compete with the ease and the tranquil of Kotor, nor with the gentle presence of Milena and her company. Perhaps I would have never written again, or only written poetry; not for profit of course, but rather for my own whims and desires. I would have come, intimately, to know Rakija, and perhaps become an expert, selling it by the crate to the tourists and expats. I could have mastered the eagle dance, and worn a Montenegrin Cap, like I was born in Titograd and swam in Lake Skadar. However, these are women I never spoke to, or met, again. I never saw Cynthia again, because of Donald. I never saw Adeline, because of Bruce. And I never returned to Milena, because of her usurper. It was thus that my dreams were just that, and my reality was Los Angeles, and Elaine.

She was born in the Spring of 1937, and was twenty-one when we had first met. She was raised, in the shadows of Hollywood, and the towers of New York. She was, by all means, a west-coast aristocrat; as her money was new and spent without taste. She loathed her father, and missed her mother. It is only the work of Hollywood's masters of spin that her father escaped the whole affair without scandal. Elaine's mother was, to the uninitiated, an erratic junkie and wanting mother. Her death, in a Skid Row boarding house, caused not as much as a ripple.

It had been three years since I had moved to California. I was made to feel exotic; like a maharaja in London. All that was known of me was that I had been a successful novelist in England, and had supposedly stolen the heart of Walter Mills' daughter. For those years, it was nice. I had written two films and a collection of poems, that were received well. America, it seems, had found a new pet. It was, in monetary terms, the greatest success I had seen. What England could offer, America could double.

Aside from my work, little had occurred in those three years. My relationship with Elaine was, for reasons then unknown to me, kept relatively secret, living only in hearsay.

In fact, the sole narrative, of any particular interest, that I can find in the years between twenty-five and twenty-nine, are the reasons for my arrival in California, and the reasons for my leaving. In my recollections, I see the latter as dominoes; one falling into the other, into the other, and into the other.

That first domino was placed on a warm Wednesday afternoon in 1962. I met with Walter, as I did on a monthly basis. Our meetings did not have the warmth of those with Balloch, nor the brevity of those with Donald. Walter was cold, calculating; he had reduced all art to business, and all meaning to marketing. I suppose he *was* like Donald in that sense.

"Robin," he said, when I was shown into the office by a young receptionist, whom I would later discover to be a lover of his. "Take a seat, young man."

"I'm pushing on thirty, Walter."

"Well, I'll be damned. You don't look a day older than twenty-four. What's your secret?"

"A zest for life, a woman I love, and a job to make ends meet."

He chuckled. "You English, always got to have the last word."

"Indeed."

Almost as if to prove his own point, he lingered in the silence for a few seconds, before snapping back into the conversation. "So, what have you got for me, Robin?"

"Well, I've been thinking about it. And I think that my last novel in England would make for something nice. '*Modern man, removes his shackles and goes out into hidden corners of the earth, in search of Eden*'. I thi—"

"No. Too complex. Let me tell you what the people want. They want to laugh, fall in love, they don't want to think about the *conditions of modernity*. That's what novels are for. Novels are novels, and movies are movies. How about this. I think it's time we wrote something for Elaine."

"For Elaine?"

"Yes. That's what I hired you for, to make her a star."

"I think she's happy doing theatre."

"No. She thinks that she's happy in the theatre. She's not. No, no. She is the romantic lead; I can just see it. *Elaine Mills*," he said, waving an outward palm before him. "*America's girl*."

"So, it's another love story then?"

"Yes! I think we can make something truly special here."

"I suppose we shall."

"Oh, Robin. There is one more thing."

"Yes?"

"You'll need to talk her into it. She doesn't seem too keen to do movies, but I know it is what's best for her."

"I'll do what I can."

"I'm thinking Al Harrison for the male lead. What do you think?"

"Al Harrison? Are you sure we can get him?"

"These actors are whores," he dismissed. "Especially those from the Mid-West, like Al. They came here on a bus with two nickels in their pockets, and they can be sent back to where they came from with one. I can afford him. He'll do it. Leave that up to me."

I left Walter's office, feeling once more that I was confined into a box of mediocrity. I didn't like my first two films, and sought to write something more seriously. I wished then that Elaine's father was from a different studio, one that took more risks. As it happened, Walter was in the business of feeling good, and not writing well. This feeling was compounded by letters from England, expressing concern for my reputation at home. I called a taxi, and went home, sullen at my prospects. All the way, I thought of the Game, and how it differed at home. In Hollywood it seemed so much more brutal; as if it were a game of life or death, success or destitution, not as it was in England; a simple matter of good manners. Threats, as I knew them, were always implied.

Elaine was not at home when I arrived. She was to be performing the following night, and was at the theatre in rehearsals. I had learned the vulgar art of screenwriting from a process of trial and error with my first two pictures. I was to show, not tell. I was to make the complex simple, and discard that which couldn't be dumbed down. After a few hours, and a bin full of crumpled-up paper, I landed on a skeleton for the story. A simple story of boy meets girl, the two bicker and argue, all the while attempting, with desperation, to hide the forces of nature that pulled them together. It was the golden mould of Hollywood in those days, a *license to print money.*

They were neighbours in a complex, with names so similar that their mail was routinely given to the wrong party. Through a series of deceptions, interceptions, and violations of privacy, the two learn more of each other; ultimately concluding that they share something like affection. I wrote the man with Al Harrison in mind, and the woman for Elaine. Much to my own amusement, their shared landlord was a portrait of Mr. Willowfall, and I'd find myself stopping after each of his scenes to ask myself what ever became of that funny old man.

Elaine returned in the evening, and we dined on a simple meal and wine. "So," she said, once her plate was bare. "Father tells me you had something that you wanted to talk to me about."

"Yes. Well, it was his idea, and—"

"He's just *dying* to save me from the theatre," she said, sarcastically. "And he's got you on his hook. He's corralled you into writing a movie for me."

"Yeah. That pretty much covers it."

"Okay, I'll do it."

"It's that simple?"

"Yes. I'd been thinking of making the step for a while, but I've been so adamant against it that I'd look a fool if I turned around and asked for a gig. In fact, I'm glad he asked you."

"Well, thank the lord. I'd spent the last hour thinking of how to convince you."

"No need. But I will let you take credit for convincing me."

"Good. I'd hate to let Al Harrison down."

"Al Harrison? He's in the picture?"

"Apparently."

"Daddy got him?"

"Supposedly. Said he can afford him."

Elaine went silent for a moment, and I could see that the joy within her was reaching a fever pitch. "You know," she said, with a giddy grin. "Al Harrison was my first crush."

"Oh?"

"Yeah, I had his poster on the wall of my dorm in college."

"He *is* handsome," I said, eager to draw an end to her fawning.

"Not just so. No, he's *beautiful*."

The next day came, and I telephoned Walter to inform him that Elaine had agreed to do the picture. "Fantastic! Good going, Robin. I've just had word from Al Harrison that he'll do the picture too. Do join us for dinner this week, bring Elaine too."

Elaine could not hide her joy when I told her. We went for dinner the following Friday. Walter was there when we arrived, but Al was not. "He should be here soon; I believe he's doing The Tonight Show. Anyway, Elaine, my dear, how goes the play?"

"Just fine, daddy. We gave the final performance on Thursday. It went well, people seemed to have enjoyed it."

"Oh, yes. I'm sorry I didn't make it, dear. Business calls. I trust that you were there, Robin?"

"Oh, yes. Opening night, and the final matinee."

"And how was it?"

"Just excellent, I really—"

"Ah, here he is!" Walter exclaimed as the doors flung open and Al Harrison walked in.

It was only when I stood to greet him that I saw how tall he was. He towered over me. His features were chiselled, as if cut from stone. His eyes pierced, and his jet black hair hung perfectly, and without a single loose strand. He was, in absolution, the leading man. "Ah, yes. *Robin the Englishman*," he said with a firm grip of my hand. "I've heard many good things."

"As have I," I replied.

"And you must be my co-star," he said, turning to Elaine.

"Ye—yes. That's me," she said with a blush.

"So beautiful! I can see why Walter here wants to get you on the big screen. Well, it is a pleasure to meet you all. Forgive my tardiness."

"Nonsense, Al," Walter chirped. "Now, enough of this standing around, let us sit, and eat—and drink."

And so, we did, food came and went, as did drinks, and by the evening's end, we each found ourselves somewhere between tipsy and foolish. Al had spent a majority of the evening addressing Elaine directly, and she hung on his every deliberate word, as I faded into the background.

"Oh, Jack?", he began, in response to a question about his appearance on the Tonight Show. "He's a bore on camera. You should see him out on the golf course. Curses like a sailor!"

"That can't be true," Elaine giggled. "I simply don't believe it!"

"He's a riot!", Al added.

"Oh, how I wish I could live your life," Elaine said, wistfully.

"Just say the word," he replied. "And I'll take you along for the ride."

On a few occasions, as I was distracted by Walter's conversation, I noticed Al lean over and whisper into Elaine's ear. Each time was received well, and only served to increase the tension that formed all around us. He was charming, much as Lucifer is, in a finely-cut suit. Midnight came, and Al was the first to stand; as if tethered to his every movement, Walter and Elaine followed suit, while I gradually rose, a clear last place.

"Robin," he said, once I had risen. "Once again, it was a treat to finally make your acquaintance. I look forward to working with you."

I just nodded. Walter noticed and jabbed Al on the shoulder. "The English," he said, with dismissal. "So cold, are they not."

"Matches the weather," Al replied, much to Walter's amusement. "And Elaine," he added, turning to face her. "You truly *are* a delight. I do so look forward to being your lover—on screen, that is."

Elaine laughed aloud, and snorted. She playfully slapped his shoulder, right where her father had.

"Hey, Robin," Walter whispered. "Let us have a word."

He took my shoulder and shepherded me outside, while Elaine and Al continued to speak. Of what they spoke, I never knew; yet when I turned to face them, he was in her ear again. We arrived outside, where I lit a smoke, and looked at Walter as if to jog his memory. "You know what," he said, after a silence. "It's completely slipped my mind; it cannot have been that important." He laughed to himself. "I'm getting up there, Robin."

The drive home was silent, Elaine smiled gently out of the window, her body angled away from me, while I just stared ahead. We only spoke for the last few minutes. "He's great, isn't he?"

"Your father?"

"No, silly! Al. He's so charming."

"Mm."

"Don't you agree?"

"Oh, yes. Very charming. Superlative."

"Do you think he liked me? Like, would he be happy to work with me?"

"I don't see why not."

"Yes, I suppose you're right. Plus, father has him by the balls."

"Mm."

"Oh, Robin. Thank you so much for writing this picture for me! You have no idea how badly I want to—work with him."

"Mm."

Elaine went to bed as soon as we arrived home. I bid her

a good night, and stayed downstairs, under the guise of working on the script, which I did. Though my sole contribution that night was to alter the final scene of the film, and to remove the planned kiss, for I knew that it would cut me deep. I picked out a bottle of California wine, and let it breathe before pouring myself a glass, and then another. I missed England, I missed Richard, and Francis; Balloch, and even Donald. I missed writing novels. I wondered if Adeline was happy, and whether Francine was in England, or in France. And as I looked over that city of angels, with a bottle in my hand; I asked myself just what exactly had I done. To what agony had I just exposed myself?

35

The sun nourishes the earth in parts, and scolds it in others. Water sustains all life, and yet can drown us too. One lesson of life that I had fought so hard against learning, was that the things that make us can break us too. Love can fill our hearts with such fine songs, on perfectly-tuned instruments, with virtuosic vocals, and angelic harmonies. Though, those same lips that sing will condemn without a moments notice. So brutal is love that the mountain of bodies stacks high, all of whom chose their fate, or rather had no choice but to fall. That is where I found myself in the Summer of 1962; the die had been cast, and solemnly I had no place to go but forward, into what felt like the surety of oblivion. And I grew warped and cantankerous, and bullish. Long gone was the cautious wonder of Hollywood. In its stead came something ugly; a creeping paranoia that arose each time Elaine was out of my sight.

Over that blistering Summer, my film was in production. Each day, I awoke, left the house, and subjected myself to a deep cut, straight into my abdomen. With each day, and each session on set, I lost more of Elaine. Her words to me came fewer, and further apart. The chemistry between Al and she became stronger, and more obvious, and we all stood by as spectators, and waited for the crescendo. Life was imitating art it seems, and on several occasions, a member of staff would remark to me of their bond, knowing not what I had to lose.

"I think it's only a matter of time," remarked one.

"Oh, yeah, it'll happen," replied another. "She wants him."

I was called into a production meeting on the final week of shooting. In the room was myself, Walter, Elaine, Al, the director, a few producers, and a studio intern, who took notes. The intern was young and nervous, and only spoke when spoken to. "So," opened the director, once we had all sat and made ourselves comfortable. "How are we all feeling?"

"I feel swell," said Al. "This has been my favourite picture so far."

"As do I!", Elaine added. "Though it's my first."

"Could've fooled me," Al replied, as their eyes met softly.

"Yes, yes, it has been very enjoyable," Walter agreed. "Robin?"

"Hm?"

"Are we having fun?"

"Oh, yes sir."

He nodded before turning to face the intern. "You," he said, clicking his fingers in a way that casually admitted he had forgotten the intern's name. "Jasper, sir," said the intern.

"Yes, Jasper. Any news for me?"

"Well," he began. "We've had some preliminary test screenings. People seem to enjoy it, but, well—"

"It's the ending," the director interrupted with impatience. "The test audiences hate it. It's too anticlimactic."

"Too anticlimactic?", I asked.

"Yes. It's artsy and restrained, too *European*. People want passion."

"Passion?"

"Yes. Passion, *amour*."

I was eager to not look like a desperate man, fighting tooth and nail to prevent what was now inevitable. I knew it, and so unbuckled the seatbelt, and shifted into the passenger seat of the car, as it rolled to the cusp of the cliff's edge. Instead, I decided on a practical approach. "And what of the codes?", I asked, feigning ignorance and concern.

"The codes?", asked the director.

"Yes. The morality codes."

"Jasper," Walter said, glancing over at the intern.

"Well," he said. "We should be okay on that front. The codes cover gross indecency, violence, nudity, and Communism."

"Yes," Walter continued. "I cannot imagine they'd work themselves into a state over a kiss."

"A kiss?", I asked.

"Yes. It is the most logical conclusion."

"I'm not sure about that."

"Robin," Walter interjected. "Your ending is good, but it's not what the people want. We are in the business of giving people what they want. Elaine and Al staring deeply into each other's eyes, as the screen fades to black is all well and good, but it leaves too much to the imagination. You have to remember that we cater to——if you'll pardon the phrasing, idiots. No, this ending is much better. That is, of course, if the cast are willing."

With that, all eyes in the room except for mine swivelled and fixed on Elaine and Al. "Well," said Al, with a sickening smile. "I sure don't mind. Elaine?"

I looked up at her, Elaine just looked down, aware of my gaze. "No," she said. "I don't mind either."

"Perfect!", Walter exclaimed. "That settles it then. We shall schedule that in for tomorrow, and finally get the shoot finished."

In hindsight, I should have left there and then, and never returned. I should have gone back to England, with my tail between my legs, for I had been defeated. Al had won. He had won the room, the nation, and Elaine was his final conquest. To all concerned, I was merely in the way. His civility towards me was a mere facade, a mask that covered the truth at the heart of the matter; he wanted

Elaine, and Elaine wanted him, and it was only the vague civilisational affect of *manners*, and myself, that separated them. After the meeting had ended, and its attendants had dissipated, I went to Elaine's trailer. I knocked twice and cheerily she called back. "Come in!"

"Hey," I said upon entry.

Her tone and demeanour changed completely. "Hey," she said, with a fraction of her earlier enthusiasm.

"I need to talk to you about something, Elaine. I'm really not sure about this. I—"

"Stop, Robin. Jealousy really doesn't suit you, dear. In fact, it is an absolutely rotten aesthetic."

"I—I just know what a kiss can do."

"Robin! You are truly being an unbearable ass right now. This is my break, my moment. And you are ruining it with your sickening envy."

"I—I'm sorry."

"Just leave, please? I need to prepare."

"Okay."

I returned home alone that night. Elaine never came. I knew not where she was, and could not face the prospect. I drank myself silly, as to push the thoughts away. The next day came, and with it a deadly dread, that slapped me across the face at the crack of dawn and woke me from my slumber. I made no hurry that morning, and ate breakfast slowly. I arrived late to set, and had missed the rehearsals. Though I was told that the kiss had not gone ahead; the director wished for it to be '*real*'. It all felt like a sick joke at my expense, that they had noticed my absence, and decided that the kiss served only to torture me, and my not being there was a stay of execution. They read their lines one last time before the cameras were on. I watched with a nervous intensity, awaiting the catastrophe that I was now powerless to stop, having exhausted my arsenal. I chewed my fingers to the bone. The lights came on, cameras rolled and '*action*' was called. They recited the words I had written for them, and moved in the way I had envisioned. The final lines of dialogue came slowly, and then all at once.

She kissed him with fire, as if she had waited

her entire life to do so. She wrapped her arms around his neck, and he placed his hands on the back of hers. As '*cut*' was called, and all of the crew cheered, I felt dizzy, like I had been punched. I could not watch the second take, and by the third, I had stepped outside.

Los Angeles is a city of lonely souls; lonely souls, who arrive every day by the bus-load, with empty pockets, and a wealth of delusions. The lion's share were to be condemned to forever be waiters, and bartenders, and drivers. Perhaps a few would become interns; like Jasper, who was the leading man of his school theatre. For me, Los Angeles was Elaine and Elaine was Los Angeles. Without her, there was little point in staying.

That night, all of the cast and crew went to celebrate, while I went home alone. Looking back, I can almost call this decision my final act of self-sabotage in America. In that act I was saying '*here you go, Al. Take your shot. Who am I to stand in your way*'.

I took a bath and moped around the house, feeling sorry for myself. I consumed some wine and listened to the Korsakov recording, desperately trying to make myself feel something. Elaine returned shortly after midnight. She carried her shoes and gently swayed from side to side.

"Hello," I said when she entered.

"Hey!"

"Did you have fun?"

"Oh, so much! I drank a little too much and had to get a cab. My car is still at the studio."

"Do you need money?"

"No, it's okay. Al paid for the cab. He's so lovely."

"Mm."

She scowled. "Oh my God, not this again."

"Fine."

"Just drop all the paranoid shit, okay. It's weird, and intense."

"Okay."

"Ugh, fine! I'm going to bed."

"Okay."

A few months passed, in which we had fluctuated,

quite violently, between cold distance and warm affection. We had put up an appearance for Christmas, though the night ended in another argument. I had spent the new year alone, as per my request, and I knew not where she went, nor what she did. By then I didn't care. I knew that it was over, and with my head placed firmly in the guillotine, I waited for the chop. In January, she began to do press for the film, and I was not invited.

February came, and the film was released in time for Valentine's. On a bitter night, we attended the premiere. Elaine was the queen for a night, and this was her coronation. As soon as we arrived, she became swarmed by a crowd of reporters, who pushed me aside so that I could not see Elaine, only hear what she said.

> "Elaine, Elaine," said one reporter, forcing her way to the front of the crowd. "A few questions?"
>
> "Of course," Elaine said with a smile.
>
> "You're the star of the most anticipated romantic comedy of the year. It is expected to shatter box office records, how do you feel?"
>
> "Oh, yes. It has been such a wonderful experience. Hollywood has welcomed me so kindly."
>
> "This film was written by Robin Fitzwarwick, a celebrated novelist in England. Rumour has it that the two of you are an item, and have been for some time. Is this true?"
>
> "Well," she said, as the crowd hung on her every word. "Robin is a great guy, and we have a lot of fun together. But a girl must keep her options open, right?"

The crowd laughed, seemingly unaware that I was stood right there. Perhaps they did know, and the entire city had conspired to force me out of its midst. "How about some photos?", another reporter called. "Hey, Robin is right here," he continued. "A photo of the writer and the star?"

The crowd gave me passage through to Elaine, and we posed, side-by-side for a photograph. Elaine leaned away, and shimmied her body from my hand to the open air beside it. While I smiled for the cameras and flashes, and with each flash my smile was contorted in upon itself. I could not help but feel a nausea that rose up, and tickled my skin from the inside. It was, I think, the most humiliating moment of my life.

"Al!, called a third reporter. "Al Harrison! A photo with your co-star?"

"Of course," he said, in a confident tone. He brushed me aside without contact and wrapped his arm around Elaine's waist, holding on tight. I watched the film without passion or pride for my involvement. I closed my eyes when they kissed, as the audience roared with approval. Later, Elaine and I drove home, in silence. Occasionally, I would glance over at her, and feel only contempt and shame. On one such occasion, she caught my gaze.

"What?", she asked, coldly.

"'*A girl must keep her options open*'? Am I some kind of fool?"

"Oh my God!"

"Is that all you can do, all you can say? Just huff and puff and groan? You knew exactly what you were doing. You know exactly how it looks; to me, to everyone! Do you expect me to just stand there and take it, while I am cuckolded in front of the entire world?"

"You are so fucking insecure. It's pathetic!"

"Really?"

"Yeah! And you're paranoid."

"Yeah?"

"Yeah!"

"Well, you wouldn't be here without me. So you can call me whatever you like."

"What's that supposed to mean?"

"Nothing."

"No, go on, tell me. What is that supposed to mean?"

"Perhaps I misspoke, you wouldn't be here without me *and* your father."

"And why is that?"

I said nothing, as the rage built up inside her. "Why is that Robin?"

"Because you can't act!"

The words threw themselves out of me, before I could form them. Possessed by vitriol, I continued. "What do you think this is, your coming out party? It's a fucking rom-com, for ugly people who get to watch pretty people pretend to fall in love and imagine that it's them. It's a joke, a practical joke on them. I've accepted that I have to write tosh, when are you going to accept that you have to act in tosh? It's tosh! It's all tosh! All of it. You're not doing Shakespeare, because they won't have you, because you cannot act. You only did off-Broadway shows because you cannot act. You couldn't get any work in London, because you cannot act, and you had to trick me into writing something for you, because you cannot act. Your dad got you a role, acting out *tosh*, because you cannot act, and you made him make me write a movie for you, because you cannot fucking act. I mean, really, did you *really* think that forgetting five takes in a row made you endearing? Did you think it made you Hepburn? No. All you did was make the sound engineer miss his son's birthday. And you know what? One day your daddy won't be there to pull strings for you, and we'll see how you do then. You'll see how ugly *fairness* can be."

She went silent, and I carried on driving. Buoyed by the seeming victory, I pivoted onto my own grievance. "You spoke as if we'd been on a few dates."

"So?"

"So? So that means something."

"If you are so miserable with me, then why don't you just fuck off?"

"You'd like that."

"Perhaps I would. I cannot keep reassuring you, Robin. It is exhausting being with someone who is so damn needy."

"You act like this is coming from nothing."

"It is!"

"Don't do that?"

"Don't do what?"

"Just stop, okay. We are nearly at the gate."

We pulled up the gate, where the security guard met us. He was old, and frail, and seemingly incapable of preventing unwanted company. Much like Mr. Willowfall.

"Ah, hello Mr. Fitzwarwick, Miss Mills."

"Hello," I said.

"Robin, a message has arrived for you," he said, handing me a slip of paper. "From England. It says it's urgent."

"Thank you."

He nodded and opened the gate. We drove through and pulled into the driveway, without saying a word. Still in silence, we walked into the house. I made way over to the desk in the corner and flicked on a reading light. As I read, my body fell limp and numb and I had to sit, my face was drained of all hue and contorted in horror. Elaine saw, and grew concerned.

"What is it?", she asked.

36

I returned to England a week later. In the four years that I was gone, London had become quite unrecognisable. I did not stay in the city for long, and after a day or two, boarded a train set for Cornwall. Francis waited for me at the station, and I entered the car before we had said a word. He was mourning already, and I knew then that Richard was not long for this world.

"How is it looking?" I asked, after a few miles of country lanes.

"Not good."

Francis spoke little, and it seemed as if he had not said much for a while. There was, quite understandably, much on his mind. "I didn't know he was ill," I said, eager to break the silence.

"It all happened very quickly."

"Is Adeline there?"

"No. She wrote a letter."

"Oh?"

"Hm?"

"It's a pity."

"Quite."

We arrived at the house. It was still precious and ornate, and yet something was off; as if a ghost roamed these halls, forever searching for something lost; as if death himself waited in the wings, searching without aim for something lost. We walked into the drawing room, where Richard's parents were sat. Charles held firm, whereas it was clear that Mary had been crying until quite recently.

"Robin," she said, creeping forward and giving me an uneasy hug. "It has been so long."

"Regretfully so."

"Yes," Charles added. "How long has it been?"

"Just shy of a decade."

"Yes," said Mary. "Ten years, wow. We had always enquired, but Richard told us that you lived abroad. America, is it?"

"Yes. California."

"Oh, that is very nice. Isn't that nice, Charles?"

"It's very nice."

"Where is he?", I asked.

"He's in the guest house."

"May I go and see him?"

"Please do."

I walked through the house and into the garden. On my way to the guest house, I passed the pond and thought of Adeline. Richard looked sickly and thin when I saw him. His beautiful head of golden hair had faded, and he was deathly hollow. He lay under a duvet, from which he sweated greatly, and I could hear his coughing and wheezing from outside.

"Hello, Richard."

"He—hello, old boy," he said, between dry and heaving coughs. "It's— so good to see you."

"How are you feeling?"

"About as good as I look."

"You look like shit."

"Then that is how I feel."

We shared a strange moment of muted laughter, before Francis walked in with a cup of tea and some biscuits. "Ah, Francis, my dear boy."

"I thought you may have been thirsty."

"Most intuitive. Please, leave it by my side. I must speak with Robin about a matter of grave importance, if——if you'll pardon the pun."

"Very well."

Francis brushed my shoulder as he passed me. We shared a smile of mutual mourning. It was clear that our friend did not have long left. His sentences were slow, slurred, and delivered in raspy whisper. "So you stuck to calling him Francis?"

"I—figured it was a parting gift, to give the old boy his name back."

I smiled at my friend. His attempts to return the smile faded quickly into a fit of coughs. "Robin," he said, regaining his breath. "There is something that I must tell you."

"Yes?"

"It's the American girl. She's no good."

"Is that so?"

"She propositioned me, the last time you were in London."

"Oh?"

"You do not seem so surprised."

"I think my dealings with her are over. Everyone has tried to warn me, everyone but Francis."

"He," Richard began, with a chuckle and a cough. "He wouldn't tell you if you were on fire, he'd think it rude and condescending. You wouldn't have listened anyway. It's impossible to listen when you're——in love. Jarves—Jarves warned me about Eleanor. It is—s-so funny isn't it, how we let these things happen to us. Love offers so few things beyond pain, and yet we go back, again, and again, and again. Perhaps we were born to love—and born to suffer. We just get the two in a single, neatly-wrapped——parcel."

"We are also destined to feel joy, Richard."

"Well, of course. It's—the joy that brings us back. We have gin and wine too, for when love does not s-suffice."

I just smiled at him, with misty eyes, at the sight of my friend; so emaciated and pale, sprawled out before me, waiting to die. "Send Francis in, would you?"

"Of course."

"Thank you, Robin. I—I am so happy to see you."

Francis waited outside the guest house, and I gestured for him to go in. I began to walk back towards the house, but stopped myself upon seeing Richard's father, sat by the pond. "Robin," he said when he saw me. "Do sit with me."

"How are you holding up, Charles?"

"I feel sick, hopelessly weak, as if my arms could not carry something as light as an apple. I cannot prevent my wife from crying, or my son from dying. I cannot induce my daughter to return home from a man she loathes, and who loathes her. I feel as if I have failed, really quite dramatically, as a father."

"I'm sorry."

"It's okay."

"Do you know how long he—"

"Could be weeks, could be days. Anyway, I do not wish to speak of my son's mortality any longer. Do tell me of America. I haven't been since I was a boy."

"It's not here, I can tell you that much."

"Here? This crummy old palace?"

"I spent the happiest Summer of my life in this crummy old palace."

"Is that so?"

"Yes sir."

"It's not what it used to be, you know."

"I heard."

"Did Richard tell you?"

"No. It was Adeline actually."

"Did you, by chance, find yourself *entangled* with her?"

I hesitated for a moment. Charles noticed and gave a little smirk. "It's okay, Robin. I shall bring you no repercussions. Did you?"

"I did."

"It's a pity she ended up with that brute. I should

have known. I should have put my foot down."

"How did you know about Adeline and myself?"

"I read her diary once, just before she left. She wrote of that Summer you were here, a young fellow who wrote poems for her. It cannot have been Francis."

"She and I did grow rather close."

"And closer I wish you had grown, perhaps you could have saved her. I liked you, Robin. You'd have made a far better husband for my little girl."

"When did you see her last?"

"The wedding. That oaf has taken her and does not intend on giving her back."

"I'm so very sorry, Charles."

"You know," he began, before pausing to consider his words. "I knew your father."

"You did?"

"We were at Camford together, and had a friend in common, a chap by the name of *Crowe*. He was a fair few years younger than me, but it was him alright. You don't meet many chaps named *Fitzwarwick*, so you remember the ones you do. He was a good man."

"So I've heard."

"You look like him."

We spoke for a while longer, and he told me a few tales of my father, before he left to check on his wife. A month or so passed, in which there was a general unease around the house. One-by-one we ventured to the guest house, and kept Richard company. Doctors came and went, each offering a varying prognosis of days and weeks. Yet, Richard outlasted every prediction. Each time one of us was summoned, we assumed it would be our very last conversation with him, and braced ourselves for such, yet a few days would go by and we'd be summoned again. However, in the middle of April, 1963, I would have that final conversation.

I was in the dining room, sharing a cup of tea with Francis. He told me, dispassionately, of the botany room, and how it had fallen into disrepair. I had not thought to enter that room since arriving, nor the library. Charles and Mary returned from the guest house, carrying on their faces a mourning and resolution, as one does after saying goodbye.

"Robin," Charles said with an arm around his wife, who began to cry once more. "Richard would like to see you."

By now, Richard could hardly speak, and hardly move. Both he and his bedsheets were drenched in sweat, and his eyes had become deathly sensitive to light. The room was dim, lit only by a lamp with a cloth over it, and the curtains were drawn, when I entered. The scent of death lingered upon the walls and ceiling.

"Robin?", he whispered into the dark, "Is that you?"

"It is."

"Come closer. I wish to see you, my dear friend."

I stepped into the bedside light, as Richard made a little noise of recognition. "Robin."

"How are you holding up, chap?"

"Like I could die."

"Then I have some good news for you."

Richard gave a few chuckles, which gave way to dry coughs. "Yes, you always had a wit about you, didn't you Robin?"

"An impulse."

"And a good one at that. Tell me about California, before I die having never seen it."

And so I told him. He considered my words, and cleared his throat. "England was always your home, Robin. Wherever else you ventured off to, you always returned. Everyone you love is here."

"Not everyone."

"Perhaps. May I ask you a question, Robin?"

"Of course."

"Did I ever annoy you?"

"Many times."

"Oh, really?"

"But it was always endearing."

"Those days were fun, were they not?"

"They were."

"Those halcyon days. Or should I say 'daze'. D-A-Z-E. For that is what it was—a wonderful daze."

"You know, Richard. You could have been a writer too."

"Oh, no. Heavens no. That was *your* destiny, Robin, mine is elsewhere."

It was the line that broke me, and I buried my face into my hands. Stirring after a few moments, I took his hand into mine. "I shall miss you, Richard."

"And I shall miss you, Fitzy. Although, let us save the tears for after I'm gone, you—look so ugly when you cry."

We laughed together again, and for the final time. He gave my hand a squeeze. "Eleanor," he whispered.

"Yes?"

"She married and became mother to a gaggle. I read it in the Tatler, the night we climbed the bell tower. Do you remember that night?"

"Of course I do. We skipped graduation and drank all day. I decided to move to London that night."

"I did love her, truly."

"I know you did."

"I fear, Robin, that I was never a serious man. But I did love her."

"I know, Richard."

"Whatever happened to the girl in Paris?"

"I have no idea."

"Such fools we were. Oh well, you must correct these things, Robin. You're the only one who can. Where I'm going, a man's mistakes are already forgiven."

Richard closed his eyes for several moments, before opening them again, weakly. "It was the drink that got me, Robin. It was the drink, *the sweet drink*—and I don't regret a single drop."

After that, he went comatose again, and came to a few minutes later. "Robin."

"Yes, Richard?"

"Look after the old boy, won't you? I fear that he will take my death quite harshly."

"Of course."

He smiled. "I know that you will. Could you send him in?"

"Yes."

"Farewell, Robin. You have been such *delightful* company."

"Enjoy the other side, Richard. I'm sure they'll have hot water there."

"They'd better."

I leaned over and kissed my friend on the forehead, before turning to leave the room; knowing with certainty that I would never see him again. I would never have to make, order, or see a gin and tea ever again. It was then that, barely above a whisper, out came his final words.

"What a sweet, fleeting treat it is——to love."

Of all of Richard's traits, quirks, and charms, it was his unflinching love that I recall most to this day, and recall with the most fondness. Each day, as if crafted by Bacchus himself, was but a chance for fun, for mayhem, mischief, and for laughter, and all were words that he loved. Even as he grew older, and more burdened by responsibilities, he never lost his love.

I walked back to the house, as a few lonely tears were scattered upon my cheeks. I sent Francis to the guest house, and took a seat alone. Looking out the window, I saw the pond, and a bizarre sensation came over me. I ventured back out into the garden, stripped to the waist, and jumped in. I swam around on my back, looking at the sky. For the first time since I had arrived back at Belling House, I thought not of Richard, of mortality, or death, I just watched the clouds that cut apart the ocean blue sky.

Thirty minutes later, I crawled out of the water and dried on the grass. I rose to my feet when I saw Francis approaching. His face said all that was necessary, and yet he still spoke.

"He's dead."

Richard took the laughter with him when he went.

We buried him at the mausoleum. Just beyond his plot, a painting blessed the wall. In it, Richard stood in a *forever* of youth, just as I had known him; when he had been at his best, and so full of life. The placard beneath, on a shiny-new golden face had, etched upon it, *Richard Belling and Uxby*.

Adeline did not attend the funeral, despite rumours that she would. Perhaps she had intended to, but got cold feet the night before, or the morning of. Perhaps she was prevented. From all that I had heard then, and heard after the fact; the latter seemed more likely.

I had resolved to return to Los Angeles, even if only briefly, as I had unfinished business there. I drove with Francis to London, where I told him of my desire to return.

"You must do what makes you happy, Robin."

"I think I need to chase misery before I can chase joy."

"I understand."

"Will you be alright?"

"I'll manage," he said.

And so, I departed for America, blind to the fates of those I left in England. All through the journey, I planned and plotted what I would say to Elaine, though I knew that it was over. As it occurred, all of my plans and plots would come to nothing, as when I arrived at the house, it was shared with Elaine no more. For she, and all of her belongings, were gone.

37

I walked around the house in a stupor, not knowing why I felt the sadness that I did. The affair had ended the day I left for England, and our love had died long before. There were no happy memories. Even the objective reality of our at-times blissful union was now tainted beyond repair. All that remained was my own idiocy, and lust, and betryal of a good woman in Milena.

My mind was filled with delusions of narrative; all the possibilities of rectifying the situation, or of my situation rectifying itself. Perhaps I had been spotted in the airport, and Elaine had been made aware of my return. Perhaps she would see some error in her decision, and return. Alas, and obviously, this was not the case.

My greatest fear, it seemed, had come to fruition. That I was an imposter; superficially charming and interesting until the day one truly knew me, after which I was a bandage to be removed and cast off. Elaine, as my mind told me with a wicked glee, had, at first glance, found me to be quite charming; only for my sorry self to be remade, over the course of our affair, into an insolent little puppy who needed putting down for his own good. Like a splinter that needed to be ripped out; a plaster on healed skin. A cyst, a pimple, a blocked drain. I knew she was gone the moment I saw the house, for her presence had left some time before. In the months before my departure, I had failed to excite her. I am one to notice that sort of thing, anomalies, and little breaks in the trend. I'd become so familiar with the cycle, that it happened right before my eyes, and I let it happen. I knew that my response would only exacerbate things; shorten the breaking of my heart from six months to one. I was pathetic; undeserving and needy. I needn't be loved, it was a waste of time for all involved. The first blow of anguish was set in motion by the first smile of mutual attraction. What disturbed me most was the realisation that the sole commonality, in all of my failed romances, was myself.

I stayed in that house for three days. There was barely any food, and three bottles of wine, and I had almost consumed it all. I must have looked like a cadaver, reanimated alone by lightning. My hair grew greasy and unkempt, a beard had begun to form, and I stunk of stale wine and smoke.

On the fourth day, I resolved to speak with Walter, in lieu of Elaine; for what I desired was not realignment, nor remonstrance, but closure. I showered, shaved, and ate at a small diner, before making my way to the studio.

"I'm afraid he is away from the office right now," said a bewildered receptionist, who had seemingly been warned of my arrival.

"Then I shall wait until he is here."

"He will not be returning today."

I went back on the fifth, sixth, seventh, and eighth days, and was told the same each day. The ninth day was a Sunday, and the lot was empty and locked, so I returned on the tenth. There, I found Walter. He had not drawn the curtains in his office, and could be seen, clear as day. I walked straight for the door, and had opened it before he could rise, or his secretary could stop me.

"Mr. Fitzwarwick! You cannot go in there."

"No, no. It's okay, Amber," Walter said with a straightening of his jacket. "Robin, I guess you'd better come in."

I took a seat; flustered, slightly manic, and desperate

to speak. "Are you going to tell me what's happening, Walter?"

"What's happening? You won't leave well enough alone, that's what is happening. Now listen to me and listen good. You have been relieved of your duties, is that clear?"

"Is that really necessary? I—I have projects, we just made arrangements for the next picture, I——"

"That picture is on indefinite hold."

"Why?"

"It is easier for everyone if you just accept this and move on."

"Where is she, Walter?"

"That needn't concern you."

"I just want to talk to her. Believe me, I don't want to reconcile, I——"

"It needn't concern you, Mr. Fitzwarwick."

"Is she with him? With Al?"

"Let's just say that she is moving up in the world and leave it at that. She is where she belongs. Actors belong with each other, and we civilians belong with the uninitiated."

"So that's just it?"

"Go home, Robin. You are a hero there."

"You'd be surprised."

"I was just being polite. I am fully aware of your circumstances."

"Then you know what you're doing to me."

"Afraid so."

"I—"

He silenced me with a gesture of his hand. "It's been a pleasure, Robin. I'm sorry it had to end this way."

One thing that made the transition into life after Elaine easier was the ease at which business could be done. Her name was not on the deeds of our home, and I could sell it without her input or objection. And so, within a week of that meeting with Walter, the house was on the market, and I had left California behind, having been chewed up and spat out of its smokey highways. I found myself back in New York, where I tried to write a play. In my delusional state, it would have been my final parting message, to a land I had come to despise; not in spite of its charms and idiosyncrasies, but because it had treated me so poorly in the end. What took me there was a sort of clamouring, a clawing. I saw fit to reclaim some semblance of a profile. I drank in fashionable bars, and on occasion was recognised. One day, I was photographed alongside some poets and folk singers, and featured in a trendy magazine. I had taken cheap rooms in the Greenwich Village, and poured myself into the play. At the centre of it was my jilting. While I mourned my friend, others schemed and hatched plans of escape. They were executed flawlessly and I found myself a stranger in a strange land. I had managed to carve out some happiness in New York, and remained in the company of my fashionable friends. And yet, fate can be so violent, and two events on consecutive days finally sent me home.

One day, as I read the paper, I saw news of Elaine. She was to marry Al, after a *'year-long courtship'*, according to Hollywood insiders. The next day, I received word that my house had sold, and the money was in escrow. And so, battered and blue, with the fact that my time in America had come to so bitter an end, I ventured home.

The reputation I had gained would mean that I never returned to America. I would forever be known, at least there, as a brief light that burned out; a victim of industry politics, a victim of Al Harrison, and of Walter Mills.

Within a couple of years, stories would circulate of the precise nature of my humiliation, how Al had stolen her from me, while I tended to a dying friend in England. In spite of this, and the patronising sympathy I'd receive, Al would escape the scandal, and become the leading man of his time. He would receive accolades, awards; and at the time of my writing this, and therefore of my death, he is still alive and still beloved. Soon, he would bore of Elaine, and would divorce her after Walter's bankruptcy in 1970. And it was thus that, with my tail between my legs, and with little else to fight for, I came home in time for the Christmas of 1963.

38

When I arrived into London, on the eve of Christmas, I was welcomed in by cold streets and billowing smoke. I was thirty, and yet held the progenies of prejudice befitting only the elderly. I had become hardened and stiff, made cold by neglect, and semi-unrecognisable on account of my beard. News of Adeline's passing, which had occurred some four months prior, reached me on Christmas morning, as I lounged alone in the Papal. I mourned her in silence, and felt an intolerable pity for Charles and Mary. Fate is violent, and it declared so that the Belling name would now die with them.

It was not until I had been back for a week, and not spoken to a single soul, that it occurred to me to check in on my old rooms. I rode there in a cab, and had my first real conversation in months. The driver, a dishevelled veteran of Korea shared my lamentations of what London had become.

> "America, was it? Should've stayed, mate. England is a nation in retirement," he said, over and over again. "We are finished, done."

I arrived at the building. On the way there, I had noticed that the King's Road, much like the city as a whole, had changed beyond recognition. The pub was gone, as was the restaurant; though this did not displease me, as I had feared the provocation of seeing them again ever since I landed. The pub was not the same without Richard's lust, nor was the restaurant without Elaine in the window. In the months since the end of our affair, I had felt every emotion that it is possible to feel. I had missed her, loathed her, and now felt little more than resentment; a bitter scar of wasted time and wasted breath.

"Hello," I said, upon leaning my head into the ground-floor flat, and seeing a stranger inside. I did not expect Mr. Willowfall to be there, and alas he was not.

"Good day," replied a short, stout man, around forty years in age.

"I'd like to enquire about a room."

"I'm afraid I can't help you there, mate. The building is coming down in a few months."

"Oh, really? Why?"

"The old man snuffed it a couple of years ago, left the building to me. I put it up for sale and some suits bought it. I think they're putting an 'otel up."

"Death seems to be in every direction," I whispered.

"What?", the man asked.

"Nothing."

"Okay."

"Are you his son?"

"Adrian's?"

Suddenly, it seemed so funny that I never knew Mr. Willowfall's first name. To me, he had always just been *Mr. Willowfall.*"

"Adrian Willowfall?"

"Yes."

"Then yes, him."

"Step-son. The old boy never had any kids of his own."

"Right."

"Listen, mate. If you are looking for rooms, there's a building just around the corner. Decent price on rent.

"Oh yeah?"

"Yeah. It's part of a white terrace, green door."

"Thank you."

And so, it would transpire, in the sheep's clothing of irony, that I would spend the next five years of my life in

Richard's old flat. Francis was not there when I enquired of his whereabouts. His status was not known and had not been known for some time. He had left with Richard, but never returned.

"Odd fellow, that Uxby chap," said the landlord as he followed me up the stairs. "Very quiet, kept to himself mostly, him and that posh chap. Then one day, they both left. I think the posh one got ill. Mr. Uxby left most of his things behind."

"Are they still there?"

"No. I had to get rid of them. It's hard to sell a flat around here anyway, let alone if there's a bunch of old jackets and books scattered about."

As I entered the flat, for the first time since 1959, I felt a tremendous guilt. And so, alone, and without guidance, I sought out the sole remaining figure of authority I had left.

"My, oh my. Robin Fitzwarwick!", Donald exclaimed when I arrived at his home, a week later. In my absence, he had changed dramatically. His marriage to Cynthia was consigned to history, and he fully embraced the lifestyle of a bachelor. This was evidenced by the half-dressed woman, clearly in her twenties, who made no effort to hide her presence.

"How long has it been, my dear boy?"

"Some time, Donald."

"What a bizarre thing. Last I heard, you were in America; making movies?"

"Yes."

"And how was that?"

"Well, I returned. Let that say all that is needed."

"Must've been five years, wow. Just incredible, you haven't aged a day."

"And you seem to have gotten younger, Donald."

"I suppose I have, that's what divorce will do to you. Have you met Addie? What a wonderful remedy she is."

"I see."

"You disapprove?"

"Honestly, Donald. It isn't my business. Do you hear any from Cynthia?"

"Her? Oh, no. That's long gone. It was an ugly affair, really. One too many—*trips abroad*, if you know what I mean; from each of us I that is. Besides, it's a new time, divorce, mistresses, it all isn't as frowned upon as it once was."

"No. I suppose not."

"Anyway. How may I be of assistance?"

"I was hoping to get back to writing novels."

"Really?"

"Yes."

"You?"

"I *am* a novelist, Donald."

"Yes, I suppose you are. There's just one slight issue."

"Oh?"

"Andress House is no more. I've closed it down."

"Wow. Times really *have* changed."

"May it never grow old."

"What a pity."

"Perhaps I can find something for you at Firebrand. Though, it is a little bit more—*vibrant* than your typical work."

"I can do vibrant."

He laughed, before noticing my demeanour. "Oh, you're serious?"

"Mm."

"Well, come to a party with me tonight. There will be a lot of the younger crop there. They'll be the chaps you'll have to impress. I'm sure they'd be amused to have you around, you're something of a cautionary tale in these parts."

"Okay," I said, ignoring the slight. "I'll be there."

"Okay."

I left Donald's, as a wave of sullenness came over me. The Albert Village was not a place I took much of a shine to. Each wall was covered in murals, to this thing and that. Whatever politics were fashionable, whichever cause displayed status and being *in the know*, was etched into the centuries-old stone - like a gangrenous wound. I took to walking east, and kept going until I was well into Kensington. I found a tea shop and made camp. In the subtle warmth, general silence, and unassuming clientele, I fell into a daydream. And then, just as an hour passed, I was interrupted.

"Hello, chum."

I looked up and was surprised to see an old familiar face. "Jarves?"

Whereas I had grown a beard, his had been chopped off, and his smooth cheeks almost reflected the light. We were both thirty, and yet he seemed much younger than me.

"I see you're back in London."

"Yes. I see you're out of the army."

"*Out*? I was hardly in, mate. My family is poor, but the name still goes a way. I just milled about in Germany for a bit. Got an honourable discharge, now I work at the Ministry."

"And here I was expecting shell-shock and horror tales."

"Not from me. Are you alone?"

"Yes."

"Well then, I suppose I'll join you."

I shuffled along the settee, and he sat on the other end of it. He lit a smoke and offered me one, which I took. "*Robin Fitzwarwick*," he said, with a thin air of mocking. "I hear you've made something of yourself since I saw you last."

"Something, and then nothing."

He chuckled. "You writers are all the same. Say, fancy buying me a bottle of wine?"

"Excuse me?"

"You don't recall, do you?"

"I don't believe so."

"Back in Camford, at the end of first year. The night Belling fell off the bridge, I bought you a bottle of wine. Do you remember?"

I did remember, and nodded. "Come on," he said. "I know a good joint."

We left the cafe, and rounded the corner. There was a small tavern, under a bridge and Jarves walked in ahead of me. I repaid my debt, and before long, we were sipping on wine. The strangeness of the situation was not lost on either of us. Jarves and I had, at the best of times, been on the periphery of each other's vision, conjoined only by Richard and his ways.

"I take it you heard the news," I said after a half-hour's idle chat.

"Yes."

"We buried him in the mausoleum—the one at Belling House."

"So I heard."

"Where were you, Jarves? Did it not seem appropriate to make an appearance. I know that Francis wrote you. Maz came to the funeral, Portnoy sent flowers."

"Oh, come off it, we're having a nice drink here, Fitzy. Don't spoil it with chatter about death. I don't want to think about the old boy dying. Though, I bet his last moments were a scene. Poor chap must've been guzzling the gin, knowing it was the last time and all."

"What?"

"Relax, mate. What's gotten you so worked up?"

"In this moment, Jarvis, it's you. How dare you say that about him. He was your friend, he was my friend. Does that mean nothing to you? How long had you known him? Since prep, right?"

"More or less."

"And his death is a subject of jokes?"

"Robin, I—"

"Fuck you. He may have had his ways, but he was the joy in our lives. And that joy died with him. And what about Francis, did he ever cross your mind? Just what the hell's he going to do. And you know what? I haven't a clue where Francis is. He could be dead. And now——and now——oh, God, I don't have a friend in the world. Enjoy the wine, you—you orange bastard."

I rose, and readied my coat. "Robin," Jarves protested. "Christ, Robin, it was only a joke. Where are you going?"

"To a party."

I was not angry at Jarves, such as it were he was true to form; and for that I could not fault him. He was simply in the wrong place, at the wrong time, and became conduit to my madness and grief. I stormed throughout the city, back towards the Albert Village. Donald had written the address of the party on a slip of paper. After an hour, I found the place and climbed the steps. It became apparent, almost immediately, that I had come overdressed; and there was not a tie in sight. Embarrassed, I began to take mine off, just as Donald noticed me and came over.

"Come with me," Donald said, pulling on my arm. "Let us mingle."

Donald dragged me around the room, introducing me to various twenty-somethings, who recognised me, but didn't seem to care. "Ah yes, Fitzwarwick," said one after another. "I think my mother reads your books."

"Oh. Thank you," I'd say, and feel a little smaller with each repetition.

This continued through the evening. Around eight, it seemed as if a switch had been flicked, and the natural cap on debauchery was lifted. Soon enough, the scrambling of restraints and limitations had been elevated to an art form. Everything had descended.

"This is literature, Robin. Art! This is where it's at. What a wonderful collection of souls."

"There's a naked man over there."

"Yes! Rodrigo Salmas. A brilliant painter."

"Really?"

"Oh, yes. I don't really understand any of it, but I hear it is very good. I take the kids' advice on this sort of thing."

"From whom exactly?"

"Those in the know; students, etcetera."

"Right."

As I wandered around the room, bewildered and slightly afraid, it became apparent that I was a stranger in this land. Thoughts began to swirl in my head, questions too; do I adapt, or do I walk away? Before I could think any more, there came a tap at my shoulder. I turned to see Elias Woodbridge, grinning with pomp.

"Robin? Robin Fitzwarwick?"

"Yes," I said, shaking his limp hand.

"Charmed," he purred. "I believe this is our first meeting. What a bizarre thing, two generations of literature, side by side. We have then, and today. Now we just need to find tomorrow. Maybe Salmas can be our tomorrow, if he can get his *wood* good to go and spit out some progeny."

"I believe I'm somewhat younger than you, Mr. Woodbridge."

"What even is age? What even is anything? All is as all does, that is all. Oh, to hell with all that nonsense. You are an old man, and I am but a baby! A teeny weeny baby!"

"Excuse me?"

"What is age if not candles? A young man is young if he lives young, and an old man lives, such as it were."

"I don't know what that means."

"How tragic for you. I shall pray, feverishly, that some day you *do* understand. It's the only hope for you, my sweet bitch of a duckling, that one day you do understand."

He rubbed my cheek with the back of his hand, before slapping himself and scurrying off, and I was left in a chasm of his confused and jumbled sayings. I stood in the centre of the room, watching all who came and went; I was within, and without. Fragments of conversation wafted through the air like a scent. I'd pick up on one, follow it until I was interested no more, and then pick up on another. One such conversation brought my evening to a premature end.

"Oh, christ. Is that Robin Fitzwarwick over there?"

"You know, I think it is."

"What on earth is *he* doing here?"

"Haven't a clue. Do you think he's lost?"

"He might just be!"

"How sad. Someone should get him a job in a library, put the poor bastard out of his misery. And send Andress with him if the old trout still thinks he's in the loop."

They laughed to each other, while I stared into my drink and pretended not to listen. Their words were true of course. Culture moves quickly, and one must keep pace. There is, quite simply, no room for stubbornness. If one is not parroting the times, one is invariably behind them. I saw a large arching window, with a balcony on the other side. It became my target, and I fled to it in search of refuge. The cool night air hit me in a moment, and I lit a smoke as the Albert Village grinned at me, sardonically, from the street.

"At last," called a voice behind me. "Someone sane I can talk to."

I turned to see Matheson, aged ever so slightly, and happy to see me. "Matheson, my God!"

"I believe it's been a while, Robin."

"How are you?"

"Unemployed," he said, without skipping a beat. "Yourself?"

"Out of ideas," I sighed in resignation.

"America not the dream you were expecting?"

"Something like that," I muttered.

"So I heard. It happens."

"No. I don't believe it does."

"Yes, you're right. I was just trying to comfort you, but you're right—you really got shafted there."

"I most certainly got *shafted.* I cannot tell you just how good it is to see you, Matheson. I figured I was losing my mind."

He looked back at the party, that had only descended further in my absence. "It's a zoo, isn't it."

"Oh, yes. The worst kind."

He leaned against the stone balcony, and lit a smoke of his own. "Oh, dear God, look at us——the *unemployable* and the *unpublishable*."

"How can so much change in five years?", I asked, clicking the lighter. "I used to be at the centre of these things. Now—now I'm just——"
"The spectre at the feast," Matheson interupted.
"Precisely. All eyes are on the naked Spaniard."
"*Rodrigo Salmas*."
"Rodrigo Salmas, yes."
"At least you're not alone," he began. "I too am a victim of Donald Andress; his wondering eye and grip-less hand. He pulls you in, of course, makes you feel special. And then, by the end of it all you're made to feel like one of half-a-dozen toys, being mulled over by an impudent little boy. And he *never* picks you in the end. And then you're yesterday's news. I could live with it if we'd been replaced by interesting people, but have you met any of the kids in there? Have you spoken to any of them? They are pitifully dull."
"And vacuous," I added, discarding one cigarette and lighting another.
"Yes. You know, Robin. I can tell you this because you're the only person I know anymore who'd find it amusing. I found myself at an art show, not too far, just at some hole-in-the-wall gallery down the road, but that's the sort of place the new lot go mad for. All you'd need to tell them is that it used to be a public toilet, and they'd trample eachother to have an exhibition there. You can see it from here, just over there. It was some sort of showcase from the art school, and they had a little contest between them. Do you know what won?"
"Tell me."
"First, I'll tell you who didn't win; the only half-decent artist in there. He had this very peculiar series of self-portraits, titled *Vices*. He painted himself several times over, however in lieu of his head were a series of common vices. One was a cigarette, one was a bottle, one was——a gramophone I believe, it was really quite fascinating; modern, woefully

modern, but the sort of art that makes you think; and there was a good degree of technical skill."
"It didn't win?", I asked.
"Didn't even get a mention. But, here's the kicker; let me tell you about the winning piece. It was a blue circle."
"A blue circle?"
"A blue circle."
"What could you mean?"
"I mean a blue circle, on a white canvas."
"That's it?"
"Yes."
"Christ."
"And you know the worst part?"
"What?"
"There was a little plaque on the wall next to it, on it was an essay-length justification for putting a blue circle on canvas and declaring it to be art."
"What did it say?"
"I tuned out after the first paragraph. But if I recall correctly, there were three minutely different shades of blue. Allegedly, it means that the artist has three flavours of depression, or whatever nonsense they teach the kids now. One is high-functioning, one is totally dysfunctional, and the other is some blend of the two. '*That's just being alive*', I thought. I ended up in the pub after the show, talking to some undergraduate, and the piece came up in conversation. I told her that I didn't think it was art, and that any old sod could do that. I said that one is meant to look at a piece of art and feel something, feel awe in the face of technical greatness, and imagination. I told her that when I go to Rome, or Paris, or—the Wallace Collection, and I look at the pictures there, what strikes me far more profoundly than the beautiful imagery is that I know that I could never make it. I could have all the time, and instruments, in the world, I could have infinity, and still I'd never recreate those works. Yet, give me a studio, a canvas,

brush, and a tub of blue paint, and I could make a piece so identical that not even the artist could tell the difference. Good art, I told her, does not require justification, it speaks entirely for itself. If art requires justification, that must be spoon-fed to the observer, then it is bad art. Well, I got myself into a little pickle there, as it turns out *she* was the artist. But my point still stands."

"So, that's the secret, is it? Just to make utter tosh?"

"Effectively, yes."

"I dread to think how successful I'd be if I were willing to write tosh. Real tosh I mean. The petty romances feel like biblical poetry in comparison."

"Why aren't you?"

"There are many reasons."

"I'm serious, Robin. Why not? You come from means, correct?"

"I do."

"A family of history."

"Yes."

"And are you currently a wealthy man?"

"Hardly."

"Well, ignore that part. It is up to you, Robin, to show the upstarts that you can do what they do, without even trying. With virtually no effort, you could write what they write. Their life's work could be a slight twitch of your finger. How funny it would be; how little they'd know, how easily their greatest works can be replicated, to such an insulting accuracy. Show the little shits up, and make a pretty penny while you're at it. It'd be—revolutionary."

"I figured *they* were the revolutionaries?"

"Them? Oh, no, no, no. They're the establishment now. It is therefore not only justified, but required of all able-minded men, to bloody their noses."

"Very well, Matheson. *Viva la revolution.*"

He made a mocking symbol with his fist. "Viva la revolution."

"Viva la revolution!", called a third voice from within the

party, as a chorus of similar repeats rung out. Matheson and I laughed, happy with the irony of our achievement."

"And what'll you do, Matheson?"

"I always fancied the idea of going into the theatre. Heck, it's the last place where one can find sanity these days, and even there it's sparing."

"Then I believe we both have someplace else to be."

"I believe so, Robin."

"Godspeed, Matheson."

"And you, Fitzwarwick."

We shook hands and each bore the grin of battle to come. And so, buoyed by our respective missions, we parted once more, and each went home. I left with only a nod and a gesture to Donald, who by then was drunk. My typewriter had not been used for some time, and had rusted a little. I removed it from its case, and placed it upon my desk. '*What is the worst, most vulgar thing that I can write*?', I asked myself.

I spent the entire night writing; without any sort of plan or skeleton. At times, I made myself laugh with the outlandish nature of my words. It was, in short, the crudest, and most needlessly profane thing I had ever put to paper. It should have been controversial, scandalous even; but it was not. By sunrise, it was complete.

The story was fairly sound, by my estimation. A group of Bohemians - a naked painter, a poet who speaks in tongues, and their friends - seclude themselves in a London flat, and debauch themselves until each has completed a work of perceived brilliance. Everything else from that point was empty. The descriptions were gratuitous, the reasonings empty, and the eros unfiltered. I wrote until the sun rose, and then I wrote some more. By ten in the morning, something was there. My eyes had grown weary and sensitive, and I slept through the day. When I awoke, I decided to name it *Lost and Found.* I named it so for no particular reason, almost as if I was protesting something, I saw fit to put as much effort into the title as I did to the whole thing.

I phoned Donald the next day, and told him that I had something he'd like to see. "I forgot how quickly you work when inspiration strikes. How marvellous."

"It's quite unlike anything I have written before."

"Is that so?"

"Yes. It is gritty, *filthy*."

"I like the sound of that," he said with a chuckle.

The call ended, and I delivered my work the next day. Although it was the afternoon, the flat was suspended in a haze of forever-morning. Through the musky air that carried the sickly-triplet scent of smoke, spilled-wine, and *intimacy*, Donald rose slowly with a grumble, as a half-naked woman, wearing but a robe and a beret, and aged some years younger than myself, painted in the corner. She did not so much as glance over when I entered, nor did she when Donald stirred and greeted me; on her canvas, lay a red circle. I took tea and lunch while Donald read it, and decided on a course of action. That evening, he agreed, enthusiastically, to publish the novel.

"They all loved it," he said, gesturing towards the mess left behind. "They refused to believe that it was a *Fitzwarwick*."

"I have just one condition," I said.

"Yes?"

"Publish it under a pseudonym."

"Well, of course. I was going to suggest doing so anyway. I think it'd be rather difficult to market your name to the Firebrand audience."

"Yes. As you said, I'm not exactly *Firebrand material*."

"No, I don't suppose you are. It also eases the need to tour the novel; a piece of raw smut, by an enigmatic, unknown author. It's brilliant. I anticipated this, Robin, and the animals who were here last night have all been sworn to secrecy, if they even remember that is. I doubt they even have, much was discussed last night. And more was done. Oh, you should've been there, Robin. Though, perhaps not. It probably isn't your scene."

"Mm."

"Any ideas on the pseudonym?", he asked.

I thought for a moment, until a skinny grin formed on my face. "Susan Denim."

Donald laughed. "I'll call her '*Sue*'."

We each gave a short chuckle and looked at each other for a moment. When it had passed, both of us knew that the conversation, and in turn our very association, was over. "Donald," I said.

"Yes, Robin."

"This is the last novel I shall ever write for you."

"Well, yes. I suppose it shall be."

"Thank you for everything you have done for me, Donald."

"You're very welcome," he said, readying a cigarette. "I roll my own these days, it's what the young chaps do, it is so much purer. Goes right to the brain."

"I suppose this ends our association."

"Yes, yes. I suppose it does."

"Thirteen years."

"With gaps in between. Best of luck, Robin. We have made a lot of money for each other."

I left Donald's house, and in faith to what I had said, would never see him again. Not too long after that day, he would be ousted from Firebrand by a takeover of the young, and would scurry into the countryside; to live out his days in exile. I too had committed myself to exile, what I affectionately knew as my *exile from creation*. I would not publish another novel for fifteen years, and it would be eleven years before I next put pen to paper. From that day, I had ceased to be *Robin Fitzwarwick the writer*, who had captured England's eyes and ears for a few short, halcyon years in the fifties. It was the sixties now, and I was old news; though not old enough to loop back around, and be an object of interest again. The novel would eventually do well, and I would receive annual royalties until 1974, when the public would eventually bore of it. That novel, which I had written with such contempt, was to be my sole lasting connection to the legacy of Donald Andress.

As I approached the station, I was ambushed and accosted by a small set of vagabonds, six in total. Their faces were dirtied and unsympathetic, and they spoke with a deference that seemed to me a paper-thin cloak, covering clumsily a wealth of ill-intention. My path to the Tube station was blocked, and there were five around me, and a sixth faced away, as if keeping watch. I gave what I could and stumbled out of the crowd, and just as I did, a familiar voice rung out from behind me. It was the sixth man.

"Hello, Robin."

I turned, feeling my eyes widen and my jaw drop at the sight that stood before me. "Francis?"

39

"It is good to see you again, Robin."

"Francis. I—What on earth happened to you?"

"Oh, one thing led to another. Life hasn't been the same since Richard——went away."

The months had indeed not been kind to Francis. His face was swarthy and gaunt, and his hair long and scruffy. He had a thick beard, which had gathered frost in the Winter wind, and his clothing was not enough to keep it at bay. I could not stand the sight of my friend, so withered and torn, at the mercy of the elements.

"Come with me."

I hailed a cab and took Francis back to the flat. He walked around it, as if he were in a museum dedicated to several years of his life. In a sense, he was.

"You live here?", he asked.

"Yes, it was an accident."

"Oh, okay."

Francis took a shower, possibly his first in months. I lent him some razors, and he hacked away at his beard. When he was done, and had put on some clothes of mine which were too big for him, we went for tea.

"I'm so very grateful for all of this, Robin."

"Francis, how did you end up here?"

"Oh, I suppose I took Richard's—going away rather

harshly."

"But why the streets? Could Charles and Mary not have helped?"

"I didn't want to bother them; they've been through so much."

"Yes, I suppose they have."

"Did you hear the news of Adeline?", he asked, stirring milk into his tea.

"Yes, quite recently."

"It's very sad."

"Both of the Belling children," I said. "Gone in one fell swoop——how intolerably sad."

"Yes."

"Francis, I am sorry."

"You are?"

"Richard asked me to take care of you, and I didn't. I take responsibility for this."

"Oh, that's okay Robin. You had things to take care of."

"That was all taken care of months ago. I was in New York, brushing up against folk singers."

"And you were healing. Please, Robin, do not beat your own back with these things. All is forgiven, all did not even require forgiving, but it is forgiven nonetheless."

"You're a good man, Francis."

"Thank you, Robin."

We finished our tea and sandwiches, put on our coats and stepped out into the brutal English Winter. "It has been lovely to see you again, Robin. I hope that I shall see you again soon."

"Wait, Francis."

He turned, with the simple and trusting grin that naturally fell upon his face. "Yes, Robin?"

"Where are you going? You're not going back to the street. Come with me."

"With you?"

"Yes. I have abandoned you once before and I'll be damned if I do it again. You are to come and live with me and that is not negotiable."

"Really?"

"Yes."

"Well, okay. May I go and get my clothes?"

"No. We'll get you new clothes."

"Okay."

We walked back to the flat. Francis lingered in discomfort, as if he wished to speak, but feared his own demands. "Is everything okay?", I asked.

"Yes. Well, it's just that you appear to be sleeping in my old room."

"Is that an issue?"

"Not on its own, no. But I don't think that I can stomach the idea of sleeping in Richard's old room."

"I understand. Here, take your old room, I'll move."

The room that once belonged to Richard had not yet been furnished. I had intended for it to become a study of sorts. In the days and weeks that followed, both rooms became furnished as bedrooms, Francis had acquired new clothes, and we settled into a comfortable routine of nothingness. We both became idle with leisure, and spent our days reading and listening to music. On occasion we would drink wine and lament the modern day. Francis held the same disdain for it that I did, and we bonded over our shared sense of alienation.

"It's a much rougher town at the bottom," he said. "I cannot count on both hands the number of times I was robbed."

Whenever Francis mentioned life on the street, my guilt grew too large to withstand, and I could only listen, for no words could rectify in my mind the great evil I had done. He would not allow me to apologise, for he genuinely saw no reason. And so, I resolved to apologise to him in a different manner.

I visited Monty, now a father of two, and senior lecturer at a university in the city. We had corresponded, via letters, throughout my time in Los Angeles. He knew of my misfortunes, perhaps more intimately than any other soul on earth. However, as his life gave way to domestic affairs and fatherhood, our letters began to slow down, and had ceased by the end of 1962. We met at a cafe, close to the campus.

"I must admit, Robin. It is very bizarre to see you in the flesh."

"Indeed. We represent the duality of thirty-year old men."

"How so?"

"Well, you are married, with children. Meanwhile, I—well I—"

"Am not."

"Yes."

"It has its ups and downs, like anything really."

"But are you happy?", I asked.

"Tremendously so. You must meet the kids, Vera too. She asks about you a lot."

"Does she know of what happened between myself and Elaine?"

"Oh, Robin," he said, with a slight chuckle. "*Everyone* knows."

"I feared as much."

"Would you come for dinner, sometime soon?"

"Of course."

"Wonderful. I shall let Vera know tonight. Where are you living these days?"

"Richard and Francis' old place."

"Oh really? How'd you score that?"

"Accidentally."

"Did Francis come with the furniture?"

"No, I had to go out and find him."

"Whatever could you mean?"

"He was homeless, I found him by accident one day."

"Homeless? How'd he manage th—oh. Oh, yes. Of course. I was very sad to hear of his passing,"

"It happened very quickly. Though I believe he went peacefully—eventually."

"I heard as much. Behind all of the shenanigans, he did have a heart of gold."

"Indeed."

"Anyway. What are you doing with yourself these days?"

"I'm retired."

"Retired?"

"Yes."

"Already?"

"It would seem that the world has moved along without me."

"It has been a number of years since your last book."

"Actually, I wrote one last week."

"So, you're not retired."

"I am. I just retired after writing it."

"I haven't heard any news of your return. Besides, didn't Donald close down the publisher?"

"It's under a pseudonym, for his new publisher."

"Ah, it makes sense now. You had to stoop, and now you've taken your ball and gone home."

"Precisely."

"Well, do you need a job?"

"Do you have one to offer me?"

"A teaching gig. The university is launching some new courses and we need to staff them. One of the courses is *creative writing*."

"Creative writing?"

"Yes."

"One can obtain a degree in creative writing?"

"Yes."

"Oh, God. What a waste."

"You think it's beneath you?"

"A little."

"Do you want it?"

"Sure."

"Okay, I'll put a word in. It'll be from the Autumn."

"Okay."

The afternoon stretched on, and we spoke of the past, present, and future. Food came and went, and wine was consumed by the bottle. Our time together drew to a close by mid-evening, and we lingered outside, waiting for a car.

"You should get the cigarettes out of your life, Robin. They'll kill you."

"The biggest cause of death is being born."

"Alright, don't get clever."

"There is one more favour I must ask of you, Monty."

"Oh?"

"Does your father still sit on the board at the Royal Horticultural?"

"Yes, I believe he does."

"Do you think he'd be hiring?"

And so it was that both Francis and I became *gainfully* employed. I was to be a teacher, and he a guide and archivist. Our idleness had morphed into long days and short evenings. The Spring and the Summer passed in that way, and we said very little. One day, as we read in silence, I suddenly stopped and stiffened.

"Francis," I said.

"Yes?"

"I'm thirty-one. Thirty-one, and I believe the joy has died."

"I'll make us some tea."

By September, I was a teacher. My students were mostly ignorant, and dragged their feet as they walked in and out. They sought not literary esteem, but rather comfortable jobs at newspapers and magazines. Those who did wish to write novels, wished to write for Firebrand, for it was where the best parties could be found. For two years I trudged along. My expectations were limited, and my days were bereft of event. I had climbed the hill and found the plateau. And yet, the view sickened me some, for I knew that I could climb no higher. I felt, in those days, like I had at Charterhouse; in purgatory and without a ladder to heaven. And yet, life just has a funny way of throwing debris into one's path, and I was not destined to solitude for long.

40

By the start of my third year as a teacher, my life as a writer seemed of another age entirely. A rot had set into the pillars, and that part of me that one could call an *artiste* was rusted to the core, and rendered immobile; and soon I thought of writing only in sparing episodes. In truth, it would have been almost impossible to continue regardless of how I felt. I was a writer of the *fifties*, and it was the *sixties*. My brief career in cinema, considered by all to be a total failure, compounded this. As it happens, my sordid novel for Firebrand had sold remarkably well, and a great game was unleashed by amateur sleuths to locate the identity of its author. My name had been mentioned in a few theories in various periodicals, citing my prior relationship with Donald Andress, but each suggestion was laughed off. '*Robin Fitzwarwick*?', they'd chuckle at any suggestion. '*There is simply no way*'.

The term began much in the same way that my first lesson at Camford had, some years prior. I gave my lesson, and scanned the room as I did so. When I spoke, I put everything into the emulation of Balloch. I borrowed his passion and copied his wit. Alas, my words fell upon deaf ears.

"—and so, Maugham concludes, through the final decision of Philip Carey, that sometimes the simplest life is that which brings us the most joy. Find someone that you love, and never cease to love them. Enjoy the little rituals of life, enjoy the gentle passing of time, if you expect simplicity; then life will not disappoint, and moments of passion will enthral. And we shall leave it there for today. Please have your short stories prepared by the end of the week, and we shall go over them in tutorials. Thank you, and I shall see you all on Thursday."

The room groaned to its feet, as individuals trudged their way to the door, the uncaring and uninterested. I stood at my podium for a while longer. A part of me expected some sort of conversation, reminiscent of my first with Balloch. Perhaps some neurotic fresher, compelled to write, would make an uneasy approach and we would wax lyrical, long into the night. Perhaps I would become Balloch, and this fantastical, wide-eyed student would become me, and we'd meet on Friday afternoons. I would take him to university events, and help with his first novel.

This was not to be the case, and instead I found myself melancholic for my old friend and mentor. 'Whatever became of that old, drunken playwright?', I'd ask myself. I knew that the drink had got him, just not to what extent. He would've been in his fifties by then. After ten minutes of silent thought had passed, a knock came at the door.

"Hello chap," said Matheson, entering the room and taking a seat, as if he were a student.

"Matheson?", I asked, surprised to see him. "Is something the matter?"

"What do you mean?"

"Well, I hope you don't think it rude of me to ask, but what are you doing here?"

He chucked, stood, and walked towards me. "That's funny. Are you ready?"

"Ready for what?"

He stopped, and saw the look of genuine confusion on my face. "Oh, you silly bugger, Robin. You've forgotten, haven't you?"

"Forgotten what?"

"The symposium. *An Evening with Robin Fitzwarwick.*"

"Shit! Was that tonight?"

"I haven't moved it. I thought you said you'd put it in your diary?"

I retrieved a diary out of my bag, and scrambled through the pages until I found the day's date. Sure enough, there was, encircled in red, '*Matheson's event*'. It was the sole booking I had made for months, and it was cast away in that brown book, left isolated by sheets of blank white paper on either side. "Am I late?", I asked.

Matheson checked his watch. "No, but we should leave soon."

Sure enough, we left, and chatted idly while we walked to, waited for, and rode the Tube. Matheson was now director of a small theatre in the West End. He had fulfilled his end of our *little revolution*.

"Thanks for doing this," he said as we arrived. "I know it's not your sort of thing anymore, but it helps."

"That's alright," I said, as a rolling anxiety brewed within me.

"Wait here," he said, ushering me into a small room by the stage door. "I'll take a look at the crowd."

I hadn't expected much from the evening. The prospect of literary esteem was now so far behind me, that I was surprised to have even heard from Matheson. We'd lost contact quite quickly after Donald's party. He was, in trying to stem the tide of declining showings and sales, running a series of literary symposia, hosting whichever writers he could. I was the fourth, and there were to be six in total. Soon enough, he returned, though there was a grave look on his face, which I had anticipated. "How bad is it?", I asked. "How many?"

"Well, these things are—"

"How many, Matheson?"

"Eight, uh—"

"Eighty?"

"Eight."

"Eight?"

"Eight people, yes. Ten if you include us."

"Funnily enough, I don't include us. Oh, Christ. I can't go out there, that's humiliating. I may as well busk outside."

Matheson had taken another look into the auditorium while I lamented. "Six. Two just left."

I paced back and forth. "Hey," Matheson said. "Don't take it out on them. There may only be eight—"

"Six," I corrected.

"Six. There may only be six, but it's six people who've come to see you. Just remember that."

"Well I can't give a symposium to six people. That's not even a symposium, that's just speaking to six people."

"Do you want me to send them home?"

"No. I think I have an idea."

I walked past Matheson and into the auditorium. The six who had remained smiled politely, and sympathetically.

"Okay," I began. "This is—so remarkably telling. Thank you all, firstly, for being here, but this is a sign that my career is over. I'd figured it was over, but now I know. The defibrillation has failed to revive the patient. So let's do away with the symposium, and have a wake instead. If any of you wish to join me in the pub, the drinks are on me."

Two of the crowd refused the offer, and left the room muttering about refunds. And so, I went to the pub with Matheson and four strangers. Two were older than me, and two were younger. The elders left after humouring me over a polite drink, and one of the younger's left after a second. Then it was just Matheson, myself, and her. She was in her early twenties, with a symmetrical fringe of blonde hair, that covered her brow. She wore a light dress, and a cardigan.

"You don't need to be here," I said to her. "I appreciate it, but I think the night is over."

"Nonsense," she said. "Besides, I was hoping you'd sign something for me."

"And what would that be?", I asked.

She went into a satchel, and retrieved - much to my shock and amusement - a copy of *Lost and Found.* I stared at her, dumbfounded. "It was you," she said. "Wasn't it?"

"How did you—"

"I recognised it."

Matheson was amused as well, and chuckled to himself. "*Viva la revolution,*" I heard him whisper to himself. I signed the book as '*Susan Denim*'.

"I was going to ask you at the university," she began. "But I figured I'd find you in a bad mood."

"Do you study there?"

"Yes, I'm a postgraduate, English Literature. There was actually something else I wanted to ask you."

"Yes?", I asked.

"I write for the university paper, and would love to run a profile on you."

"On me?"

"On you, yes."

"And you can see that my current—let's just say *occupation*, is quite a fall from where I once was."

"I suppose one could see it that way."

I looked to Matheson for approval. He finished his drink and stood. "I don't need to be here for this," he said.

"Adieu, Robin. Until next time. And you, I'm sorry, I don't know your name."

"Elsa," the girl said, shaking his hand. "Elsa Sullivan."

"Goodnight, Elsa Sullivan."

And with that he was gone, and I was left with *Elsa Sullivan.* She moved closer and removed a notebook, in which I could see an interview that was laid out and plotted meticulously. "And what if I'd said no?"

"You wouldn't have."

"Why is that?"

She blew upwards, and the wind cut her fringe down the middle. "Right, shall we begin?", she asked, ignoring the question.

"Sure. How long will this take?"

"Not long at all. I only have enough column inches for several questions."

"Okay."

"Why did you retire from writing?"

"Wow. Straight in with the googly."

"I have a straight bowl, generous bounce, if you'd prefer that?"

"Which is?"

"Your favourite book."

"No, it's okay. I suppose it comes down to a question of does one stay at a party, at which he is no longer welcome. I felt that literature, or rather the culture around literature, had simply moved beyond me, what I wanted to write was not in demand, and I did not want to write what was in demand."

"It sounds like quite a practical decision. Is there anything you never finished?"

"Yes, the first novel I ever started. I couldn't quite crack it, put it in a box, and never looked at it again. I should like to finish it one day."

"Do you think that you will?"

"Perhaps when I am on my death bed."

"That sounds like a premonition."

"No. I'm accepting my own limitations."

"You went to Hollywood."

"Yes."

"Would you consider your time there to be successful?"

"It was, until it suddenly wasn't."

"Is that why you returned to England?"

"It was and it wasn't."

"Can I have a straight answer."

"I believe that the world already knows. Look, if you want to understand why I'm where I am, it's really quite simple. I was just confined to an epoch. It's important to note that I grew up in the war; I saw it, heard it. My father died at war, it's—sorry, what year were you born in?"

"Forty-two."

"Okay. So, you were alive during the war, but you don't remember it, correct?"

"I suppose not."

"I remember life before, during, and after. And I think in those days that people just wanted something that was warm, and beautiful, innocent and young. In a single word, they wanted love. I was able to give it to them, while satisfying my own urge to write."

"So what changed?"

"Everything. In the blink of an eye. One day, I simply awoke to find that *conquest* was the word of the day. Sex conquered love. Brash youth conquered precocious youth. Nuclear heat conquered warmth. And lust conquered beauty."

"I see that you haven't lost your instincts."

"Like I said, I may write again."

She smiled, satisfied.

"May I ask you a few questions?", I asked.

"Of course."

"You're young, right? How old are you?"

"I'm twenty-four."

"Right, yes. You're young, and in the literary circles. I think. What do they say of me?"

"You really want to know?"

"Somehow I do."

"I thought you knew already."

"Only what's been said to me. Though I find people are much more honest in their—critique when the subject is not in the room."

"Well, firstly it is a lot more mixed than you'd presume. Many people still love your work, they see it for what it is. Some resent you for going to Hollywood. Most associate your work with their teenage years, and there's no harm in that. I believe they'll come back around because you wrote things that are permanent. You hooked them in with stories of young love, adventure, and then you filled their heads with platonic loves; art and music whatnot.

You know, I remember reading Loving Saint Anne, and the scene where you listen to that Korsakov record in the library."

"Me?"

"Well, yes, I assumed that all of your protagonists were stand-in's for yourself."

"I suppose so."

"Was that not on purpose?"

"I used those books to meditate on things. I was always unlucky in love, so I wrote myself into good fortune."

"Well, either way. I read that scene, and rushed out to the nearest record shop to find a copy, and I couldn't. I ended up searching all over town, and found one after two hours of looking. It made me cry as well."

In that moment, I felt a tugging within myself. As if some lasso, made up of lost praises and courage misplaced, had wrapped itself around my waist, and pulled me into her field of gravity. It was not lust that I felt for Elsa, nor was it a desire for intimacy - though I was lonely - but rather it was an insatiable thirst, to hear more, for she so easily spoke words that I had longed to hear.

"I think I have everything," she said beginning to rise.

"Wait," I said.

"Yes?"

"What else to people say of me? It's just that I have shielded myself away from people's words for so long, that now it's right in front of me, I can't resist."

"Like I said, there are divergent paths."

"Like what?"

"People who like you, people who don't. Though I don't think it's *you* that they don't like, I think it's *yesterday* that they wish to assail and besiege. It's the *system,* the police, their parents, schoolmasters. It;s just easier to attack a novelist. Of course, you could have easily been shielded from it. I don't think

Andress House was the right place for you. To them, you were a cash cow; bankable, reliable, popular, a license to print money at Christmas. Yet at the same time they refused to let you expand. The Yugoslavia book read like a bird with clipped wings, if I may say so. It was, if one discounts Lost and Found, your most *experimental* work, and they just let it trickle out. I remember feeling so angry about that. And then they just dumped you as soon as the new crop came along. I recall getting into a fierce debate, just a few months ago with someone who called your work petty romances. They absolutely were not. Maybe the first one, but that's to be expected from a debut. Your second novel captured young love perfectly. Your third and fourth novels were not even romantic at all. They were witty, fierce; they captured in a bottle the other side of youth, the frustration, the aimlessness. My point is that the right publisher would have done better by you."

"I'm not sure if the right publisher exists."

"Oh, they do. They're just not big names. Perhaps you should have shopped around a little."

"I was eighteen when I first published with Andress. Perhaps it's not been made public, indeed I hope it hasn't, but the Andress family had quite the hold on me back then."

"Is that so?"

I raised a brow, which told Elsa that if she wished to probe further, it would be at her own peril. "I am a firm believer in permanence, Robin. Change is inevitable, sure. But good things are permanent and one day you shall be known."

"Known as what?"

"I don't want to inflate your ego, Robin."

I chuckled. "You'd be breathing life into it."

"One of the greats."

"I fled then the iron was hot, Elsa. I've squandered my chance at greatness."

Not long after, I bade Elsa a goodnight, and

returned home with a long-forgotten sense of buoyancy. Francis read on the sofa as I entered the living room. “Evening, Francis.”

“Good evening, Robin. How was the symposium?”

I thought about the evening. “Better than I would have thought.”

41

I saw Elsa in fleeting encounters, as we skirted and danced around one another in the halls. In her I found the deep comfort of nostalgia. In her, I found the sense that I had not quite vanished from view. On occasion she would remind me of a passage she had liked in an old book of mine. At least thrice a week, an apple would be left on my desk, and I knew, instantly, the culprit.

On one such day, when Christmas and the new year had been and gone, and the Winter of 1967 slowly acquiesced into Spring, we spoke again. I was sat in my office, grading short stories when there was a knock upon the door.

"Come in," I called.

The door opened and Elsa entered, in her typical nature; reserved, yet forward; polite, yet assertive. "Hello," she beamed.

"Hi."

She took a seat and began studying some notes of hers. Confused, I enquired. "Can I help you with something?"

"No."

"Have you come to give me another apple?"

Her eyes shot up and stared me down. "You have no evidence that I have done any such thing. An apple? How abs—"

"My secretary saw you."

"Okay, it was me."

"I don't even have a secretary."

She laughed at the interaction, and I joined her for the last few beats. She spoke up after a muted minute. "What are you doing?"

"Grading stories."

"How are they?"

"Not very good. Are you sure there's nothing I can help you with?"

"Well, it's just that I wanted to invite you to something, but for some unknown reason I feel so embarrassed."

"Embarrassed?"

"Yes. It is most peculiar."

"Go on."

"Well, it's my birthday at the end of the week, and I wandered if you would like to attend a dinner for it."

"Your birthday dinner?"

"Yes."

"Would that not arouse some suspicions?"

"Only if such suspicions are grounded in fact."

"Are they not?"

"It's just dinner, Mr. Fitzwarwick."

"People talk, Elsa. Regardless of what they see or imagine."

"Well, would you come regardless?"

"Yes, I think I shall."

She grew excited and bounced up to her feet.

"Thank you ever so much!"

"That's okay."

"It'll be on Saturday." It was a Monday.

"I shall see you then," I said, readying a cigarette and opening a crack in the window.

She rose and made way for the door. Just as she opened it, Monty went to enter and the two startled each other. "Oh, hello," Monty said, bowing his head slightly.

"Hello," Elsa chipped back. They passed one another in the door frame and soon Monty was sat before me.

"A student of yours?", he asked.
"A friend."
"Is she a student here?"
"Yes."
"Be careful, Robin. I—"
"It's okay, Monty. Nothing is happening. She's from the college paper and wanted to interview me, that's all."
Monty froze, and gave me a funny look. "The college doesn't have a paper."
"Can I help you, Monty?", I asked, shaking off his revelation.
"*I* came to see if you'd dine with us tonight; Vera and the kids."
"Tonight?"
"Yes."
"Sure, I'd love to."
"Great! How long has it been since the last? Must've been two or three years by now. Vera misses you so, the children too. We'd begun to worry that you had a whole other life to live."
"I can assure you, Monty," I said, shuffling and stacking some papers. "That my life is of very little interest."

The truth of the matter is that I felt somewhat inferior around Monty in those days. While my life had stagnated and my career could be witnessed only in retrospect, Monty's had soared. He had climbed to lead his faculty at the university, and now found himself as the provost of the whole college. Within a decade, and upon the glowing recommendations of the outgoing incumbent, he'd be installed as the University Chancellor.

"I'm sure that is not true. Have you not managed to write anything?"
"No."
"It'll come."
"Perhaps. Would there be room for one more?"
"Do you wish to invite the student?"
"No. Francis."

"Oh, yes of course. Truth be told I had completely forgotten about him. How is he?"

"Somewhat lost I fear. He waits for me to give him instructions. He seems to have had the independence beaten out of him. I fear that if I were not there, he simply wouldn't eat."

"One of Richard's less savoury traits."

"Yes."

"Of course Francis is welcome."

"Great. I shall let him know."

And so, we dined,, and that night is of little in the way of meaningful recollections. Monty's children were seven and five. They were well behaved, and an object of great pride for their parents. Monty, in those days, was something of a duality. He possessed everything I wished for, yet also wished to never possess. He was comfortable, successful by his own metric, and loved beyond compare by those around him. And yet, something in his life was stale, predictable. Much like my own life, the youth had been squeezed out of it and all that remained was each passing day; seconds, and minutes, and hours.

All that is of note about that evening's meal was a comment, made in passing by Vera as we finished our food, and Monty took his children into the kitchen to fetch pudding.

"You, Robin," she began, before placing a glass of wine to her lips. "You have the ability to move people to tears, by making little markings on paper. Isn't that remarkable? That you can do that? If I could do that, I'd never stop. I'd do it all day, every day."

She was, of course, correct, and those words - then spoken to me with such a nonchalance, that she may as well have told me what water is wet, fire burns - were imprinted on my thoughts until we bid our goodbye's.

That night, we returned home and settled ourselves with a glass of whiskey. On the way back, I meditated on what Vera had said, and asked myself if I had indeed jumped ship prematurely. Perhaps there was still room for me.

"You know, Francis," I said, as we entered the flat

and made ourselves comfortable. "I *was* happy once."

"Oh?"

"Camford. I was happy in Camford."

"I know."

I thought about Camford again as we sat in silence, like I so often did. All manner of quagmires and tragedies had found Francis and I in the paltry years in between then and now. We had known death, destitution, and abandon. And yet, those years never left me, and never ceased to give me a subtle and serene comfort; like the clouds parting at last, after a long and rainy day. When Camford was at the fore of my recollection, no other blissful or rose-tinted haze could possibly jostle for space in amongst the awe-filled visions of cloisters and cupolas, and collegiate stone, and the smell of geraniums, and the sound of students roaring into gear and riding about on bicycles - the hum of reinvention. Where a thousand years of ever-moving and replenishing youth found its own way through the winding halls of adolescence unbound. Where yesterday and today cut a path in tandem, hacking through the undergrowth, easing the trail for tomorrow to saunter from eighteen to twenty-one; scribbling away in battered old journals and breezing along the waterway in a punting boat, at peace with the world and all of her tenants. And when it was buried underneath, a deep and distant ringing was always there. But that time is gone, and shall never return. And all that is left are memories that shall die with me. It is perhaps the greatest and most sincere curse of sapience; that we are blessed with memory, only to desire fiercely, and search fruitlessly for something that cannot be held. I was happy there and was not here.

'*Tomorrow*,' I said quietly to myself. '*I shall be older, where once it felt as if I were to be forever young. And the next day I shall be even older, and older more the day after that - looking back with a sterner face, scarred by lines and wrinkles, hardened by time and regret, left baffled and bemused by the world around me, which seems intent on throttling the artist and praying to the merchant and financier - more dishonest, less taken by all that is beautiful and good; more conducive to my own flavour of madness, which brews and boils with every day that passes. I do not hate the world as it is, rather for what it is not, or is no longer. I do not hate the world because it is ugly, but rather because it was once beautiful; not because it is lawless, because it was lawful. Disorganised, oriented; loud, quiet; discourteous, civil, and so on.'*

"But I can never go back, can I?"

"No," he said.

"That's the greatest curse of life, isn't it; that we can never go back."

"Is there a day you'd go back to?"

"That very first night, do you remember?"

"Of course I do."

"Jarves was telling some embarrassing story about me, at Charterhouse, and then you dropped a glass on purpose. Do you remember doing that?"

"I do."

"Why did you do it?"

"I don't know," he said, sitting up straight. "It was just the right thing to do."

"We are two sides of a coin, Francis. You always do the right thing, and I always do the wrong thing. I've squandered just about every chance of happiness I've ever had. And now, I'm in my thirties. I'm in my thirties, and my sole joy comes from the memory of my teens and twenties. What's the use of it all, Francis?"

"Excuse me?"

"This——life we've built for ourselves. Aren't you bored, Francis? Aren't you so unbelievably bored? So bored that you could kill a man, just to—feel something?"

"I don't know, Robin. I suppose I'm just happy to be comfortable. I've a roof over my head, which at one point I didn't have, as you well know. I have you for company, and this rye is very nice."

"It is nice. And yet, I am bored stiff."

"Then I think you should do something about that,

Robin."
"Do you think Monty was right?", I asked.
"Was he right?"
"About writing, how I should get back into it."
"Well, yes. That's obvious to me. Is it not obvious to you?"
"Is it?"
"Why would you choose to live in your memories, when you have the means to feel more? If you only live in yesterday, or in tomorrow, then there shall be no room for today. Answer me this, Robin. How do you feel in the morning?"
"That depends on the morning."
"The mornings when you are going to work."
"Oh, yes. I feel sick."
"You see, Robin, I feel wonderful in the mornings. Not because I am doing what I was born to do, but because I enjoy what I do. I take meaning from it."
"You're right. I know that you're right, but I fear that I'm doomed."
"In what sense?"
"I miss writing, tremendously, every day. I—I just think it's over for me."
"Nonsense," he said, getting up and joining me at the window.
"You don't need to display it in public, you know. You could just write."
"I don't know what I'd write about. I used to mine my own life for material, but there's not much in teaching, and I don't particularly want the world to know that I am a teacher. What am I to do, write another *Lucky Jim*? At least he had interesting characters. I'm surrounded by dullards. Or I could make something up, but what? My mind is so bereft of ideas. All of the space is filled up by boredom and a longing to not be bored. Should I write about God? But I don't believe in God, so do I just invent one of my own? Perhaps I should do that. Perhaps I'm just drunk. What do you think, Francis? Should I write

about a god of my own invention? And what shall he do? Curse the good and bless the wicked? Turn water into stout? Shit himself?"

"You could name him Extretius!", Francis added, taking great joy from my pondering. "But the obvious answer is that book you were working on in Paris. You see, I believe it's the one thing about writing that you truly lacked in those days, and without it you can never stop."

"And what would that be?"

"Would it be woefully pretentious to call it your masterpiece?"

"No, it wouldn't be. It's there, waiting for every writer who dares dream. But I daren't think how long I've waited, maybe sixteen years?"

"You're all wrapped up in yesterday again."

By now, we were both gazing out the window, into the street below where a light rain had begun to fall, coating the slabs in a shiny veneer of dirt. "What did you make of me back then?", I asked.

"I'm sorry?"

"You must have formed some opinion of me. It's okay, I won't get upset."

"You'd have no reason to, Robin. I've never thought ill of you. You'll have to let me think about my answer, as you said it's been some time. One thing I call is thinking that you couldn't hurt a fly."

"That's funny. I remember thinking a fly could have hurt you."

We laughed and I readied us each another glass, and sat impatiently while he thought. "I'd say that you were quite unlike the chaps I knew from school," he said. "There was this——unassuming nature about you, yet one that was inquisitive. You asked questions with your eyes, and the answers came from your observations. Your five senses, guided by reason. You were not boastful. You chose your words carefully, which makes sense. You were funny, in a funny sort of way. I'd say that I knew straight away that you were an artist. Not because of any body of work, nor any prestige, for you've built those things since I have known you. There's a sensitivity to you, even now. And by that I don't mean that you've become rigid, but you have become colder. A matter of age I suppose, though I don't believe I've changed all that much. Writing is simply what you do, and a writer is simply who you are. I think that you are lost without it."

"Am I lost?"

"Well, if everywhere you go leads you to where you don't want to be, then yes, you're lost. I dare say that you weren't entirely happy in Camford. You say that they were the happiest days of your life, and I have no reason to disbelieve you. From what I've heard, you've been through the meat grinder and back—we both have. Here's what else I remember thinking about you, that there was a distinct sadness. It wasn't the typical sort of sadness, it wasn't heartbreak, or madness, but rather a melancholy——a melancholy somewhere deep within you. It is, I used to think to myself, the sadness only found in writers and poets and painters. It is a tool, like ink or turpentine. The rest of us are just the regular sort of sad. That is what I believe that you have, Robin, the writer's curse. You are able to craft something from nothing, it's a form of magic really. And yet, with it comes an enormous pressure to——well, craft something from nothing. The artist is lonely, his head is full of ideas, and so he is dominated by his own company. I don't think it is happiness that the writer truly seeks, it is only a respite from sadness."

Francis went to bed not long after those words. I lingered and had another glass, and with the fuzz of drink came the clarity of memory, cutting through like a knife. I recalled those teenage years, all that had been scattered between that first night and this one. I recalled the excitement I felt; at life itself and any opportunity to capture it. I recalled how I'd stay up all night, plastered on merlot and two packs of smokes, and write until the sun rose, just to feel the keys beneath my fingers. And then I became unendurably sad, and knew then that I'd have cut off a limb, without a moment's thought, for one more night like in Camford, with Richard at the helm. And then came clarity once more, for Francis had seen deep into my soul, and with a delicate pinch, had extracted a tincture for my malaise. It lay in words, it always did. Memory was an old lover, rather than a progeny to bring into this world.

There was a box underneath my bed; in it were the skeletons of my old life. A copy of each of my books, and each of my screenplays, my typewriter, a few notebooks with scattered poetry and fragments of adolescent idyll. Under it all was the unfinished manuscript, from whence it all came.

'*All's Well in Winter Days*,' I whispered to myself, just as I had almost two decades earlier.

42

Saturday came and I received a note that informed of the restaurant. It was in Westminster, just shy of the Abbey and Parliament. I arrived several minutes late, and yet was the first to arrive. I noticed, immediately, the rouse I had walked into. Elsa sat alone, on a table for two. So convinced was I that some sort of mistake had been made, that I questioned if it was Elsa who was sat there. Alas it was, and she wore an expression of bespoke panic.

"Elsa," I said, while taking a seat. "Is everything okay?"

"Oh, yes. It is so embarrassing. I——well, I told the others that I was under the weather, and rearranged for next week."

"You did?"

"Yes," she said, unable to look me in the eye.

"And your birthday *is* today?"

"It is."

"Ah," I said, now understanding the situation perfectly. "Well, *happy birthday*."

"Thank you."

She had flushed red, and buried her head into her hands. "Hey!", I said, placing a hand onto her wrist. "It's okay, don't be embarrassed."

"I don't know what I was thinking."

"Don't be so silly. Here, I've a gift for you."

She raised her, head and our eyes met, quite possibly for the first time. Our gazes held as her features softened and the natural colour returned to her face. "A gift?", she asked. She smiled and I rummaged through my bag.

"Close your eyes, and give me your hands."

She did as I said, and I placed an apple into her outstretched palm. Upon opening, she laughed mightily, and it gained the attention of much of the room. "Oh, Robin. This is my favourite ever gift."

"It's only a joke, Elsa. Here, I have another."

"Another?"

"Yes."

"Do I have to close my eyes for this one too?"

"No."

I retrieved some papers and laid them out on the table. "What is it?", she asked.

"An unpublished *Fitzwarwick* novel.

"You want me to read it?"

"If you'd be so kind."

"Oh, Robin. This is so wonderful."

"You are quite possibly my biggest fan."

"I think I may just be. You know, I was there when you read *Adam of the Adriatic Eden*."

"Really?", I asked, recalling the night my career died.

"Yes! In that crummy little Chelsea bookshop. When would that have been? Must have been about nine years ago."

"Yes, I suppose it must have been."

"There were so few people there, and I felt ever so sorry for you. I also felt so angry. 'How could people be so foolish', I asked myself. 'Don't they know what they are missing'. I believe some of your friends were there. Elaine Mills was there, as was the man I met in your office on Monday. There were some people I did not recognise."

"Vera, Monty's wife. There was also my friends Richard and Francis."

"Do you still see them?"
"I live with Francis, and you met Monty the other day in my office; Vera is his wife."
"And Richard?"
"He died, several years ago."
"Oh, Robin. I am so sorry."
"If one was to tear out their hair over all of life's little heartbreaks, soon we'd all be bald."
She giggled, and quickly caught herself. "I'm sorry, I don't mean to laugh. It's just that it was very well put."
"Yes, I suppose it was."
"It is a pity that you do not write anymore. You do have such a beautiful way with words."

We ate, and drank. In Elsa's presence, I found hope for myself. Here, before me, was someone who viewed me so highly. Ever since returning from my sojourn in the Balkans, I had been met, almost entirely, with dismissal and derision. In England, I was washed, and in America a failure outright. '*Relic*', '*has-been*', '*snob*', '*public school boy*'. These were words I had heard, or read, and each struck like the very first blow of rejection, which befell me in that Avignon hotel room in the Summer of 1952. My skin did not toughen from each cut and bruise. It remained just as tender as the day of my first praises, and so each strike was a brand new agony. As such, I found her celebration to be intoxicating.

To her, my words were gospel and my poetry was communion. Perhaps it is why I fell for her in the way that I did. Not through the beating of my heart but the shrivelling of my ego. On some days, I considered myself cursed, as it had seemed that all of the relationships I'd had before simply led to the destruction of one or more participants. Adeline was dead, Cynthia a forlorn divorcee, Elaine had abandoned me and I had abandoned Milena. Francine was an unknown quantity.

"If you were to read this," I said, gesturing at the fragments of a novel. "Mind you, it'll need reworking of course. But if you were to read it, and find within it some brilliance, some of my old ways, would you expect me to finish it?"

"Of course."

"Then perhaps I shall."

"Really?"

"What have I to lose? I'm already a teacher."

"I suppose so."

And so, when I returned that night, I wrote what would become my first steps away from the barren land I had exiled myself to. I prepared myself with typical rituals, though hours passed with little fruit. I took to a few glasses of wine, and as they trickled into my blood, I found that I had nothing, I had lost my words. And then, like water trickling from a dam, with cracks beginning to show, words began to form. I poured another glass, as water beat ferociously on the cracked wall, that came undone with every passing sip. My eyes had begun to widen, as my pulse elevated and adrenaline reverberated around my body. This was the thrill that I had missed so greatly, that one true treasure that none could take from me, and yet I gave away in an act of rebellion. I came alive, as words poured from my brain to my hands, and from my hands onto paper.

Cracks became crevices, and concrete was sprayed all over the valley, as the dam burst and thunder roared. Water in the form of words cascaded, and all fears were swept away. I was alive and blind, in a fugue state and I wrote, and drank, and wrote, and drank, and smoked, and read, and marvelled, and paced around, and danced, and stretched, and when I stopped, with the sun beating through the window upon my eyes, I was shell-shocked. My hands seemed to sizzle and smoke, as I took a deep breath in and a stuttering breath out. For the first time in three years, I had written.

"Francis," I said, later that day when I had risen.

"Yes, Robin?"

"I wrote last night. An entire story, from start to finish."

"Oh, did you?"

"I did."

"I feel like a muse," he grinned, handing me a cup of coffee.

"And *I* feel like a writer again."

"What'll you do with it?"

"Maybe I'll burn it."

"Oh, I get it. Like an act of protest?"

"Something like that."

"Would you like some toast?"

"Yes I would."

I ate and left the flat, and travelled into the centre of town, where I had arranged to meet with Elsa for tea. "A story!", she exclaimed. "Oh, Robin, how exciting!"

"All thanks to you, Elsa. I did't know if I had it in me."

"I read your manuscript. Well, the half of it that is written."

"And?"

"It's brilliant. There's most certainly a naïveté to it, but it's raw, and it's——Fitzwarwick. I get it."

"Can you see why no eighteen year old could write it?"

"I do. What'll you do with it?", she asked, nodding downwards at the chapter.

"Burn it."

"Oh, like an act of protest?"

"Funny, Francis said just the same thing."

"That's funny, I hear that a lot from you, that I sound like this friend of yours. Perhaps I should meet him."

"Perhaps you should."

We walked across the street and into Hyde Park, where I produced a lighter and set the paper-stack ablaze. We gave the work a sort of funeral, before stamping out its embers and finding a bench nearby to sit on. We remained there for some time, saying little, and then a lot, and then little again. Afternoon came, and Elsa rose to her feet. "I must go, Robin. My parents are in the city and I promised to meet with them."

"When shall I see you again?"

"Not for some time, I'm afraid."

"Oh?"

"I have a thesis to write, for which I shall require total isolation. You, Robin Fitzwarwick, are forbidden from my presence. You're too much a distraction."

"When's it due?"

"The middle of April."

"So, a month?"

"Yes."

"I can wait a month."

"Okay, good. Once all is out of the way, I would really like to dine with you."

"Do you mean as we have done? Or as we are not currently permitted to do?"

"What do you think?", she said, before turning and walking away, leaving me to wonder.

From that day, and for the next few months, something else emerged from me. I was prolific once more. So utterly consumed was I in the novel, that at some point on the road a bizarre thing happened. I entered a state of wicked obsession, and formed a para-social bond with my creation. The characters on the page were my friends, and I missed them when I could not be with them; in the classroom, away from my desk. It dominated me, as I grappled back, and soon we danced a tango, that novel and I, under the moonlit, Spring night, as I waited for Elsa. And then, fate, dressed up in her untrammelled cruelty would find its way back to me. As one night, while I drank with Francis in a bar, the first seed of my fifth destruction burrowed itself into the soil. It came in the form of a stranger.

"Say, I don't suppose you're Robin Fitzwarwick?", asked the mystery man, when by chance we met in the local pub.

"I am."

"Goodness me, what a wonderful surprise. I'm a great admirer. I was saying just the other day, it's *such* a pity you stopped writing."

"Um—thank you."

"No need to thank me, I just figured someone like you would still have so much more to give. Are you writing still?"

"I wasn't until recently, but I've gone into a good patch."

"Is that so?"

"It is."

"That——is music to my ears, Robin. May I call you Robin?"

"You may."

"That is music to my ears, Robin. I knew Firebrand would see what they'd lost and come crawling back. It's a very different place now though I hear, without the *mighty Donald Andress*."

Donald's ousting was news to me, but I thought the subject uncouth to dicuss with a stranger. "I'm not signed to Firebrand."

"Oh, no? Who is it then?"

"Well, currently I don't have a publisher."

"Are you serious?"

"Afraid so."

"Well, count my lucky stars. As it happens, I'm in the publishing business. Well, I am soon to be. You see, my old man just snuffed it, he's a frog from Lyon and ran a publisher out there. It'll be mine as soon as the lawyers pull their fingers out."

"Is that so?"

"Oh, yes. I'd love to work with you. Just think of it, *the triumphant return of Robin Fitzwarwick*. It'd be one hell of a story."

It would have been, had he not played my frail and fractured ego, like a fiddle. "Yes, it would be."

"Take my card and think about it."

I did think about it, and I called him after a week and invited him for lunch. He paid, and used the afternoon as an opportunity to butter me up. He spoke as if he had only just read all of my works, in a frantic hurry; and that his interpretations, affected as they were, had been informed entirely by public reviews in national newspapers. I was seduced by his greasy wit, and shameless flattery. So much so, that I allowed myself to dream once more. Though I would not dream for long. Perhaps it was the silver tint of his tongue, or just my own desperation, but when he told me that he needed a few thousand to pay off the lawyers, I handed it over without question, and never heard from that man again. It was all the money I had left, and without it I had no choice but to approach Elsa and ask her for money. She obliged, and I fell into her debt. The day she bailed me out I burned my creation, and swore off writing again.

> '*How foolish you are,*' I said to myself, as the flames danced in the fireplace.

43

Penniless, and with my dreams dashed again, I returned to my daily habits and the nightly lamentations of where my life sat. In a fit of anger, I had destroyed one creation; though could not bring myself to burn All's Well, and instead buried it again at the bottom of the box, underneath the ghosts of my career.

Francis trudged along too, and we shared a sort of distant depression; his living vicariously through mine. We rarely left the flat except to work, and kept to ourselves. We had each other, and yet were intolerably lonely, and numb again. I had fallen silent again. Elsa was a free woman, and we dined together the moment she was no longer a student. We walked the south bank, and shared a kiss by the abbey. That night we shared a bed for the first time, in the early hours of the morning, when sleep drew near, her face contorted, and I could tell that she was deep in thought.

"Are you okay?", I asked.

"Yes. It's just, well. I want to ask you about some things, but I fear that it would upset you."

"Go on."

"Well, I wanted to know more about your parents."

"My father died when I was six, and my mother died giving birth to me, I've told you this before, surely."

"And he died in the war?"

"Yes. I fully expected my father to return. I'd even

found a banner, and spent the morning etching it with a *welcome home* message. Alas there came a knock at the door, and I ran so fast that I nearly went through it, expecting to see my father. It was an army messenger, telling me that he had died. The notice gave his date as two days before the German surrender."

"How did he die?"

"An allergic reaction."

"Oh. That's rather—"

"Ironic. Yes, I know. He used to tell me this story about my mother. He told me that she obsessed with birds, she knew all of them, every last one. And when she would see one, she'd point it out and say '*Sparrow*', or '*Falcon*'. Well, there was a storm when I was born, the very end of Summer is typically like that. And when she was dying my father was forced to just sit there, watching his beloved whimper for life, beg for just a few more minutes. She never got to hold me. She was too weak. But just as she began to fade away, a little brown bird appeared on the window sill. And with her last ounce of strength, she pointed at it and said '*Robin*'. And so that is what he named me, my father."

Elsa just smiled at me, with the crowning of tears in her eye, though none ultimately fell. "That is so wonderful."

"Life has many beautiful moments, even the sad moments. Especially the sad moments. I believe that, in a way, sadness is the most base expression of humanity. What truly separates us from the animal kingdom, to me, is that we are acutely aware of death."

"And what about your friend?"

"Monty?"

"No, the one who died."

"Oh, Richard."

"Yes, you've never spoken much about him either."

"No, I don't suppose so."

"How did he die?"

"Something with his liver. I think the drink got him in the end."

"I'm sorry."

"He was a piece of work really, but there was just this little spark in him. The sort that we all have, but lose in adolescence. I'm glad that I knew him."

By the start of May, we were together, and in the early days of the Summer, she moved into the flat. It was a Saturday in the second week of June when Francis and I carried a car-load of boxes into the flat. After it was done, we opened a bottle of wine. Two had become three.

"You know," I said, once we were onto our second glasses. "The day I met Francis, I drank this vey wine."

"Here, let me see that?", Francis enquired, examining the bottle. "Yes. Yes, we did."

"How did you know that?"

"It's an Alsace wine—reminds me of my father. It's the region of France he died in."

My father had been much on my mind as I neared by thirty-sixth year, and circled middle-age like water about a drain. Had it not been for a locket that I carried daily, I'd have forgotten his subtle features; his gently-lined face, strong arms, firm hair. I had grown to resemble him closely.

Like all do in the burgeoning days of love, we formed our own little habits, and coined our own terms. Wine had become *fuzzy*, music was *juice*, and rain was *Godspiss*. For a year, we moved along like this; in bliss and in comfort. With Monty consumed by the birth of his third child, Francis and Elsa became all that I knew. When she and I were not sleeping in the day, or spending the nights by candle-light; the three of us would take walks, go to the cinema, and talk late into the ghosting hours.

For that moment in time, that seemed to hang in the air like the very firmament we stood under, all pleasure came from them. When I was not with both, I was with one, and when not with one, I was with the other.

The teaching work fell, utterly, by the wayside. I gave my students random, arbitrary grades, with no internal justification. I gave half-baked feedback, and rarely attended tutorials; though no one seemed to care, or even notice. So consumed was I in these two different sorts of love, that all outside of it became an unfocused blur.

I was happy with Elsa, and blissful, and high. I loved her, cherished her, and then—no more.

I awoke one day to find that the love and tenderness had died in the long night. I suddenly recoiled at the sight of her, when she called my name upon entering, I would make myself busy and pretend I hadn't heard her. I stayed late at the college, drank more with colleagues, taught with reformed gusto, and dined alone with Monty; all in pursuit of avoidance. Her little flaws and quirks became a creeping and lurid noise, zipping about my ears and drawing me closer to madness. Her bad jokes and accompanying laughter, that had once made me love her, now rubbed the skin like sandpaper. When I took her to bed, I turned out the light. Soon enough she noticed, and her praise came thick and fast, and with an untrammelled intensity. One day, she'd come to me, having found *some old thing* in a box, referring to one of my earlier works, and how she'd forgotten just how brilliant it was. I was a *genius*, a *visionary*, a *voice set truly apart*. But it stunk of desperation, and I withdrew even more. For a few months more I walked about that great discombobulated palace of my mind. I walked each room, and strolled the garden in search of answers, of an altered path. In it, I found nothing. No semblance of peace or understanding. Once the Autumn of 1969 had ended, and the Winter trickled in, I resolved to end my relationship with Elsa. My home had become a prison, and the only key at my disposal was crafted from the courage and coldness required to break a human heart. At last, I set to work and plotted, and all through the day of action, I was tense and jittery, and pumped myself full of caffeine and nicotine, in preparation for the tears to come, that would surely flood the house and drown us all. When I had lingered for too long in my office, and could linger no more, I set off home.

"Robin," she said, ambushing me upon entry, "I must talk to you about something."

"Yes, me too."

"Oh, you go first then."

"No, it's okay."

"Okay. Well—"

She sat down rigidly in an armchair by the door. Only then did I see her face, which was flushed and robbed of colour. In a moment of folly, I believed that she was to confess some infidelity to me, and I would be free. Just not with Francis, I recall saying to myself.

"Elsa," I said, crouching to her level. "What is it?' Wha—"

"I'm pregnant."

The words were like a slap, and for a few seconds there was chaos, and then there was clarity. Knowing full well the gravity, and most certainly the error, of what I was about to say; but also knowing that it was the right thing to do, albeit in total contravention of my truest convictions, I asked her to marry me.

We were wed in the early weeks of 1970, at a small chapel in Kent, where our home was to be. It was a small affair. On my side of the aisle sat Francis, Monty and his family, and a few disinterested colleagues from the university. We kissed to applause, and as I was led from the church, with confetti raining down, and the deceptive Winter sun, I felt as guilty men must do. I looked at my ring, and knew that I would not remove it without committing some grave act of betrayal. And it is among my deepest regrets that such a betrayal did in fact take place. Yet, you already know this, for it was *you* who felt the blade at its sharpest. It was five months after that, almost to the day, that *you* were born. This book is for *you*, Andrew.

It is yours and yours alone. It is yours to keep, or yours to burn, or yours to sell and let the world in. I cannot influence your decision beyond my words, for by the time you read this, I'll likely be dead; and what you are reading is but the confessions of a dead man.

PART FOUR: *ICARUS FELL*

44

Late Autumn is, to my mind, the most grim little corner of the year, As the days shorten with a merciless pace, and Winter calls out for its own arrival; with it, darkness and cold and broken hearts. I stood in the Autumn of my life for several years in ambivalent suspension, and now it is time to discuss the Winter. Late Autumn's harbinger call came on the day you were born, I was a rotten father from the start and our bond was tenuous at best. You never really looked my way, nor clamoured for my embrace. In fact you cried when I picked you up. Perhaps infants have a natural way of reading the wicked, and perhaps I am the wickedest soul you ever knew. It was in such a vein that the Winter of my life began on your fourth birthday.

Friends and family had gathered at our home in Kent, far from the clutches of the city. It was your day, and yet, unwittingly, I became the centre of its attention; the centre of its ire. You may recall this day, as you were around the age at which memories form. It was warm, and we sat in the garden, vying for shade. After food had been eaten, and your well-wishes sent; it was time for gifts. In spite of my protestations, your mother took care of their procurement. All but one of them, signed '*from mummy and daddy*', came from her alone. I was afforded a single gift, and had stalked various shops in search of it. I found it in a toy shop in the city. It was a lion puppet.

I was so excited to give this to you, that I sat with annoyance and impatience as you opened the gifts of others. Books, clothing, and a painting set from Francis; who had noticed an aptitude for the arts that none other had seen. Soon it was my turn, and with great joy I presented to you this gift. I placed my hand inside of it, opened the mouth wide and let out a mighty roar. You broke into tears immediately, so utterly terrified. My heart sank and face grew neutral, and your mother carried you away from me. Within seconds, the scorn of others fell upon me.

"What on earth were you thinking!", one cried.

"He's only a child," called another.

"How ghastly, scaring his own little boy like that."

Elsa returned and took her own go in berating me for the ill-thought gift. "I cannot believe this, Robin," she groaned. "It is as if you do not know him at all."

Our love had not been rediscovered in the stresses of parenthood, there were no moments of tenderness, or shared laughter; just a thing that both of us sought to escape, but did not know how, nor where to flee to. Ours was not a happy marriage, rather one that was animated by duty alone. And with each passing day, each acceptance of scorn, each failure to be loved, and each failure *to* love, I grew further from the joy I had once known. '*Life'*, I would say to myself, '*has stopped moving now. You are at the plateau and the peak, from here, all you can do is fall.*

That was not the first day, nor the last, in which I questioned by suitability for fatherhood. It seemed that I could do no right, regardless of my intent. I questioned also if I was fit for marriage. In truth, what I gained from our relationship was someone who had reminded me that I was still capable of brilliance. However, this too had passed, and mentions of my novels and poetry were long gone. To her, just as to everyone else, I was just a teacher who once was more.

I fell silent, and accepted that in this moment,

I was the villain of the afternoon. I sulked in the corner, and observed Elsa's parents smother you with affections. Gifts came and went, and Elsa received all thanks. Monty approached me after a while, as I sat with an equally speechless Francis. "Hey," he said. "Don't beat yourself up about it. It'll be a funny story one day."

"I thought he liked lions."

"He——", began Francis.

"Perhaps he does," Monty interrupted. "From afar at least. Though for how much longer, I cannot say."

He nudged me in the arm, as I let the humour of the situation take hold. Elsa noticed us laughing and sent a scowl my way. After that day, there was no new mention of my faux pas. It had snuck, effortlessly, into the pantheon of my other ills, and soon became a face in the crowd. I was a poor father, I could do no right. I could not connect with my son, and that was to be presumed from now on. A new week came, and with it those tedious university parties that I had come to despise so much. Elsa and I left you in the care of a sitter, and drove into the city. Monty and Vera greeted us as soon as we arrived.

"Ah," he said upon seeing us. "What a treat to get away from the little ones."

"Quite," said Elsa, taking Vera's hand into her own. "Come along, Vera. Let us fetch some drinks while the dad's talk."

They made way over to the bar, as heads turned to follow their progress. Monty leaned in, as if our conversation was private and clandestine.

"Say, Robin. I don't suppose little Andrew has recovered from the whole lion debacle?"

"He won't speak to me."

"It happens. Kids. They think each little thing is the end of the world as we know it."

"I really thought he'd like it. He loves lions."

"Yes, I suppose most four-year old boys do."

Elsa and Vera returned with drinks, and then came the mingling. In those days, I found readers of my work in the strangest of places. I distinctly recall seeing an elderly man of the Orient reading my first novel on the tube in 1967; the caretaker of the university reading my first collection of poems; and a film-club screening of a film I had written at a Grammar school in our Kent town. I was never flattered by these sights, I merely felt a distant envy towards myself; an ugly, shameful little beast called resentment. How I hated middle age, how my knees hurt in the morning, and my eyesight worsened.

Throughout the evening; I spoke with a professor of modern languages, who bored me to no end, a doctorate student in literature, who insulted my work without knowing who I was, and that same caretaker, who'd gained himself a job on the side, handing out flutes of champagne. Lastly, I came across a face I'd rather have not seen.

"Mr. Fitzwarwick, is that you? My God it has been some time."

"Hello, Mitz."

He seemed to take a particular delight in where I had ended up. As he postured and probed, I could sense that he viewed me as inferior. "Yes, *Fitzwarwick*. Not a name one hears so often these days. Given up on the writing, have we?"

"I'd call it a sabbatical."

"Whereas others would simply call it—teaching."

"If I'm not mistaken, Mitz, you and I have the same job."

"Hardly. To compare Camford with some plate-glass dump is to compare a cathedral with a mud-hut. I am a Camford don, a position that one earns, not one that is simply slumped into."

"Then you share a job with William Balloch."

"*Shared*. That drunken letch was holding the department back, and I have corrected its course."

"Well then, I shan't interrupt your crusade any longer."

"I take it you haven't heard from Balloch?"

"If he's even still with us," I said, gravely.

"Oh, he is. I haven't seen him myself, though I have heard rumours."

"You enjoy your night, Mitz."

The thought of my old friend, huddled over in the worst of days, much like Francis, but without a friend to take him in, filled me with a most unspeakable anger. How the world had turned him out, and how he'd felt he couldn't see me. I shuddered when I thought of his fate, and suddenly desired to go home. I gestured to Elsa that I wished to leave. We fulfilled the remainder of our requirements, and left after bidding Monty and Vera farewell.

"Oh, Robin.", Elsa said once we had cleared the city and sped towards the Kentish coast. "You seemed so miserable tonight. Not at all your typical self"

"My typical self?"

"Yes, you know——better at hiding it."

"You know that doctorate student? The one who you introduced me to."

"Yes?"

"I asked him if he wished to write himself, as opposed to just criticising writers. Do you know what he said?"

"What did he say?"

"That he wanted to be a writer, and then saw what became of Robin Fitzwarwick, and decided that it was beyond his pride."

"He referred to you in the third person?"

"He didn't know it was me."

"Oh."

"Yes, Elsa. I am unhappy. I'm very unhappy. Miserable, one might even say. I realised tonight that the only thing that can make me happy is truly gone."

"And what would that be?"

"You know what."

"I suppose little Andrew and I mean so little to you."

"I said *thing*. Not people. And besides, little Andrew doesn't care for me, I don't even know if you do either."

"You think I don't care for you?"

"You don't see me in the same way."

"How so?"

"You saw me as a writer, an artist. It dominated our conversations, made me feel so prestigious, like I hadn't been forgotten. Now, I'm just like anyone else."

"Oh, Robin. I was young then, things change, life moves on. It doesn't mean I don't love you, I just——got older, that's all."

"Then you gravely misunderstand what it is that I desire, Elsa. What it is that I have always desired. To be seen as a writer."

"I think you need to move on from that, Robin."

"You think I should give up?"

"I assumed that you already had."

Her words stung me, more so because they were said with such a nonchalance, that they could have been intended or not. It was an insult masked perfectly. They stung because they were true. I knew that my words were still there, lurking in some dark crevice, but that they were held back, for I was sick at heart. I was not melancholic - the sort of sadness that breeds words - but something else entirely. What came to mind then was another story of youth, of my father. It was several months before war broke out, and he had taken me to the zoo. What I recall most firmly about that day was the sadness I felt for the animals. I recall seeing an Asiatic lion, laid out in a small patch of turf, no bigger than a drawing room. I recall thinking how sad that lion looked, juxtaposed to his natural opulence and straight, domineering lines - as if he had come from the art deco imagination. I recall asking myself, and then my father, why he looked so sad. And then, I suddenly knew. That lion, majestic and proud, had no business being in a cage in Regent's Park. T'was the Serengeti where he belonged. T'was in art that *I* belonged.

This reverie had taken my gaze away from Elsa, who drove the car for I had taken to wine that evening. I looked at the passing night, as the urban became rural. Elsa snapped me back into the present. "I've been meaning to talk to you about Andrew's schooling."

"Oh?"

"Well, do you recall when we were first married? And we spoke of our schooling lives, how we'd both had a rotten time?"

"I do."

"You told me that school, to you, was little more than an internment camp for children. An institution dedicated to the abuse, demoralisation, and spiritual castration of children."

"Did I really say that?"

"Yes," she said, impatiently, for she knew that she did not have my full attention. "Have you considered home-schooling?"

"Home-schooling Andrew?"

"Yes. It can be rather cheap; he wouldn't need to be in such an awful place."

"Home-schooling. Oh, yes. That could work."

"I would volunteer myself, but I know nothing of the sciences, nor of mathematics. I fear that you and I are far too devoted to the arts and humanities to give him a *holistic* education."

"No, I suppose not."

"Plus, you are already teaching, and we need the income now that your *Lost and Found* money has dried up. It'd have to be someone that we know, someone we trust."

"I think I know just who."

And so, the very next day I took Francis for lunch. He had been made redundant by the Horticultural Society, due to funding cuts, and found himself in dire straits once more. He accepted with glee, and moved in with us a month later.

"Hello, young man," he said, when I showed him into your room. "My name is Francis; I believe that we are going to be working together from now on."

You looked up at him, with your bulbous blue eyes, as I stood in the doorway. "Hallo, Francis."

Francis smiled, as he examined your small collection of books, and picked one up. "Ah yes," he said, with a beaming grin. "I remember this one rather fondly."

45

Two years of a cold distance passed. I still found myself unable to connect with you, and life seemed to be lived entirely upwind. Five days a week, I drove my second-hand car to London, and taught the uninterested. I would take lunch either alone, or with Monty when his schedule allowed, and each night I would drive home to find you and Francis in the library, giggling away while you learned of the world. Your mother was either asleep or watching television. We hardly spoke. She kept the home well, and worked part-time. We ate familiar food, and watched familiar shows. In the Summer, we'd go to the beach, or a fair. And when it rained, we sought refuge inside, and when the sun shone, we bathed in its amber glow. It should have been so idyllic. Alas, I had found the black dog, taken him in and become one with his ways.

It was 1976 when the ground beneath me had begun to shake, my comfortable spot in the plateau roared under the pressures of inevitable change and so began my downfall. The schooling year had ended a week prior, and I had spent the Saturday in my study, reading, when there was a knock on the door, and Francis came in.

"Hello, Robin."

"Francis," I said. "Come in. How can I help you?"

"Well," he said, nervously. "It's not me you can be of assistance to. It's little Andrew."

"Andrew? What is wrong with him?"

"I'm afraid he's had a run-in with the neighbourhood bullies."

"Oh?"

"He's terribly upset. Perhaps you should go and speak with him."

"Where is he?"

"His room."

You were sobbing into the sleeve of a jumper. There were cuts and scrapes on your arms. "Andrew," I said. "Andrew, what's happened?"

"Nothing," you said, in between little helpless whimpers.

"Come on, Andrew. You don't need to lie, do tell me what is the matter. Francis told me that some neighbourhood kids were being mean to you."

"Yes," you said, eventually. "They pushed me, and stole some coins I had for the sweet shop."

"They did?"

You just nodded, too upset for words.

"Well, Andrew. You need to stand up for yourself."

"I do?"

"Yes. If someone is trying to hurt you, then you cannot let them. If you do, then they will hurt you over and over again."

"But—but what do I do?"

"If they push you, then you push them right back."

"But I'm—little."

"Your body may be, but your spirit inside says otherwise. Inside you are big, and strong. Like a boxer."

"A boxer?"

"Yes, like a boxer. Here, punch my hand."

I placed out my hand, palm facing you and encouraged you to hit it, which you did. I let out a synthetic groan of pain and fell to the floor, as Francis jumped about the took on the role of announcer. "Andrew Fitzwarwick," he cried with elongated vowels. "Champion of the world!"

You giggled and became giddy with excitement, and jumped about too. "You see," I said, getting to my feet. "You have nothing to fear, Andrew. Inside, you are a warrior."

"I am a warrior!"

"A big, fierce warrior."

"Thank you, dad."

But that was my second failure of fatherhood. The first was the lion, and the third would occur some time later, in a dingy London bedsit. I smiled and ruffled your hair, before making my way back to the library. For the remainder of the day, you seemed to come around to me. Later that day, I found you lingering by the door's edge, and invited you to join me. It was a good day, and one of the few we would enjoy together. The next day, I was sat in the very same spot, when your mother burst into the room.

"Just what the hell is wrong with you?!", she cried, as I looked at her with confusion. "Are you a mute?", she repeated. "Tell me right now, just what the hell is wrong with you?"

"Elsa, what are you talking about?"

"Did you tell our son to go and fight the kids who were picking on him?"

"I told him to stand up for himself."

"Oh you stupid arse!"

"Darling, calm down."

"Don't you *darling* me."

"What's happened?"

"Those kids were twelve years old, Robin. They're twice his size."

"Oh, God," I gasped, knowing immediately what I had done.

"You need to examine yourself, Robin. You are a terrible father."

"I—I had no idea."

"You told him to be violent."

"No! I wanted him to defend himself, I thought they were his age."

"He's six! Six years old."

I got up and ran past her, towards your bedroom. When I entered, you were sat on the bed with a bloodied nose, Francis sat next to you and provided comfort in the form of his mere presence. "Go away!", you screamed upon the sight of me. "I hate you. I never want to see you again!"

Francis gave me a sympathetic look, as I slowly drew myself out of the room, weighed down by the shame of what I had accidentally done. Elsa stood silent in the kitchen. "Elsa," I said in a hushed tone. "I—I am so sorry."

"I don't even want to look at you right now, Robin. You could have gotten him killed."

So disturbed was I by the incident, that I did not care to call out what I saw as an obvious hyperbole. Instead, I retreated to the library, seemingly the only room in the house that I could call my own.

By now, my typewriter sat on top of a cabinet, and it had collected several years-worth of dust. I brushed it off, and sat it upon the table. I began to write something simple, a monologue of a man who suddenly did not recognise anyone around him, a stranger in his own land for that is what I was. That single monologue soon grew into several conversations, and by the end of the day, I had discovered these works to be the basis of a play. I slept in the library that night, as I could not face the others. I spent the entirety of the next day working. At four in the afternoon, Francis came to me with coffee and food.

"Here," he said. "Laying them down. I figured you'd be hungry."

"Thank you, Francis."

He smiled with a nod, and turned to leave. "Francis," I called, causing him to turn back.

"Yes, Robin?"

"Do they hate me?"

"They are very angry."

"I thought as much. Here, sit. I could use the conversation."

"What are you working on?", he asked, gesturing to the typewriter.

"Oh, that. I don't know yet."

"Are you writing again?"

"I think so."

"Oh," he said, as a silence descended. "That's nice."

"Do you hate me?", I asked.

"Hate you? Robin, I could never hate you. I haven't forgotten all that you've done for me."

"You're a good man, Francis. I'm glad you're here."

"As am I, Robin. Don't blame yourself for these things. Mistakes are just as common as virtues; people just seem to remember them more clearly."

I smiled at him, before ripping a page from the typewriter, and passing it to him. "It's a play. Do you recall Matheson? He was at the wedding."

"Yes."

"He's in the theatre, he said he can put it on for me when it's done."

"How exciting!"

"Would you read it? I think it could go somewhere."

"Of course."

He read the play and left some notes. He had noticed things that I did not; little flaws and inconsistencies. And with them, I finished the play, and his final appraisals, under the promises of blunt honesty, said to me that it was complete, and ready to be seen.

After some convincing, washed thoroughly in her own desire to see the back of me for a while, Elsa agreed that it should pursue its completion. And so I went to London, where I met with Matheson, who'd kept his word. He accepted my play, and staffed it with his retinue of actors. Overall, I spent just shy of three months in London, and in September, on the cusp of the school year my play was debuted.

Francis, and Elsa were there for the opening night. On that night, that part of me I had known for sure to be done, dead and buried along with all other remnants of a bygone age, came roaring back to life. The actors did what was asked of them, and my words came to life. I had exposed my heart, and all of its twangs of pain and desperation, to the world, and had not been turned away. The movement of my usurpation had itself been usurped, and in its stead came a newfound appreciation for *Robin Fitzwarwick*. I received my first standing ovation, and my first praise from strangers, in many years. And on that stage, feeling as if the years in exile had been but a bad dream, I began to weep with joy.

"I'm so very proud of you, Robin,", said Francis, once I had emerged into the theatre bar.

"It was excellent, dear," said Elsa, coldly.

It was a night of nostalgia, re-treading of steps so familiar, and the three of us stayed together a while longer, as we once had all those years ago. Later, I bid them goodbye, on the understanding that I would return home in a week. That week passed in a flash, and the final performance came. Afterwards; myself, Matheson, and the cast took to the local bars and worked our way through three of them. The passage to each bar saw our crowd dwindle down, until it was just Matheson and I in the final location.

"Cheers, Robin," he said, tapping his glass into mine. "This one shall be my last. Old timers like us cannot go on like this."

"We're not that old, are we?"

"We're certainly not young."

"Regrettably so. Anyway, what shall we toast to?"

"To your successful return of course."

I smiled to myself, knowing that what I had accomplished was something of a flash-in-the-pan; something of a fluke. "It's funny, isn't it, Matheson. How intertwined our fates have been throughout the years."

"Indeed, it is. To think, twenty-five years ago, Balloch brought a young whippersnapper writer to one of those dreadful college parties."

I grimaced when I thought of my old friend; taken away and drowned in a riptide of drink. "Whatever happened to him?"

"Haven't a clue. It seems he just vanished into the wind."

"I saw Mitz a few years ago."
"Oh really? Where?"
"At one of those dreadful college parties. He told me that Balloch was still around."
"So you do know what became of him?"
"No. I couldn't bring myself to. It'd have ripped me apart."
"Mm," Matheson grunted in agreement. "Do you recall that party Donald threw, in the Albert Village."
"I do."
"So you can see the disappointment I have for you, my friend."
"Excuse me?"
"I did my part, got into the theatre. You wrote that wickedly *ghastly* novella——good work by the way, it was grotesque and they loved it. And then you just threw in the towel, became a teacher, what's that all about?"
"Believe me when I say this, Matheson, any disappointment you may have for me is matched, and exceeded by the one I have for myself."
"Do you at least enjoy teaching?"
"Of course I don't. Perhaps I would if it was a good college; Camford, or Royal Northern, Imperial perhaps."
"And instead, it's *Ring-Road Polytechnic*."
"Yes it is."
"You'd be surprised, Robin, the upstart lot, the real horrible little bastards, didn't take over quite as much as we'd feared. Sure, they've got Firebrand, most of the big theatres, the pictures, but there's still room for us. Clearly there was still room for me."
"With all due respect, James, you're free to pursue these things. I'm not. This was really spectacular fun, I mean that, and it's been wonderful seeing you again, but I'm married now, I have a kid. I'm forty-three, James. I'm just—tired all the time."
"Forty-three," he repeated.
"I've known you for more than two decades now,

Matheson. My students were born after we met. If nothing comes of this play then—well then I think it's too late."

"And are you happy, Robin?"

"No."

"Why?"

"Because I agree with everything you're saying. I know what I am, and I wish so desperately to be it. But I am sworn to my marriage, to fatherhood. And the marriage is loveless, and my son hates me. And yet, here I am."

"He'll come around."

"I don't know what's more shameful - my son looking up, or my forebears looking down."

"How old is he?"

"Six."

"Oh, never mind then. You've fucked it up there."

We laughed to ourselves. I looked down, into my drink, and just as I looked up, I caught a ghost-like reflection in the mirror that sat before me. Before I could process what it was that I had just seen, Matheson threw the rest of the whiskey down his throat and stood. "Well, Robin. It is a matter of true simplicity. It is never too late to find the joy in life. And now I must go. It has been a great pleasure once more. I hope to work with you again soon. Will you be staying?"

"For a bit."

"Righto. Until next time, young Robin."

"Until then."

Matheson left, and I returned my gaze to the drink in my hand. I dreaded looking up and into the mirror again; my skin began to sweat, and my heart beat in odd patterns. Before I could rouse the courage to look up, a soft hand rested itself on my shoulder, and I knew its source immediately. She spoke to me in that wavering American tongue.

"Hello, Robin."

"Hello, Elaine."

She had not aged well, and her entire demeanour announced a sort of desperation."Wow, it sure is good to see you again, Robin. How long has it been?"

"Twelve years."

"Wow, such a long time."

"Indeed."

"What are you doing here?"

"I just wrapped up the run of my play."

"You wrote a play? Wow, if only I'd known, I'd have auditioned," she said, with a contrived laugh and a weak slap of my arm. "That is actually why I am in London, I thought I'd give the West End a fair go this time. You know, see what the old smoke had in store for me."

"The *big smoke*."

"Oh, yes! I meant that," she chuckled, nervously. "Say, can I buy you a drink, Robin?"

I said nothing, and gestured at the seat next to me.

"You still drink wine, I see," she continued.

"Mm."

She withdrew a purse, and rummaged through its various flaps and layers. I glanced into it to see that there was no money inside. "Rats!", she exclaimed.

"It's okay," I said. "I'll get these."

"Would you? Thanks!"

Off came the braces and into the fore I darted. And from that moment until the next morning, every word was a lie, every gesture of interest an affectation, every bout of laughter an indiscernible declaration of bitter grief. She was a husk before me, and I hated her for it. I hated that one who'd hurt me so, hadn't the strength of conviction of remain perilously beautiful. She had discarded me beautiful, and come back to me ugly. I detested her sunken eyes and greyish skin, that once was a picture of grandiose beauty, the likes of which I'd never known in the quads and cloisters of Camford; an entirely American beauty. I hated her forward-bending frame, her stale-cigarette smell, and her inch-deep reflections on what had occurred between us. We spoke not of her marriage to Al, for I knew it was over and had little to say about it. Nor too did we speak of my own marriage, though I had not removed my ring, and evidence of my looming infidelity was a mere glance away.

"Right!", called a bartender, as he rang a bell. "Last orders!"

"One more?", Elaine asked.

"No. Let's get out of here."

"Okay. Back to yours?"

"I don't live in the city."

"Oh, that's okay. I only live a few minutes away from here."

"Lead the way."

We walked through those familiar London streets, until we arrived at the little bedsit that Elaine had come to call home. Inside, we shared another glass of wine, before our mouths ceased to speak and our bodies said all that was required. Afterwards, we lay there in silence, as smoke filled the air.

"You know, Robin," she said after several minutes.

"I made a grave mistake, marrying Al. He was such a bastard to me. I only see it now."

"Hollywood is as Hollywood does," I said, giving the impression that I had hardly listened. "A grim town for grim deeds."

"Oh, yes. So grim. So very grim. Grotesque! Oh, Robin. I do so regret leaving you in the way that I did. Really, it was my father's doing, he concocted the whole thing."

"Is that so?"

"Could you find it within your heart to forgive me?"

"Of course," I said, exhaling.

"You were my truest love, Robin. And my greatest regret. Will you stay the night? We have so much to catch up on. I'm——so glad to have you back. This time, I am not going anywhere."

I lay there in silence and smoked another cigarette, until her pattern of breathing whispered that she was asleep. As soon as she was, I gently raised the duvet, and crawled out of bed. After dressing, and giving her one last scornful look, I fetched a pen and paper. I scanned my mind for words to write, and landed upon those of William Blake.

'I was angry with my friend. I told my wrath, my wrath did end. I was angry with my foe, I told it not, my wrath did grow.' I wrote. *'Take care, Elaine.'*

I slipped out of the room, and walked to my hotel. The next day, I boarded a train and returned to my family, knowing full well that I had betrayed them beyond all forgiveness.

46

"Ah, Robin. Come in," said Monty, when I entered his office in the middle of February, 1977.

"Hello, old boy."

"What can I do for you, Robin?"

"Well, I was hoping to enquire about my taking a sabbatical."

"A sabbatical?"

"Yes."

"Whatever for?"

"Let us just call it a creative endeavour."

"Oh?"

"Do you remember that novel?"

"You've written quite a few as I recall."

"Yes, and one that I never finished."

"Oh, yes. Christ, I'd forgotten about that."

"As had I."

"Yes, I suppose this profession swallows one up. How long have you worked here now?"

"Thirteen years in September."

"That's about ten years longer than I thought you'd last."

"Me too."

We lingered for a moment, Monty offered me a cup

of tea and I requested coffee instead. He gave word to an assistant, and a few minutes later we took our first sips.

"I'm very happy for you, Robin. I knew when I saw your play that we'd have this exact conversation before the year's end. In fact, I'm surprised it's taken you this long. Lord knows you were never cut out for this sort of thing. '*Teacher*?', I used to say to Vera. '*Robin Fitzwarwick*?'. '*Oh the humanity*!', I'd say, '*he belongs in books, not the classroom*'." He laughed to himself, in a way that told me he had never in fact said those words. He then steadied himself. "Of course I will grant your sabbatical. How long do you need?"

"Just an estimation, the remainder of the school year—and perhaps the Summer too."

"Yes, you work rather quickly as I recall."

"When I'm capable of working."

"So, do you think this is it?"

"How do you mean?"

"Well, if you complete said work, would that be curtains on your time teaching here?"

"Would you hold it against me if it were?"

"Oh, no. Heavens no. Like I said, you don't belong here. You belong *there*. You were born to write; write you did, and write you shall. If I were to stand in your path, and usher you back into the classroom; then I wouldn't be your friend."

"Are you my friend, Monty?"

"Don't be a fool, Robin."

"Thank you. I appreciate this."

"Just make sure it's a success. I don't think I can stomach the thought of you in a lecture hall any longer. You look terrible in tweed."

I left, and made my way home after clearing out my little office. Elsa was home when I arrived, as were Francis and yourself; though you were out of sight and in the midst of some lesson. "You're home early," she said.

"Yes. I have been meaning to talk to you about this, but I have spoken to Monty, and it is agreed that I am to take a sabbatical."

"A sabbatical? Why?"

"I believe that I can finish the novel."

"Oh, Robin. I don't know about that. I wish you'd told me, asked me even."

"I thought you said it was brilliant, worthy of finishing?"

"Yes, but that was some time ago, Robin. Things change and, well, don't you feel that the horse may have bolted already?"

"The horse?"

"Yes. You were a writer once, but now you teach. It is a noble profession."

"*Those who can't do, teach.*"

"I don't want to argue about this. It's clear that you have already made your mind up, and made the arrangements. I just wish you'd spoken to me about it. You are so very headstrong sometimes."

"Are you disappointed?"

"Yes, a little."

"I thought you believed in me?"

"Oh, I do. It's just——never mind. Yes, honey, I do believe in you. Go right ahead."

I knew full well that I had been unreasonable, and should have spoken to her first. But I was now the saboteur. I said no more and vanished out of her sight. I cut a lonely figure in that house, I glided about the halls silently, and without being seen, as if I were a ghost forever condemned to roam the house of his forebears, crying out in anguish and shock, perturbed by the new occupants. I endeavoured to spend the rest of my day in the library, but some unknown force came over me; and before my mind could reconcile with my legs, they had carried me to the brink of your room. I entered, and found you and Francis, with a series of animals sprawled out upon the floor. Both of you stopped when I entered the room. By this point, you had warmed to me slightly, and made your way over. "Hallo, daddy," you said, as I ruffled your hair.

"Hello, Andrew. Are you okay?"

"Yes, thank you. Francis is telling me about nature, and animals, and why we are the best one."

"Oh, are we now?"

"I feel I've made a rather compelling case," Francis chuckled, as he stared down at you with warmth.

"Andrew. Daddy is going to be taking some time away from work; and I was hoping you would join me for a day out?"

"A day out?"

"Yes. My father used to take me to the beach when I was a boy. Would you join me?"

"Can Uncle Francis come?"

"Actually," Francis interjected. "I think this day is best for just you and your father."

"But I want you to come too!"

"Now, now, young Andrew. A father and his son need days like this, you'd be a very good young man if you were to indulge your father on this."

"Okay. When are we going?"

"Tomorrow."

And so, we went, and I took - albeit briefly - my place in the pantheon of fathers and sons. We drove down to the coast and walked the pier, tried our luck in the arcades, and played in the sand. To my mind, it was the one and only true day we had together, and one of my happiest. I do sincerely hope that you recall that day, as well as I do. For memory is my theme, and despite the pain I have caused you since that day; it is one that we shall always possess.

That day was one of rediscovery. And in the joy I felt, or the respite from misery, I found peace from which I found words. And I wrote throughout the Spring. And life felt as it did when I was young and in Camford. I took my notes to the local tea rooms, where I sat in the corner like some urban hermit. When I was done, I'd walk home and draft the prose in my head, make way for the library and write until the day was gone. Admittedly, I saw little of anyone in those days; and my closest companions became the staff of said tea rooms. By the dawn of Summer, I had built my skeleton, the outline of my house of words. By Summer's midst, I had begun to populate it with scenery. Each day was as productive as the last, and I felt something that had been alien to me for quite some time; fulfilment. And then, as the good things in my life tend to do, it went away, and the land grew barren and still. Desperately, and with a steadily increasing anger, I fought to find words in the deepest trenches of my mind. Ultimately I found nothing, and misery came back into my life, like a long-lost lover. August came, and with it the looming threat of my returning to work. So numb was I, that I had ceased to eat, and ceased to speak.

There came a brief phase, where I had something that I knew to be bad. And yet, longing for something, anything, I wrote on. I tapped away, as if I had been lobotomised. That is when you came to me.

"Daddy?", you called from the door's edge.

I said nothing. I just continued to stare at the keys. "Daddy?" Nothing again. "Daddy?"

Once more, I said nothing. I heard you, clear as day. I knew you were there, what you wanted, and that I could not give it to you. After a few minutes, the calling ceased, and when I turned around you were no longer there. Your mother also came to me one night, as I stared at an empty page.

"Robin?"

"Yes."

"Do eat something, you've been in here for days."

"I'm not hungry."

She closed the door, and ventured in. "How long have you been staring at that page?"

"Three days."

"Oh, Robin. Please stop this, it is killing you."

"I cannot go back. I must finish it."

"No. You know what? No. This is not good enough. I won't have you moping around obsessing over words like you're a young man again. I let you have this little experiment, and now it's over. You have a son, a family, have you forgotten that?"

Suddenly, and from where I know not, a tidal wave

of anger consumed me and I turned to face her with fire in my eyes. "Fuck off! Just fuck off! You irritable little thing."

"Robin—"

"You don't believe in me, you said as much. If you don't believe in me, then why on earth did I bother marrying you?"

She looked stunned. Her face seemed to shiver, in terror and in hurt. She rose to her feet with caution, as if I were some wild beast, with her in my sights. Still maintaining my gaze, and backed toward the door until she bumped into it. With jittered hands, she flung it open and disappeared.

In the years that have passed; and with it, hours of reflections and meditations on my life and how I have lived it; I consider those words to be the ghastliest that ever left my mouth. I slept in the library that night, unable to face her, or what I had said. When I awoke, a note sat on the desk, it was by her hand. '*I have taken Andrew to my parents for some time. I don't know when I'll return.*'

47

That Summer ended in isolation, and I returned to the university. I said not a word to Monty, nor to Francis, nor to you or your mother, who had since returned. I turned forty-four in muted silence; without so much as a gift or a cake. In those late August days, I barely slept or ate. I kept to myself, and uttered no more than a few sentences a day. I was a spectre in my own home.

September came, and I returned to the university, without a thing to call my own; no novel, no joy to speak of, no true friends, and no desire to carry on the life I was living. Each day served as a reminder of what I was no longer, like a knife that circled a wound, etching out as much agony as possible before the final incision.

When I entered my office, I noticed a parcel on the table. It was addressed to me; and inside it was a manuscript and a note. It was from a third-year student of mine.

> '*Mr. Fitzwarwick,*' it read. '*I would be forever grateful to you if you were to read this short story I have composed. Your feedback, insight, and potential mentorship would mean a lot to me*'.

I read the text and found it to be brilliant. This is what I had been waiting for, and yet it filled me with a great, inexplicable rage. In the years since, I have come to regret almost all of the actions dated to this chapter of my life; and my response to this story is a particularly shameful example of where my mind sat. Without restraint, reason, or respect, I ripped his story - that I knew to be of great quality - to shreds. I attacked the language, the tone, the message and the meaning. And when I was done, I trembled. Knowing then, and knowing now, that I had committed a great injustice. I had robbed the world of an artist. I did not see that student any more after that; not in my lectures, not in my seminars. I never heard the name again.

At the end of that first week, I trudged home. I found the place to be exactly how I had left it; and it carried that same vague stench of resentment and desperation. That night, as well as on the Saturday, and the Sunday, I said virtually nothing. You and Francis chatted away with gaiety, while your mother looked on, while I sat in the corner as the ghost at the feast. You told her of your lessons, and how Francis had made the most complex of things simple.

"I'm taking Andrew to my parents next weekend," Elsa said to me coldly.

"Oh, yes."

"I figured you'd be too busy around here, so I told them that you're too busy with work."

"Yes. Thank you."

"Mummy," you said. "Can Francis come with us?"

"I'm afraid not, dear. Francis has a life of his own."

"Francis, please?"

"Your mother is right, young Andrew. I must stay and take care of your father."

"Father? But he doesn't do anything. He just mopes around the library all day, he's like a ghost in that way."

"Well, someone has to keep him company."

"I don't think father is capable of being happy. That's what you said, right mummy?"

Elsa shuddered and looked over at me with nerves. I shrugged it off and let you continue. "Mummy says that father *used* to be a writer, a really good one. But he doesn't write anymore and that is why he doesn't smile. I think that he's sad because he's old, and wishes he was young again."

"Your father was an excellent writer," Francis said. "I've read all of his books."

"Can I read one?"

"I'm afraid they are a little bit too mature for you," I said.

"Oh, okay."

I spent the next week as I usually did, waiting for the weekend. And when it came, I bade you and your mother a farewell. You may recall that day, and how a rare modicum of humanity came out of me that day. You and I both know why, but it is important for me – as a confession of the dying man – to give you my perspective.

On the Saturday night, on the eve of your return, I sat in the garden and drank beer alone. Soon enough, Francis joined me. He approached me sheepishly, as if something grave was on his mind.

"Good evening, Francis."

"Good evening, Robin."

"Before you ask, no. I am not okay."

"I didn't think that you were. But still, it is polite to ask."

"Indeed."

I paused for a few moments, now that something grave was on my own mind. "Francis, can I ask you a question?"

"Yes?"

"When was the last time you knew me to be happy?"

"Do you mean the last time I saw you happy, or the last time you were consistently happy?"

"Both."

"I believe the last time I saw you to be genuinely happy was not that long ago, when you were writing."

"And for consistency?"

"Well, when Richard was still with us. Before you went to America."

"Yes. I suppose that's true. He took the laughter with him."

"I miss him greatly," Francis said, with a slight quiver of the lip.

"There are times where I convince myself that I've forgotten what he looked like. And then it all comes back to me, his golden hair and shiny skin. He was beautiful, wasn't he? Almost otherworldly."

"Yes," he said, turning the words over in his mind. "*Otherworldly*."

"You're right, Francis. I don't believe I've laughed truly since then. Can you imagine that, Francis? All these years without laughter, just——breathing, and eating, and sleeping, and shitting."

"I can. But one learns to move along."

"Have you?"

"I don't believe one ever truly gets over grief. But one does learn to live again, to live anew."

"It's a rather sad state of affairs, is it not?"

"Which part?"

"Everything. How I can't do the only thing that makes me happy. How far I've fallen, how my wife can't stand the sight of me. How ghastly a father I am."

"It can go one of two ways, growing up without a father. It either makes us wonderful fathers, or completely ill-equipped."

"Did you never want children of your own?"

"I can't have children of my own."

"Oh. I'm sorry."

"It's okay. I made peace with it some time ago. Truthfully, I take great enjoyment from Andrew; from watching him grow."

"I fear he never liked me."

"He fears that *you* never liked him."

"It all started with that bloody birthday present. The lion. I still cannot understand why he had such a bad reaction to it. The boy loved lions."

"Wolves."

"What?"

"He never loved lions. He loved wolves."

"Oh."

What followed was a pregnant silence, as it dawned on me that I never truly knew you. And that you never truly knew me. Numbly, I finished my beer and grabbed another. Francis waved me away when I offered one to him. I took a sip and searched within me for the courage to say what I said next. "Our love was internecine."

"I know," he said.

"Yes. I must confess something, Francis."

"Yes?"

"I don't love her. I don't know if I ever did."

"Then, why did you—"

"She got pregnant. I was going to break things off, but she got pregnant, and it felt like the right thing to do."

"I suppose it was in a way."

"For a while she made me feel alive again. Maybe that's what I felt. Not love, just—alive. The world had forgotten me, Francis. I don't suppose you'd know what it's like to be up that high, and then to crash and burn. It's funny really. When you have it, it's such a rotten thing, but losing it is just——devastating."

He said nothing, and just placed a hand over mine. "Francis," I said after a minute."

"Yes, Robin?."

"If something happened to me, that meant I had to go away, and perhaps never return, would you look after my family?"

"I would."

"I know that you would. I just needed to hear it."

"Do what you must, Robin. Just know that you would be inflicting a great deal of pain. Even if what you say is true, and they hate you, that is what you would do to them. You would be making a boy spend the rest of his childhood asking where his daddy is. You may find happiness elsewhere, and you probably will, for you know in your heart that there is none to be found here. But just remember that if you are to find joy, then you must inflict misery in order to reach it. You said as much yourself when Richard died. *I must chase misery before I can chase joy.*"

And with that, he rose and went back into the house. I just sat there, and examined my surroundings. This little world I had carved out of earth and stone, for a family I never asked for. I knew that I could stay no longer. I packed my things in silence, moving from the bedroom into the library, taking all that I could fit into two bags and two boxes. Lastly, I entered the kitchen, where there was a drawing of yours. On it, was myself, Elsa, and Francis. You stood between the others, holding either of their hands, while I was cast off to the side. I took it with me. And as I made my way to the front door, carrying all that I owned, Francis emerged from the shadows. Our eyes met, and held one another for a few delicate moments. He was my dearest friend, the most patient of my follies and foibles. I had saved him, and in turn he had been the loyalest of friends. As I looked at him, and saw the gentle cut of betrayal bore ever-so-slightly into his skin, I knew then that I hadn't just broken your heart, nor your mother's. I had broken his too - it was written in his eyes, plain to see. So too was something I had never before seen in Francis, a brief flicker of hatred. We said nothing as I turned, opened the door, and vanished into the Autumn night.

48

A month had passed since that night. I had taken rooms in a London bedsit, as it was where I could not be found. I neglected to go into work, and the mere act of leaving the room filled me with enough dread to make each excursion brief and only in pursuit of the baseline essentials. I knew that I could stay in England no longer, for its spectres were too great and too numerous, and hidden away in too many corners. As fate escaped my grip once more, I rifled through my belongings one day, in search of a sign, a ticket to wherever next. In one of the boxes I had taken with me were the skeletons of my years prior. There were my manuscripts, old letters from old friends, the Korsakov recording, and underneath it all, I found Milena's necklace.

Travel had evolved greatly since I was last in Montenegro; and I flew into Belgrade, and then to Titograd. I knew of no address, and had only memories to guide me. When I was last in Kotor, twenty years prior, and when I had gotten lost, I knew that in order to find the house, I'd locate the bay. There was a little white hut on its right-hand side, and from there I'd walk straight with the water to my western flank and it was only a matter of minutes from there. As it happens, such a method still worked, and I recognised the house from afar, it sat over a small ridge. I had not come here for romantic pursuits, nor had I come here to apologise, or make amends. I simply wished to fulfil a promise, as I had forged a habit of breaking them. I had promised Milena, on Christmas night, 1957, that some day I would return her necklace.

On my approach, up and over the ridge, I heard the scattered laughter of children running around, and flung myself back a few feet until I was peering over the mound. There I saw three such children; two girls and a boy, playing. They were no younger than eight, and no older than thirteen, and for a few moments I watched them, until a voice rung out from the house. In the intervening years I had forgotten all of my Serbian, and could not make sense of what was said; but I knew that voice. I have forgotten a great many things, but the souls once bound to my own were never allowed to slip. Even today, the faces and voices of all whom I have known are as clear as day, as crisp as the sun's glaze on the Montenegrin bay water. Richard and Cynthia, Francis and Francine, Balloch and Matheson, Elaine and Adeline; all were clear. That is how I knew that Milena had spoken those foreign words. Her voice had graduated, from a precocious young woman, to a mother of middle age. I watched the door, and sure enough she emerged.

She seemed to have barely aged. Her innocence and grace had only increased with what I had assumed to be her motherhood. She greeted her children, with arms around each shoulder and spoke to them in that alien tongue. I found myself grinning as I observed. Yet, sensing that I had no place here, and satisfied that she was happy and content without me, and not hindered by my memory, I placed her necklace on the branch of a tree, and walked back down the ridge, never to see Eden again.

I returned to England two weeks later. The guilt and shame greeted me with a slap, and I desired another to converse with. And so, I sought out Monty. Like a ghost, returning to haunt an old abode, I set foot on the campus and walked towards the chancellor's house.

"Robin," Monty said, coldly, as he shook my hand

but averted his eyes.

"Monty, may we speak?"

"I may. You may not. You may have witnessed your wife crying by your own hand many times, but I have not. So you can imagine my distress when she turns up at my house on a Sunday evening; crying her eyes out and asking if I knew where you were."

"Monty, I—"

"Shut up. You abandoned her, and you abandoned your son. He's eight years old, you bitter, ghastly old thing. Do you have any idea what you have inflicted upon that little boy? I thought you were a man of honour, Robin. How wrong I was, how deceptive the wicked can be."

"I know."

"And yet you did it anyway."

"Yes."

"Was it really so terrible? Married life? Were you really that miserable?"

"I was."

"Well that's irrelevant. You married her, no one made you do it. You made your vows, swore your loyalty."

"Monty, I can't. Even if I did go back—"

"Oh, this matter is not for debate. You *will* return to your family."

"I can't."

"Robin. Return to your family."

"No."

"Well then, it would appear that you have left me with no choice but to relieve you of your duties. You may leave my office now."

And so, I stood, and turned to leave. With one hand on the door, I turned to my oldest friend in the world, not knowing if I should ever see him again. You see, when I made the decision to abandon you and your mother, it was not just you I turned my back on. In fact, I had turned my back on everything I knew on that Autumn night.

"Monty," I said as the door opened. "Will I ever see

you again?"

"Time heals all things, Robin. So, I cannot speak for the distant future. But in the immediate, I do not wish to see you for quite some time."

"I understand."

And that was that. With a final, chilling contact of the eyes, I turned the door and left the campus. There were two months of pay in the office, and I left half with the request to deliver it to my wife. And then I left, having closed the door on this chapter in my life. It's almost funny to think about it now, how in spite of my initial reservations, inevitable miseries, and eventual sudden escape, that part of my life, that of a lowly teacher at a lowly college, covered more of my time than any other pursuit. I was a writer for ten years, and a teacher for thirteen.

There was an eerie silence in my head as I walked home. I'd compare it to the numbness one feels after breaking a bone, before the shock wears off and the agony ensues. *I could not be happy in England*, I said to myself, *and so I must leave.*

For the next few days, I reflected on my life. How at times I had been so full of joy, and others so full of misery. I thought of the ghosts of my past; of Cynthia, who I had heard was dying in pastoral exile; Adeline, who was dead; Milena, who was happy; Elaine, who was sad. Elsa; who I had broken and betrayed, and you, who I had failed. There was one whose fate I did not know of, who was a mystery even when I knew her; and yet she never left my mind, even when I was in the depths of love elsewhere. I gathered what little I had, sold what I could spare, and took myself to Paris.

49

The sun shone handsomely through Parisian days and nights. Paris, as I took my daily walks, brimmed with romance and a knowledge that this was the place to be. A lot had changed since I was last in France. A revolution had come for those riverside streets and winding alleys. Its catacombs and dishevelled churches told of a city reborn, as it had been reborn, again and again. It was in Paris that I rediscovered that rarest of things, that which I thought I could find no more. Unbeknownst to me, two things had happened since I was here last, my name had lingered and it had not been tarnished. While I was not quite known by face, I was by name, and it did not take me long to find a publisher, and to write once more.

By the time I had fully reacquainted myself with Paris, and what she possessed, four months had gone by. I had explored every crack and crevice, with the sole exception of the Latin Quarter; whose company I still hadn't the courage to request. I had written a novella, and had agreed to serialise it with a local magazine. I heard that it had been received well, and read well, though not widely, and soon word spread to England, though I would not know this for many years to come, of my resurfacing. No attempt, however, was made to find me and bring me home. In France I had formed a dedicated niche. This was due, partially, to a misreading of my works as being of the political; this came as a surprise as, to my mind, my work contained not an ounce of politics in any syllable or stanza.

I lived alone, and had no friends. I dined alone, and drank alone. I orbited the expats from afar, and knew none of their names. Occasionally a face I did know would make itself known; some writer, or artist, or actor, who had found himself in the soaring peaks of his own fifteen minutes, would enter the room with an enormous gravity, and all eyes would point east. Like I, they'd fallen from grace in their own lands, and Paris had scooped them up, and led them out from the underworld like Orpheus with his lyre.

I had hoped to see Francine by chance; reading by the Seine, or playing gaily in a brasserie. Though I knew that fate would never be so kind as to do all of the work, and that I would need to seek her out. I had avoided the Latin Quarter, and the little cafe until I had been in Paris for longer than I can recall, long enough to write. Perhaps I believed that it would be an affectation of fate. Though one day, as I walked without aim, I glanced around and realised that my wandering thoughts had guided my feet, and I was there. That is when I saw it; Le Coin.

I ordered a black coffee. When it came, I asked the teenager if I could speak with the owner, and that it was a matter of great importance. It was the first full sentence I had uttered in several weeks.

I had come to Le Coin, and requested to speak for the owner because I believed the cafe to still belong to Francine's uncle. Perhaps he'd know where she was, and from there I would write her a letter; one of such bluntness, brutality, and honesty, that it would perhaps yield no results in my favour. Yet, I had to. I had to tell her everything, all of my deeds and misgivings, what had made me flee from her, and what I had done ever since. As it happened, I would not need to write such a letter.

"Qu'est-ce que tu lis?"

I smiled to myself, as I recalled that question with a great warmth. It was only when it repeated, that I realised the words to be real, and not mere recollections. "Qu'est-ce que tu lis?"

I felt a pulse in my face, and was completely stunned. I turned around slowly, to see her. "Bonjour, Robin. I was wondering when I'd see you again."

I could hardly speak. So surreal was the moment, and so present was I in it, that I could almost not participate. I could only utter her name. "Francine."

"How are you?", she asked with a smile. "It has been so long."

But I had prepared for this moment. I had spent cumulative days, and weeks, and years thinking about this moment. What I'd say, how I'd say it. And so, in preparation - for some part of me had always known that it was always Francine, that I'd set fire to my own life, and my own happiness when I flipped that coin - I had taken to learning French, at some midway point in my thirties, and I had rehearsed, to the syllable, what I was about to say.

"Ask me in French," I said.

"Comment vas-tu?"

"J'en perds mes mots..."

I gestured for her to sit, which she did with ease and a simple grace. We sat only a few inches apart, both utterly fixated on one another. She looked me up and down before she spoke next. "Tu n'as pas changé, à part les quelques rides sur ton visage," she said, with a smile.

"Et toi tu es encore plus belle qu'avant," I replied.

"Es-tu en train d'impliquer que je n'étais pas belle que nous nous sommes rencontrés?"

"Je n'oserais pas!"

She let out a small laugh, and I did too. There were these small breaks throughout the conversation, where some involuntary function or spasm would overwhelm us both; as if the strangeness of the situation carried symptoms. Softly, she broke the latest bout of silence.

"Je savais que tu reviendrais, mais je ne pensais pas que ça te prendrait si longtemps."

"Je ne t'ai jamais oubliée. Je n'ai jamais oublié tes yeux, et la façon que tu avais de me regarder… Je n'ai jamais oublié tes lèvres, la manière qu'elles avaient de bouger, des'adresser à moi… Je n'ai jamais oublié comment tu m'embêtais, ni l'impression que tu m'as faite la première fois que nous sommes rencontrés… Malgré toutes ces années..."

"Vingt-cinq…"

"Oui, vingt-cinq. J'étais un idiot à l'époque, et, je crois que je le suis resté. Ce jour-là, à Paris, quand je t'ai appelée, je t'ai menti. Il n'y avait pas d'urgence, je t'ai quittée pour une autre. Une autre qui m'a blessée. Et depuis ce jour, je crois que je suis maudit. Condamné à ne jamais trouver le vrai amour. Toutes les femmes que j'ai connues m'ont trahies, et quand ce n'était pas elles qui me trahissaient, c'est moi qui les trahissait… Toutes ces années à me demander «Pourquoi ai-je fait ça ?», «pourquoi a-t-elle fait ça ?». J'avais une femme et un fils. Et malgré ça je ne pouvais pas échapper à cette malédiction."

"Quel nom donnes-tu à cette malédiction?"

"Qu'aucune d'entre elles ne portaient ton nom. Il n'y a pas un jour où je n'ai pas pensé à toi pendant ces vingt-cinq années. Et toi, as-tu pensé à moi?"

"Oui," she said, after a pause that seemed to last forever.

"Toutes ces années perdues…"

"C'est le problème quand on trouve son chez soi en l'autre, peu importe où nous allons après dans le monde, peu importe qui nous rencontrons… Nous sommes condamnés à chercher, à être des chercheurs. Des astronautes dans nos propres têtes. Tu as parcouru le monde, et moi je suis restée ici, en sachant qu'un jour tu allais revenir. Mais je t'ai déjà dit tout ça au téléphone, ce jour-là, quand tu m'as appelé. Tu t'en souviens ?"

"Can we speak in English now?", I asked.

She chuckled softly. "Of course."

"I cannot believe my eyes."

"You should," she whispered. "They're not lying to you."

"I fear that they might be."

"Do not give in to such things, Robin. You have waited all these years—"
"Twenty-five."
"Yes. Twenty-Five years. You have waited all this time, do not let fear get in your way. I am sure you have told yourself many times that if you were to see me again, that nothing would prevent you from saying what you had to say."
"How did you know that?"
"Because *I* have done just the same."
We smiled at each other, before I took a glance around the café, effectively empty and preparing to close for the day. "So, you own this place now?"
"I do."
"Since when?"
"About five years ago. My uncle passed away and he left it to me. I was in Avignon at the time, but I always missed Paris."
"Avignon?", I asked.
"Yes."
"How funny."
"Why?", she asked with a giggle.
"No reason. I-I'm sorry for your loss."
"It's okay. I'm sure you have experienced that side of life as well."
"I have."
"Then you will know that words do nothing, although they are appreciated. I want to hear of you, Robin. What happened to the *great Robin Fitzwarwick.*"
"The great?"
"The thing about your name, Robin, is that it is quite distinct. So, when you write a few famous novels, or make a few films in America, people recognise the name."
"You've—"
"Every book, every film, every word."
"You were always there."
"I used to say to people; *Robin Fitzwarwick, I knew*

him. I was one dinner away from loving him."

Her accent had shifted from chirpy and English, to a buttery French. It was clear that she had been here for many years, and had perhaps not spoken her native tongue in those years, until now. It made her tone hard to decipher. "I have lived with that reality for a long time," I said.

"Twenty-five years."

"Yes. Twenty-five years."

"So, you became a writer."

"I did."

"And then you were no longer, and then you were again. I saw that you'd come back to Paris a while ago, I was sure you'd have come to see me sooner. Tell me, Robin. What's Hollywood like?"

"It was one of my biggest mistakes."

"Did you do that for a girl as well?"

"Yes."

"Oh, Robin."

"I know."

"Okay, now you ask me something," she said.

"I didn't realise we were playing a game."

"What is life if not a game?"

"Okay. You said that you knew I'd return."

"Yes."

"Why?"

"I just had a feeling that you would. I told you on the phone. I'd see you again."

"Hm."

"You do not seem satisfied with my answer."

"It feels like a—well—"

"A leap of faith?", she asked.

"Yes."

"I agree with you. There is no reasoning to it, no rationality. But the best things in life are often lacking in such things. Reason, ration, these words are the death of love. You and I are the same in that respect."

"In what respect?"

"In that we are passengers. We are the ones for

whom life just seems to happen, without reason. Everything we do is in reaction. And whenever we do take life into our own hands, it does not end well."

"Passengers?"

"Yes."

"Did you ever marry, Francine?"

"Now you get the hang of the game. No, I did not."

"Because you knew I'd return?"

"Yes. Men came along, and I entertained a few for dinner. But none ever left an impression on me."

"I came back you know, not long after I left."

"I know. One of the other girls told me that an Englishman had asked about me. I knew that it was you. Perhaps this is why I waited. I figured that you'd give it another go."

"Would you entertain me for dinner? Perhaps tonight?"

She smiled and gave me a sardonic look. "I think you know the answer to that question."

And so, a quarter of a century after we had agreed to do so, Francine and I dined together. I lingered in the café while she closed up, and sent her staff home. After which, we took a walk to the river, and to a bistro that she had come to adore. We spoke more over dinner, and I felt vindicated in every mistake and misfortune that had taken me back to her. After we ate, we walked the river and found a scenic bank to sit on. She had aged wonderfully, and looked hardly different from the café girl I had met in my youth. She was just as funny and charming, and her ability to make my knees feel weak had not lost any ground. That night still lives, as clear as day, in my memories, though it would be forever tainted by what was to come. Francine had a secret. She was dying.

50

And so began our finite year. When the lavender seemed to be in bloom through all seasons. And yet, the peace and love I felt was tinged by a distant, creeping sadness, as the black dog picked up my scent. There was a landmine down the road, some twenty paces away. I could see it, for it was marked clearly and surrounded by tape and bollards, with a flashing neon sign overhead. And yet, I could not do anything, except to walk decisively into my own total dismantling. I knew, with more clarity and conviction than I had ever known anything before, that once my sojourn in the sun was over, a misery beyond words awaited. And so within days, I had left my shabby rooms and moved in with Francine. And from that moment, until our last together, we were one continuous thing. Our movements, words, thoughts, all fell into one direct stream. She knew everything now; all of my mistakes and misgivings. She had experienced every lurid night as if she too was there. She knew what I had done, what I had endured; and yet she understood.

In was in that familiarity of routine, and the decades of time we had to make up, that I settled in for my fifth and final love affair.

We grew impatient in the company of others, and waited until we were alone. People came and people went, wishing her well in between. They toasted to her health, knowing exactly what we knew. That it was little more than an act of grace for the dying. There was no saving her, all efforts had been exhausted long before I walked back into that cafe.

We would spend our days in the café, and when we were not there; we were in bed; reading in silence, talking about everything and nothing, or walking by the river. I didn't write in those days, for I did not need to, and I had no desire to. I wrote to escape, and escape was the furthest thing from my mind. I had precious little time with her, and little else mattered. One month became two; and then three, four, five, six. All I had, and all I wished to have, was right in front of me. When she could, we'd dance, and when she could not, we read and listened to music on her antiquarian gramophone. So engrossed were we in our comforts, that we aged, day by day, without so much as noticing. In spite of what was to come, I was very close to heaven; or perhaps the upper ridges of purgatory.

On one day, I accompanied her to see the doctor, where she was told what she already knew. I sat in the waiting area, while she was attended to. As I sat there; my body numb and my head vacant, it suddenly occurred to me that perhaps I was condemned to be alone. You see, on that front, very little had changed. It was, as I realised then, my truest form. I had a lonely childhood, a lonely adolescence, and a lonely adulthood. Loneliness is not some constant sensation, but it is never far away. Whether I was on my own, without a soul in sight, or in a room full of them, I felt alone. In misery, or in joy; sickness and health, til death I shall not part from that cunning black dog. The door opened and Francine shuffled out; stern and seemingly indifferent, as what she had heard was of no news to her.

"Wait here, darling," I said, ushering her into a seat. I would like to speak with the doctor."

"Monsieur?"

"Anglais?"

"Non. Francais."

"Peut-on parler?"

"Oui, mais je n'ai pas beaucoup de temps."

We walked into his office, where he placed the files pertaining to Francine and her health into a cabinet. "Je vous écoute?", he said once I had seated myself.

"Est-ce que vous pouvez faire quelque chose?"

"Pour sauver sa vie? Non. En revanche, on peut la lui rendre plus facile."

"Comment?"

"C'est très simple… Francine a accepté qu'elle allait mourir. En revanche, ce qu'elle a du mal à accepter, c'est de devoir renoncer aux petits bonheurs de la vie… Voilà comment vous pouvez l'aider: en la faisant rire, en la faisant sourire, et, peut-être même, lui faire oublier, l'espace d'un instant, qu'elle va mourir."

We said little else for the rest of the day, we just meditated on what we had left. Soon, she grew too unwell to manage the café, and handed the responsibility to a nephew of hers; who himself had come to Paris to find something. "Wine?", I asked her one night, before we got into bed.

"No, thank you."

I poured myself a glass and threw it down in one, before pouring another. "Robin," she said, with a cautious tone. "Please stop lobotomising yourself. It won't dull the pain."

"It seems to do the trick."

"Please, my dear. Come and join me."

And so, I did. She wrapped her thin and emaciated arms around my chest, and pressed her face, so white and marked by jagged bones, into my shoulder.

"Are you afraid?", I asked.

"Afraid of what?"

"I don't know. The lights going out, I suppose."

She removed her head from my shoulder and looked at me in silence. "No," she said after a while. "It's funny, really. I used to fear death, every single day, until I started dying."

"Why?"

"I just know that I'll be alright. I don't know. Perhaps it is my body, and my mind, preparing me for death. Perhaps it is some unknown force calling me to come home."

I could not speak, I just smiled at her with misted eyes and implored her to carry on. "It's just one of those things," she continued. "You think you can understand it, but you cannot. It's better to just let go, enjoy what's left, and hope for the best."

"That is what breaks my heart. That we could have had all this time together."

"Don't, Robin. You will never find peace if you let these thoughts in. Do not think that you have done me a disservice. I will not die alone, and that is all that anyone can do for me. And I wouldn't have anyone but you here."

"Without fear?"

"Yes, without fear."

"Would you prefer to die as you are, or to just go out in a second?", I asked. "No pain, no looming, just, gone."

"I'd change nothing. There is something to dying this way, you think each day is your last, and then you wake up the next; and it is this little treat. I go to sleep, and ask myself if my body can survive the night. My breathing is so shallow, and my lungs do not fill. My heart beats so slowly, and my brain gets foggy. So foggy. And then, I wake, and you are there. And you kiss my head, and fix me some coffee. You see, when you are dying, the morning is the best part of the day."

"It is for me as well. Seeing your eyes open."

She smiled, before leaning over and kissing my cheek. "My beau parleur."

We fell into a silence, in which thoughts of death, and heaven, and hell had begun to circulate and spiral. Francine had a sense for inner conflict, and saw it on my face. "What concerns you?", she asks.

"I——I find your philosophy on death so—unspeakably beautiful, but I just know it won't —"

"Make it hurt any less?"

"Yes."

"I think you are looking at things in the wrong way. It is not a matter of knowledge, or empirical evidence, it is faith. If you are searching for confirmation, or evidence, in proof or in proof of absence, you will not find it, and will spend the rest of your days clutching at pixie dust. I do not believe because I have seen God, or because I read it in a journal of the sciences, or because a friend went there and wrote me a postcard. I believe in it because it fills my heart with a most unspeakable joy, and it makes me not fear death. I believe in it *because* it is beautiful."

"And what do I do when you're gone?"

"What you've done any other day. Wake up and live. I can't, so you must."

"And where will you be?"

"I shall go to a little field in the stars. Built just for me."

"And me, eventually."

"Oh, yes," she said with a little grin, all that she could muster. "I shall reserve a seat. You shan't get rid of me that easily."

"I'd never—"

Her smile disarmed me, and soon she was asleep. And while she slumbered, that unspeakably beautiful piece of music, that I knew only as the Korsakov recording came to me, as it always did when I felt the extremities of love, and passion, and sadness. I just looked at her sickly white flesh, and her chest that seemed to stutter as it rose and fell.

"I would do anything for you. I'd kill for you, die for you. I would conquer lands for you, and force the subjugated to pray in your name, and build great, towering temples. I would drain oceans, flatten mountains. And if a cure to your ills were buried in my own chest, I'd rip my flesh from the bone, bore through the muscle and ligament, dismantle my ribs, and pull it out for you."

"*Beau parleur*," returned a faint whisper. "Those all sound lovely. But," she said, turning slightly and smiling with all the strength that she had. "You can just hold me as I go. That's enough for me."

I recalled what the doctor had told me. His advice reverberated in my mind, and woke me each morning like an alarm clock. I did what he said and tried to bestow upon her as many little joys as possible. I prepared coffee and toast for her in the morning. I made her laugh, bathed her, and listened when she spoke. When her feet could still carry her, I drove us to Versailles for the day. But they would not carry her for long. And soon, she grew too weak. I cooked all of her meals, and washed her body and clothes. It was just her and I.

Six months became nine; and then ten. We awoke one morning, and I carried out my standard morning duties as she slowly stirred and gained strength for the day.

"Robin," she whispered, as I lay down her breakfast.

"Yes?"

"Do you feel ready for me to die? Have I become a burden?"

"My dear. Where do you get such thoughts?"

"Is some part of you not longing for the day in which you can eat breakfast at your own leisure?"

"Do not be silly. I cherish each day I have with you, toasting bread and boiling water is hardly a price too great."

"Okay. Good."

"You are funny."

"Am I?", she asked, in between soft chuckles that quickly gave way to coughs.

"Oh, yes. Hysterical."

"So, you don't feel ready for me to die?"

"Not at all. And I don't think I shall have to worry about that for a while longer," I said, knowing that she had weeks. "Besides," I continued. "I am doing all that I can to make what time there is left true and beautiful."

"Everything?"

"Yes, I believe so. I feed you well—"

"As if I were a cat?"

I laughed. "Yes, like a pampered cat. I make you smile; or, at least, I try to. I make you laugh—"

"Or at least you try to."

"Yes. I read to you, bathe you, express how I love you so. What else would you have me do?"

"You could make an honest woman out of me."

"Oh?"

She giggled and gave my shoulder a little slap. "I speak in jest, Robin."

"Even if we were to do such a thing, I think I'm still legally married in England."

"I'm sure no one would notice."

"Are you proposing?"

"I want to marry you, Robin. I always did."

"I want to marry you as well."

"Who cares what the courts say? To us, it is real."

"Okay. Let's get married."

I turned to the kitchen counter and fashioned a ring out of tin-foil. "Francine Jones. Will you marry me?"

"Hmm—", she pondered aloud. "What can you offer me? Fertile lands? Piles of gold?"

"A loving husband."

"Sold."

I knew that by loving Francine as much as I did, and by staying with her in those dying days, I had opened myself up to the totality of destruction. And yet I did not care, nor seek to escape the inevitable drive into my chest, of a blade so sharp that I could not quite fathom, as much as I anticipated, the agony I would feel. For a day in her heart gave me more joy than a lifetime in any other, and because love is the most addictive of drugs. And so it was, that I was to be wed again. This time, it was without the jurisdiction, or recognition, of the church, the state, or the registry office. It was just for us. I held Francine tight as we kissed, and she held me back with arms so thin and frail. "Thank you," was all that she said.

51

There come certain days in life that one repeats, and one is doomed to repeat. Without let, or mercy, every moment is played back in memory; every decision, every word uttered; everything consumed, built, destroyed. I recall, with a sinister, snarling repetition, that seems to ambush me at will, even now, the day I lost Francine.

It began like any other; I woke and made breakfast, held her while she stirred. I read her a magazine, and some poetry. And when she took her mid-day nap, I left the apartment to walk. In those final weeks, the walks I took during her nap became a daily meditation. I did not busy myself with practical matters; such as the looming question of my staying in France or returning to England; I simply focused on comprehending what was happening, and what was about to happen. However, it is a thing that cannot be truly comprehended by the non-believing mind, and I found no answers. I stopped on the river and observed a young family. The parents were no older than their mid-twenties, and the child was an infant. I thought of you in that moment and wondered how you were. I wondered if you had forgiven me, or if my absence had been a relief. A blessing in disguise. Perhaps your mother had remarried, and that you had more siblings. Soon enough, the thought had been exhausted and I desired to be at home once more.

Though nothing could have prepared me for what awaited. “Robin!”, was the first thing I heard when I entered. “Robin! Is that you?”

I ran up the stairs and found her, sprawled upon and floor and writhing in pain. “Francine!”, I yelled. “What happened?”

“I fell. Robin, I can’t move. I can’t walk.”

I knew right there, and right then, that the day had come. I picked her up, and she was so light. I carried her into the street and called, frantically, for a taxi. After a few minutes of maniacal waving, one pulled over and I carried her into it. In flustered and broken French, I bribed the driver to get to the hospital as quickly as possible. He obliged, and we were there in minutes. I carried her body, which felt like a sack of feathers, into the reception. In what felt like seconds, she was carted out of view as I was brushed to the side by a flurry of doctors and nurses. Pre-emptive grief took all of the strength that my legs had so far mustered, and I fell to the cold floor in a heap. It was fifteen minutes before I could stand, and another ten before I could find the words to ask after her.

She had stabilised, and was asleep when I found her. A gentle beeping hum indicated her shallow pulse, and it was only the flickering of her eyes that told me that there was still a person there. I made the necessary calls, and what remained of her family came by to say various farewells. The whole thing seemed orchestrated, so that I would be the last to be with her. By the evening, her time had come.

“Robin,” she whispered, as her eyes fluttered open.

“Yes, my love.”

“I cannot see. It is too bright in here.”

I rose and dimmed the lights. Her breathing was raspy, quite like Richard’s on his last day. I could not speak; I only held her hand.

“Robin,” she continued. “I am so glad that we were able to have this—time together. You have no idea how much it means to me.”

“If it means as much to you as it does to me, then I do have some idea.”

"Now is not the time for your cleverness, my love. You are so *clever*."
"I'm sorry."
"I do not want to hear you apologise, Robin. You treat yourself like a wicked man, but you are good. You must forgive yourself for the mistakes you have made."
"I don't know if I can."
"You must. It is the only way that you will ever know happiness again. If you dwell on misery, you will only ever invite it in."
"What do I do?"
"I have left instructions. They are at the apartment. I wrote them down because I fear that I will not have the time to say all that I need to say. But you must promise me that you will forgive yourself."
"But I've done so much wrong."
"And so much right as well. There is one more— thing. Try to reconnect with your son, it would do you so much good."
"And if he doesn't allow it?"
"Then at least you have tried. It is all that one can do."
"Then I shall try, my love."
"Good," she rasped. By now her words had gotten slower, and the distance between them had grown greater. "You rescued me from loneliness, Robin, as I feel I have done for you as well. I have no prouder accomplishment."
Fighting through tears, all I could say was "thank you."
"We'll see each other where there is no pain, no sadness—no broken hearts. I shall wait for you when I get there, but do not hurry. Live on, find joy, forgive yourself and you shall know some semblance of peace. And then, when it is your time, we'll meet again. We were always passengers, Robin. But I think that it is time to take fate into your own hands. Perhaps it'll be kinder to you this time. The world

isn't an ugly place, my love. It has so much beauty, you just have to want to see it."

I pressed my forehead into hers, and kissed her nose gently. She smiled under the pressure, as droplets of a tear began to form in her eye. "Do not be sad, Robin. I am going to the most wonderful place. No pain, no sadness, no—broken hearts. You rescued me from loneliness. And I—I rescued you as well, I like to think. I have no—prouder accomplishment. A good life is—happiness shared. That's it. We have each rescued a good life out of one wasted. I waited for you, and you—came."

Those were the last words, and she lost consciousness not long after. Within an hour, the beeping had ceased, and her death was formally declared. I stayed in that seat as they took her away, and the room was cleared of her presence. When the time came to return home, I avoided it for as long as possible, and I sat by the riverside until the morning sun rose. When I returned to the apartment, I collapsed into the bed and wept until I could cry no more. And then I slept until my body woke itself, and with the entry of the day into my senses, came the realisation that she was gone. Every day from then began in the same way.

There will come a time where you too come to know death; its finality, bluntness, impoliteness, the poor timing. When that day comes, take comfort in this; that no moment is more difficult than the first morning after; that first realisation that what is gone can never return. However, with this comes a sort of peace, as no day will be more difficult, things do get incrementally easier from that point.

Once I had given myself that day or so to comprehend things, I found the manilla envelope in her bedside table. In it were instructions for her memorial. She wanted a funeral for her family, in which her body would be put to rest, and she wanted a second funeral, for me and me alone. In the envelope was a letter for my eyes only, its contents I shall not repeat, and her copy of White Nights, the one that I had given her all those years ago. I was to bury the book, alone, in the hills that surround Versailles.

The first funeral came, and with it little of note or consequence. Family members; to whom she had just been a distant aunt, paid their respects, and reminisced on her moments of kindness. Her body was laid to rest, next to the plots of her aunt and uncle. A week later, I found my way to Versailles, and dug a hole in the hills. I buried the book, and a bottle of our favourite wine.

> "There is no true way for me to explain, in the simplicity of words, what your presence has meant to me," I whispered. "I was lost, and then I was found, as I know was the case for you as well. This year we have had together will never leave me, nor too will your memory; your gentility, your goodness, even in the face of such suffering. I wish, for your sake, that there was no land beyond our own; for if I could have you again, even just for a single day, then heaven would be tantamount to hell when compared to the kingdom that I would build for you on earth. Of all the souls I have known, I loved you the most. And I could never love a living thing quite as I loved you. You gave me that rarest, most sacred thing, a respite from loneliness. And for that, I shall always be thankful that I chose your little cafe to read my book in."

And with that, I bade her farewell, hoping with all my heart that we would meet again in that fabled field in the stars. I would never again return to that plot in the hills of Versailles, as I had no need to return. Wherever I would go next, whatever I would do, Francine would be there. She would live on in every act of kindness. I glanced back, one last time, at the upset soil I had created, and then I returned to Paris, where I would see my darkest days.

52

I recall almost nothing from the days and weeks after I buried Francine. It was a time in which I stumbled and slurred through each day, waiting for it to end so that I could wait for the next day to end, and the next day after that. I was drunk almost all of the time; and when I was not drunk, I was hungover, or asleep, or fetching more drink. My hair had grown long, my beard bushy, and I resembled Francis when I found him at his lowest. In the throes of my broken heart, I had uglified my once harmless demeanour.

I remained in the flat; and had so mastered the art of seclusion, that those in the cafe would sometimes forget that I was even there, and would greet me with surprise when I did appear. Theirs was a look of puzzlement, and then one of sympathetic knowing. I became an urban legend, an old wives' tale; the sad old Englishman in the flat above Le Coin, who wails at night for his lost lover. It was a time of self-harm in slow motion, as my grievance was brutal, and my promises to Frances ignored. I was stick-thin, pale-faced, and a most unseemly sight.

Three years passed in that manner. I drank away the pain, and slept off the isolation. I had not a friend in the world, and was running out of pennies to my name. By the Summer of 1983, and my fiftieth birthday - though I had not noticed then - my funds ran out.

Somewhere in that dark age, on days where it had seemed that my grief had left me, and I was on the mend, I began to write again. I figured that, in the act of writing, which I had never forgotten how to do, I'd find some form of purpose; though I was also content to drink myself to death. Perhaps I would find my name again, as would the world, yet I was also happy to remain a ghost.

As it happens, my latter preferences would prevail. Sensing that I would die in Paris, sooner rather than later, I did what I had become accustomed to, and silently fled in the night; making my way to Calais, and then back to England with the last of my pennies. It had been almost five years since I was last in England. Once more, she had changed. Everything seemed more grandiose; the buildings were taller, greyer, and made more of steel and concrete. The cars seemed to be more opulent, driven faster, and people spoke more of money, and made more of an attempt to show that they came from it. There was no longer a trace of my lot, we had been firmly usurped, and this land now belonged to the swindlers and the Bruce's.

In those early days, once I had arrived and re-settled in the capital, I walked around in a haze. This was mostly due to my constant inebriation, which I had made no attempt to conceal; though under the floorboards lay a shock and awe at the brightness and opulence. I had meagre lodgings in the east end, and it sat above a corner shop, which served me well as the wine was cheap. I survived on sandwiches, and the occasional piece of fruit.

By October I had written a rambling ode to death, which to my mind - broken and battered by drink and by grief - was a masterpiece. Though as I would come to realise, having read it back on the other side of that wall, it was wholly nonsensical, a mere delusion of grief. This delusion was not shared by the first publisher I had approached, nor the second, the third, fourth, fifth, or the sixth. I bounced from one to the other, my mental state worsening with each trip; at the end of each road that I travelled stood a single word; 'no'.

The seventh road I travelled; the one that would take

me to the offices of Firebrand Books, would be the most damning, the most destructive. In my state of unwell, it had not occurred to me to arrange a meeting with any of the publishers; and my sudden presence was most unwelcome. My face was a stranger, yet my name was not, as despite a brief resuscitation in Paris, I had become a cautionary tale for young writers. Donald's presence had been scrubbed, almost entirely from Firebrand; and all that remained was the acknowledgement that he had founded it.

I walked in; shabby, underdressed and with loose documents spilling out of every hole in my ripped leather bag. I smelled of stale cigarettes and cheap wine. A secretary baulked at me.

"Can—can I help you?", she asked, nervously.

"Yes, my dear," I said with the confidence of a warped mind. "I am Robin Fitzwarwick, and I would like to publish a novel."

"Mhm. And do you have an appointment?"

"Oh, heavens no," I exclaimed. "I don't have a phone."

"Is everything okay here?", called a male voice. I turned to see a man, significantly younger than me, in a clean blue suit with slicked-back hair.

"Yes, my fine sir. I am Robin Fitzwarwick."

"Oh, yes. I've heard of you. And how can I help you, Robin Fitzwarwick?"

"I've written a novel."

"Oh, have you? That's *very* nice."

"Indeed. I believe it to be my finest of works."

"Right. I just have a few questions."

"Go right ahead, young man."

Before speaking, he glanced behind each shoulder to make sure that he had an audience. He did, and every set of eyes was fixed upon us, upon me. I had unwittingly become the lunchtime entertainment. It was rather likely, now I think about it, that word had travelled among the various publishers that I was on the loose.

"Yes," the young man continued. "I just wanted to

know if you've hit your head, and become rather confused. Why on Earth would we be interested in anything written by *Robin Fitzwarwick*?"

Scattered laughter began to rise around the room, as the young man grew encouraged by the reception. "I mean, you're not just a has-been, you are *the* has-been. We have a reputation to uphold and this isn't a charity. So why don't you take yourself back to whatever hovel you've been hiding in for the last twenty years, and we can all forget that this ever happened."

The laughter grew louder and more uniform. Suddenly, I felt as bulls do to matadors; afraid, angry, embarrassed. Spurred on, he continued. "Look at you, for Christ sakes. You smell like fresh shit, look like three-day old shit, and I'm sure whatever it is you've written is month-old shit."

"Is that really him?", called a voice from the back, as the laughter ramped up again.

"I think it actually is!", called another.

I was cornered and my natural defences kicked into to gear, and my head shot around the room, taking in each potential threat as the laugher ramped up and echoed around my head. There was the ringleader, who was getting a high from the ordeal he inflicted; the scattered voices around, who added injury to insult; the receptionist, who had taken the first opportunity to flee, and was there no longer; another young man, dressed remarkably casually, who was sat in the corner behind me, and had not spoken yet, had begun to furiously take notes.

"Look at his shoes!", called a third voice, as all eyes, including my own shot down. They had been my sole pair for three years and had become shot-up and covered in holes.

"Behold, all!", the leader announced. "The great Robin Fitzwarwick, the most exciting writer of—about thirty years ago, blessing us with his presence, and in his Sunday best too!"

The room broke out into its loudest laughter yet. I felt my chest tighten, as my heart broke again. From that, a surge arose in me. It started in my feet, and worked its way up, until it reached my lips; and from there it could only go outwards.

"H-H-Hey!", I screamed, at the top of my lungs, as the room fell deafeningly silent. The silence gave me a few seconds to think, and to articulate, though I did neither. "Not a single fucking one of you knows what I have seen, f-f-felt. You," I said, pointing at the leader. "Have you ever loved someone, who died in your arms? Or you," I pointed at a face in the crowd, who'd been particularly vocal. "Did your parents d-d-die before you could ever know them? W-Were you raised by people who called you a m-murderer? Do any of you know what it is like, to be told over and over again, that you are just a cash cow? And then to be told that n-no-one cares anymore? Do any of you know what it is like to have your best ideas destroyed! And your worst ones elevated? Do you know what it is like to be eighteen, and be thrust into fame, alone, at eighteen! I have been in this, alone, since I was twelve years old, twelve! Since that day, I have walked through hell! Alone!"

"Was that before or after you abandoned your family?", asked the voice behind me. Of all the words thrown at me that day, those were the ones that broke me, and I hadn't even the courage to turn and face the accusation. He had asked it without effort, and he had broken me without effort. My knees buckled, gave way, and I fell to the floor and wept, having finally hit rock bottom after tumbling for a decade. "I'm sorry!", I wailed. "I'm sorry! I'm sorry! I'm sorry! I'm sorry! I'm sorry, I'm sorry, I'm—I'm—"

Eventually I simply rocked back and forth, muttering incoherently to myself. The mood seemed to change in the room, and I became a point of concern over mockery. I was helped to my feet, and handed the bag I had dropped a few minutes earlier. I staggered out of the building and collapsed in a nearby alley, crying uncontrollably until I could cry no more and fell asleep. When I awoke, my wallet had been stolen. And yet, the worst was still to come. As it happens, the young man who had posed me that final question, and who had written away with such glee, was a journalist. The next day, an article about my state was published in the Herald. I never read it, and never sought to. I didn't have to, as I knew what it was. I knew that everyone I had left behind would read it, and know that my leaving was ultimately a good thing.

It was, simply, my darkest day. And yet, as I have outlined before, one's predicament is never fixed. And before long, Winter would give way to the Spring.

PART FIVE: *FABULAM DE NIHILO*

53

> *"Death? Why would one ever dwell on such a thing, I want to talk of life! That empty canvas, with a handy painter at its fore. You see, Fitzy, we are all very good painters in some sense, and we all have a beautiful, barren canvas in front of us. Just—reach out and paint."*

Those were words that Richard had said to me, as we drank alone one night in 1953. I had forgotten them then, almost as soon as he had said them; yet they had inexplicably come back to me long after he had died. I suppose it had taken me this long to see the sense in them. It is now time to discuss the final chapter in my life. So far, you have seen my rise, and my fall. What follows is my redemption.

It came with another recollection, of my sixth birthday. It fell right on the cusp of war, and would be the last before the war took my father to Europe, and kept him there. I awoke to find him stood at the end of my bed and grinning with delight. He was a good man, and the prospect of doing good filled him with a most immeasurable joy. Once I had stirred, he approached the bed and gestured for me to take his hand, and follow where he led. Downstairs, fast asleep and grinning to itself, was a kitten; no more than a few weeks old. "This is yours, Robin," he said. "Yours to love and look after. War is coming, my dear boy, and it is my duty to go and fight. And whether I shall return or not, England shall rely on you, Robin, to keep it ticking after this grizzly affair is through. If you can keep a kitten in good humour, then you can do the same for your country some day."

And then he left. First to the countryside, where he learned to kill, and then to France, where he was killed. In between, he came home briefly after the evacuations at Dunkirk, and as I had heard from an uncle, he was briefly in North Africa before being seconded to the Normandy front. These details are of little consequence, as only one fact of the matter is salient, I only saw him once more after that. And when he was gone, and I was left in the care of my cold and callous relations, that kitten became my joy. So much so that Joy is what I named her. Joy and I would spend each day together, and I would talk to her. I shared my problems with her, my fears, and my moments of bliss. For a while, she was my only friend. We'd listen to the radio, and hear reports from the war. When my father returned home after Dunkirk, we greeted him together. And then, one day in 1942, a bomb landed nearby and she vanished. For weeks, I searched for her, walking the streets, as planes flew overhead, with a tin of sardines, calling her name to no avail. Soon, I gave up, assumed the worst, and returned home.

It was in those days, that I learned perhaps the greatest lesson of life, that so much of it existed beyond control. I could not prevent Joy from running away, I could not prevent my father from dying. I could not make a woman love me, or preserve the love that I once felt, nor keep a friend or a lover alive.

I thought of Francine daily, and missed her with such a force that it sometimes hurt; as if her absence was a hot stick, that poked me at disparate intervals. It was a brand, that marked the word '*alone*' over my scarred and battered shell. I had no control over the sad things in life, and yet I also had no control over the little miracles that come around; two years after she vanished, Joy inexplicably returned. And when I had reached my lowest low, another old face would return.

Each day, when I would take my walk along the south

bank, I'd invariably come across London Bridge. Each day, I'd stand on it, and gaze down into the blue abyss below.

"You look like a chap in the midst of a bad week," called a voice on one such day. I turned to see the source, and found it to be a man of around eighty. He was frail, and yet carried no object of assistance. It was the first time since I wailed on the floor of Firebrand Books that any concern had been thrown my way.

"Bad week, bad month, bad year," I replied.

"Let me give you a piece of advice, kid," he said, edging closer to me. "Enjoy the misery you feel, it is a compliment."

"A compliment?"

"Yes. You see, most people will live their entire lives in the middle. They will only ever be content, 'alright', 'decent'. They will never know the heights of euphoria, or the depths of despair. Life will be unremarkable, predictable. To feel absolute joy, or utter misery requires a certain complexity of mind. Never be unremarkable. You may be down in the dumps, and think that the music has stopped, but I bet you have quite the story to tell. You don't write by any chance?"

"I used to."

"Yes," he said with a knowing smile. "You have that air about you."

"Can I ask you something?"

"Of course," he smiled.

"If you had lost everything, everyone you loved. If your name had not been forgotten, but something so much worse; only known for your ills. If you had spent your entire life, waiting to be reunited with the woman you knew to be the one, only for her to die in your arms when you found her. If you were completely alone, standing on this bridge, would you jump?"

He scoffed and nodded his head, as if he knew what I had lived, and had come out the other side of it. "I lost my wife, about ten years ago. We were married for fifty years. Which, I dare say is a longer innings that your own. On some days, I come here and ask myself that very same question. '*What is life without love*'? We tell ourselves that we shall never love again, but that is not true, for we can love in many different ways. Friendship is love, appreciation of the arts is love, petting a cat is love."

He moved closer, until he was within touching distance. "You see," he said, placing a hand onto my shoulder. "I believe I have been asking myself this question longer than you have. And my answer is no. I would not."

I went into my pocket and withdrew a note I had scribbled some weeks earlier. It was a simple goodbye, to no one in particular. In fact, it simply read *goodbye*. With a smile, I held my hand over the railing and released. The paper fluttered and danced in the breeze until it hit the water, and was evaporated immediately. "What's your na—"

I turned, and he was gone. For the rest of the day, and on many days since, I asked myself if he was real, or if he was some figment of my weary mind. Perhaps he was a ghost of my past, keeping me alive.

A year had passed since that episode in the offices of Firebrand Books. In that year, I had signed onto the dole, and lived the life of a quiet hermit. I lived on tinned food, typically cold, and murky tap water. A man by the name of Hyde had taken pity on me, and had added me to his retinue of showcases. We'd tour the country and its newly-built universities, running meet-and-greet stalls at Freshers fairs, literary societies and other hubs of the young and the mocking. It was the Spring of 1984, when I found myself at the university I had once taught at.

It was a humiliating affair; I heard the snickering of those mocking young, who saw my name, and then my dishevelled appearance. I had not shaved in some time. By the third hour, I had not shifted a single book.

"Tough crowd," said a man in the stall next to me, who had once been a prolific author of spy novels.

One group of four took particular glee in my presence. They lingered for a while as I shot nervous glances over every few minutes. I saw the others egging another on to approach my stall, which he did.

"Hello," he said.

"Hi."

"I must say, I'm a big fan."

"Really?", I asked, as a distant ray of hope appeared.

"Oh, yes. All of your books. I particularly like the one about——something, but it was excellent, very clever. Would you sign one for me?"

"Of course!"

"Great!"

"Name?"

"Imy."

"Imy?"

"Yes, pronounced '*eye-me*'"

"Okay," I said, writing it down.

"And the surname is 'Relevant'"

"Imy Relevant?"

"Yes, you are."

A chorus of laughter shot up as the young man turned to face the adoration. "I can't believe he fell for it!", he called, triumphantly.

"I know," said another. "What an absolute twat!"

The ringleader, who'd duped me so, marched towards his friends, like a gladiator freshly released from victory, before carelessly tossing the book I had signed into the bin. From that point, I simply looked down; unable to face the public, by whom I had been rejected so cruelly. A few had noticed what happened, and made an effort to get a book signed. Though I knew their reasons, and I loathed their pity, which was a sharper knife than the derision, and still could not look up.

"Name?"

"Margie."

"Here you go."

"Thanks."

"Name."

"Gerald."

"Here you go."

"Thank you."

"Name?"

"It's for a friend of mine, by the name of Icarus."

I paused, stunned by the word. "Excuse me?", I said, still looking down.

"Icarus. And could you tell him to be careful? I fear he's flying rather dangerously."

Slowly, and with a great caution, I looked up to see him. Sure enough, it was Balloch. His hair was now grey, though he looked healthy and vitalised. "Hello, Robin," he said.

"Balloch."

"I go by *Bill* these days; I haven't taught in quite some time you know."

It was too surreal. To see Balloch before me was like a dream, and I expected it to swiftly become a nightmare, or that I would wake up. All I had were questions.

"But—But——Why are you here?"

"Because I think you need me."

"I—"

"It's okay, Robin. Save your breath," he said, looking scornfully at the mocking group, who had lingered to scrape what little laughter remained. "Be gone, the lot of you."

They scattered, and he turned back to me. "Come on, let's get out of here."

"But I only get paid if I'm here all day."

"I think you've sold enough of your dignity for one day. Come on, lunch is on me. Oh, and leave the flask here."

We left, not caring that I had just lost my sole income. He took me on a short walk, around five minutes, until we arrived at a cafe. "Order whatever you want."

I did, and before long a Full English, with toast, coffee, and orange juice stared up at me from the table. Balloch just watched me as I gulped it down with a ravaging hunger. He waited until I had finished before he spoke.

"How long has it been?", he asked.

"Well, I believe I saw you last in—1953."

"That's not what I meant. How long have you been on the drink?"

"I've always been on the drink."

"No, you haven't. Some of us reach a tipping point, the edge of the cliff. You were not there in 1953, but you are in 1984. Dare I say it, my dear boy, that you are, in fact, in the ocean below."

"Four years."

"Yes, that sounds about right."

"How did you know?"

"You mean aside from the flask at your desk? And the fact that you are clearly drunk right now?"

"I suppose so."

"You've lost the shine in your eye, your innocence. It has been ripped out. Only drink can do that."

"Well, I don't see a shine in your eye either."

"Yes, I suppose you're right. And I dare say it won't ever return. I was lost in the drink for decades, Robin. But I'd say you already knew that. It's very hard to hide these things."

"Yes, it is. Do you not drink anymore?"

"Not anymore, no."

"How did you do it?"

"I asked for help."

I thought about it. My head throbbed with little bouts of agony, as it had since I first began to drink like this. "Bill," I said, looking him square in the eye. "Please help me."

"Of course I will. But you need to want my help, and ignore the siren's call to flee in the night and drink yourself stupid. It is no easy feat."

"How long ago did you kick it?"

"A decade, as of last week."

"A decade?"

"As of last week."

"Why didn't you come and find me a decade ago?"

"I looked you up, and learned that you were married with a kid, teaching at some pile of bricks in the city. The one we were just at as it happens. I figured you were happy, and at peace."

"I wasn't."

"I know. Happy men don't drown themselves in gin."

"Or wine."

"Well, at least you still have your wit. I suppose that part hasn't been sold for a bottle just yet. It was the misery that carried me over in the end."

"Were you really so unhappy?"

"Oh, dreadfully so. Not even you could have pulled me out."

"So, what happened to you?"

"You want me to recall events, in which I was drunk, that occurred thirty years ago?"

"Yes."

He sighed, before readying himself to speak. "Well, I made a tit of myself at one of those Summer parties. You must've been off somewhere because I don't recall you being there."

"I was in Cornwall."

"Right, yes. With that loud fellow. Whatever became of him?"

"He died."

"Oh. I—"

"It's okay. Please carry on."

"Well, I always used the drink to mask the pain I felt. I suppose I never quite recovered from my career going to tat. Teaching felt so— humiliating."

"Yes, it's quite the sponge."

"Indeed. Oh, how I hated teaching! Not even the faux-prestige of being a Camford don would have saved me. I numbed myself to avoid the pain of my reality, the true pain I mean, a little bit always got through, especially when I saw you take those first—steps. A superior, probably egged on by Mitz, gave me an ultimatum; give up on the drink, or leave. And so, I left. I took the severance, and fled into oblivion. I roamed around the continent; Spain, Italy, Germany, and then I ended up in Scotland around 1968, from there it all becomes a bit of a blur. Until, I woke up one day in a hospital room. Apparently, I'd been on the side of a motorway, daring cars to hit me. It's funny, I never felt suicidal, but I also never cared if I lived or died. That was until I came so close to death; not from the cars, but from alcohol poisoning, that I decided to pick one. I picked life. That was the 28th of March, 1974, and here I am. How about you?"

I told him of my life since I saw him last, in that little Camford office. I told him of my final year of schooling, my own gallivants around Europe, and my misadventure in Hollywood.

"Yes, that is the last I heard of you, making movies."

We graduated to dinner, and I told him of my plateau, and my life of teaching. I told him of my married life, and how it came to end in the middle of the night. I told him of Francine, and our year together; how her death had broken me, and how I hit rock bottom in the middle of the Firebrand offices.

"So, you found her?", he asked.

"I did. But it was too late."

"No. If she'd died while you were off gallivanting, then yes, it'd be too late. But you found her. And you were able to have that time with her, fate may have taken her away from you, but it cannot take your memories."

"The worst part is that I tried to purge them out of my mind. I've had a drink every day since I lost her. I only stopped when I ran out of money."

"I know the feeling."

We lingered in silence for a few moments, and I could tell that he was thinking. After a while, he came to some conclusion and snapped his eyes towards me. And so it was that as I drifted alone in the sea, a boat came. I moved into Balloch's flat, and entered a regime of sobriety. On occasion, he would find me weeping over an empty bottle of wine, and we'd start again from step one. On other occasions I would break down, and cry until it felt as if my vocal cords may snap. Soon enough, eight months had passed, and I had gone four without a drink. With the clarity, came inspiration, and I found myself able to write once more. It began with a few short poems; but soon I lusted after an old, familiar bedfellow.

"What's it about?", Balloch asked, once I had compiled a paragraph.

"Fatherhood, I suppose. Death, drink."

"Superb. Family is a trove of storytelling. You can write the funniest comedy, the bleakest tragedy. There's so much there, an absolute goldmine."

It was like Camford again; we would stay up, long into the night, and discuss the work that gradually bore fruit. And one day, a week shy of Christmas, it was finished.

"I must say, Robin, it is excellent. A tad rusty in the early chapters, but nothing that cannot be cleared up. Once you found your footing, it's—it's classic Fitzwarwick; delicate, witty, charming, funny, sad. It's real. See, that's what your writing always was, it is what caused your brief flame to burn so bright, how real it all felt. I could never crack the minutiae of daily life, perhaps it's why I failed."

"You really think so?"

"Of course."

"So, what now?"

"You tell me. Do you feel ready to face the world again?"

"I believe so."

"Then it is time, and I know just who to show this to."

54

"Robin!", cried Matheson, when I was shepherded into his office. "We meet again. I must say, it is so very bizarre how we keep meeting like this."

"Hello, Matheson."

"Christ alive, how long has it been?"

"Almost a decade, I'd say."

"Yes, the last I saw of you, we were sat in some grim little pub in the West End."

"That's the one."

"And now for a bit of discomfort, I'd heard about your——*episode* at Firebrand, and was so very worried about you, old friend. But I hear that you are well now, or as well as can be. Is this true?"

"I hope so."

"And you're certain about that?"

"Yes."

"You're off the drink?"

"Yes."

"And you find yourself in good mental health?"

"I believe so."

"You're not going to go spare, are you?"

"No."

"Right! I suppose we'd better take a look at this then. Leave the manuscript with me, I'll give it a once-over and see where we stand."

I nodded before leaving the room. Balloch waited for me in the hall. "Well?", he asked.

"He said he'll read it."

"Ah. That'll be a few weeks then. It's probably for the best if you busy yourself for a while."

"Busy myself?"

"Yes. Are there any affairs you wish to get in order? Before you are flung back into public view."

"Well, there is one thing."

"The boy," he said, knowingly.

"It's something Francine said to me, right before she—went. She said that I should at least try."

"Now seems like a good time to try. Do you know where he is?"

"No. I just know that he doesn't use Fitzwarwick anymore, or Sullivan."

"Perhaps Elsa has remarried?", he asked.

"Yes, I presumed so."

"Do you have anyone who may know where they are?"

"Francis, but I don't know where he is either."

"Hm. That is tricky. How about that Monty chap? You said that he'd taken on some of your old responsibilities."

"That is true."

"I don't suppose it's worth a shot?"

"Yes, I suppose it is. It's just that I—"

"Fear he won't accept you?"

"Yes."

"It's not about his acceptance, Robin. It is about ridding yourself of this burden. You've conquered mightier tasks on this journey, my boy, this shouldn't be much worse."

He was right, and I looked Monty up. I found that he had retired from the university, and was managing the estate of his ailing father while awaiting his inheritance of Barony. We met for lunch in the June of 1985, on a street that had changed entirely since we met last. We sat in silence for a minute that felt like an hour. Monty was the first to speak.

"I must say, I am relieved to see you in good health. Word travels quickly, and I learned of your unfortunate circumstances. But it all seems to be behind you."

"I'm on a better path, Monty."

"Good. I knew we'd meet again; but also, that it would only be when you came to me. You were on the precipice of a great and unfortunate journey, and you had to embark upon it."

"And I did as much."

"And how was it?"

"Great in length and unfortunate in nature."

"You haven't lost your wits then?"

"I did, but I found them again."

"Good. It was the only thing you ever liked about yourself."

"Listen, Monty, I—"

"Didn't come here to catch up with me? Yes, yes. I suppose you want to know about little Andrew. The boy is just fine."

"Is he?"

"A few scars here and there. One on the arm from some older boys in his neighbourhood."

"Mm."

"I'm just pulling your leg, Robin. He's okay. Really, he's a good kid. I don't see him all that often, but when I do, it's a treat."

"Does he ever speak of me?"

"He asked about you a while ago, but I didn't know. It was before the Firebrand incident, which he is aware of."

"I don't suppose he'd like to be called a kid at that age. What is he, thirteen now?"

"Fifteen."

"Right."

"Have you looked him up?"

"Yes, but I couldn't find him."

"Really?"

"Yes, no Andrew Fitzwarwick, or Andrew Sullivan with his details."

"Mhm."

"Has Elsa married again?"

"Do you really want to know?"

"Yes."

"She has."

"That's good, I'm happy for her. Is he a good man? A good father to Andrew?"

"He is."

"Who is he?"

"Come on, Robin."

"What? I want to know."

"You really haven't figured it out yet?"

I held his gaze, and shook my head slowly, eyes slightly widened. "Robin, I find that the word I call you more than any other is '*fool*'. You are a fool sometimes, a blasted fool, the smartest fool I know. It was right under your nose the entire time. Think about it, who was there for him? Who stuck around?"

Suddenly, it became so clear. "Francis."

"He's a good father. They have a daughter now as well."

"I thought Francis couldn't have children?"

"Miracles happen, I suppose."

"Could you put me in contact with them?"

He sighed, and acquiesced. "I want no direct part in this, I won't play the mediator. I can give you a phone number, but under one condition."

"Yes?"

"That you only call *once*. And whatever they decide to do, you accept."

"Okay."

He took a sheet of paper and scribbled down a number. He motioned for me to take it, but pulled it back as I approached. "You promise? Only once."

"Yes, I promise."

"I want to hear you say it."

"I'll only call once."

"Okay. I believe you."

I called twice.

I froze when I heard your voice; so much deeper, so ravaged by puberty, yet I knew it straight away.

"Andrew?", I said, once my courage had returned.

"Yeah?"

"Andrew, it's—it's your father."

The line clicked almost instantly. I froze again, wounded by the rejection, and reeling from the fruition of my fears. When I called again, fifteen minutes later, it went to the answering machine.

> "Hello, I do not know who is listening to this, but whoever it is, this is for you. It's Robin. I know that I am almost certainly not welcome, but I have fixed many aspects of myself, and wish only to make amends. To speak to my son, even if just once, is the most important thing—" I gave my address, before putting the phone down, and waiting.

A week later, while I sat with Balloch in an easy silence, there was a knock at the door. Balloch rose to get it, while I listened intently. "Robin, it's for you."

All of a sudden, three paths stood before me. One in which it was your mother, one in which it was you, and one in which it was Francis. Like all other facets of my life, I had no control. I would walk one of these three paths, not knowing who would stand at the end of it. My legs trembled, ever so slightly, as I rose to my feet and approached the door.

"Hello, Robin."

"Hello, Francis."

For a moment, all was suspended in frozen time. As I stared at a ghost, and a ghost stared back at me. It was he who broke the silence. "May I come in?"

I opened the door to its full width, and gestured for him to pass me by I led him into the lounge, where we sat facing each other.

> "Shall we have some wine?", he asked. "For old time's sake?"

"I don't drink anymore."

"Oh, yes. I'm glad to hear that, it is probably for the best. What do you have in?"

"Coke."

"Marvellous," he said. "May I have one?"

I had always known what to say to Francis, and I should like to think that he always knew what to say to me. However, on a day like today, our minds were blank, and we searched without luck for inspiration. At least, not for fifteen minutes that seemed to last an hour. Francis spoke abruptly.

"I'm afraid to say, Robin, that Elsa was quite perturbed by your calling. She contacted Monty and gave him a right old earful, apparently he'd given you the house number on the condition that you only call once. You were very naughty calling twice, Robin."

"I know. I'm sorry. I hear that the two of you are married."

"Yes, I would have written to inform you, ask your blessing and all, but not a soul knew where you were. We just got the divorce papers, and assumed that you were still with it. Beyond that, we didn't kno—"

"I was in Paris."

"Oh, wow," he said with a little chuckle. "Yes, that does bring up some nostalgia, that Summer by the Seine."

"It was a wonderful Summer."

"As was the one in Cornwall."

"Oh, yes. Have you heard much from Charles and Mary?"

"I'm afraid they're both long gone. A pity really, but such is life."

"Whatever became of that wonderful house?"

"I believe the National Trust have taken it over. It belongs to England now."

"It always did."

We smiled at each other, and it was clear that both of our minds had become picture houses; and each replayed those foggy recollections of youth and of innocent folly. "What were you doing in Paris?", he asked after a while.

"Francine."

"You found her?", he said, with a smile of shock.

"I did. But she was ill, cancer too - just like Richard. We had a year together, and were married, right before she——you know."

"I was very sad to have read that article in the Herald. The one about the state you found yourself in. I do not wish to pry, but I figured that some terrible thing had happened to you."

"A fair few. But then again, I have done some terrible things."

"Nothing that shan't be forgiven."

"Do you not resent me?"

"How could I? I have what I had always dreamt of. No good thing comes without bad, and no bad without good. You did hurt them; Elsa and Andrew, but out of it came something wonderful."

"Is he happy?"

"Is anyone truly happy?"

"I suppose not."

"It is not a question of if he's happy, as all things are fleeting, and run in circles. I have seen him happy, so happy. I have seen him sad as well. He gets sad around the time of year that you left. What matters is his character, and he is a most excellent young man."

"Tell me more."

"He is a painter, of remarkable talent. He does these landscapes, and one would swear that they were photographs."

"A painter?"

"Yes. He's a natural really. He's sort of like you in that sense, he will go into a state of fugue for a couple of days, and emerge with something truly wonderful."

"I'm glad that he has you."

"And I am glad to have him."

"What'll he do next?"

"He wishes to attend Camford, '*like his father*', he says."

I smiled, and looked down. Though over the course of several seconds, my face shrivelled and straightened, as it dawned upon me what Francis had meant. "He's referring to you, isn't he?"

"Yes."

I knew then all that I needed to know. That the life I had created was in better, more stable hands. And with that, I was content. We stayed in that lounge for another hour, and spoke of lighter things. We laughed and reminisced about Richard's various escapades, Summers spent together, and Summers spent apart.

"I'm glad that you found her, Robin," he said, once the evening had come to an end. "Love is such a funny thing, to have it, and hold it, even briefly, is a blessing. It is a virtue that rights all wrongs."

I patted his shoulder and smiled. "You are the greatest man I ever knew, Francis Uxby."

"You were the first to call me *Francis*, you gave me my name back, Robin, and I never forgot that."

Those were the last words we ever shared. Content in the knowledge that some amends had been made; he returned to his family, and I returned to my recovery. He waited while I fetched some things from upstairs. I returned to him and handed over a pair of letters; one for you and one for your mother. And with that, I could do no more. When I walked into Balloch's room, he rose and addressed me with a smirk on his face. "I have some good news," was all that he said.

55

"*You may know Robin Fitzwarwick for a multitude of reasons, and in recent years, few of them would be positive; his highly-publicised breakdown in the offices of Firebrand Books, his ill-fated move into Hollywood, or the rumours of his marital infidelity and rampant alcoholism. However, I, like so many others know him for what he truly is, the premier romantic novelist of his time. A wickedly fierce and witty writer, who combined the comedy, tragedy, and romance of life with such an ease, that any punter who picked up one of his books would fancy himself capable of writing too. However, few, if any, could replicate the vivid scenes and realist dialogues he composed, twinned with the dream-like surrealism and playful energy of his body of work, mostly confined to the 1950s. It is safe to say that, at long last, and having travelled a thunderous path, Robin Fitzwarwick is back. 'At Least I Tried to Try' is the must-read novel of the year. In it, the one-time-prodigy, now in his early fifties, makes a triumphant return to the literary scene; and I shall be the first to say that he has been sorely missed.*"

Balloch closed the newspaper and looked at me with a smirk. "Looks like you're back," he said, placing the paper into my outstretched hand. "The critics are a fickle sort, are they not?"

"Better late than never, I suppose. How'd they know

about the—drinking?"

"I suppose it was obvious to anyone who'd ever been tight."

"Which would be everyone."

"Alas it is no longer a mystery."

I laughed and went back over the review. "So," he said, leaning forward. "How does it feel?"

"Odd. I don't think I trust people when they say nice things to me, or about me. Except for you, of course."

"Yes, I can see that. Consider yourself a lucky man, Robin. Few earn their old spot back. Thank the Lord for Matheson, he really pulled it off."

"Any word from The Herald?"

"Why?"

"It was their journalist who wrote the piece, about my little episode."

"Not that I know of. You know I don't read the Herald either. *Never read the Herald.*"

"I suppose it is of no consequence."

It had been a handful of months since I had seen Francis, Christmas approached and the trees were bare. Matheson had done me well, and the book had been marketed, to expert effect, as the triumphant return of a once-cut gem. The Game had changed, so much so that now it hardly existed. It was a starkly different world to the one that I had fled in 1959. The industrial politics of literature was no longer played out at opulent parties in opulent rooms. Instead, it was done in print. Publishers didn't command the press, because there were now so few, and those few were largely American, without the means or the interest in the affairs of the English. Literature still had the ability to make well of a man, but one truly interested in the jackpot would have made movies, or television. Christmas came and went, the new year too. I spent both with Balloch, and we sat in a general ease, occasionally sharing a glance of mutual affection; and more often lamenting our boredom.

"Sometimes you just want a drink," Balloch said

after one bout of silence. "Just to make the time go a bit faster."

Despite this, and despite my agreeing, neither of us ever cracked. We sipped cranberry juice, to replicate the sting of drink, and made ourselves dizzy to replicate the euphoria. We read poetry and recited theatre to replicate the camaraderie, and danced because it was the same if one was sober or not. Some months passed like that. Our two souls, seemingly destined to be alone, had found companionship at last. Money trickled in from the novel, and with it my financial burdens were eased, and soon I had paid off the various debts that I had accrued. Naturally, I shared my rediscovered wealth with Balloch, for I considered it to be the repayment of another debt, one far greater than rent or utilities.

"Is money not the funniest thing," Balloch stated one day, when we had decided to spend well on dinner. "It makes the world go round, it is what we dream of at night; it affords so much freedom, and enables so much good, yet it cannot make one happy."

"Is the caviar not to your liking, Bill?", I asked.

"It is not the caviar, dear boy, but the company. I'd be just as happy eating porridge. And to answer your rhetorical question, this caviar tastes like salty dirt. I never saw the appeal."

"No, nor I. I suppose it is just a status symbol."

"Yes, what pair of twats would be eating Caviar in the Ritz on a Thursday?"

We laughed together, as that was exactly what we were doing. We took such sardonic joy in the pompous and ostentatious things in life. How ridiculous we found it all to be. It was now deep into the April of 1986, and I felt as I did when in my twenties. I could laugh again, smile without force. "You know," he said, as we left the restaurant and hailed a cab. "I think we may have just completed London."

"You think?"

"Where else is there to go when one has just eaten caviar at the Ritz, and not even finish the plate?"

"Elsewhere, I suppose."

"Do you have any ideas?"

"I do, as it happens."

"I'm all ears."

"Cornwall," I said.

"Cornwall?"

"Yes. I was happy there."

"That's good enough for me. Let us go and be hermits."

As my fortunes picked themselves up, and dusted themselves off, there was to be one final twist in the tale, one final jerk on the shoe-string of fate, London said goodbye with a final bowl at the stumps. As the cab approached the drive, Balloch noticed - before I - a lonesome figure sat on the porch, waiting patiently.

"I say," he gasped, pointing. "There's a young chap there on our doorstep."

It was you.

Nervously, we approached, as you looked up and shot to your feet. There was a few seconds of silence, to which Balloch was an unwilling participant. He had deduced instantly what was happening, and who you were. "I'll go in," he said, politely brushing you out of the way and entering the house. You doubtless recall this conversation, as it wasn't too long ago, but I shall recount it anyway.

"Hello," I said.

"Hello, Robin."

"You can call me dad, you know."

"I think that's a bit too informal. After all, I don't really know you."

"I understand. Lord knows I sacrificed that right."

"Mhm," you mumbled in agreement.

"How are you?"

"Do you care?"

"I called you, didn't I?"

"More times that Uncle Monty said that you must."

"Did you come here just to insult me? Of course I care."

"I actually don't know why I am here. I was passing

through London, going up to Camford to take a look around."
"Oh, yes, I hear you're planning to go."
"Yes."
"Did you want to come in?", I asked, placing a hand on the door.
"No. I just wanted to show my face."
"Thank you for that."
"Mhm."
"Would it make a lick of difference if I said that I was sorry?"
"Half a lick. I read your letter, they were all right about you."
"In what sense?"
"You write very well, so well that it's where all of your humanity is."
"Is this the first thing of mine that you've read?"
"Aside from your letter?"
"Yes, aside from the letter."
"It was. Mother was very strict about, there was to be no mention of your name, no copies of your books, she nearly killed Francis for seeing you when he did."
"I suppose she would have. Did she read hers?"
"No. Burned it, still in the envelope, you can imagine that Francis wasn't best pleased about that. He accepts that we won't have Sunday tea together once a week, but it still didn't sit right with him."
"Shan't we have Sunday tea?"
"No."
"I have a question, Andrew."
"Yes?"
"What made you come? You hung up when I called."
"It just seemed a slap in the face at the time, but I've had time to think about it, and I spoke to Francis after he saw you. He told me about what happened, with that lady in Paris. He didn't say much, I don't think he knows much outside of the most basic de-

tails, he said that you'd fallen in love with her when you were eighteen, and that she had cancer when you found her again. And then that you'd become a dipsomaniac, and had a breakdown. I was happy when I first heard it, but then I realised that would make me as cruel as you were. Perhaps I don't mean it, I don't know you well enough to know if you're cruel or not. I know that you never loved my mother, and that you only married her because of me, which is honourable in a way, and cruel in another. Maybe I'll spend the rest of my life arguing with myself about you.

"You can get to know me if you wish."

"No. It'd hurt mum too much."

"Is there anything I can do? To make this right?"

He thought about it for a moment. "Do what you do best, dad. Put it in writing. You're no good at speaking, or so I've heard. You get all—fidgety and doubtful, but I'd like to know."

"Know what?"

"Everything."

And then you left, not looking back, Satisfied, though a little shell-shocked, I entered the house again, and found Balloch sat by the phone. There was a message on the answering machine, from an number we didn't know.

"It's an American number," Balloch stated.

I called the number back, and after navigating the quagmire of switch-boards, time-zones and office hours, spoke with an executive in Los Angeles. She had found my script; the one that Walter Mills had spiked over twenty years earlier, and found it fit for production. At last, my final work of that strange sojourn would see the light of day, and while I refused the offer of a job, I was paid handsomely for the script, and would live on the royalties until my dying day. And with that, I had been redeemed in public eyes. Shortly after, I had been approached by Firebrand about an anthology, and later that day I signed an exclusive deal with Matheson. And so, I resolved to leave the civilised world behind.

56

We lived as nomads in those first few Cornish months. We rambled down to Penzance and back up to Molt Bay, where I fell in love again and desired to build a home; finding beds wherever they could be found, and making friendships that lasted the night and seldom beyond. It was the youngest I had felt since my year with Francine. We tried our hands at surfing, became intimate with the folklore, and learned fragments of the local tongue. Balloch truly loved the beach at Molt Bay. "If I die in this water," he'd say, floating each morning for hours on end. "Leave me here."

In accordance with our leaving London behind, Balloch's house was sold, and all of our affairs had been settled by the Spring of 1987. We sold all that was of no use, and packed all that was into a little old car, and drove down over two days.

In the third month, I returned to Molt Bay, where little had changed. Here, I was met with an impulse, most bizarre, that whispered to me that I must visit Belling House. Just as Francis had said, it belonged to the National Trust now.

Belling House was exactly how I had found it, and as I walked each room, the memories of each came back. I walked the upstairs landing, where Adeline had once bludgeoned my wrist with a hammer. I walked the massive yard, where the pond was intact, but the guest house had been demolished. I entered the library, where I had wept to the music of Korsakov. Finally, I found myself in the drawing room, where so much had happened that it fell beyond the remit of brevity. On the wall were paintings of the Belling family, including one of Richard and one of Adeline. Though they were replicas, the originals being in the mausoleum - which as I had been told, was reserved for the sole inhabitant of the estate - I found the visitation of ghosts hard to withstand, and would not look at either of the Belling children without a great thump in my heart. Their hair, golden blonde, and preserved on canvas, forever. Just as I had known them. At first it licked and lapped, but then it just bit me and I stepped outside. Balloch was there, admiring the stonework on the portico. I sent him out to the garden, under the premise that there were nymphs etched into the stone.

"How do you—oh, yes, *Belling House*. How could I have been so dim."

Balloch obliged, and I took the moment to examine the facade once more. I felt, in that moment, transported in time. I was nineteen again; naive and hopeful. As my gaze rotated, and more of the house came into view, I fell upon that small, rounded hill, just off to the left, where I had only been once.

The servants halls were empty, for they had mostly been dismissed some decades ago, and those who now worked at the house would drive in from elsewhere. It seemed abandoned, as if some pathogen had wiped all life from the place. So lost was I in recollection, that I hadn't noticed the rocking chair outside of the furthest cottage to the right, nor its occupant, who swayed back and forth.

"I was wondering if you'd ever return," he said, causing me to spin in his direction.

"Bilkins?", I asked. I could hardly believe my eyes. He must have been eighty by now. He smiled, nodded, and gently rose to his feet. I rushed to help him. "I figured that you would return someday. I wouldn't dare hazard to guess how long it has been."

"A long time, Bilkins. So you're the final inhabitant, they said that only one person lives here still. I don't know why I hadn't assumed it."

"I knew it was you, Robin, as soon as you came up the hill. No one ever seems to pass this way. I'd say it makes sense. It's the big house they come to see. Everyone has seen a cottage, though not everyone has seen—", he poked his walking stick in the direction of the house. "That."

"It is the most beautiful house in England."

"Yes," he agreed. "Not the biggest, nor the most lavish. But it has the most heart. That is why I gave it to England, because England needs to see what she threw away. Oh, you should have seen it in its day. 1925, that was the Summer to have been here."

"That is before I was born, Bilkins."

He gave a chuckle. "Late to the party, as ever, Mr. Fitzwarwick. Would you follow me? I think there is something else that you would like to see."

He led the way, and I knew where he was going as soon as he mentioned something of my interest. He led me, unsurprisingly, to the mausoleum, and using that key, which I was sure had never left his side, opened its large door. We had stood in this very room, more than three decades prior. He had shown me the Belling men and their helpers, their portraits through time. "Just as I said to you back then, one day there would be another painting up on this wall. Here it is."

I followed the point of his stick, and fell upon an image that I had pictured in my mind for many years. There on the wall, preserved in eternal youth, were Richard and Francis. Just as I remembered them. "This is just how I like to remember, Richard," Bilkins said. "Before that horrid disease came and took him away."

"I've seen this one before. It had been finished before the funeral, the replica in the house pales in comparison. One could almost feel him."

"You know," he said. "Francis came to visit, not too

long ago in fact. He mentioned you, as it happens. He feared that something awful had happened to you. You shall have to let him know that you are okay."

"I already have, Bilkins."

"Oh, good. It is so sad when friends fall out."

"They're buried in here, aren't they."

"Yes. All four of them are. Would you like to see?"

"I would."

I came into the section of the building, reserved for the bodies, and found that the family had indeed been reunited. There were four marble graves, identical in size; each inscribed with a name, and the years of life. "I do miss them greatly," he said, removing his hat. "They were *such* wonderful children."

"Yes. They gave me something, this family. Something I fear that I lost when they died. Some little spark, that made each day an adventure."

Bilkins chuckled. "That was their gift to the world. They made it all seem so unserious."

I thanked Bilkins for his time, and bid him a farewell. Walking down the hill, I found that Balloch had wondered back to the facade, and our paths crossed on the gravel.

"Are you okay?", he asked. "You look as if you've seen a ghost."

"I've seen three."

"I can see why you stayed down here all Summer. It's a wonderful place."

"It is. Though, Bill, I think that I must leave now—and never return."

"Is that so?"

"Yes. I've just said goodbye to the place."

"Is there anywhere you'd like to go? A happy place?"

"Yes," I said, recalling a particular memory that had remained uncorrupted by loss. For there was nothing to lose, only decaying walls and barren windows.

"Is that it?", Balloch asked, when we had arrived after a walk of some two hours. "You dragged an old man all the way out here, to look at an abandoned old house?"

It was just as I had seen it last, all of those years earlier. It had not grown any more decrepit, yet was no closer to salvage. It was simply the same.

"This is the old Boden House," I said with a solemn brevity.

"The old Boden House?", he enquired.

"Yes. The Boden's, they used to be the other great family in these parts, them and the Belling's. All of the sons and heirs died in the Great War, and the house burned down in the 20s. The patriarch decided it was more harm than worth to fix the place up and took up residence in Bath. It has been empty ever since. And now, both families are gone."

"It's a bit small for a country house."

"I think it's just perfect."

We sat on the grass and ate the lunch we had prepared. Soon, the afternoon grew into its latter stages, and it was nearing evening. "Are you ready to move along?", Balloch asked.

"No, not just yet. I can't quite bring myself to leave."

"Oh. Then perhaps we have arrived."

"Arrived?"

"Yes."

"What do you mean?"

"It is no secret that we've been rambling about without rhyme or reason. Did you not ask yourself why?"

"You know, for the first time in many years I have not been concerned with yesterdays or tomorrows."

"Well, perhaps we have not been so aimless, just—flying blind. We've been searching for a home, and today we very well may just have found it."

"This place?"

"It's probably cheap. The council, or whoever owns the land is probably desperate to get rid of it, all the better if the place gets done up."

"You're serious about this? You want to buy this place?"

"I'd dare say, Robin, that it is you who wants to buy it. You said it yourself; you simply can't bring yourself to leave. So how about you don't leave?"

"This place? This dilapidated old thing?"

"Yes. Besides, you like dilapidated old things. You *are* a dilapidated old thing."

"And you're aware of the magnitude of work this place will require?"

"Magnitude? I wouldn't go that far, a few licks of paint here and there. I mean, just look at this place, you'd get a most wonderful airflow for a start. What? What are you laughing at?"

"Oh, nothing. It's just that I've heard that one before."

Balloch was right. It was cheap, and I bought the land for a modest sum, and work commenced in the sweltering June. There were two corners of the house which were still covered by something vaguely resembling a roof. Naturally, these became our rooms.

Eventually, we tired of working alone, and hired men from the local village to help. Soon, it became a fixture of the community, an event that all could believe in, and contribute to; fixing up the old Boden house. I had never built a house before. For what it's worth, I hadn't ever really built anything before; yet Balloch knew how and I did as he commanded.

"I had to feed myself somehow," he'd say whenever I asked of his prior unknown skillset.

And so, that dilapidated old thing slowly grew into a home. As the house grew more and more into something liveable, we naturally migrated from our corner and into other pockets. By September, a ceiling was up. From that day onwards; we ate breakfast in the kitchen before the help arrived, and entertained ourselves in the lounge after they had left, each relishing in the other's friendship once more.

"Aha!", Balloch would shout to me when I woke

each morning and made my way into the kitchen. "I win."

"One of these days, Bill, I will rise before you do. And when that day comes, you'd better believe that I won't let you forget it."

"I'll believe it when I see it," he'd say.

We carried on in that routine of comfort for a while longer. We'd rise, eat, and talk until the men from the village arrived. Then, we'd spend the day building, before evening came and we'd have each other once more. The work came to a halt when the Winter arrived, and we took an empty cottage on the village outskirts until Spring came. And in the May of 1988, it was finished. Just in time for the sweet and succulent airs of the dancing embers of Spring, and its final descent into Summer.

There came a night, two weeks after the work had been finished, and we had settled in. I awoke from an early evening nap to find Balloch sat on the porch, with two rocking chairs dragged out onto it. The sky was cloudless and moonshine danced upon the water of the lake. There were stars in the sky, thousands of them.

"There you are," he said with a grin. "Awake at last, do come and join me, Robin."

I did, and we occupied either rocking chair. "It is such great fun to rock back and forth," he said. "Don't you agree?"

"My knees hurt."

"Oh, stop moaning. You have paradise at your feet, and a true friend to share it with."

"So, this is it then?"

"What is what?"

"This. Here. This is where it'll all end?"

"I suspect so. Does this bother you?"

"No. I just wonder what the others are up to. I fear sometimes that I am cursed,"

"If I were to hazard a guess; I'd say that they spent some of their time in a state of joy, some in a state of misery, and for the rest, they're asleep. Cursed how?"

"Most of the people I know are dead. Cynthia died last year, Donald the year before. Richard, Adeline, Francine. Milena, I think, will live to ninety, so she's well and good. Elaine may be dead, or wishing that she was, best to keep that book firmly shut. That just leaves Francis, Elsa, and Little Andrew, who seem to be well. Did I tell you that little Andrew is a painter?"

"You did."

"I have one of his drawings. I took it from the fridge when I left that house."

"Your priceless piece of art."

I laughed to myself. "Yes, quite."

"Do you still feel guilty about the matter?"

"I do."

"Even now, that you've made amends?"

"I haven't just yet, he wants me to write him a memoir of my life."

"When'll you write it?"

"When I'm dying, I suppose. If I beat him to the punch, that is. But he doesn't smoke, so it's likely."

Balloch then let out a noise that seemed part laughter and part whimper. "Two old men, sat on rocking chairs and talking about death. We really have reached the final chapter."

"Speak for yourself, Bill."

He took a moment to examine the house with pride. "You know," he said, once he had turned back to me. "It really is quite remarkable what we have done here."

"It truly is."

"Consider it my parting gift."

"Bill!", I exclaimed. "Do not say such things!"

"It's a mere fact, kid. I'm getting up there."

"I must be the first man in his mid-fifties to be referred to as *kid*."

"Oh, Robin. However old you get, and whatever old man things that you do; to me, you'll always be the eighteen-year-old who just wanted to talk to me about Maugham."

"That was a heck of a day."

"And one I replay in my head."

"Really?"

Balloch seemed to snap his tongue at me, as he sat up straight. "Oh for Christ's sake, Robin, when are you going to view yourself in any form of positive light? You ooze self-doubt, I never understood that about you."

"Excuse me?"

"I replay the day we met, and you know why? Because you're a good chap, one I am honoured to know. You seem to have this idea that every relationship you have is some form of charity, with you as the sorry recipient. Do not fail to see what it is that you give. On that day in 1951, I was a washed-up drunk. I'd lost something, and you replaced it. Your enthusiasm, your excitement, respect. For those few years, before the drink carried me away, it was all that kept me going. And it isn't just me; it's Francis, it was Francine. You do ten good things that are subtle, and one bad thing that is harsh, and think that it makes you the devil on horseback. Well, it doesn't, it makes you a human. Do you know who is good every moment of the day? In every interaction? Nor do I, but I can imagine that they are a most frightful bore."

"Bill," I asked sometime later, when the matter had died down. "If we're on the subject of reproaches. There's one thing I've been meaning to ask you."

"Yes?"

"When you vanished, why didn't you let me know? I can understand vanishing from the others, but why me?"

He sighed. "I couldn't face you. I saw the way that you looked at me, like I was your hero or something. You losing that admiration would have broken me."

He rose to leave, as he was one to do when it was suddenly time for bed. "Hey," he said, from the doorway. I looked up and he continued.

"Do you remember that dinner we had in Camford, the first one?"

"What about it?"

"I asked if you wanted to be great."

"Yes?"

"You are. Forgive yourself, kid. Before it is too late."

I thought about his words as I lay in bed. Perhaps it was time that I took the burden of forgiveness into my own hands, rather than giving it to others to gift and withhold at their own whim. That night, I did something that I had not done, perhaps ever before; I prayed. I prayed for forgiveness, that I might forgive myself. With it, came a sort of rapture, as I felt what seemed like my parasites of self-hatred leave my body, and fly through the window, out into the night. I slept like an infant after that. The next morning, I walked into the kitchen to find that Balloch was not there. Gleefully I walked along the hall and into his room.

"Aha!", I cried with the spoils of victory on my tongue. "I told you that one day I'd beat you."

But there was no response. Just the outline of his body, under the blanket. I could see no head, limbs, or feet. "Bill?", I asked, approaching the bed, and raising the duvet. When I saw him, I knew right away that he had slipped off in the night.

"Bill," I whispered to myself.

It is difficult to quantify the good that Balloch had done for me. He was a father, a friend, a mentor, a saving grace. When I think of the pantheon of souls tethered to my own - Richard, Francis, Cynthia, Donald, Matheson, Adeline, Milena, Elaine, Elsa, you, and him - each has imparted something upon me, and from each I had gained something priceless and irreplaceable. Although, none other than Balloch had done so twice. He had built me, and he had built me back up. He was cremated, and scattered by the beach at Molt Bay, where he had wished to always be. And now, wherever the tide shall carry that water, he'd be there for the ride.

On that day, another miracle occurred. Through the thickets and hills that separated the beach from the rest of the world, emerged the village folk who had helped us to build the house. One by one, they took a handful of ash and sprinkled it into the wind. It had been two weeks since my friend had passed, and on the day of his scattering, I was able to smile for the first time.

"You were the father I never had," I said to myself, as the last ashes left my grip, and the coastal wind carried my friend to his final place of rest; out on the water he loved so much. I picked up a stone, placed it in my pocket, and returned to the home we had built. And there once more, I was alone in the world.

57

In the time that had passed since Balloch died, that familiar state of nothingness had returned, as I floated through each day; doing the bare minimum to ensure that I awoke the next. It was not for a handful of months that I snapped myself out of it, and lived as the departed had wished me to. I consumed food and water, sat on the porch, and read poetry when my heart could take it.

Thus far, I had resisted the urge to drink myself into stupor. Yet, for reasons unbeknownst to myself, a crack emerged on my fifty-fifth birthday. With all the strength that I could muster - and there was little left - I left the confines of the house, and ventured into the village. I was met by the locals from afar, who had seen me on the horizon. They offered sympathetic smiles, and little nods. Those who came to the beach had formed some distant bond with the sad old writer who now walked through their town. A few fell into step with me, and escorted me to the village shop. They helped me to carry my items of purchase; a week's supply of food, a month's of cigarettes, and a bottle of potent wine. None had failed me, for none knew that I was a dipsomaniac. I was escorted all the way home, and wished well.

Once they had left me, I placed the bottle on the dining room table, and stared at it in contemplation as hours passed in the guise of minutes. In the lowest depths of my addiction, I had not bothered to drink with a glass, for I had no one to share it with, nor was anyone there to witness it. Instead, I simply drank out of the bottle. And so, I unscrewed the cap, and carried the bottle to my lips with a shivering hand. So close was it to my senses, that I could smell the wine, and thus I could taste it. Though once the bottle had been tipped, and it was on the way to my throat, there was a noise that shook me still, and caused the bottle to slam into the table, somehow not breaking. It was a hollow thud upon the kitchen floor, I looked down and saw that the stone I had picked up from the beach had fallen from my pocket. The physics of such baffled me, and I was thrown into a fit of self-reproach.

Shame was a more apt word, perhaps *guilt*, as if I had betrayed my friend, and spat upon his final achievement. I poured the wine into the sink, and watched it paint the basin red. I discarded the bottle and walked around the house in a daze. Before long, I found myself at the door to Balloch's old room. I entered, and found the place to be exactly as I had left it. The first thing I had done once his body was removed, was make the bed. I had not, however, thought to examine any other corner. Perhaps my grief had rendered me myopic, or given me a tunnelled vision.

On the desk, sat neatly in a typewriter, were a few chapters of simple prose. At the top was a title: *We Built a House for One*. It was a novel, there was no doubt about it. All of a sudden, a thought entered my mind and entrenched itself, as ideas are one to do. This, it had occurred, was Balloch's final gift to me. On several prior occasions, in the first phase of our association, I had suggested that Balloch and I write something together, for I wished my success to find him as well. He always refused, stating firmly that he was retired. As it happens I had been searching for something that would give me closure, peace in the face of another aching departure; and now I had it.

Like I had so often before, I entered the state of mind in which I wrote almost all of my works; one of rapture, fervour, obsession. For that brief window in time, I lived, ate, slept, and breathed the words that lay before me, and they had formed an orderly queue in my head. Nothing else mattered, and I wrote through the Autumn, and into the Winter as village folk noticed my absence and brought me food. On Christmas Day, they returned and asked to join in with their celebrations, which I did. After that, and before the new year, I was a member of society once more. I sang the local songs, refused the local ale, and danced the local dances. On the second of January, 1989, I returned to the novel.

As much as I had paced through the bulk and body of the work, its finale came at a crawl. Not because I was bereft of words, because I was not. Rather, it was because of what finishing such a journey would mean. This would be the last time that Balloch and I would work together on something, ergo the last time we would be together. To finish it would be to say a final goodbye, and to leave my friend behind.

Though, all things must pass, and by March, it was finished. I made one last excursion to the beach at Molt Bay, and to the very spot from which I had sent Balloch into the wind.

"*I am not sure if this is what you had intended,*" I said to myself. "*But I have finished what you started. You shall be a writer once more.*"

And then I left, with Balloch now confined to the cinema of my mind. I made arrangements with Matheson, and boarded a train for London. I had telephoned him the afternoon of that trip to the beach, to inform him that I had something to show him.

"Oh, thank God!", he exclaimed over the phone. "Things are really starting to dry up in the city."

In search of alleviating Matheson's strife, I made my way to his office. "I cannot stand the sight of these four walls any more, Robin. Let's go and get something to eat. We can talk about things there."

We left, and moved around the centre of London with slow, anaemic steps, until we found a place that was to his liking. London had changed again, as it had done every time I had been away. Once more it seemed taller, greyer, bleaker.

"So, this all really happened?", Matheson asked, once he had read several pages. "You really fixed up an abandoned old country house? And Balloch—— he's gone?"

"We did," I said. "He is."

"Why?"

"Natural causes."

"No, the house."

"I went down to Cornwall when I was nineteen, and found the house then. And then, when I was old and greying, I returned and found it just as it was all those years ago."

"No deviations then," he remarked.

"No."

"Cornwall," he added. "What a magical place. Nothing ever seems to change, unlike this place. Uglier by the day."

He fidgeted uncomfortably before continuing. "I've been meaning to say actually, I was very sad to hear of Balloch's passing."

"It's okay, James. You know, I genuinely believe that he died a happy man."

"How rare a feat," he remarked. "Truly enviable."

Our lunch came to an end, and I returned to my hotel. A few days later, I was once again in Matheson's office. This time, he had made the necessary arrangements.

"I think it shall make a fitting tribute, Robin. A fitting tribute to a great, and very misunderstood man."

"I think so. What would you say to putting his name on the cover too? 'We Built a House for One, by Robin Fitzwarwick *and* William Balloch."

He smiled. "That, Robin, has already been taken care of. I figured that was what you wanted."

"Thank you, James."

"So, what'll you do next, Robin?"

"Nothing," I said with a simple smile. "I shall return

to Cornwall, and do nothing until I'm dead."

"*The final retirement of Robin Fitzwarwick.*"

"Yes. I feel that I have written all that I can. For once, I am content to simply be alive."

I got up to leave, safe in the knowledge that mine and Balloch's story was in safe hands. You see, Matheson held a genuine love for literature, quite unlike any other I had known on the business side of writing. He was quite unlike the others, who craved money and notoriety. Matheson had walked many paths, and almost all of them had intersected with my own. He was there in sunshine, and in rain. He was a critic, and reviewed my books. He was a publisher and put them out. He was a producer, and hosted my plays. And now he was once more in publishing, this time with a company of his own, when I made my return.

"You know, Matheson," I said, as I lingered by the door. "I think you may just be my last friend in this world."

"You've come a long way since The Fox," he said, as a smile grew across his face, connecting one ear to the other. "*The great Robin Fitzwarwick*, my friend."

And with that, I closed the door behind me, ready to live out my remaining days in peace. I left London that day, and would never again return to the city of my birth.

58

Five years had passed. I had checked out of polite society, and now lived alone, in a sea of familial comforts. I grew vegetables in the garden, and busied myself with music and poetry. I walked, weekly, into the village, and lunched with the locals, and no longer spent my birthdays alone. Word of my name had finally travelled south, and the villagers became starkly aware of who I was. As such, I would spend my sixtieth birthday in their company. The world beyond my rural life had simply ceased to be.

That was until the Summer of 1994, when I received a phone call from London. It was the BBC, who wished to invite me to a televised interview. I accepted, on the condition that the interview would be conducted in my own home, as I had no desire to travel.

A month later, the production crew arrived, and I was met by another familiar old face. "Hello, Robin," she said, with a grin as our hands met.

"Eleanor Andress. It has been a long time."

"And a long time since I was *Andress*."

I welcomed Eleanor and the crew into my home, and prepared drinks with her as the crew got set up. "Before we begin," she said, as we took our seats. "I must say that it is good to see you in such health. I read of your predicament and was worried for you."

"I have certainly sat in some dark rooms, Eleanor. But it is safe to say that I am in a far better state these days. I was sorry to hear of your parents."

"Such is life, it always ends the same way. Right," she said in a brisk tone. "Shall we begin?"

We were fitted for microphones, and Eleanor received confirmation that the cameras were rolling, and the microphones were on, and began: "Thirty-nine years after the release of Robin Fitzwarwick's seminal novel Growing Up, it has this week been added to the British Library's list of Great British Novels. I'm joined by the author; whose journey through the public eye has been turbulent to say the least. Though his personal troubles are behind him now and he enjoys a glowing, albeit resurrected place in the hearts and minds of the British public. To many, he is the novelist of their youth. He is one of Britain's most celebrated post-war novelists, and if he won't mind me saying, an old friend. Robin, we'll begin with the house, as you insisted on not coming up to London. Am I correct in that you built this home yourself?"

"I believe restored is a better term. It used to belong to a prominent family, but fell out of sorts after the great war. I restored it, alongside a good friend of mine."

"Yes, William Balloch, the playwright, and co-author of your latest book. He was a mentor figure to you?"

"Yes. He taught me at Camford for two years. It is thanks to him that I was able to write at all."

"He and my father, I'd dare say."

"Yes, your father did a lot for me as well."

"You were eighteen when you wrote your first book."

"Yes. It was a collection of poems that I published with your father."

"Are you proud of those early works?"

"I am now. I wasn't always."

"Why is that?"

"It's not the typical sort of thing that teenagers do,

is it?"

She laughed. "I suppose not. And do you miss those days in Camford?"

"Immensely. But I'm sceptical of wishing for the past, such desires cannot be fulfilled. But if it were a movie, I'd watch it."

"Well, we shall come to movies later on. What do you miss about those years?"

"I miss being young. I miss—being free. I miss my friends, I miss wine, and smoky pubs, and the college bell tower. I miss the little flat we used to live in."

"It was rather different from your childhood?"

"Well, there was no war to think about, but yes. I never felt that I had lived in a home before that flat."

"Have you been back?"

"I never returned to Camford again."

"Why?"

"Like I said, what's gone can never return. I—knew that I could never have what I once had there. Camford, for me, was spontaneity, it was youth, because the people I had there were truly spontaneous, and we were young. The grown up world is so—contrived in comparison."

"Do you feel that you became famous too young?"

"Meaning?"

"Well, did you know how to handle it."

I chuckled. "No. It was like a bullet. But, I don't see how else it could have happened. Perhaps I maybe should have waited until I was older, but it was right there. I was offered my dream, and took it. I'd have taken it at any age. Though I wouldn't say I was ever famous; at least not in the way that those in other vocations become famous. I never drew crowds, only eyes in privacy."

"You were at least in the spotlight."

"I was. And yes, perhaps I was too young. But, you see, I don't think I was ever really a child. I recall my father telling me that I was always a little old man. As if I was born eighty, just in the body of an

infant."
"Believe it or not, I was told the same."
"I believe it."
"But he died in the war. And my mother died giving birth to me. Perhaps I wasn't quite a man when things took off for me, but I wasn't a child either."
"I'd like to move along, if you please. And discuss the novel that really put you on the map. Growing Up was the best-selling novel of the nineteen-fifties. How do you feel about it in retrospect?"
"It is my least favourite novel."
"Why?"
"Because it is the only one I wrote for money. Not initially, but at some point in writing it, I realised that it was very marketable, and I knew that it would sell."
"Is that such a bad thing?"
"Perhaps I leaned into it. I figured it would buy me some freedom."
"And did it?"
"It did. But that's where things went wrong. You see, I went away for a long time, because of the fame that Growing Up brought with it. It was a bullet. And I went away because I wanted to write something truly for myself, that was my gravest mistake."
"Why?"
"Because back in those days, we had a thing called the Game."
"I remember."
"And the most key thing about the Game, is that it evolves quickly and violently. Step away, even for as little as a year, and it'll be quite unrecognisable when you return. That is what pushed me out, as I see it now. Th——"
My words trailed off. "Are you okay?", she asked.
"Y—yes. I just spoke for too long, ran out of breath. It's been happening a fair bit lately. Must be the smoking."
"Yes. Are you alright to continue?"

"Of course."

"Okay. Well, I'll ease you back in with a simple question. "What is your favourite novel? Of yours that is."

"It wasn't always. But now I'd say it was my first."

"Yes, okay. The Way We Went."

"Yes."

"Why?"

"Sentimental value, I suppose."

"You're a writer who mines your own personal life for stories. Growing Up being written as you had left college; and more recently with books on fatherhood, and the building of this house. Was the girl real?"

"She was," I said, diverting my eyes and shielding myself away. Eleanor noticed the cue and swiftly moved on to a question regarding my travels.

"No, no. It's okay. Her name was Francine, and we met in Paris in the Summer of 1952. Though I was a fool, and I left her. And for the rest of my life, I knew, sometimes in the front of my mind and sometimes in the back, that she was the only woman I could truly love. We met again in 1977, just after I had left my wife, and married a year later. Though she was ill when we met, and died not long after. That is when I began to drink seriously."

Eleanor was stunned, so too were the filming crew. Eleanor had to furiously consult her notes for a contingency. "Uh—when you——-I'm sorry, it's just that you caught me off guard there."

"I'm s-sorry, E-Eleanor. I—"

I began to speak, but the words trailed off again, as a bizarre sensation descended. A great fog emerged inside my head, and I grew disoriented, and short of breath. Tinnitus erupted in both ears and my hearts' beat felt strange.

"Are you okay?", she asked, more concerned than before. I could not hear her words, but I saw them on her lips, as I fought to drag some focus back to my senses.

"Y—yes, it's just, I-I feel funny all of a sudden. In fact, I've felt a bit funny all day."

"Okay," she said, turning to face her crew. "Let's take five here, give ourselves a little break."

The crew dispersed, and Eleanor went into the kitchen. She returned a minute later with a glass of water. "How are you feeling?"

"I'm alright. It must be the lights or something. I never did too well in the heat."

She got up again and opened the window. A fresh Summer breeze rolled in, and I felt some semblance of composure returning.

"Mind if I smoke?", I asked.

"Of course," she said. "It's your house."

Shakily, I withdrew my cigarettes and lit one. The process drew some focus back in, and by its end, I had regained control over my body. "I think I'm okay," I said.

"Finish your water, and I'll call the others in."

I finished the water and put the glass in her outstretched hand. She strolled into the kitchen, coming back with the crew, and a replenished glass of water. The interview had resumed within minutes.

"Do you view your career in stages?"

"I do. My early books, Hollywood, and my later books."

"You wrote the last of your early books after you'd left the game. And gone abroad?"

"Yes, to the Balkans."

"Did you find that much had changed in the years you were gone? I don't mean in literature, or publishing, but in society as a whole."

"It was another society entirely."

"Is that a good thing or a bad thing?"

"Most change is amoral, some like it and some don't. It wasn't my cup of tea, let's just say that. To me, it were as if all that mattered was to shock and appall. Granted, I do feel that writers are there to challenge things, poke little holes and whatnot, but there is a sense of fair play that the old writers had, a line in the sand."

"Was there a sense that you were no longer welcome?"

"Yes, it was like a decade had passed. I had gone from writing best-sellers to niche. There was a new crop by then, and they wrote in a very different manner."

"Are you referring to the Firebrand set?"

"Yes and no. It wasn't just Firebrand."

"And then you went to Hollywood."

"Indeed."

"Would you do it again, if given the chance?"

"No. I don't quite share the view that my time was there a total failure, but it was more harm than is worthwhile."

"It seemed to be studio politics that forced you out, rather than matters of your output."

"I agree."

"Do you have many regrets?"

"Many, yes. But they grew fewer by the day. I have learned to forgive myself, to let things go."

"What would you consider to be regrets?"

"I didn't drive the car very well."

We spoke more of those years; and how I awoke one day to find that I was thirty. How I became a teacher, and the decline of my married life. We skirted around my time in Paris, before going further into my issues with the drink, and my nervous breakdown. Lunch came, and with it a break. The crew had prepared sandwiches in the kitchen, and I ate well before excusing myself to the porch. I was there for ten solitary minutes, before Eleanor came out.

"Mind if I sit here?"

"Not at all," I said, before gesturing at the cigarette. "I couldn't give up drinking and smoking."

"That's fair. Listen, Robin. While I've got you out here, there was one thing I was meaning to ask you about."

"Oh?"

"Richard. I-I know that he passed, some years ago

now. Was it a painful death?"

"No. As far as death's go, it was somewhat peaceful."

"Did I break his heart?"

"You did. I never saw him with another woman after that."

She just looked down, as if she had pictured in her mind, on numerous occasions, what a life with him would have looked like. "Are you married still?", I asked.

"Yes. Just about."

We sat there for a few moments, each playing a film in our heads. She broke the silence. "What ever became of Fucksby?"

"Francis."

"Yes, Francis. Whatever became of that funny little man?"

"He's raising my son."

"Isn't life strange," she remarked.

And then she told me of Cynthia.

"What exactly happened in there?", she asked, after a silent interlude. "You seemed completely out of it for a minute or so."

"I—I have these episodes sometimes, when I think about her. My pulse doubles, and my arms feel so weak, and my chest feels so tight, like it could burst. And my head fills with the ghastliest thoughts."

"It sounds like a panic attack," she said.

"A panic attack?"

"Yes. A rather grim experience, as I've been told, but apparently no threat."

"The human heart is such a terrifying thing, is it not?"

"How do you mean?"

We all have this little—instrument inside of our chests, no larger than a fist. And it just goes, and goes, and goes; when we are in utero to when we die. It doesn't stop, and if it does, then you are completely fucked."

"Hm. I never thought of it that way."

"Ready when you are," called one of the voices

inside.

"Shall we?", Eleanor asked.

"We shall."

We returned to the house and took our seats again. A half hour passed, the matters of which I cannot recall. What I do recall is how the day came to an end. The when the fog returned and my breath left me again, worse than it ever had before. I stumbled and slurred through final questions; answering briefly and forgetting the question immediately after. Eleanor noticed, and gestured for the camera to be switched off. "Robin?", she asked, as my eyes began to water and her figure grew distorted. "Robin, are you okay? Get those lights off!"

"Y—yes, I-I feel—I just need s-some fresh—air—"

I rose to my feet clumsily, and staggered toward the door. As it came to within reach, all that kept me standing was there no more, and I tripped on nothing. All that I remember was seeing the floor approach, and then, nothing.

59

I awoke in a room that was sickly white, and stunk of sanitation. For a moment I asked myself if I had died. The sound of a low, mechanical hum slowly eased into my senses, and told me that I had not. My eyes felt as if they had been glued shut, and I forced them open at a great cost. Once they had been pried open, and my eyes adjusted to the light, I surveyed the room. There were wires that entered and exited my arms and chest; a clock that read a quarter past seven; a muted television, that played the news; and in the corner, fast asleep, Eleanor.

"Francine," I groaned, and Eleanor's eyes shot open. "Robin!", she called, bouncing to her feet. She paced over, and thumbed a button next to my bed. Within minutes, a nurse entered.

"Ah, Mr. Fitzwarwick, you're awake."

"Where am I? Where's Fr—oh. Where am I?"

"You are in the hospital. Do you remember anything?"

"I—I fell over."

"Yes, and you gave your friend here quite the scare."

The nurse turned to Eleanor. "Could you excuse us, Mrs. Fletcher? I'm afraid I must speak with Robin in private."

Eleanor agreed, and left the room. The nurse's demeanour shifted greatly once we were alone. "Robin," she said in a grave tone. "I'm afraid to say that I have substantial news."

I said nothing, and waved for her to continue. "You see, your friends thought that you had suffered a heart attack, but your heart is fine. We initially thought it to be a stroke, or something similar, but your brain seems to be doing just fine as well. So, we ran some tests, and commissioned an X-ray, while you were sedated, and it would appear that you have a tumour on your left lung, quite a large one in fact. And, I am afraid to say that we fear it to be malignant."

The words seemed to leave her lips in slow motion, yet they hit me like a rapid punch. "*Cancer*," I said, almost chuckling.

"It is in a very, very early stage, but yes,"

"Lung cancer," I whispered..

"Typically, we'd show a bit more decorum about it, maybe even wait until you've fully woken up before telling you, but time is of the essence. You face a long and arduous road, but you can be treated to a much higher probability of survival if we operate immediately."

"Immediately?"

"Yes. Now, this is a small hospital, and we only have two surgeons, both of whom are currently in surgery. The earliest we can have you in is tomorrow afternoon."

"Tomorrow afternoon."

"Yes. Now, it is very important that you do not despair. Try to get as much rest as you can, and we will return in the morning for your preparation. Okay?"

"Okay."

The nurse left, just as Eleanor came back in. She looked as if she had seen a ghost; the ghost of someone she knew well. "Oh, Robin," she said. "They just told me, out in the hallway."

"*Cancer*," I said with another chuckle.

"Yes, but they said that it can be operated on, maybe even

removed entirely."

"And then what? I spend the rest of my life with half a lung, needing some instrument to breathe?"

"It's better than dying."

"Is it?"

She recoiled at the question. I just smiled at her. "I'll be alright," I added.

"Do you mind if I go back to my hotel for the evening?", she asked. "You've had plenty of rest, but I've had none at all."

"Of course, go ahead."

"I shall see you in the morning, Robin."

"You don't need to stay."

"Yes, I do. You—you don't have anyone else, do you?"

"No—no one else."

"Wait, Eleanor, there is just one last thing."

"Yes?"

"Could you get a nurse to remove these wires? I feel quite alright, and they are such a burden."

I couldn't sleep that night. I just lay there, staring up at the ceiling. In my head, a great battle took place between two impulses. I thought of my life, sixty years of drifting. Sixty years of spectating, reacting, observing. Sixty years of failures and successes, all of which seemed to have ambushed me from some hidden vantage point. And then, the battle had been won. I couldn't clear my mind of the conclusion; that I had never taken true control. I had never put my foot down; only ran away from, made the best of, adjusted to. However, on this night, all of that would change. And for what seemed like the first time in my life, I would take my fate into my own hands, even if it was the last decision I ever made.

I changed and made myself as inconspicuous as possible; before slipping out of the hospital. I lit a smoke on my way out. As I exhaled, I looked at this little white stick of puffs and plumes. It looked so innocent, so harmless.

"So," I said, to the cigarette. "You're the little bastard who killed Robin Fitzwarwick."

I laughed to myself, and hummed a little tune as I slipped out into the Cornish night. A bemused taxi driver agreed to take me home, on the promise that there was cash at the house. I spoke with him as I would with an old friend, and tipped him generously. And so, I settled in, knowing that I was to die in this home that Balloch and I had built up from the ashes. I slept long into the next day, and was only woken when there was a pounding at the door.

"Robin! What on earth are you doing here?", Eleanor cried upon seeing me. "You're supposed to be in surgery in an hour. I went along to show moral support, and they said you had vanished into thin air."

"I know. I chose this."

"Robin, you—"

"Eleanor, I know what you are about to say. You are going to implore me to give life another chance; that it can always get better, and it's the little things that make life worth living. I don't expect you to understand what I am doing; I just need you to acknowledge that this is what I have to do."

"You're not thinking straight."

"The tumour is in my lung, Eleanor, not my brain."

"So that's just it?"

"That's all she wrote."

She wanted to protest, but Eleanor understood. I saw the process by which she understood. Perhaps it was the calmness in my voice, or the austerity in my eyes, but she knew that I could not be convinced. It was written on her face. She went to speak, but caught herself, and instead flung her frame into mine, and gave me a tight hug.

"You're going to look so bloody good when the interview goes out."

I laughed, genuinely amused by how she had coped with the grief of it all. "Is there anything that I can do?", she added

"Could you drive me into the village?"

Our voyage was silent, as we both had much on our minds. When we arrived, she got out of the car with me.

"Here," she said, retrieving a walking stick from the boot. "It was my father's'. It's been sat in the boot all this time, I'd never thought to remove it. Funny old thing that."

"Thank you, Eleanor. Are you going to be alright?"

"You're asking me? Yes, I think I'll be okay. I feel very sad, but it'll pass."

"Just remember me as you once did."

"A dipsomaniac?"

"*Young*. Remember me young and foolish. That'll do the trick."

"It'll make it worse," she said, before she withdrew to her car, and drove it out of sight. And that was the end of Eleanor. I spared a thought for the pantheon of souls, whose company had, invariably, come to define me, and how they slipped away. Cynthia left with a letter, Adeline with a record, Bruce with a punch, and Milena with a necklace; Elaine with a betrayal, your mother too; Richard with words said, you with words unsaid, and Matheson with them written; Balloch with a house, Francis with a handshake, and Eleanor with a walking stick; Francine with a life of reproach, now corrected piece-by-piece. Monty would be the last farewell, and again that is a story for another time.

Summer airs sang away and Summer flies danced and twinkled as I trudged into town, and the crickets formed a symphony. A young man, also named Robin, whom I'd come to know came trotting out of his cottage and took one of my arms. Locals nodded my way and I was sure that word of my dying nature had been spread, like spores and seeds, and the knowledge that I would soon be gone had pollinated the village chatter. I am not sure why, but instinct took me towards the parish church, which was empty and still.

"I should like to spend some time in here alone," I said to the other Robin.

"Of course, Mr. Fitzwarwick. I'll be in the pub if you need me."

I walked in and sat in the pew, trying to recall the last time I was in such a church. And then, my seeing Eleanor had unleashed memories of Richard, I recalled something that he had said to me, at the end of my first week in Camford, and I smiled, giddily at the memory.

"I have the sense, old boy, that this place shall never quite leave us. And when we do leave it, we shall never return, for nothing will give us keener joy than the youth we shall undoubtedly take for granted."

How right he was, and how I missed him. I hoped, in that moment, that I would go with the grace, and acceptance, and the humour with which he had.

"Hello," whispered a voice behind me. I was not startled, as the word was uttered so gently, that if anything I was made more relaxed by it. I turned to see the vicar, who wore a face of unassuming welcome.

"Hello."

"It's a wonderful church, isn't it? I find that I often come and sit in the pew, even when there is no service on."

"I'd have thought that would be the one time you weren't sat in the pew."

"That's good. I shall have to write that one down. But do you agree? About the church?"

"I do. I've never been a Christian, yet churches have always been my favourite sort of building."

"It is a testament to those things larger than oneself. Do you often sit in the temples of beliefs that you do not hold?"

"No. But today felt like an exception."

"Any reason?"

"I'm dying."

The words left my lips with such an indifference that it were as if I had known this for years, not days. "The logical conclusion of living," the vicar joked.

"Are you often this macabre?"

"I find that people are so squeamish about death. Granted, not all believe in the eternal soul, and for them I can imagine it is rather terrifying, and not a subject for mirth. But, I see no thing that is beyond a little joke."

"You are quite unlike any vicar I've met before."

"Have you met many?"

"No."

"There is more to us than cucumber sandwiches at the village fair. May I ask you a question?"

"Of course."

"Were you christened?"

"I cannot recall. I don't think so, my father wasn't very much into religion either."

"There is to be a baptism tomorrow, I've spent the morning readying the pool. It's just around the back of the church. Would you let me baptise you?"

"Me?"

"Yes. You know, *just in case*."

"When my wife died, she told me that she was going to a *little place in the stars,* built just for she and I. I don't suppose that this would get very much in the way?"

"It'd help if anything."

And so, behind the church, with only the Vicar, the Verger, and God himself as my witness, I was baptised into eternal spirit, though all I craved on the other side of death was Francine. I would have taken damnation with a skip in my step if it was to be spent with her. We spoke some more, and he gave me a bible to take home. When I left the church, it was seven, and the Summer sun was still out. Village life is quite unlike any other, and with it comes a uniformity. In this case, it was the pub, where the other Robin had told me he'd be. Doubtless there too would be most of the village folk. I walked, slowly, and impeded by several fits of coughing, towards it, and opened the door. All eyes turned and fixed on me when I entered. Although I was no stranger, and had come to know some of the villagers rather well, they were still surprised to see me.

"Hello," I said, to no soul in particular. "I—I just wanted to come here and say thank you to you all. For helping to build the house, and for everything since. I—I'm going now, and I dare say I shall never return. Bless you all, and goodbye."

With that, I turned and left. As I hobbled across the village centre, I heard the door fling open behind me. I turned to see Robin stood there, almost in tears. "Mr. Fitzwarwick," he said, as his look of fluster met mine of a quiet, content, acceptance. "Where is it that you're going?"

"Me?", I asked, as a smile flashed upon my face, and I accepted death wholeheartedly. "I'm going to a little place in the stars."

Though my farewell to the villagers had not been so final, and they had refused to let me go. Once a week, several, including Robin, would arrive at the house. They'd bring me food, and cigarettes, and we'd drink coffee on the porch and tell old stories. They'd come to know Richard quite well, for he was there for my funniest of tales. It was in those chats that I learned of something that warmed my heart to no end; that the re-building of the old Boden House had reunited that community, where it had once been fraught, and marred by familial rivalries, Balloch and I had unwittingly put them to bed, and turned out the light. The tale of the two outsiders, who had exhausted their lives elsewhere, returned to this land, so far south, and that ever-fleeting thing; joy.

And so came the end. It is now time to finish the story. My story about nothing, *fabulam de nihilo*. Here I stand at the water's edge. Though, where it will take me, and to whom, I do not know.

60

I awoke on the first of June, 1996, and knew that today I would die. This day began in coughs and splutters, as had each of the last hundred, but today, I *knew* I would die. And after pulling the covers back, and hauling myself into the bathroom, I made uneasy eye-contact with myself in the looking glass. There I saw myself as I was; old and haggard, thin and weak, sickly and pale, made ugly by the disease which ravaged me, and would soon come back to collect a final offering. My beard was unkempt, and my hair knotted and greying. And then I saw myself as I had been; curious and sharp, and young with deep brown eyes that gazed about the world in a state of cautious wonderment; I saw the stories forming behind those eyes, and phantom words dancing on the tip of the tongue and the purse of the lips. I was beautiful once, in a way that asked nothing of the world. So I saw myself as I was, and the way I had been; that I was beautiful once but ugly now, and knew that today I would die.

It was four weeks earlier when, sensing that I hadn't long left, I summoned Monty. By then, I had been cancerous for almost two years, and was weak and frail, and knew that soon the music would stop. He arrived a week after I had written to him, and as soon as we met, all was forgiven. Every ill-thought word, and careless betrayal lingered in the air no more. He hugged me, and I hugged him, with all the strength I had. The slight quiver in his frame told me that he was crying, and so I cried too.

"Oh, Robin," he said, over and over. "I had no idea."

"It's okay, Monty. I keep a good secret."

"It isn't just this, Robin. It's everything. I think about the last time I saw you, every day. I was so cruel, so petty and vindictive. I wanted to see you suffer, break, I wished such wrath upon you and you had to endure so much. I am so sorry."

"Monty," I said, removing myself from his grip and looking him in the eye. "It's okay, really. Come in."

He followed my lead and we came to the room in which I lived. By now, I did everything from that one room. My bed, desk, and panoramic view of the lake; they all emanated from one spot. It was close to the kitchen, and the front door. "How long do you have left?", was the first thing he asked, once we were seated.

"I don't know."

"Weeks? Months?"

"Could be either, could be days."

"Oh, Robin. Why are you doing this to yourself?"

"I'm afraid it's too late now, old boy. I wouldn't have it any other way."

"Why?"

"It's just my time."

Monty smiled as a tear left his eye. "I was thinking on the drive down, do you remember the first time we met?"

"Of course."

"Those older kids had me cornered, and you stepped in. You tried to say '*stop*', but you stammered on the 's'. And they laughed at you, right in your face. And then they left, and you walked over, and helped me to my feet. You jumped on a grenade for me. You didn't even know me, and you put yourself in harm's way for me. And from that day, those kids made your life hell, the teachers too. You brought all of that upon yourself, for a kid you didn't even know.

I never knew how significant that was until now. I never acknowledged just what you did for me."

"It was a fair deal, Monty. You helped me through it all."

"I'm sorry that we drifted. I think about all that has happened to you. You may have needed helping through some more hell, and I wasn't there. I don't know what happened, life just —"

"Moved along."

"Yeah."

We came to a little pause, as neither of us knew what to say next. "Tea?", Monty asked after a while.

"Please."

He returned, and I posed to speak. In his absence, only one thing had been on my mind. "How is little Andrew?"

"Not very little. He's taller than you, I'd say. But he is well. He got married last year."

"Married?"

"And a kid on the way."

"Wow, and he's twenty-five?"

Monty smiled. "Yes he is."

"Well, he got there younger than me. Did you go to the wedding?"

"I did. It was a wonderful day."

"How are Francis and Elsa?"

"They seem happy; happy as can be."

"Do they know that I'm dying?"

"No, I don't think anyone knows. Should they?"

"Not just yet. I have instructions for you, Monty. But they can wait."

Monty stayed for another two weeks, during which I was waited on hand-and-foot. He had picked out a room upstairs, and tended to me as I grew weaker. We had many more conversations like the one we enjoyed on that first night. Like Eleanor, he had attempted to convince me to live, but I would not move, for it was my fate, forged by my own hand. And on our last evening together, we sat together one last time.

"What are my instructions?", he asked once he had packed the car.
"I need you to speak to my son. Everything I own; the house and all within it, shall belong to him. All of my money, the rights to all of my works, my home, all of it. Can you do that?"
"I can."
"He may sell it all if he sees fit, but he needs to know that it all belongs to him."
"I shall do my best, Robin."
"Then that is my dying wish to you, Monty."
"It shall be done," he said, as his eyes misted again. We retired to bed not long after. Morning came, and so too did Monty's time to leave. We found ourselves outside, and by the lake.
"Okay," Monty said, as I turned to face him.
"Monty," I said. "I can assure you, I am fine. I will be fine."
"Death is making me think about life. It is all just so funny, is it not? By every metric, I'm a success. I had a good upbringing; I'm a father, a grandfather, a godfather. I rose in my profession, all the way to the top. For Christ's sake, I'm a Viscount now - not that it means anything. And yet, I don't know what I have to show for it. I fear I'll be forgotten not long after I'm gone. Remembered only in—fucking Debrett's."
"I don't know what I have to show for it all either. Save for this house."
"Your novels. Did the news ever make it down here?
"What news?
"They're being taught in schools now."
"They are?"
"Yes. I fear, Robin, that your awareness of the world never went beyond your immediate surroundings. You, my friend, are the mortal enemy of teenagers around the country, who have to study your work. Do you remember telling me that? That it was your dream? You see, Robin, that is what you possess;

what so few others do. It is something that not even death can take from you. For better or worse, you have a legacy. You will live on, in the half-baked essays of schoolboys."

With a nod and a smile, we returned to our silence. And when it was time for him to go, we said little, for it had already been said. He turned to leave; however, he stopped himself, and turned back. "Did you ever finish that novel? *All's Well in Winter Days*?"

"No."

"Well, now would be a good time."

That was to be Monty's parting gift. He reached for the car the door and opened it, before stopping, and turning one last time. "What's it like? Dying."

I thought for a moment. "Like waiting for a bus."

"Robin," he said, with a crackling wave.

"Yes?"

"Wherever it is that you're going, I hope she's there."

I smiled at my oldest friend, knowing that this was it. And then he was gone, and no one stood between myself and the end. At great physical expense, I found the manuscript. I pored it over, words I had written in flashes, with entire decades in between.

And then, it clicked. I was searching for an ending, yet I never found it. In that moment, I knew why; All's Well was the story of life, and what it all meant. All's Well was my life. I wrote the beginning when I was young, the middle in middle-age, and now I had reached the end. In that moment, it was so obvious. A good life is happiness shared, and the simple creation of memory. Richard had told me as much as we drank alone one morning in my first Michaelmas Term, as had Francine on our last day together.

I finally wrote those words of conclusion, and with it I had completed the last of the Fitzwarwick novels. And once it was done, I placed it in a drawer that I have not opened since. If you do read this, then go to the desk, and open the left-hand drawer, it will be in there. And then,

I had just one more thing to write, one more promise to keep. And so I sat, and considered my life. It truly did begin at Camford, with one, sole, piece of familial context.

I was born on a Tuesday in the August of 1933. On the Wednesday, my mother died. My father died too on a Wednesday, twelve years later.

And from there came all of my memories. And now it is time to complete my story. After a few days of rest, I recounted everything that I could recall, for your eyes only, upon your request; so that you may finally come to know me in some way. Some things may not have happened quite in the manner that I recall, yet I can say with honesty that I have been honest, as honest as I can be. I have not exaggerated my good days, nor minimised the bad. Every conversation happened as I recall it, though perhaps with different words; for so few have the gift of words. Every place I have seen was real, every woman I have loved and brother I have cherished were made of flesh and blood and bone. Everything I did or say had real consequences; good and bad. I have told you; without filter, dilly, dally, or discretion, the story my life, in every detail I have committed to memory. It all happened; my bitter youth in the war, and my idyllic college years. I have told you of my travels, my time spent in various little corners of this world. I have told you of my career as a writer; its rise, plateau, fall, and redemption; my marriage to your mother and my fatherhood of you, however brief they both were. I have told you of my year with Francine, and of her death; of restoring the old Boden House with Balloch; my years as a teacher, and my descent into the bottle; my flirtations with Hollywood, my return home, and my simple, silent end.

And now I am writing in the present tense. With each passing day, I grow weaker. And so, with that in mind, I shall write to you one last time. It is my greatest hope that one day you too will be sat in this very room, reading these words. I hear that you are married. In this, I wish you the best, and pray that your decisions will not echo my own. I hope that my story has been something of an education, a rallying cry to pursue art, and beauty, and truth, and love above all other things. I hope that you take control of your fate, and guide it firmly, and with prudence.

I am not a good man, I am not a bad man, I am just a man. And there are many things that I regret, and many things that I do not. I do not regret the friends and lovers that I have known along the way; for they saw me in the crowd, and each gave me something that I never parted with. Balloch gave me my life's work; Francis was the man I could have been; Richard kept me young. Monty, raised me; Matheson always found me.

I do not regret loving Cynthia, for the pain she gave made me a man; nor Adeline, who taught me tenderness, and kept me young all the same; nor Milena, through whom I saw paradise; nor Elaine, who made me go home. Nor Francine, who made an honest man of me. Nor Elsa, for through her, my blood shall live on. And lastly I do not regret you, for I am sure that you will shine light into this world; into cracks and corners that I could never quite reach.

I have lived, and now I shall die. I have loved, and now I shall love no more. I have seen the world, and now I shall go beyond it. I have written, and danced, and drank, and smoked, and sung. No more. I have travelled, and now I shall be still. I have suffered and now I shall know no pain. My race is run, and now I rest.

My sole reproach of this life is that I did not stop enough, to look around, and appreciate all that I had, and saw, and felt. It is all so beautiful when you stop.

In my final years, I have asked myself many times; if I lived a good life or a bad life. And in my final days, I finally have an answer; I do not know. I was simply a passenger.

The End.

Thank you.

Printed in Great Britain
by Amazon

56178339R00279